WOLF OF CRIMSON

The Crimson Flame Series

Whitney Thorn

WHITNEY THORN LLC

Copyright

This is a work of fiction. Names, characters, places, and incidents either are the product of the author's imagination or are used fictitiously. Any resemblance to actual persons, living or dead, events, or locales is entirely coincidental.

Copyright © 2025 by Whitney Thorn LLC

All rights reserved. No portion of this book may be reproduced or used in any manner without the written permission of the copyright owner, except for the use of quotations in a book review.

For more information, address: author@whitneythorn.com

First paperback edition November 2025

Cover by: Get Covers

ISBN 979-8-9939018-0-0 (paperback)

ISBN 979-8-9939018-1-7 (e-book)

whitneythorn.com

To my mate, Trevor, thank you for all your love and support along this journey. Most of all, thank you for gently telling me to find a hobby. XO Whitney

Author Note:

Trigger warnings: Women's abduction/trafficking. Mention of suicide. Sexual content and explicit language.

Definitions:

Werewolf: A massive, immortal wolf that walks on four paws.

Lycan: A massive, immortal wolf-like beast that walks on two legs.

Crimson Wolf: A form of werewolf who wields fire magic with deep red, crimson-colored eyes.

Goddess Blessed Wolves: Shifters who die, and the Moon Goddess, Selene, sends back with enhanced abilities and connections to her to fulfill a purpose.

Old World: Eden, sister planet to Earth. It has two moons, Alpha and Lycaon. This is where Lycans and a type of werewolf known as Alphas originated.

The Crossing: The mass migration of supernatural races to Earth from Eden, which allowed the innocent beings of Eden a chance to flee and avoid mass genocide during the Scorch Wars. These beings were liberated when the last remaining Guardian Angel of Eden opened portals to Earth in 1870.

The Guardians: A military operation led by the Guardian Angels of Earth, consisting of all supernatural races.

Moonborn Pack: A military operation and the largest wolf pack located in the state of Oregon, aiding North American werewolves in need.

Broken Stone Portal: One of the last remaining open portals connecting Eden and Earth, ruled by the Wolf Demigod, Ezekial, and guarded by the Moonborn Pack.

The Dragon Empire: A supernatural safe place owned by the dragon shifters, where supernaturals are granted housing and protection at the cost of their servitude in a magical binding contract. Located in Las Vegas, Nevada, and consisting of large supernatural hotels, casinos, fight pits, a brothel, and clubs.

Werewolf Ranks (Highest to lowest): Alpha, Beta, Gamma, Delta, Omega

Werewolf Naming: A person's first name is their human side's given name, and their middle name is the wolf's given name.

Fated Mate Bonds: A gift from the Moon Goddess, Selene, to any werewolf or lycan born on Earth under her moon. A werewolf or lycan can sense their fated mate when they turn eighteen and their animal awakens. At any age, someone may feel that their fated tie to another has ended, whether through their mate choosing another or through death. It causes a small sensation in the chest and a soul-deep knowing that they are no longer connected to another.

CONTENTS

PROLOGUE

Dana

April 19ᵗʰ, 2008, Pearl Mist Pack, Mississippi, USA

The clock on my nightstand glows a bright red, disrupting the darkness as I read, 12:01 AM. It's finally here, my eighteenth birthday. Tonight, my wolf will awaken, allowing us to shift for the first time, and if we are lucky, we will sense our fated mate.

Psh, fated mates, what a bunch of horseshit.

The purple cotton sheets tangled around me rustle as I roll away from the obnoxious crimson reminder. My thoughts grow more aggressive as they force me to relive, on loop, Bobby's stiff, rehearsed confession after school today.

"Dana, I know tomorrow is your birthday. I wanted to tell you myself that we're fated mates."

The Moon Goddess, Selene, chose Bobby, the future Alpha of the Pearl Mist pack, as the other half of my soul. However, one three-letter word holds the power to undo everything – but.

"But the day of the lycan incident, I felt the signs of a bond break, and that's when I saw you on the ground…"

He felt our fated connection break? Of course, I wouldn't have any recollection of that, seeing as I was dead.

"I believe our bond breaking was for the best. I'm in love with Ashley. Her Alpha bloodline will make her an excellent Luna fit for the pack. I've already been in talks with her father, Alpha Rick, who has agreed to a merger of our packs, seeing as she is his only child. This would be an extremely beneficial strategic move for us."

Alpha Bloodline. Pack Merger. Beneficial. Strategic. Fit. All the qualifications that you, Dana Jo Johnston, are lacking as his mate.

"I'm sure you can understand that I must put the pack first. Dana, I wish you the best."

My fated mate wished me the best. While polite sounding, the words rang hollow. A silver bullet to the heart would've been less painful to endure.

A broken bond could be repaired if we tried, and his unwilling-ness is what hurts me the most. Fated mate rejections are uncommon among shifters, leaving me feeling ashamed and betrayed. My flight instincts hit hard, hollering at me to run away from here as fast as possible. My pride would rather see me walk away than stay, and plead for the love he's unwilling to give.

My Memaw June's childhood lesson brings a small smile to my face. *"Dana Jo, now there are two things we Johnston women never chase: top-shelf tequila and men. If a man is too stupid to see your worth, don't bother with the fuss; move on. Oh, and Sugar, make sure you do it with your head held high, and your heels even higher."*

That is precisely what I'm going to do. I've been contemplating relocating to Moonborn Pack in Oregon to join their military ranks after graduation. It's been something I've wanted to do ever since I attended their junior military program last summer. My talk with Bobby gave me the push to submit my application for admission. I want to focus on my bright future, but instead, my brain decides it's better to rewatch the highlight reel of my mate's rejection. Again.

Sleep seems like it won't relieve me from this cruel memory anytime soon. A feeling of agitated pacing within my mind makes me unable to settle.

My younger brother, Davey, sleeps soundly next to me. My Irish twin, my ride or die. He held me the entire evening, listening to my tears and easing some of the heartache.

"No matter what you do, I'll always be your number one cheerleader on the sidelines. Kickin' splitin' cartwheelin' for you. Shit, who

am I kidding? My ass will be parked in the stands next to the cutest boy, while I stuff my face with nachos, but I'll still be cheerin' for you no matter what you do. Whatever happens next, let's do it together, okay?"

Davey is right, no matter what happens next, we'll stick together. He, too, deserves more than to stay and be subjected to daily bullying due to his sexuality. Our wounds will never heal until we create space from this bond, this pack, and our mother, who has never seen us as enough.

I need to persuade Pa to let Davey come with me to the Moonborn Pack now. I can serve as his guardian while he finishes high school next year. I think Pa will understand. Ma will pretend she's not secretly relieved to see her two blemishes move away.

"Dana Jo, a man will never mate a wild thing like you. Do you want to become the pack spinster?" My mother's words from the past whisper.

"I am in love with Ashley," Bobby's deep bass follows.

My evil thoughts hold me captive. No one is going to save me from them, and I can't break free. Internally, I scream at my tormentors. A surge of anger ignites within me, overwhelming me. Something claws forcefully at the walls in my mind. This angry energy is electric; it fuels the raging storm within.

STOP! STOP! STOP!

I can't take it anymore. I grab my iPod, jam my earbuds in, and start scrolling through my music.

Fuck, I'm feeling hotter than a stolen tamale. What's happening?

My heart begins to flutter wildly, causing my pulse to quicken. Wolves don't awake until the night of your eighteenth birthday, not in the early morning hours. Anger at Bobby feels like wildfire in my chest. This rage has nowhere to go. The circular clicking pauses over Metallica's "Enter Sandman." My mind goes straight to that day.

No. Why is THAT song even in here?

Irritably, I scroll on. Drowning Pool's "Bodies" starts with an ear-splitting volume. I exhale a sigh of relief as the singer's scream cradles my rage like a lullaby. I pause my pacing, which I didn't realize I was doing. Davey's still out cold.

Okay, so it can't be that loud.

A gentle caress grazes my mind. *"Yes, I like this,"* a voice whispers, startling me.

I yank the earbuds out and look around my eerily still bedroom.

"I liked that," the voice repeats. *"Doesn't it make you want to kill something, or someone, perhaps?"*

"What? No! I'm not killing anyone, crazy voice in my mind."

"But you have killed before," the voice reminds me.

When the haunting memory resurfaces, my heart starts to jack-hammer. My temperature follows, amplifying quickly by several degrees.

"Are you my wolf, Jo? Um, Jo is your given name if you're not aware."

The voice giggles. *"Of course, it is I, your strong, fearless, and beautiful wolf, Jo, but I prefer Joey. I'm not sure who else you would expect to share consciousness with."*

"I thought wolves awakened during the moon's rise on my birthday, not now."

"I do what I want, and I decided I want to come now."

Agony overcomes me, causing my legs to give out. Crumpling to the ground, I gasp for air, each breath a battle. Everything feels on fire. I clutch my stomach and wonder how I'll survive the first shift.

"Dana! What's happening? Are you okay?" Davey's warm arms wrap around me, trying to pull me off the ground.

The pain is so intense I can't speak.

"PA! Help! Something's wrong with Dana!"

"Look at me. It's going to be alright." Davey freezes. His body locks in place as confusion catches in his gaze.

"What?" I groan out through the painful tremors.

"Your eyes are red," he murmurs.

Red? My eyes are red? The meaning behind this is stuck, lost somewhere in the agony.

My father bursts into my room moments later, with sleepy eyes and wearing only his boxers.

"What is it?" Pa heaves out, a tremble laced in his voice.

"Dana is shifting already, and her eyes are red."

He, too, pauses on my face. "Goddess be," he mumbles.

Pa's safe arms lift my withering body, holding me tight as he sprints out of my room. My eyes are unfocused as I try to take in my surroundings as we move from the house to outside. The moonlight washes over me like a soothing stream, taking some of the burning inferno within. A mixture of my growls and choking disrupts the calm of the night. My exhausted body gently meets the cool ground. I lay there trembling, wishing this would all pass quickly.

"I can't let go," I tell the impatient black wolf with red eyes, who I can see so clearly now in my mind's eye. It's like we're taught in school. Once your wolf awakens, you can easily visualize them in your head. But this isn't the first time I've laid eyes on her. I saw her years ago, on that day when I died.

"Trust me, Dana," she urges.

Closing my eyes, I place all my trust in my wolf and let go. Our shift is painfully slow as our body rearranges itself for the first time. Blinking my eyes open, I see fire dancing around the midnight colored fur of my paws; Joey's paws. Davey and Pa stand in complete shock. Our head tilts slightly, seeing them through newly enhanced eyes.

Davey switches from shocked to crazed villain. "No frickin' way! Dana, you're blessed by Selene! Jo's a crimson wolf. Stick that up your overly inflated ego ass, Bobby. You so fucked up, man!" he yells to the heavens above.

Jo raises her muzzle, alight with fire, towards the glow of the moon. She lets out a long howl, fiercely declaring she has arrived.

CHAPTER ONE

Ajax

The Assignment

September 2024, Guardian Military Secret Complex Europe (Custos Lands)

Something pulls me from my sleep, causing me to wake with unease. It's not even 5:00 A.M., after a late night out with my squadmates to celebrate the start of a five-day rest and recuperation break. The cheerful bird songs outside my bedroom window slightly calm my racing heart. I close my eyes, letting my heightened lycan senses search out signs of a threat, but there are none. They conclude that one of my flatmates is up, likely Evan, returning from a hookup with the cute fae he chatted up all evening. That could've been me with her attractive friend. However, Mars wasn't on board, so I had to take the lonely road of self-care.

Mars lets out an annoyed grunt. *"Their scents were too sweet. I didn't want to fuck fruity pebbles,"* he complains. *"I'm tired of mindless flings, I want a mate."*

Ah, yes, there it is, the core of all our arguments lately, my lycan wants to settle down. I make a very non-committal noise in the back of my throat. I understand the stress of our work is taking a toll on him. We've been a part of this military operation for a decade, witnessing both the dark and light sides of the supernatural community. It has been harder to hold onto the good amidst the bad, especially after losing friends in the process. It's becoming more difficult to compartmentalize, making it impossible to ignore. We may be reaching a point where we need to step back from the organization for a while and perhaps take some time to travel and re-center ourselves.

Mars disagrees, *"I don't think we need more travel. We need a pack, family, friends, and even better, a mate to center us."*

"Honestly, those seem like some pretty big commitments, buddy. I'm not sure I'm ready for that."

"Maybe we should start seeing the therapist again to talk through these commitment issues," Mars gently suggests.

I make another non-committal sound. *"Listen, you know there isn't an overabundance of mateless female lycans milling about, so I don't think we should put all our hope into finding one."*

Lycan women made up a significant portion of the casualties in the numerous wars of the Old World, Eden. Our numbers still haven't fully recovered since our kind made the crossing to Earth in 1870.

"Jax, I know we can find someone if we take the time to look within packs. What if we could find our fated mate? The one made for us by the Moon Goddess."

"Do us both a favor and tone back the optimism a wee tad. We need to be realistic about the chances of simply finding a compatible mate."

Watching a former Guardian teammate leave to settle down with a mate sparked something instinctual in Mars, making him adamant it's what we need. There was a noticeable change in our friend once he met his mate. The heaviness we all bear as soldiers was lifted, and everything about him seemed lighter.

Mars refuses to drop the subject. *"Tell me we can at least put effort into trying."*

It's complete shit having an internal debate with an animal whose primal desires can easily override their logic. It's obvious we disagree on a course of action to help us break out of this slump.

"Sergeant Blackclaw, are you available to come to my office?" Andy, an archangel and Guardian General, mindlinks me. Her voice holds its usual underlying tone of strictly business. The unease returns, coiling around my nerves.

"Yes, I can be there in fifteen," I respond.

"Excellent, see you soon." She cuts our mental connection.

Tossing my covers aside, I get out of bed and head to my dresser to find a clean uniform. Anxious energy runs through me, while a surge of excitement pulses from Mars.

"What's exciting about being called into the big boss's office at 5:00 A.M.?" I ask.

He shifts around like an excited puppy. *"A change, and I think one's coming."*

Change. The word echoes around my mind, something about it resonates, and I'm not sure how I feel about it, even though that might be exactly what we need.

Tiptoeing, I walk softly through the small four-bedroom military apartment to avoid waking anyone. On the couch, I find Evan indulging in an extra-large pizza and the supernatural fight ring channel.

"Hey, where are you headed this early?" he asks around a mouthful of meat lovers.

"Andy wants to see me, but after that, I want to hear about your night."

There's no suppressing that devilish smile of his. "You missed out, man."

"I figured. I can't wait to hear about it when I get back. See you soon."

"We didn't miss out," the stubborn beast protests.

I can discern Mars' growing irritation from being out of sync lately. We've been through this before, when we spent years traveling until he could no longer handle the solitude. That's when we joined the Guardians, and it was exactly what we needed at the time. As a high-born dominant lycan male, we needed the exertion of battle, as well as the bonds of friendship we've established.

On my walk to Andy's office, I try to mentally prepare for what's coming next. I run through scenarios that might require a call during a break, and this early in the morning.

"Maybe she knows we've been struggling," I admit.

Mars sits patiently, eagerly awaiting what lies ahead. *"That angel doesn't miss anything."*

"I wonder if it's a blessing or a curse to know everything?" I ponder to distract myself.

"I'd wager you'd think it's a curse to take away the spontaneity of life."

"I think you're right, my wise, hairy friend."

As I approach my destination, I keep my sights set on the gleaming white marble tower accented in gold trim, rising higher than any building in the Guardian lands of Custos. It's been nicknamed

Heaven's Staircase. Typically, I find the most beauty in nature, which is a fleeting moment in time, rather than in man-made creations that can endure centuries.

There's something about this tower's graceful, tapered design, which segments into tiers separated by ledges of gold and gemstones, that makes it one of my favorite sights. The top of the tower transcends into an open columned gallery crowned by a golden dome. A gleaming angel figure stands at the pinnacle, its wings spread wide, gazing toward the heavens above.

At the bottom of the wonder, there are no visible doorways. I press the pad of my finger into one of the five fist-sized opal stones that run the perimeter of the tower. Taking a step back, I wait for my gateway to appear. A golden sheen of mist creeps from the stone wall. It takes the shape of a feather as it spins, creating a direct transport to Andy's location. Stepping through the portal, I enter a vacant hallway outside a large wooden door with carved angelic markings. On the wall next to the door, an elaborate nameplate reads, "Archangel Andreena." The back of my knuckles tap twice against the door before it opens itself.

"Ajax, come in," Andy's feminine voice rings out.

Inside the door, an inquisitive orange cat with a blue polka dot collar sits. The fluffball weaves between my legs, meowing up at me for attention. I bend down to stroke its silky coat, and its back arches into my touch.

"She didn't strike me as a cat person," Mars mentions.

"Me neither," I agree.

"It's my granddaughter's cat, Mango. I am animal sitting." This makes me smile. I've never heard this ethereal being say anything so human.

"It's a sweet cat," I comment.

"Yes, it is, but I am more of a reptile person, myself," Andy says.

The cat brushes along my legs once more before shifting its focus to a toy Andy tosses. My attention shifts back to the angel, noticing the faintest lip twitch. I've never seen her smile before. Her deep brown eyes hold a mix of ancient strength and concealed warmth.

Andy sits behind her rich mahogany desk that matches the room's aesthetic. Books and ancient forgotten treasures rest atop shelves that span the room. Floating orbs of pure angelic energy pulse gently, casting a soft glow.

"Please, take a seat." She gestures to the seats in front of her desk. "I'll jump right in. In your file, you listed your home pack as Highland Pack, but you have ties to the Silverthrone Pack in Canada as well, correct?"

"Yes, that's correct. I was born in the Silverthrone Pack and still have family there. It's a complicated history, and the new Beta has a deep grudge with me, given my bloodline, so I decided not to list it as my home."

"Do you visit often?" she inquires.

I think about it. "Well, as much as I can, which isn't often."

"Excellent. I require your assistance on a current matter within the Silverthrone Pack."

This piques my interest since Mickey and Miguel check in regularly, and I haven't heard of any drama that would warrant Guardian involvement.

"This would be a solo mission gathering intel on pack members," she states.

"Like spying?" I feel hesitant because that's not my specialty. My stomach drops at the thought of living there for an unknown amount of time. Am I ready to face some of those past demons head-on that led to years of depression and PTSD?

Mango returns, jumping up onto my lap, pursuing more attention. The cat's a good distraction. Andy scowls at the loud purring feline who starts rhythmically kneading on my stomach.

"Precisely spying. Investigations have led us to believe a top player within a large female trafficking ring may reside there. What I need are your inconspicuous boots on the ground gathering intel. You have natural ties to the pack, so it will not raise suspicions if you move home to be closer to loved ones. We also need assurance that the new Silverthrone King is not involved in these crimes."

Mars is overjoyed with these orders. "*This seems like exactly the change of pace we* are looking for."

I, on the other hand, am distracted by Mango. What is this cat doing?

"ACK! Mango! There will be no sin biscuits in my office," Andy's raised voice catches me off guard. The cat slowly blinks, not bothered by the angel's outburst. She narrows her eyes back at the feline in challenge. "I will take you down to the exorcism department to check you for a demon incumbent," she warns.

I lift the ball of fur off my lap and set him on the ground, giving his butt a little pat with my foot. He shows me his teeth and hisses before trotting off.

"Andy, you know I'm more of a muscle guy, not a spy," I retort.

"Yes, well, we will move you off your current squad and into an advanced, specialized training in preparation for this mission."

I hold back my objection, wanting to admit I'm not the right person for this assignment, but that's not how you speak to an archangel who gave you direct orders.

Instead, I tell her, "Okay, I'll do it."

CHAPTER TWO

Dana

Cheers to Beautiful Packages

April 26, 2025, Moonborn Pack, Oregon, USA

I fidget restlessly in the backseat of my hired ride's car, growing anxious to meet up with my brother, Davey, and his mate, Charles. The cool spring air from my cracked window helps chase away the scent of the cheap air freshener waving at me from around my driver's rearview mirror.

Watching the sights of the pack pass by stirs up memories of the day Davey and I officially joined seventeen years ago. The anniversary always brings both welcome and unwelcome memories from my past to visit. The most prevalent unwanted one is Bobby's rejection. As the years continue to put space between me then and now, the loss of our fated connection cuts me less. Around this time, I always find myself wondering about him and the life we might have had together. *Who would that version of me be? Would she be happy?*

Ugh, piss off and die unwanted thoughts. I'm too tired to deal with you.

"Remember the first day you arrived? Our first day was a good day," Joey encourages my brain to redirect from the annual pity party.

The day we arrived was nothing short of intimidating. With 15,000 members spread across 20,000 breathtaking acres, the Moonborn pack is massive. We were a couple of broke teenagers then, with more hopes than belongings we could cram into my beat-up 1996 Saturn. It took a little over a week after my eighteenth birthday for the proper paperwork to be filed, allowing me to join their military ranks. Then we hit the road, never glancing back at Pearl Mist.

Driving up the Moonborn Pack's excessively manicured entrance, lined with oversized signs to direct visitors through the city, was enough to make two small-town kids feel out of our depth. Military personnel could be seen at every turn. Davey had bounced around like a puppy who had heard he was getting a treat. A tall, handsome treat in a uniform that could be seen milling about.

I did extensive research on the pack before joining in April 2008, and the large military presence is what drew me. The Moonborn pack was known for assisting wolves across North America and safeguarding one of the few remaining active portals connecting Earth to Eden. The Broken Stone Portal must be secured at all times to prevent threats from crossing through the worlds.

Our first night at the pack, we treated ourselves to a celebratory dinner at The Rogue Capt'n Saloon, a quaint pirate-themed bar nestled along a flowing river. Ever since, it's become our tradition to frequent this joint every year around the end of April to celebrate our liberation day. Somehow, here we are, seventeen years later, still honoring that tradition.

After bidding my nose blind driver goodnight, I hustle inside. At this point, it feels like I'm running on fumes. The long days I've been putting in are catching up with me. Being a Commanding Officer over one of our Elite Military Squads has placed more responsibility on my shoulders and taken up more of my time. Achieving my rank has required a lot of blood, sweat, and maybe a few tears I'm reluctant to admit. To me, it's all been worth it.

"Well, we're forty minutes late. They won't be pleased," Joey states the obvious.

All I can do is groan in response. She's right, like always.

"Tell them we were getting laid, not working late...again. That excuse will earn their approval," she suggests.

Incredulously, I stare at her in my mind's eye. *"They'll never buy it. They know I'm in my vibrator only era."*

While I'm not a prude, it has been a minute. With my busy and stressful career, I needed to simplify other areas of my life. Take out, wine, and my vibrator collection do a fantastic job of helping with that. Not to mention, it's been wonderful not having the awkward "sorry, it's not you, it's my wolf" conversations.

It doesn't take long to spot the back of Davey's golden hair and Charles' rust-colored hair, lounging with a drink in hand on the deck. The dynamic duo makes me gag with how undeniably perfect they are for one another. I'm grateful that my brother found his fated mate at eighteen. For him, it was a love written in the stars. There's no more deserving of a soul I can think of. While Davey, along with most of our family, struggled with his sexuality growing up, Charles's Delta family welcomed Davey with open arms; no questions or judgment. Those sweethearts even adopted me into their family as Auntie Dana.

"Happy seventeen years of freedom! Sorry, I'm late, lovies. Bad guys here, there, and everywhere. No time for margaritas, unfortunately," I joke, trying to lighten the situation as I take my seat.

"Dana Jo, how are you ever gonna find a nice man to settle down with if you keep working all those long hours? You'll put yourself in an early grave, and I wanna see my adorable niece or nephew pups runnin' around. Ya hear?" Davey, clucks with his sweet-as-pie southern accent. His impression is spot on for every southern mama back in Pearl Mist.

"Sorry, Ma," I call him. "But men will have to wait."

His nose wrinkles in disgust at the mom reference. "Oh, no you didn't. Don't you make me look like a fool while trying to kick your ass. I'm not above clawing and hair pulling." He sticks out his tongue playfully.

"Hun, no one wants to see you going all cat-fight mode," Charles chuckles.

Though Davey ranks higher than Charles by blood, Charles is the better fighter. Instead, Davey's fight comes as a verbal assault. It gutted him when our former pack Alpha denounced him as the next Gamma solely due to his sexuality. After that, he refused to train or fight, claiming he was choosing to be a lover, not a fighter.

I, too, chuckle at the thought of Davey's fighting antics. "Okay, low blow calling you ma, I'll admit it."

"But in all seriousness, my favorite sister-in-law. I know that blessed crimson DNA of yours drives you to protect others above yourself, but know you're allowed to choose yourself and your happiness." Charles' voice is a soothing baritone. He and Davey are teachers in the pack schools, but Charles doubles as my unofficial therapist. The man is too good to me.

"Somewhere out there, the Goddess has created the perfect were-man who's well packaged and has an extra big heart." Davey's eyebrows wiggle suggestively. "And who will also be able to handle our girl, Joey, without crying."

Our group bursts out laughing at the inside joke. These two have learned the hard way not to play matchmaker for me after numerous failed attempts. They finally accepted defeat after a date with a kind Omega math teacher ended briskly in tears. And they weren't my tears.

"Cole still won't talk to us," Charles sighs, with genuine sadness shining in his eyes.

"Ah, Cole, that poor lamb. I only wanted to play," Joey giggles innocently.

"Yes, well, he didn't know that and thought he was going to meet our Goddess after you shifted into a full blaze of glory," I argue with my inner wolf.

"He had so many cool hobbies, whereas you have none. I thought showing him our fire ability would earn us some cool points. How was I supposed to know he'd be that upset?" she shoots back.

"Well, lesson learned. Warn us next time."

"Yes, yes," the fire beast mutters.

"It's hard being an extremely dominant female," I mumble before taking a swig of Davey's mango margarita.

"We know, Jalapeno," he says, yanking his drink back. "I still think you should visit some of the crimson packs in Europe. Now, they'll give Jo a run for her money."

"They can try," Joey says overly confidently.

"Yeah, maybe," I tell Davey very noncommittally.

"Just promise us you'll at least consider putting yourself out there more. You're too amazing not to have someone special in your life," Charles compliments while handing over his watermelon margarita for me to try.

"Thank you." I gladly accept the sugary drink. Loneliness pangs deep in my soul, causing me to flash my best smile in hopes of masking it. "Yes, I'll do my best to try men again soon." Another problem for another day. I'll file that away in the "ignoring your problems" cabinet for another month, since *soon* is subjective.

"Maybe they are right and we should start giving men a chance again?" Joey proposes.

"You do know 90% of the time it's you. You're incapable of playing nice with others in the sandbox, so that's why we stay home," I fire back at her.

"Ah, rude!" Joey acts offended.

"Ah, truth!" I parrot back in the same tone.

"I can't help it; I'm more dom. Men need to get over themselves and accept it." She huffs, raising her nose in the air.

"Truth." I can get on board with that statement.

Our sole problem with were-men is our dominance and assertiveness have unintentionally left some men feeling emasculated. This is how we were created, and we won't change the core part of ourselves.

Most male wolves prefer a less dominant mate, hence why female Omegas and Alpha males tend to gravitate toward one another. An Omega balances the Alpha, whereas we seem to be the equivalent of castration to an Alpha male.

I've tried being with less dominant wolves, but those relationships have all left me unfulfilled. I went so far as a foursome with three Omega males while in Vegas, who worshiped me as their Queen. Looking back, I'm pretty sure they were in an all-Omega male cult seeking a strong Alpha female to serve. That was not my finest judgment.

Then there was a vampire who was fun in bed until he nearly choked to death on my blood, stating it was unbelievably hot. Davey still sneaks in the "Big & Rich's Jalapeno" song while out at bars to honor that fond memory.

At this point, I should probably start a blog on my bad sexual encounters. Maybe someone, somewhere, could at least find amusement in them. *Ugh, we're so screwed and not in a good way.*

Thankfully, the waitress arriving to grab my order halts my unwanted trip down bad-dating lane. After she bustles away, I turn to Charles, steering the conversation away from me.

"So, how's the adoption process going?"

"Well, it's going," Charles tries to sound positive, but his shoulders slump and he looks deflated.

"Yeah, nowhere fast," Davey replies with a sarcastic snort.

They have been hoping to adopt for seven years now. They've explored additional options in other countries but still haven't found their pup. My instincts stir, telling me it will happen soon.

Our waitress drops off my margarita and a restock of tortilla chips. *Sweet coconut margarita, come to Mama.*

"Everyone says adoptions take time. Good thing time is on our immortal side. Now, cheers to your future pup, I know you'll be getting soon." I extend my glass over the center of the table and give them a confident look. They both smile back with hope in their eyes.

"Yes. And to your future man, Dana, what did you call him, Hun? Large packaged, were-man?" Charles dodges as Davey swats at him.

"I said nothing about the man's actual package," Davey defends.

Charles gives him an incredulous look. "Babe, your mind is never not in the gutter. We know you weren't talking about anything large aside from his cock."

A large smile spreads across Davey's face. "Fine, you know me too well."

Laughing, we all raise our glasses, drinking in hopes of future babies and giant packages.

CHAPTER THREE

Dana

Captain Lumen

"*D*ana," a faint voice calls in my mind.

Buzz. Buzz. Buzz.

"*Wake up, Snoring Beauty, our phone's buzzing,*" calls that same snarky voice.

"*What?*" I mumble, rolling onto my back. I swipe away a rogue strand of hair from my mouth, realizing that it had been clearly hanging open. My mouth currently feels like the Salivaless Desert. *Need water. Now.*

Buzz. Buzz. Buzz.

"Work phone, buzzing! Get up!" Joey barks.

Shit! I spring up so fast, I see stars. Ugh! Five margaritas, five shots, three or more moonshines, and a poor karaoke rendition of Spice Girls' "Spice Up Your Life," because Davey and I stick to the classics, has left my brain feeling a little sluggish this morning.

"A little sluggish? It's basically '90s dial-up internet in here without that annoying sound. The porch lights are on, but no one is home." Joey huffs.

"We're in the wrong profession, seeing as you're a comedian," I say dryly.

Grabbing my work phone from my nightstand, I quickly scroll through several missed messages from my direct supervisor, Captain Brutis Lumen. *Shit on a stick.* According to his latest text message, I have eleven minutes until I'm due in his office. Launching my covers off, I stumble my sluggish ass into the bathroom. There is no way I can roll up to my Captain's office smelling like a stale bar.

Brutis and I have a stupid, overly complicated past, which makes him all too happy to report on any incident, big or small. We matched on a dating app when I was younger, which led to casually hooking up. One of those young, naive, and horny cluster fucks you look back on wishing never happened.

He was older, which made it more exciting. He was also the first person I met who had experienced a broken mating bond, which created a sense of camaraderie. Those who experience a fated connection break describe a slight squeeze followed by a pop around the chest. It's not painful, but it does cause temporary grief and a soul-deep knowing. Either one's fated mate has died or taken a chosen mate, forever bonding them with another.

The man's idea of a woman's place in the pack was more traditional than mine. A beautiful picture was painted of how, if we mated, I could stay home to raise our pups. Pretty life, but not for me. I quickly realized it would never work and hightailed it outta there lickety-split. He wasn't too keen on breaking things off.

His parting scorned ex-monologue to me was, *"You'll regret this."*

Cliché! And yeah, still no regrets over here.

Fast forward to our professional careers in the military, forcing us to cross paths. When the Captain position opened, I challenged him and beat him in a fight. This embarrassed him and wounded his pride. That day, I witnessed his loathing of me transform into hatred. Of course, the old ballsacks making the decisions still chose him for the role over me, but clearly, he has never let it go.

"And neither have we," my salty wolf grumbles. *"We were the better choice for the position."*

When I arrive at his office, he wastes no time with pleasantries. Instead, he thrusts a tablet into my hands.

"Scan this regarding your next assignment and then get out."

Gladly, coffee breath. Wait, what? I'm on scheduled leave starting tomorrow for an entire week. *Damn it. Why am I getting an assignment? This better be world-ending shit.*

The top of the report confirms Squad 13 is assigned to this case and that it's been classified as a Tier 3 incident level. That's neither my squad nor a tier level we handle. Each situation is rated based on specific criteria to ensure we send the right teams for the job. Our military operation consists of twenty lower-level squads that manage Tier 1-3 assignments and eight elite squads, like mine, that handle more serious threats classified as Tier 4-5 assignments.

My eyes quickly scan the intake form, noting a pack located in Alberta, Canada, encountered rogue wolves last night, resulting in five females being abducted. A team is needed to secure the pack while also launching an investigation into the missing women.

The pack is described as small and peaceful, with no known enemies or history of internal conflict. It's noted that two young adult females went missing in the late '90s. They were never found or heard from. Situations like this happen too frequently in werewolf society. I know all too well, having spent over a decade within the lower-level squad ranks.

"Sir, per these field notes, this situation falls below the threshold of elite squad deployment. Squad 13 has already been assigned," I state as a matter of fact.

"Correct. Good to see they taught you how to read in backwater Mississippi. You, along with Squad 13, will be handling this situation."

Is that smugness I detect?

Joey growls, *"It sure is."*

My brain, still processing slower than usual, can't compute how I fit into this equation when this is not my squad. *Wait, am I being demoted?* The bastard has been waiting to take his shot for years. Maybe he finally got what he wanted. Panic rises in my gut, causing my internal well of fire to flare to life. Swallowing the panic, I hold his gaze, pretending I'm composed while silently urging him to say more.

"As much as I wish I was delivering the joyous news of a demotion, it's not. This is Luca Black's first assignment in the field. You will accompany Squad 13 to ensure everything runs smoothly while maintaining a low profile. Squad Leader Kyle will oversee the entire operation. You're to keep your mouth shut and not interfere unless prompted by immediate danger directed at Luca. Do you understand?"

Joey shakes her head. *"I can't believe we just got placed on pup sitting duty!"*

"Yeah," I agree with her. *"And that's insulting to Luca's abilities."*

"Sir, does Luca know or want the added precautions?"

"He doesn't have a choice in the matter. I decided to send someone to ensure his first mission goes without a hitch. You will say nothing. If anyone finds out the truth of why you are there, it'll be on your head."

Gosh, what is that smell? Oh, just some good ol' brown nosing.

I know why Captain Lumen would want to ensure Luca's first mission goes smoothly, but the kid has been training since he was in the crib for fuck's sake. Luca's father holds a prestigious role as one of the personal bodyguards for Ezekial Moonborn, the Pack's Alpha. As a descendant of Eden's Moon God, Alpha, Ezekial carries the status and power of a demigod. With that status, he's the kind of man everyone is obsessed with being noticed by.

"Is there no one else who can oversee this task as I'm on approved leave for a week starting tomorrow?" I ask, trying not to sound desperate.

"No, Commander. I chose you for this task since you are available today."

My blood boils. *Available?* He knew damn well I had scheduled leave time. A belated birthday vacation to Napa Valley with my girls, and an unlimited supply of wine, isn't what I'd consider available.

"Sir, I'm sure one of my competent team members would be willing to step in." Goddess, I desperately need this vacation more than I need air, but I'll not grovel or beg this man.

He stares at his computer screen, looking bored. "No. Leave time is subject to change when urgent matters arrive. Now get out of my office."

"This isn't classified as an urgent matter. Taking time off is highly encouraged to help us stay vigilant and prevent stupid mistakes. I've had only a handful of days off in the past year, so I'm long overdue for a proper break. I'm confident I can find someone else to handle this assignment discreetly."

He leans back in his chair with a smirk. "You spend your nights home alone with takeout. That's plenty of recharge time. You'll have to submit a request for a different week off."

How does he know what I do with my evenings? Has he been keeping tabs on me? Unease washes over me.

"What I do with my personal time is none of your business, so I suggest you stay out of it," I snarl. Malice flashes in his eyes at my disrespectful tone. I know the man hates me, but the thought of him spying on me takes this to a new level of discomfort.

"Don't you dare speak to your reporting officer that way. I want you to be ready to leave at 0900 hours. Now, get the fuck out!" His finger points to the door.

Hold your tongue, Dana. I can't... It's slipping...

"Maybe we should see what Ezekial thinks about this little pup-sitting arrangement of yours?" *Damn, that tongue of mine is a slippery one; it's hard to hold back.*

"Enough!" he bellows as his fists connect with his desk, causing it to groan from the impact. "Don't undermine my authority! I swear, I'll write you up again for insubordination of your commanding officer. Eventually, they will throw you out, bitch."

Jo bares her teeth in displeasure. A low warning snarl emanates from my chest before I hastily retreat from the office. I grit my teeth while holding Joey back. Internally, a firestorm is raging. She wants to take this outside to show our commanding officer who the bitch really is.

I try to make her see reason. *"It's not worth the fight or getting kicked out. We can't give him more leverage on us."*

"Let's kill the bastard when no one is looking. It'd be doing everyone a favor. His soul is corrupt, and he knows how to hide it well," she spits. Her anger fuels our crimson gift.

Strong emotions are the equivalent of tossing accelerants into a fire. Internal flames lash out at me as I try to fight them back. I've learned to treat them similarly to another being within my vessel. Verbally reasoning with them is not an option, but I can assert dominance or guide them with my controlled feelings.

The farther I get from his office, the more the flames simmer down, slowly returning to their origin within my center. Reflecting more on what transpired leads me to believe I'll probably receive another write-up to add to my overflowing file. Brutis and I have become a running joke among those who process reports due to the sheer volume of complaints we've submitted about each other. It's the same old song and dance between us.

Brutis is a patronizing, misogynistic prick with sexist remarks, and I won't roll over to this behavior. One time, he asked me how often I was sucking Ezekial's dick to get him to turn a blind eye to my behavior. Or his favorite, reminding me that a woman's place in the pack is to raise the young, not hold positions of high rank. Regrettably, there have been no witnesses to Brutis' behavior toward me. Investigation findings have boiled down to one person's word against another's. The cunning bastard has internal connections, resulting in the blame always being unfairly placed on me. My appeals have either been ignored or vanished entirely, with no records of my submissions.

Fine, I'll admit I have an authority problem, so one could easily make assumptions. Whether I was born or blessed this way remains unknown. Everyone in our military ranks seems to have heard of me. The female wolf who is immune to the pack dominance hierarchy, stirring up trouble wherever she roams.

Even the mighty Wolf Demigod, Ezekial, can't use his godly power to make me do anything. It royally burns his ass, but we've managed to form a sort of friendship over the years. I genuinely don't wish to be his number one pain in the ass, but I guess the title must go to someone. I treat him with respect, but respect doesn't mean staying silent. I'll speak my mind when I see things differently from him. Everyone needs checks and balances. He won't say it out loud, but I know he appreciates my unsolicited opinion.

On the bitter trek back to my apartment, a quiet voice within urges me to leave and join the ranks of the Guardians. It whispers I might find my place there. *Flip this place the bird, girl, and don't look back. You deserve better.* My headstrong nature screams that is what Brutis wants me to believe: that I am not valued. My brother's face, Charles, as well as those of friends, teammates, and thousands of wolves I have aided over the years, come to the forefront of my mind. Because of all that, I won't let one asshole be the reason I walk away from all I've built here.

CHAPTER FOUR

Ajax

Karissa

Pounding on the outside of my bedroom window rouses me from sleep. *What the—?* Groggily, I open one eye to note the time, 9:00 a.m. Scrubbing a hand over my face, I wonder how I've managed to sleep this late. All the late-night investigations I've been putting in must have caught up to me.

"Get up, man, now. We need your help," Mickey's familiar voice calls as he continues to bang on my window.

"Are you sleeping? When the fuck have you ever slept in this late, child of the rising son?" Miguel complains.

"Meet me at the kitchen door," I shout while tossing on a pair of joggers.

What kind of trouble are my brothers up to this morning? While we are not blood related, I consider both my family. Their kind-hearted parents took me in, raising me as their own for a time after I lost mine. Pain pierces my heart, the same way it always does when I think about that day. Quickly, I shut that train of thought down.

An unnerving sense of trepidation crawls in as I make my way towards the kitchen. Flipping the lock, I fling the sliding door open. Both let themselves in as I head toward my coffee maker.

"What's the fire?" I ask through a yawn.

"Karissa White, a seventeen-year-old girl is missing. Her parents reported it to Gamma Dolken about thirty minutes ago. They assumed she was sleeping in until they checked on her, and she was gone. No signs of foul play, her window was unlocked, and all her belongings appear to be there, like her phone," Mickey relays, standing tall with his arms crossed over his broad chest.

With both my brothers serving as pack guards, they would be the first to be notified about a situation like this.

"They've confirmed she didn't sneak out to a friend's or a male's house for the night?" I question.

Mickey nods. "Yes. So far, no one has seen her since yesterday evening."

Son of a bitch. Frustration builds inside me, but I tamp it down, trying not to give away my poker face. Here it is, the reason I'm back here. Internally, I start chastising myself for not having flushed out this scum bag already.

"Most of the pack is already out searching for her, which concerns me. Those drunk old fuckers who probably just left the bar won't know their ass from their elbow and will muck up evidence. Dolken's working to corral the chaos. Karissa's family panicking is contagious, and no one is thinking rationally right now," Mickey pauses for a breath, allowing his twin, Miguel, to cut in.

"What our dear brother's ramblings are leading to is that we could use your help. Gamma Dolken already cleared it," he tells me.

I eagerly agree, glad I'm getting an easy entry into the situation so I don't have to insert myself another way. "Of course, let me quickly get dressed."

They believe I've worked as a mercenary for the past ten years in Europe, which is an easy explanation to give. While Miguel usually has good intentions, he's a walking security breach. If someone who shouldn't know learned I work for the angels, I might get stabbed in the back with a silver dagger. Guardian agents are seen as either valuable or the next target of an assassin. Many dark supernatural entities try to infiltrate the angelic order. As a security measure, all agents are bound by a silencing spell that makes it impossible for us to share mission details with outsiders. However, you can tell trusted individuals about your affiliation with the organization.

The angels of Earth's extremely cautious behavior has helped keep their numbers stable, unlike those of Eden. Aside from Andy, all the angels of Eden were lost in the Scorch Wars that led to The Crossing. New angels can't simply fly down from the heavens to join their brethren in the mortal realm. The supreme deities of the worlds specifically created the Guardian Angel race to live throughout their mortal realms, serving as their protectors within. Only through death can a Guardian Angel enter the divine realms beyond, never to return to the mortal plane again. With the Eden angel's eradication, the ones of Earth and their supernatural military do their best to aid both worlds.

Our trio sets off toward Karissa White's home to speak with her parents after I am dressed. There's a buzz of energy that flows through my body, making me feel alert and ready. I've been back here six months and have not uncovered anything substantial.

On our walk over, I learn King Anders, his Beta Matt, and a few guards are currently away on pack business. The timing seems extremely convenient if indeed this female was a targeted abduction.

Guided by my brothers, we arrive at the White's home. The buttery yellow house provides an illusion of comfort and warmth.

There's no warmth as Karissa's dad, Ben, greets us with a hollow expression and barely concealed fear.

"Mickey, Miguel," is all he says in a way of greeting. "Demi told me you would be heading over with someone who could help."

Karissa's mother is sitting on the couch, wrapped in a woman's arms, uncontrollably sobbing. "Someone took my baby! My sweet baby! Goddess, hear my prayers and help us find her."

Mickey tears his gaze away from the heartbreaking scene to focus on Ben. "Yes, this is Ajax Blackclaw. He's not a member of the Guard, but he has extensive outside experience."

Karissa's mother's eyes dart to mine. "Did you work for the angels? Can they help us?" Her eyes hold so much hope that the urge to tell her the truth sits on the tip of my tongue.

"Ah, no ma'am, I apologize. Mercenary work." Keeping the truth from her is nearly as painful as watching the light of hope drain out of her eyes.

"We'll take your help." Ben extends his hand to me. "You're Brun's boy?" he asks.

"Yes, I am." The mention of my father's name instantly causes a lump to form in my throat.

"He was a good man and pack Beta. One of my father's closest friends. My dad was gutted when your parents died. Know your father was a strong man for having the courage to stand up to that tyrant."

"Yes, he was." That's all I can manage to say. An overwhelming swarm of emotions bubbles up inside like it always does when I speak with people who knew my parents. They bang on the bars of their rusted, neglected cage, begging to be set free.

"Anyways, why don't you follow me? I'll take you to my daughter's room so you can get her scent," Ben says, gesturing for us to follow him up the stairs.

On the way, we pass decades of family photos. They have an older son, Demi, whom I've been acquainted with through Mickey. He appears to have been well into adulthood by the time his younger sister was born.

Letting my mind wander, I think about what it would've been like to grow up fully with my family. It would've been filled with love and memories from simpler times. Instead, my siblings and I were forced to walk paths we did not choose. The trauma of my past is something I am forced to carry with me like silver chains, painful and heavy. *Fuck, this isn't the time for this. Keep it together, Blackclaw.* Mars stirs, tenderly brushing against my invasive thoughts, acting as my silent source of strength. It's a reminder I don't carry this grief alone.

Pulling my focus back, I try to memorize Karissa's features from the photos hanging on the wall. She has inherited traits from both parents. Large, wide-set brown eyes with high cheekbones like her mother's, and ashy blonde hair the same color as her father's. I wouldn't be surprised if she were a targeted abduction.

"Wait here," Ben instructs. "Gamma Dolken thought it was best if as few people as possible entered her room until they're able to search it."

"We understand," Mickey replies.

He walks to her closet and grabs a sweatshirt. I can already smell her vanilla and dull lemon scent from standing outside her room. Ben hands over the shirt, and I bring the well-worn garment to my nose. I take a deep pull of scent, committing it to memory. Mickey and Miguel follow suit before we make our way outside the cherished family home. Mars comes forward, helping to enhance our senses. A trace of her scent lingers on the ground below her second-story window.

I turn to Ben. "Have you caught her sneaking out before?"

"No," he replies quickly. "If you want to follow me, I'll show you where her scent trail ends. There was no one else's scent present around hers this morning."

Ben leads us toward the pack's southeastern border, where her lemony trail abruptly vanishes. My mind races with potential causes: entering a vehicle, a scent-masking potion, or using a portal. Quickly, I rule out a car as there are no tire indents in this grassy area. Unfortunately, we lack the ability to track a portal ourselves. That would require assistance from a powerful witch.

"Scour this area and look for anything that could hold a scent-masking potion," I instruct.

"How or why would my daughter have that?" Ben frowns. I see the internal struggle inside him as he tries to understand what could have motivated his daughter to leave the safety of the pack lands undetected on her own. The White's don't seem to think she would have gone willingly.

"Maybe she didn't have a choice and was forced to take it," Mickey suggests.

"I'll not pretend to know motives. I know the only way her scent would go cold like this is if she entered a portal or took a scent-masking potion. Our best course of action right now is to look for signs of scent masking until we can get a witch to help us." Both my brothers look thoughtful before they spring into action.

"A portal," Ben murmurs. His eyebrows draw together as he turns it over in his mind. His fear is back and breaking through his composure.

Forty minutes of sweeping the area pay off when I find it. A small glass vial lying tucked under some shrubbery. I quickly shed my clothes, letting Mars take the lead. Our shift happens within the course of a few breaths. It's a fluid transition from man to lycan after decades together. I love the sensation the change provides, like a stretch to a sore muscle you welcome.

"*What is it?*" Mickey's voice enters my head.

"*I believe this is a potion bottle,*" I mindlink to both of my brothers and Ben.

Crouching to ground level, Mars leans our long snout in to smell the mundane object. The cork plugging the top smells strongly of birch, allowing it to easily meld with the scents of the forest. Birch is a commonly used ingredient within these types of potions, confirming my suspicions. Sniffing again, we pull the slightest trace of lemon.

"This has her scent on it. Someone grab a secure bag that we can put this in," I instruct.

Without a word, Mickey takes off in search of one. Ben wastes no time shifting, allowing him to confirm his daughter's scent. Both of us shift back to our human form and begin dressing when Mickey returns with Demi and Dolken in tow.

Demi is gruff and demanding. "What is it?"

"A potion bottle. Highly likely, given the heavy birch fragrance, it was used on a scent masking spell," I answer.

"It has your sister's scent on it," Ben confirms somberly.

Demi's sharp eyes move from his father to me. "Are you insinuating my sister ran away on purpose?"

"No, but she did mask her scent either by force or choice. If it was by choice, there might be some clue she left behind as to why," I say.

Treading lightly, since I hold no authority in this pack, I turn to Dolken. "Someone should search her room for signs of anything out of the ordinary, like more vials of scent masking."

Ben agrees. "I can start searching it now."

"Beta Matt asked us to wait until he returned later today, but I agree it's too critical to wait. We'll search her room now. Give her phone to Abe to hack into." Nodding at Dolken's orders, Ben starts back toward his home.

A group of us decides to continue in the direction the cork was leading, which is to neutral ground outside pack territory. We grab additional weapons and men before continuing in our search. The farther we walk off the pack lands, the more Mars starts to prowl like a caged animal. His anxious energy is putting me on edge.

"What is it, buddy?" I ask, unable to ignore his change in behavior.

"I'm not sure why, but it feels like something major is coming."

CHAPTER FIVE

Dana

Canada

An hour after I visit Brutis's office, I arrive via portal to the small 110-member Crescent Moon Pack in Alberta, Canada. The pack borders are surrounded by dense forest, emitting the perfect heavenly Christmas tree fragrance. I slowly inhale a large breath of the clean forest air.

Wow, that's lovely, but not as lovely as Napa, I think bitterly.

What I wouldn't give for a big ass glass of wine in my hand right now, without a care in the world. My amazing friends were disappointed, but they understood that duty called, each being part of the Moonborn Pack's Military. Still, I can't shake my own disappointment over the whole situation, which is souring my mood.

The pack's Gamma leads our troop through the heart of the secluded pack. Tiny wooden cottages with tin roofs litter the area. Pack members with grim expressions meander about, catching curious glimpses of us. The main Alpha house is a beautiful rustic lodge in the center of town. The Gamma escorts our group through the residence, where we'll be sharing bedrooms for the duration of our stay. This news does nothing to help the dark storm cloud hanging over my head.

Taking ten personal minutes, we split off to claim bedrooms before reconvening in the largest conference room for a debrief with their Alpha. I enter one of the rooms, noting there are three queen-sized beds all nestled side-by-side.

"Do you have a preference, Commander Johnston?" Behind me stands a young Beta Private, and next to her is an Omega who specializes in technical functions for the squad.

"The one closest to the door would be great. Thanks for asking," I reply.

All three of us quickly claim a bed before storing our belongings. Neither of them speaks, but I pick up their unease around me. No doubt they are wondering what the hell I am doing here.

Nervous tension has been thick among the squad members since they found out a chaperone would be tagging along. Glances from teammates have left pricks of awareness along my skin since we arrived. Not being allowed to share the real reason for me tagging along has increased the unease. I intend to give the impression that I'm here to evaluate performance. I will sit back, observe, and then provide constructive feedback at the end of this endeavor. Team members can choose to learn from it or piss on it, whatever they wish.

Okay, I can do this. Time to put my big girl pants on and suck it up. Positive attitude, girl. You're not salty.

"You are the equivalent of an ultra-processed meat loaded with sodium right now. *Stop lying because I ain't buying it,"* Joey scoffs before she dramatically plops down. *"You can tell yourself what you want, but we are here as damn babysitters and we hate it."*

"Aw, there's that favorite optimistic voice in my head," I coo at her. *"You're right, but we are losing perspective. Some asshole needs to be castrated for kidnapping women."*

She bares her teeth. *"I'm happy to help with that."*

"That's my girl."

I slip into the hallway, searching for the pack's Alpha and Beta before our meeting in the conference room. Speaking with them privately is ideal to explain my presence. Being a more dominant wolf in their territory will make their wolves instinctively see me as a threat to what is theirs, so it's best to nip that in the bud. Lucky for them, the only Alpha I'd ever consider challenging for a pack is Bobby, in hopes of seeing that bastard cry. Following their scent, I find them in the Alpha's office. Their heads both snap in my direction as I enter after a quick knock.

"Alpha James, Beta Zane, may I have a quick word?"

"Yes," Alpha James replies, waving me in.

I walk swiftly over to them, extending my hand for them to shake. Both men have fatigue etched on their faces, their clothing is unkempt, and there is the unmistakable odor of stress sweat emanating from them. According to the report, the Beta's future chosen mate was among the females taken. Their mating cere-mony was to take place on the next full moon. The man looks like he hasn't slept in a year, aging his handsome young face.

"First off, I want to say I'm truly sorry for the attack on your pack. Moonborn Pack will do what we can to aid in retrieving those taken." They respond with somber shakes of their heads.

"Second, I wanted to make my presence clear. I'm Comman-der Dana Jo Johnston of Moonborn Pack's Elite Squad 2. My boss has asked me to tag along for training purposes. Squad Leader Kyle will be your main point of contact, but if there's anything I can do to help while here, please don't hesitate to ask." They both look at me with unreadable expressions.

"Thank you, Commander Johnston," James says politely.

"It was nice to meet you both," I tell them before turning to go.

"Are you a crimson wolf?" James asks as he studies me intently. "Sorry if that is rude to ask."

"Yes, I'm a blessed one." Interest sparks in his eyes at the mention. Blessed wolves are a rarity.

"My father told me stories as a pup of crimson wolves, mentioning they all carry a signature smoky scent. I've never had the pleasure of meeting one before. You're most welcome here. We'll take all the help we can get to bring our women back," James tells me.

"The pups would love to see your wolf if you can find time. I think it'd be a big morale boost," Zane adds, trying to force happiness into his words.

"Of course. Jo can never pass up an opportunity to showboat."

Small talk continues between us as we head toward the conference room. The space has been selected as the optimal location for a temporary command center. Inside the tight quarters, I spot Luca, then quietly retreat to a side wall. Since space is limited, it's best to become an invisible fly on the wall.

Alpha James begins by recounting how four rogues lured the pack patrol, himself, and Zane to their northern border. "A scuffle broke out among the rogues just beyond the border. It was close enough to put us on high alert if anyone dared to cross into our lands. Shortly into the altercation, five more rogue wolves joined the scene. The rogues hurled taunts, trying to get us to take the bait and leave our posts, which we didn't.

Shortly after the five additional rogue wolves showed up, two houses on the eastern part of the pack caught fire, splitting our pack's enforcement in two. There were no witnesses or injuries during these fires. The cause is still unknown."

An unknown fire is strange. If a rogue had come onto the pack lands to start it, they surely would have left a scent trail or evidence of how it started.

"During what we believe were suspected diversions, five females, last seen at a party near the southwestern side of the pack, went missing. The party halted when news of the imposing threat was shared through a pack mindlink. Most went straight home or to the border to assist. No one witnessed the women leaving the pack. Their scents led toward the neutral ground outside the pack lands before vanishing. No additional scents were detected in that area. There were no signs of a struggle or calls for help heard by any of the pack members. The five females ranged in age from seventeen to nineteen," James shares with the group, and you can visibly read his heartbreak.

Two are minors, meaning their wolves have not emerged yet. A common trait among wolf traffickers is to take underage females before they gain their wolf's full strength to fight back. Furthermore, mate bonds *require* the wolf's presence; without them, no connections could have already been formed. Linked soul bonds are nearly impossible to break, unless you have the dark magic to do so.

Something must have compelled these women to leave the safety of the pack land. They wouldn't have done so willingly, knowing there were threats around the borders.

Joey tosses around a thought. *"Witches, likely dark ones if they are working for traffickers."*

A chill runs down my spine. *"Damn it."* I rub at my temples, which are throbbing thanks to the lack of sleep and the over-consumption of alcohol. This just got a whole hell of a lot more complicated if dark witches had a hand in this. A higher-level squad such as mine might need to take over this investigation.

"How do we best track down these rogues if they left no scent behind? It feels like too much time has passed already," Zane asks, trying to keep the desperation out of his voice.

Agony rolls off the guy. Reading his emotions of genuine concern and regret makes it easy to rule him out as a suspect. I've seen too many forced mating situations that have led to foul play during my time in the military, but that is not the case here.

"That is a valid concern, Beta. Luckily, it's still within the first 24 hours," Squad Leader Kyle tries to reassure him. "My team will conduct reconnaissance around the area where the women's scent trails end, checking for signs of anything your patrol may have overlooked. I'd like my team to move deeper into the neutral territory to scout, while your pack handles the reconstruction of the lost homes."

I know I'm supposed to be a shadow on the wall, but when have I ever followed the rules? The circumstances we're facing aren't great. The Alpha and Beta need to understand the odds here.

"If I may, a half-feral pack of rogues wouldn't have been able to orchestrate something with this level of detail. This was likely the work of a well-organized trafficking organization. The attack was well planned, specifically targeted given the age and accessibility of the women, then executed perfectly," I remark, letting the facts speak for themselves.

Kyle agrees with a curt nod, but keeps his emotions tightly in check. Zane's fists clench as he fights to hold back an enraged snarl. His wolf is close to the surface. James studies his Beta briefly as a worried line creases his forehead.

"So what does that mean for Emmaline and the other women taken? How do we find them?" Zane grits out as his wolf's eyes reflect for all of us to see.

"Fabricating facts isn't something I do, because if roles were reversed, I'd want to know everything. Highly organized trafficking cases like these have a solve rate of less than 50%. The keyword is highly. Random cases of rogues taking women are usually easily resolved. But if you start adding witches—"

"Witches!" Zane shoots up, snarling at me. "There were no witches present!"

Raising my hands, I give him a silent warning with my eyes to remain calm.

"Let's hear her out, Zane," James places a hand on his shoulder, squeezing it subtly.

"Whenever other supernatural beings are involved, the solve rate goes down substantially. And let's be clear, this case reeks of witchcraft, with unknown fires starting, women leaving the pack lands, and scent trails going cold. Since the Moonborn Pack has some witches in residence, we can request their assistance. If you know of any magical beings with the ability to create locating spells, I recommend you call them. We could also explore passing the case over to The Guardians. They can't always investigate immediately since they have many priorities overseeing all of the supernatural races." I leave out the part about how these women will likely be mated off by the time the case reaches their hands.

"FUCK!" Zane roars as his chair goes sailing into the nearest wall. I notice Luca slightly flinch at the sudden outburst. Newbie. The rest of the squad is well-trained for situations like these. They remain professional while Zane works through his anger.

"Zane! Calm the fuck down, your anger won't help anyone," James bellows at his second in command.

Zane starts pacing around before he drives his fist through the nearest wall. Pieces of drywall crumble easily under the immense force, leaving a hollow hole behind. My heart aches for him.

"Zane!" James yells again. Jo surges forward as I walk toward him. Reaching up, I pull his hands down from his messy hair, forcing him to look me in the eye.

"Calm down," I command. He bares his teeth, but I feel his body naturally respond to my dominance. "We're going to try our best. Right now, Emmaline needs you to stay strong."

His chest heaves as he sucks in a lungful of air, trying to calm himself further. A mixture of potent emotions continues to pour off the male. Luckily, he's no longer assaulting the wall, so we can move forward.

"Alpha, how far are the closest neighboring packs?" Kyle asks, trying to get the conversation back on track.

"The Glacier Pack is run by my cousin about twenty miles west of here. They're about double our size. Our lycan neighbors, the Silverthrone Pack, are southeast of here. The lycans keep to themselves, never involving themselves in any wolf affairs, so I don't know much about them. Though I did meet their new King and Queen when they took the throne about three years ago now," James says thoughtfully.

The mention of lycans piques Joey's interest. We both carry a hidden eagerness to spend time among their kind, which is driven by the unusual similarity we share.

"Can you provide a list of all the packs within a 100-mile radius, along with your current standing? We can't rule them out until we investigate." A smart call by Kyle.

The discussion about the packs in the area continues for a little while longer before Kyle gives his team their orders. Assignments are handed out to contact nearby packs, increase border patrols, and search the neutral ground. The eleven members of Squad 13 jump into action after receiving their squad leader's orders.

James, Zane, our Omega tech support, Angela, and I remain. Thankfully, the dense air in this compact room is finally beginning to subside. Angela is head down, vigorously typing on her laptop, pulling maps of the area to determine the best route for a drone. James and Zane look even more worn out. They appear lost and unsure of how to contribute.

"I need to find a witch to place security wards around the pack. My family has been foolish for far too long, by only having sound-proofing and human deterrent ones in place." James shakes his head, clearly berating himself.

"Private Angela, please provide Alpha James with a list of witch allies," I instruct.

"Yes, Commander Johnston." She radiates eagerness. I love the young ones.

"Alpha, Beta, you're in good hands here. Why don't you take a moment to recharge with rest and a bite to eat?" I suggest. They're reluctant but agree a break will help them return with a clear head.

Fresh Christmas tree aroma greets me when I step outside on the front porch of the Alpha's lodge. I wonder where I'll be most beneficial.

"Joey?"

"Let's have a run around the southern neutral grounds," she answers without hesitation.

CHAPTER SIX

Ajax

Search Party

Ten of us make our way through the neutral unclaimed lands, looking for anything that stands out. We find a fresh trail of disturbed foliage leading us a mile deeper into open territory.

"Here, does she own a pair of Nikes?" I ask, pointing to a muddy print resembling a female size with a partially smudged Nike logo.

Demi quickly replies, "I'll mindlink my mom."

"What teenager doesn't have a pair of white Nikes these days?" Miguel deadpans.

"Karissa does own a pair of Air Force 1s; ask your mom if they're missing," Noah, Demi's good friend who eagerly joined our search party, suggests.

Demi hits Noah with a critical glare. "How the fuck do you know what shoes my sister owns?"

I'm not sure how Demi is late to this party. It's clear to me why he'd know that tidbit of information.

"Just a random observation." Noah shrugs him off, attempting to play it cool. He misses the mark as we watch him squirm under the weight of our sudden scrutiny.

Demi's stare looks hot enough to leave a mark on Noah's face. "Is that all it is? At first, I thought you were torn up about this because Karissa's my sister, but now I think there's more to it."

"Come on, don't be a dick and make him say it out loud. You know it's bad juju," Miguel whispers conspiratorially. It's clear he came to the same conclusion I have.

"Tell me!" Demi pushes, his tone dangerous. His body vibrates with tension as he refuses to break eye contact with Noah, silently challenging him.

"That's cold, man," Miguel mutters.

Demi snarls, "Shut the fuck up, Miguel!"

"I will, in fact, not be shutting up, thanks," Miguel throws back.

Demi's right hook misses my brother as he expertly sidesteps it. This scenario is typical for Miguel, considering his highly perceptive and sarcastic nature.

"Stop it, both of you! She's my mate. There I said it," Noah's deep voice rumbles over the scuffle, showing his lycan is near the surface. Demi halts, losing his Miguel ass-kicking momentum.

Karissa isn't old enough to sense her fated mate, but Noah is. The poor bastard has grieving-mate written all over his disheveled appearance, making it clear to all who look close enough.

"Does she know?" Demi's tone holds an accusatory sharpness.

"Don't be an idiot. Everyone knows not to break the underage mate rule. I like my head right where it's at, thank you!" Noah is correct.

The unwritten rules are simple: don't tell anyone if an underage female is your fated mate. The moment you do, a price might be put on your head.

After The Crossing, fights for female mates became a sport. Savage competitions decided who would earn the privilege of carrying on their bloodline. Early on, some tried to claim younger females due to sensed bonds. Those individuals often met the afterlife sooner than expected. Killing a mate before the female was old enough to solidify the fated bond forced them to take another, and often not of their choosing. Our kind has made strides out of that dark age in lycan history, but the fear is so deeply rooted that it has been hard to fully extinguish.

"You're one of my best friends. You and my sister? How did you manage to keep this to yourself?"

"Unwritten rules, Dem."

Dolken interjects. "Noah, do you have any ideas where she might have gone?"

"Dolk, I swear to the Moon Goddess, I've kept my distance. I have no idea where she would've gone." Dolken nods once, clearly sensing the truth behind Noah's words.

The wind rustles softly through the forest canopy as we continue for another few feet. Silently, we follow the breadcrumbs of crushed greenery along the forest floor.

We emerge into an area where fresh spring vegetation lies limp and withered in muted shades of gray, having had the life stolen from it. My stomach drops at the sight. Decay hangs heavily around it as it rots before our eyes, falling to the ground with a pitter-patter. The putrid smell is impossible to ignore.

"This isn't good," Mars says. *"Andy will need to hear of this."*

"Agreed, I will message her an update once we get back."

"Strange. Has anyone seen something like this before?" Noah asks the group. Most of the guys gather around, shaking their heads no.

Dolken inhales deeply. "Smell that stench? That's dark magic, and it was used here."

"Yes. I believe they used it to open a portal, based on the way the affected plants form a perfect rim," I point out my observation.

"Fuck," the colorful word rushes out of Demi's mouth. Noah crouches down on his haunches, no doubt trying to keep his lycan from raging.

"There are wolf scents up here," Miguel calls farther ahead. "They head toward the direction of the Crescent Moon Pack."

Demi is boiling with rage. "I'm going to fucking kill all of those dogs if they were involved!"

Noah jumps to standing. "Agreed!" The two men take off in haste toward the direction of the pack.

"Wait!" Dolken hollers after them.

I lace as much dominance as I can into my words, and I command the entire group to stop moving. Everyone listens, halting in their tracks. Demi and Noah look taken aback, while others don't seem surprised. My family may have been stripped of its Beta title within the pack, but that level of dominance runs through my very blood despite the circumstances. It can't be stripped away even if a tyrant king says so.

"Everyone needs to pause for a moment," I say calmly. "Let's be rational and talk about this strategically. Storming a wolf pack would do nothing but ultimately declare war between the packs and take time away from this investigation. We need proof, not assumptions. And trust me, no one wants the weight of harming an innocent hanging on their conscience. My suggestion is we request a meeting with their Alpha."

The majority of our group agrees easily. With a firm glare, Dolken's eyes pin Noah and Demi, giving them the option to settle down or return home. After receiving assurances from both of them, we proceed on toward the pack lands.

Mickey is correct; there are numerous wolf scents in the vicinity, but these scents belong to rogues. Wolves that have left their pack or were born to rogue parents exhibit specific characteristics, such as a sharper, muskier odor due to poor hygiene. While scenting the area, I can distinguish at least ten unique scent trails, which could possibly indicate a rogue wolf pack.

As we reach the border of Crescent Moon, we encounter unmistakable tension. Pack patrol wolves, along with several armed soldiers in matching black uniforms, hold us in their barrels' sights. From twenty feet away, you can smell the fear of the younger pack patrol members. Their petrified eyes jump between our group of ten fully grown lycans. The three soldiers can hide their emotions better, not giving away their uneasiness so readily. Unlike the pack pups, they appear to be well-trained, as if they could put up a decent fight. Mars perks up at the sight of them.

"I wonder what they're doing here," I ask him absently.

"Something's going on. Stay vigilant," he advises.

"Stop right there," a female wolf calls from behind her raised rifle.

"Everyone hold," Dolken orders through our mindlink.

Demi starts vibrating with impatience as if the inconvenience might make him explode at any moment.

"Those are Moonborn Pack emblems. We don't want to do anything that warrants the Wolf Demigod up our asses," Dolken points out to the group.

"Speak for yourself. He's very much welcome up mine any-time," Miguel quips.

Joel mock gags. *"Gross! Not a visual we need right now."*

I inwardly chuckle at my brother's antics. Dolken shoots him a stern "that's enough from you" look before announcing to the patrol, "We wish to speak with your Alpha regarding an urgent matter."

No one has time to respond before a fierce growl emanates from behind the pack members. A stunning, sleek black wolf with piercing red eyes charges to the borderline. With fangs bared, it snarls warnings in our direction. Fire snakes from its midnight paws across the grass, creating a defined border line. There's a clear threat in the wolf's body language, stating that if we step a toe out of line, our asses will become ashes.

An unexpected, overpowering aura bulldozes us with its immense force. Instinctively, we all take a step back. Low snarls of unease are heard throughout our group. Our lycans dislike the threat this wolf is posing. The aura continues to feel like waves crashing into us, not giving us the chance to come up for air. Strangely, the feeling alters from chokehold to a soft caress. It slides over my skin like silk, feeling almost intimate. *I like this feeling.* Over my shoulder, I see my pack members do their best to hide their distress.

"Holy shit balls!" Miguel mindlinks the group.

"Have you ever felt a fucking wolf with this level of power before? Who the hell is this guy?" The strain in Demi's voice is apparent.

I tsk. *"Not a guy,"* I confidently reply, unsure how I know, but deep down, I do. The she-wolf has the height and build of an average Alpha male wolf. She is extraordinary. Mars surges forward, rumbling in agreement as we both stand captivated by her.

"Go to her, now!" Mars encourages me.

"A she-wolf? I don't believe it," Demi sneers.

"Can she-wolves be that big?" Joel asks, also skeptical.

"Never call a lady big, especially one with fire magic, it won't end well for you," Miguel helpfully adds.

"Jax, how are you unaffected right now?" Mickey grumbles from beside me.

Ignoring all the internal chatter, I let my voice ring out while raising my hands to signify that we mean no harm. "Everyone, please stand down. We just want a word with whoever is in charge."

I hold the crimson wolf's gaze, hoping she will see the truth in my words and understand that I will not submit to her in fear. Her appraising red eyes narrow at me, making my heart skip a beat. I struggle to comprehend what is causing this reaction within me. After a couple of breaths, her eyes continue scanning the rest of our group.

Sweat mixed with anger drifts around my pack mates, who still strain under her vice-like aura. The wolf lifts its nose, sniffing the air. Once satisfied that we don't pose an immediate threat, the heavy aura recedes. Guns remain pointed in our direction as the wolf retreats behind nearby trees. Mars whines when we lose sight of the black beauty. I can feel he is in total awe of this woman.

"I don't like that she's leaving," he admits.

"She'll be back, buddy," I reassure him. Oddly, I, too, feel a weight of her absence inside.

CHAPTER SEVEN

Ajax

My Angel of Fire

My emotions overwhelm me to the point where it's hard to formulate a coherent thought. I'd never understood the phrase "rendered speechless" until the most beautiful woman with a mess of blonde, silky hair emerges from the forest's cover. Her natural beauty matches that of her surroundings. She is tall, strong, and as sharp as pine needles.

As she gracefully strides over, we wait in the calm before her storm. An oversized T-shirt is all she wears, which is not uncommon after a hasty shift and clothing grab situation like this. It does little to conceal her womanly figure underneath. The shirt clings to her otherwise bare chest.

"Thank you, universe, for this small victory today." Mars is basically drooling over this woman.

Long, ivory-toned legs are on full display. One thigh has a decorative trinity symbol tattoo. Christ, she looks like she'd be a fucking kindergarten teacher with that angel face. She is the definition of a wolf in sheep's clothing.

Her pretty pink lips are turned down in an adorable scowl. That sweet mouth draws me in. I want to see it begging to take me deep... *Whoa. Fuck. Focus Blackclaw!*

The breeze carries her scent my way, it's a perfect blend of smoky bonfire with lavender undertones. She is downright mouthwatering. Mars' energy shifts from enamored to hyper-focused on this female. He urges me to let him come forward. There is a quiet desperation driving him to be acknowledged by her. She needs to see us and only us. His thoughts grow to borderline obsessive with each and every step she takes towards us. Possessiveness over her starts to overwhelm everything else I am feeling.

"Wow, she has surely captured your interest. Stand down," I scold the overzealous beast.

"No," he challenges back.

"Stand down, now!" I tell him again.

Snarling, he pulls back, resorting to pacing.

"Speak your business, lycans," the beauty calls with a southern twang.

My cock suddenly springs to attention at the sound of her authoritative voice. *Whoa, you're not getting any, so you better stand down too, soldier.* Shifting ever so slightly, I reposition my gun to conceal the growing bulge in my pants. Mars helpfully shows me images of exactly what he wants us to do to the pretty she-wolf. Us ripping that thin shirt off and licking every inch of her body so everyone here knows who she belongs to. The bastard is not helping the problem down south.

"Listen, we're on a job. We can't have the pretty wolf. End of story!" I hiss at him.

"Get closer," he begs. *"I want to scent her better. I sense a lycan quality about her."*

"Like she's a hybrid?"

"I'm not sure," Mars replies honestly. *"That's why we need to get closer."*

Wolves and lycans have a complicated history that prevents them from coexisting harmoniously. Each was created by a separate lunar deity, deities who didn't get along. Eden, unlike its sister Earth, has two moons. The legend states that the Moon God, Lycaon, wanted to outshine his brother, Alpha, by creating a race of supernaturals that were similar but superior to his. Being the larger of the two moons, he had the means to do so. Thus, wolves are like the weaker cousins of lycans. Lycaon gave his creation the ability to walk upright like a human, not on all fours like an animal. Lycans are an ideal mix of beast and man. We are stronger and faster than a werewolf. Our kind often keep to ourselves rather than coexist, as the majority believe that cohabiting with wolves doesn't offer us any value.

We are proud, arrogant bastards, thanks to our original creator. Even with all our futile feuds, there are were-lycan hybrids in the world. *Could she be one? Or maybe she has a lycan chosen mate?* The thought makes my stomach churn. *Great, even worse, I'm so fucking turned on right now by a mated female.* Internally groaning, I force myself to get my head out of my ass and focus.

"We need to speak with the Crescent Moon Pack Alpha, not their hired security guards." Demi's tone is condescending and laced with his lycan aura, causing a few soft whimpers to escape from some of the patrol wolves.

I might fucking skin the bastard alive, and luckily, Mars is on-board. Turning toward him, I send a low warning growl that I hope conveys how displeased I am with his pointless show of disrespect. Several shocked expressions from my pack members are sent back my way. The crimson wolf, however, stands unfazed. She raises one delicate eyebrow at Demi. Her facial expression turns from annoyed to playful.

"Right," she drawls. Turning, she slowly strides in a small circle until she returns to the spot where she stood originally, all mirth gone from her face.

"Hello, I'm Commander Dana Jo Johnston of Moonborn Pack military, and as such, I'm the highest-ranking individual here, even more so than the pack Alpha, who is currently indisposed. Now, if we can shake our dicks of this pissing contest, I'd like to get back to business. First, if you use your aura against my wolves again, I'll take it as a direct challenge against the Moonborn Pack, and I'll seek to eliminate the threat. Is that understood, sir?"

A smirk creeps across my face, which I quickly work to school. Strong wolf with a sassy mouth. This woman is more than a wolf with magic; she is fire. Demi stares at her, dumbfounded, as if he can't comprehend a wolf ever having the backbone to speak in such a way to a lycan.

"Yes, it won't happen again," Dolken thankfully interjects, keeping Demi from speaking further.

She nods in approval in his direction. "Thank you, sir. Now, please tell me what I can do for you, fine gentleman."

"A female has gone missing from our pack, and the investigation has led us here," Dolken tells her.

"Oh, I'm truly sorry to hear that. When did she go missing?" she gently asks.

"Karissa went missing sometime between last night and this morning," Demi responds, managing to hold back his emotions.

"She's your family." A statement, not a question, from the fiery commander.

Surprise emerges in his eyes. "Yes, she's my sister."

With a genuinely thoughtful expression, she asks, "How did your investigation lead you here?"

"We followed what appeared to be her tracks through the neutral ground. There we found scent traces of wolves heading in this direction," Dolken recounts.

She lets out a soft, "Hmm," as her eyes scan the trees behind us.

"We," Dolken continues, but she raises a hand, silencing him as she takes a deep, inhaling breath.

Her eyes scan the forest behind us with intensity. I, too, feel an uneasy prickling sensation along my back as if being watched. Following her lead, I scan the area but come up short. Mars pushes our heightened senses out, and still, nothing.

His hackles rise as we continue to come up short. *I don't like this feeling of being watched,* he whispers as if this invisible threat can hear our thoughts.

"Gentleman, this conversation needs to be taken to a more private location within the pack. I can't allow all of you onto the grounds, and no weapons will be permitted," Commander Dana tells us.

"No way in hell we're agreeing to split up our party," Demi openly expresses his displeasure.

Mars sighs, *"We should've left him home."*

A softened expression quickly replaces the commander's anger as she meets Demi's gaze. "I can assure you we're not your enemy. It might feel that way as tensions are running high due to an innocent female missing. This pack also had women recently abducted, which is why the Moonborn Pack military is assisting here. We might be able to help one another if we can all cooperate. You have my word that no harm will come to you unless warranted by your own aggressive actions."

Her eyes lift once again to sweep the forest, seeking the unknown threat. Fire sparks hop along her graceful fingertips as if silently daring anyone out there to cross her.

"Thoughts?" Demi mindlinks the group. Most of us agree, although it causes some unease. We are placing a lot of trust in one person's word.

"I don't trust any of these mutts, no matter how nice they are to look at," Joel sneers.

Mars angrily surges to the surface, snarling at Joel. *"That bastard better stop calling her a mutt."*

Using all my strength, I yank Mars back, although the urge to rip Joel's head off is mutual. Mickey gives me a "What the fuck is wrong with you?" look. I've been wondering the same thing.

Miguel just smirks before replying to the group. *"Christ, Joel...don't go saying shit like that out loud unless you want to get lit up by the Commander."*

My voice through the connection is deeper, thanks to Mars' presence. *"She's speaking truthfully. They won't harm us, though it's always good to stay alert."*

Dolken also agrees that we should speak with them. "Alright, you have our word we'll remain civil unless warranted by aggression from anyone in the pack that threatens our safety," he tells her.

"Fair enough. You, sir, who appears to be overseeing this operation, may enter, along with the brother," she says, pointing to Dolken and Demi. Moving on, she points to my brothers, "Twins, you can come. With your troublemaker vibes, I'll want to keep a close eye on you."

Mickey snorts, "Well, as long as you know it, we won't have a problem."

Finally, her beautiful ocean blue eyes find mine, "And lastly, you, sir, may come. You're at least level-headed. The rest of you can wait here. Be on alert; something is lurking. Follow me this way, gentlemen."

"Yes! She picked us!" Mars looks like a happy dog who was just adopted from the animal shelter.

I can't lie, there was instant gratification when she chose me. *What is wrong with me?*

The fire playing along her fingers dies before she gestures us forward. Our weapons are left in a pile near our remaining pack members. Mars hums with eagerness to be near her, to smell her, and hopefully touch her. Vastly outnumbered by wolves, I'd expect him to have hackles raised with complete focus. Instead, he only wants to sniff the fucking Commander. Unbelievable. Perhaps it has been too long since we've enjoyed a woman's company. *Yeah, that's likely it.*

"I don't think that's it," Mars tells me as if it's the most ridiculous idea in the world.

"Well, what is it then?" I push back.

The urge to connect with her intensifies as I watch the gentle sway of her hips. They make me forget my train of thought. Striding purposefully in her direction, I surrender to Mars' desires. Discreetly, I scent the air, searching for her unique fragrance. That smoky lavender crashes into me like a bullet train.

"She's our fated mate." Mars declares with certainty. He starts to lose his shit as if our favorite football team just won the European Cup.

Blood drains from my face, my breathing hitches, and the world might have stopped spinning. *My mate?*

"I, um, it can't be. We're more likely to find Santa Claus than our fated mate. She probably uses some good smelling campfire shampoo or something," I mutter.

One muscle above Mars' eye lifts. *"You can keep telling yourself that, but I'd like to get closer to our mate now."*

I attempt to reason with logic. *"She's not our mate. She's a wolf, I'm sure of it. I've never heard of a wolf-lycan goddess fated pairing."*

Lycans and wolves born under the moon of Selene on Earth are bestowed with the gift of a fated mate, unlike those born in Eden, who can only sense their compatible partners. As I was born on Earth, I would have a fated mate somewhere in the world, but could she be a wolf?

"Jax, do you not feel the pull to her? Tell me how there could be such a physical pull to a female and our body's natural reactions without a mate bond at work? I'll wait patiently while you continue to struggle with this."

I want to punch the smug bastard. *But is he right? Is that what this feeling in my chest has been since I caught her faint smell? And the reason for the deep-rooted desire to be closer to her?*

"I'm not sure. Maybe you're right and I should speak to her," I tell him, feeling suddenly an influx of nervousness.

Mars gives a little huff. *"Yes, finally we agree."*

She pauses for a hushed conversation with a man in a Moonborn Pack uniform. He doesn't look pleased with the situation. Our team also pauses, giving them space. Another woman rushes up to her, handing over a uniform and boots. She quickly pulls on her pants, but not before I get a better look at her tattoo.

I notice the symbol of the Moon God, Lycaon. There appears to be scarring that resembles a bite mark next to the intricate tattoo. Given the size, I'd put money on it being from a lycan. Thoughts start to flood my mind. *Why a tattoo of the lycan creator? Why wouldn't the bite have healed itself? Did someone hurt her?*

My whirling thoughts cause my gut to clench. The idea of someone hurting her sends indescribable anger coursing through me.

Fuck, breathe, just breathe. I should not care. I should not care. In the name of the wee man, Mars is probably right.

"Of course I am! Now get your head out of your bullocks and go talk to her!" Mars shouts at me because he is sick of my indecisiveness.

After she finishes dressing, we continue deeper into the pack lands, all of us silent. Internally, I criticize myself for not having spoken to her already. I've never had trouble talking with women or anyone else, for that matter. However, I feel like this moment will undoubtedly change my life. *Am I ready for that?*

CHAPTER EIGHT

Dana

Mr. Blackclaw

Our unexpected lycan visitors agreed to speak in a more private location, after also sensing a hidden presence that couldn't be seen, heard, or smelled.

"I'm picking up more witch vibes."

After hearing Joey say that, I must physically resist the urge to close my eyes and scrub a hand over my tired face.

"I was concerned about that," I tell her.

This mission is far more complex than we thought, especially now that lycans are here. It's probably best I came along – though I'd never admit that to Brutis. The handsome, dark-haired lycan who caught my attention earlier comes closer, interrupting my thoughts. *Damn, he smells amazing.* My body hums to life. *Whoa, thank the Goddess I just got dressed.*

"Hello, I'm Ajax Blackclaw, the level-headed one." A brilliant smile and playful wink light up his attractive face.

"Well, isn't he a tall drink of iced tea?" Joey giggles.

Typically, winking is a massive turn-off for me, but not his. My body likes it, and being this close to the gorgeous stranger, a lot.

"It's nice to meet you, Dana." He forgoes the formalities of my title.

That blatant disrespect would usually piss me off, but from him, it doesn't. Hearing my name come from his mouth makes my insides gooey. *How odd.*

"Imagine him screaming our name in pl—"

"STOP, horny wolf!"

It was too late to pause that steamy fantasy. My body began to heat the moment he spoke to me, and now it's ablaze with need. *Hello, lady bits, glad to see you've joined the party.* There's a change in my scent. *Fuck.* Whenever my emotions are heightened, the flames respond, giving off a stronger essence of burning wood.

As an extremely dominant Alpha female, it takes a lot to get me this turned on, and this guy only had to say hello. I notice the flare of his nostrils. *Ugh, this is so embarrassing. Why couldn't I have met him anywhere else but here?*

"It is nice to meet you, Mr. Blackclaw." My professional greeting feels forced and too formal. I want to bury my face in the crook of his neck. *Shit, who's this guy and what's he doing to me?*

Mr. Tall Drink of Iced Tea stands at least 6'8" with dark blue eyes framed by long lashes. Confidence and charm radiate effortlessly from him. Thick, muscular arms, with eclectic tattoos, are prominently displayed. He can't conceal his perfectly toned body, even in his looser-fitting T-shirt and tactical pants. Some shifters are bulky, but not him; he's lean yet lethal.

"Please call me Jax."

My eyes snap up from his lower region, which I was admiring. "Okay, Jax." Given that damn smug smirk, he knows I was checking him out. Heat rushes to my face. *What is happening? Get it together. You've never been this unprofessional.*

In an exuberant manner that feels so like him, he gestures to the handsome, older lycan. "This is Dolken, our pack Gamma and King Anders' grandfather. Then we have Demi, Miguel, and Mickey." All three give a greeting accordingly.

"Nice to meet y'all, though I'm sorry about the circumstances for this meeting," I tell them. I'm genuinely upset another young woman is missing from the area.

Every person we pass on the way to the pack house seems uneasy about our guests, except for me. It's clear that everyone, including

Squad Leader Kyle, is unhappy with me for allowing their passage onto the lands, but they aren't the real threat. I'm surprised Alpha James isn't out here as well, expressing his displeasure.

Jo agrees, *"Yeah, we're gonna get an ass chewing alright."*

Jax brings himself into my personal space. "Can I ask you a question?"

Please ask if you can touch my happy fun spot. My hormones cheer in favor of this request while doing the damn can-can. My entire body vibrates with anticipation of his hands on me. The strength of his leathery scent this close is too much, making my brain short-circuit.

Thankfully, he asks his question instead of waiting for me to formulate a coherent response. "I couldn't help but notice your trinity tattoo. May I ask what the meaning behind it is?"

Yes, you can touch me. Oh, wait, my tattoo?

"He's gone and tripped your breaker. We need to restart your circuit box right quick, human," Joey chuckles to herself.

"Yeah, we'd love to hear about your tattoo. It might help distract from the lack of a welcoming party we're receiving," Twin 1 pipes up. *Um, is that Mickey?*

"No, it's definitely the other one, Miguel," Joey corrects me.

Shit, get it together. We can't have everyone knowing how turned on and flustered this guy is making you. Think of disgusting things. Mucus, the smell of cat urine, porta potties, cottage cheese...

"Captain Brutis, piece of shit, Lumen."

There it is, lady boner destroyed. Joey comes through with the assist. Okay, this man needs to back up because he is leaning into my personal space as if he owns it.

"And maybe you should request he wear a paper bag over his perfectly sculpted face while you're at it so your brain can function properly."

"Shut up, Joey."

I narrow my eyes at Jax, deciding to ignore the irritating presence in my head. "Excuse me, but haven't you heard of respecting personal space?" I attempt to make my tone sound sharp, but it falls short.

"She could BBQ you in a second, man," Miguel chirps in again.

The corners of my lips tip up. I knew I'd like the twins. Miguel is right. Leather and cedarwood here has a very sexy ass, which I could fry, but that'd be a tragedy.

"Agreed, such a waste of a good ASS-et," Joey chuckles to herself as if she's just killin' it with her jokes.

"Sorry." Jax raises his hands in mock surrender before taking a few steps aside, allowing me to breathe slightly easier. "Your tattoo with God, Lycaon's symbol, has made me genuinely curious."

"Tell him how it's one of a kind like us," Joey says eagerly.

"Girl no. That sounds like a tacky jewelry store ad."

Jax's patient eyes hold my gaze as he silently waits for my response. Deciding now isn't the time to relive the story, I reluctantly break eye contact and continue walking. A powerful urge deep down makes me want to fall into those strong arms and share all my secrets with him. It takes only a few steps for Jax to return to my personal space. *WTF?* That leather sent wraps around me, just so damn yummy and welcoming.

"So you're going to leave me hanging like that?" he asks.

I don't miss how he emphasizes the me. There's no doubt that Mr. Charismatic here is used to getting what he wants. The thought irritates me enough to make my internal fire take notice. The magic inside springs up, ready to eliminate the cause of my distress. I force a warning glare, hoping it conveys he needs to leave my personal space—again! Snickering, Jax takes a few steps aside, back into his lane.

Why did you agree to let him come? You just had to choose the attractive one. Now you need to ignore him, Dana, because you have a job to do. I can tell Jo is enjoying my internal self-directed pep talk a little too much.

"Come on, Commander, now you've got the rest of us wondering," Twin 2, I mean, Mickey, inserts himself.

Miguel pipes in, "My guess is, it's your first tattoo you randomly picked because you thought it looked cool."

I chuckle lightly, "Well, Miguel, it sounds like you have experience with that."

A rich laugh escapes Mickey. "Oh, Miguel does."

"Listen, I'll make y'all a deal if y'all can be on your best behavior for the Alpha, who'll undoubtedly chew my ass for letting five lycans onto his pack without his permission. I'll tell you the story behind it on the way out. It's not random and does involve one of your kind, which is why Lycaon's mark is significant. Do we have a deal?"

"Deal." Jax's response is immediate.

"I want to clarify that I didn't agree to anything," Miguel hastily adds.

"I don't believe the word 'behave' exists in Miguel's vocabulary," Demi says dryly.

"And haven't you ever heard the saying well-behaved women seldom make history?" he shoots back. With that, I can't contain my laughter as we finally arrive at the main pack house.

CHAPTER NINE

Ajax

Alphahole

*"G*oing real smooth with your lady, Casanova,*"* Mickey mindlinks me.

"I don't know, I'm picking up some 'let's get freaky' vibes between them. She's into him but playing hard to get." Miguel gives me a double eyebrow wiggle.

"No way he is getting anywhere with her. Out of even your league, man," Mickey argues.

"Let's make a bet: the winner gets to pick the loser's next tattoo," Miguel wagers.

Mickey makes the mistake of quickly agreeing. *"Deal."*

"You two need to shut the hell up and get the fuck out of my head," I snap.

Miguel's cackle is the last thing I hear before I cut the mindlink. There's no way I can divulge to those two that she's my fated mate. They're already over the top without life-altering information in their clutches. Dana is my fated mate. I believe Mars, given our reactions and how her smoky scent calls to me. She seems to be playing it coy, likely not wanting to draw attention to our situation with everything else happening right now. Okay, little wolf, I'll play along.

It's challenging to keep the doubt from creeping in, given her lack of reaction. Yes, I scented that sweet arousal of hers, but not for long. There's also the fact that she's a wolf, and cross-species fated mates are only something I've heard mentioned once.

"She is ours, as we are hers," Mars rumbles, upset that I'm still debating what I know to be true.

"It's not what I expected. Most fated couples sob tears of joy, while our mate acts as if she has no idea. It's disheartening," I admit.

"I know. The timing isn't great. You need to talk to her the second the moment seems right."

"I will, buddy," I agree with the beast's urgings.

Our group remains silent as we walk up the steps of the main ski lodge. The Moonborn Pack soldier Dana spoke with earlier brings up the rear. He still looks as displeased as before. Trepidation lingers in his scent, although he tries to hide it outwardly. We follow Dana directly to the Alpha's office, passing a makeshift command center with several large monitors and a woman frantically typing. Given the pack's small size, it lacks meeting areas.

The Alpha's office is a decent size, but with five full-grown lycans, we quickly make the space uncomfortable. Dana stands to the left of a massive desk. I take the open space to her right, making sure to get a little too cozy. Mars is extremely pleased to be so close to our mate. Wow, our mate. The concept is so foreign to me. We actually found her. Dana rewards us with sharp eye daggers. Does she think her annoyed glare is going to make me move? Because I find it quite adorable.

Feeling cheeky, I purposely cross my arms over my chest, causing my bicep to brush against hers. For the briefest moment, I feel those electric tingling sensations everyone goes on about radiating from the point of contact. Her head snaps down to the spot where we touched, then back to my face. Our eyes connect, and I hold her intense gaze. Her expression is a perfect mask, though I can tell she is struggling to understand.

"Does she truly not know?"

Mars contemplates. *"Actually, I don't think so."* The moment is short-lived as the pack Alpha and Beta storm in.

"This wee Alpha pup is pissed," Mars points out the obvious.

"Commander Johnston!" The Alpha roars. "I don't appreciate being notified that you've allowed five lycans onto *my* pack lands without thinking to ask me. You better have a damn good reason for it!"

The Alphahole rages at my mate, pouring his dominance into the room. This only causes his Beta to bare his neck in submission. *That's not a good look.* Irritated by the way he spoke to our mate, Mars releases a low warning growl to ensure the Alpha recognizes his displeasure. Quickly, I stifle it, trying to cover it with a cough. All of my group's eyes shift to me. Dana doesn't waver from her intense staring contest with the Alpha.

"Mars, don't do that shit again. We can't start anything here; besides, our girl can take care of herself," I remind him.

"What the hell was that?" Demi snaps through our group mindlink.

I lie poorly. *"Just a little tickle."*

"Bullshit," he shoots back.

"I told you I was picking up heart-eye vibes between the two," Miguel teases.

Dolken intervenes. *"For fuck's sake children, enough. Jax get your dick in line before we have an angry neighboring Alpha to deal with."*

"Yes, sir," I assure him.

Still holding the Alpha's gaze, Dana explains her actions in a deadly calm manner. "Alpha James, I assure you they're not a threat to your pack. They, too, have a missing female, which they're investigating. My intuition tells me this isn't a coincidence, but related to the same trafficking ring we believe took the women from here. I sensed an unknown presence lurking in the woods, so I asked them to speak here in private."

Annoyance rolls off him in waves. "I won't risk more of my pack's safety on some 'blessed' woman's feelings."

In a blurred second, she's positioned inches from his face. Given the woman's impressive height, the two stand eye level. Her dominance blankets the entire room, causing everyone to remain silent. *Goddess, that dominance is a turn on.*

"I'll not be spoken to in that way again. Is that clear, Alpha?" Fire dances in her eyes as the signature crimson wolf smoke scent spreads, immersing the room.

"Crystal," he bites out.

His eyes lower in a sign of submission, and sweat has broken out along his forehead. I can tell she is holding back, keeping him on the edge where she wants him.

"Good. Now, Dolken, can you share what you have found regarding your missing female with us?" she asks.

Both sides recount the events in detail. The two situations share similarities, leading us to believe they're related. By the end of our meeting, Alpha James seems to have come around to us. Dolken and he exchange contact information and agree to keep each other updated with any new information. Dana suggests to Squad Leader Kyle that he should request reinforcements.

I mentally logged as many details as I could from the discussion to share with The Guardians. The thought of admitting my shortcomings to Andy feels like a kick to the gut. She's counting on me, but here I am, late to the game, since someone was taken on my watch after months of not being able to identify this bastard.

CHAPTER TEN

Dana

Blessed

For heaven's sake. Stop fixating on Mr. Blackclaw. Women are missing. Get your head out of the gutter! That mantra has been on loop the entirety of our time in the Alpha's office. Leather and cedarwood stood so close to me as if he knew how much that boyish smile affected me. *And what was the electric feeling when his arm brushed against mine? Nothing, it was nothing, because he's completely off-limits, at least while we're working.*

Exiting the Alpha's sauna of an office is a relief. Outside the lodge, the fragrant air is a small welcome piece of joy. Their group agreed to show me where they believe Karissa was taken through a dark magic portal. Kyle didn't seem pleased when I chose to let ten lycans escort me to an unknown location within the woods outside the pack lands. With an unknown presence lurking, the rest of the squad should stay behind to ensure the pack's safety.

Deep down, I know we can trust the lycans. Strangely, I feel at ease around this group, especially with one handsome lycan in particular. Their cooperation has been refreshing. Dolken demonstrated he's an exceptional leader who prioritizes our shared goal rather than getting caught up in the complexities of our cross-species politics.

I turn over what just transpired from our meeting. An altered image of Jax bending my naked body over the Alpha's desk and having his way with me conjures in my mind.

"Joey!" I hiss, scolding my brat of a wolf.

"You know you want to. There must be cobwebs down there by this point," Joey mumbles the last part dryly.

"Any cobwebs present are in part due to you scaring off men."

She snorts, *"At least I'm not the one making them doze off."*

"What are you insinuating?" I snap.

"You're BORING!"

"I'm not boring!"

"Name a hobby besides work," she challenges.

"Well, I um, like to drink wine with my friends."

She huffs at me. *"Not a hobby."*

"Fine, knitting while Netflixing and drinking wine." That has become a favorite pastime of mine. *Gesh, when did I become such a hermit?*

"Really helping your case, Grandma. Maybe we should adopt some cats. At least they might be fun to play with. Or better yet, move us into the retirement home now."

My wolf is such a drama queen.

"Excellent idea, Jo, because I freakin' love bingo and watching game shows!"

"Whatever. Just try not to scare off our fated mate. I prefer to move in with his fine ass instead of old wrinkled ones."

"Our what?!" I choke on my spit, then snort in disbelief, followed by a cough to cover the deranged sounds coming from my mouth. Five pairs of eyes with varying expressions flash my way. *Damn it.*

If a wolf could facepalm, Joey would've at this moment. *"WOW. Real smooth... I'll go pack my bags now for the retirement home."*

Mickey walks over and pats my back like I just choked on a bug, not soul-scrambling news. "You okay, Commander?"

A deep, threatening growl escapes Jax's plump, full lips. Lips I wish to taste so badly. His eyes bore holes into Mickey's hand resting innocently on my back.

My mind fights to comprehend that I have another fated mate, and one who is already showing possessiveness over me. This isn't male behavior I'm accustomed to. *Mate.* I send the thought out into the universe, hoping Ajax Blackclaw somehow gets the message that I now see what he is to me.

I give Mickey an awkward nod before stepping out of his reach. "I'm fine, thank you," I tell him.

Distancing myself from Mickey seems to work, and I can see Jax's tension slipping away the farther I put distance between us. Miguel's face is lit up like the frickin' Eiffel Tower. That mischievous smile tells me he's on to our secret.

"Jo, WTF was that 'our fated mate' bomb you just dropped?! Why am I just hearing about this? Does he know?" I have so many questions for her.

"Yup. He knows," she chirps with the 'p' in yup making a popping noise. *"His lycan has been reaching out, but I haven't responded yet. I want my man to work for it."*

Now it's my turn to facepalm at her ridiculousness. *"I still don't understand. Bobby was our fated mate."*

Wasting time thinking about that man leaves a sour taste in my mouth. My insides clench at the thought of another potential mate's rejection. I'm not sure I can relive that again.

"Explain to me how we can have another? Oh, no, do you think we have even more out there? Are we destined for some poly, brother-husband shit? I once read a fantasy fiction romance novel where

the FMC had five mates. Five mates! I don't want that. With all their needs, I'll never get sleep or a moment to myself, no thank you, ma'am." My thoughts continue to spiral straight down the crapper.

"Who's being the drama queen now? I knew right away he was our true fated mate. I was seeing if you were smart enough to figure out the signs. Clearly not, hooman, proving I'm the smarter half of this partnership."

Never have I wanted to strangle my wolf more than I do at this moment. Why, goddess, was I chosen as the vessel for her? Taking a calming breath, I ignore the dig since there are more pressing matters.

"Alright, well, Almighty One, you still haven't explained how we can have two people who complete our soul."

"I had to reach out to Selene to understand. Think of us being similar to a Phoenix. The first version of ourselves permanently ended the day we died, and we were reborn. Our rebirth changed our soul, altering our destined life path. No longer were we a Gamma ranking werewolf with no magic, and Bobby was no longer our soul match. We'll always carry a small part of Bobby with us, but fate decided it wasn't meant to be. Our Moon Mother created our new bond to Ajax, meaning he's our true mate. It's another blessing, one for which we must send her our gratitude."

"I, ah, well, um." I stop. Truly unsure of how to process all of this.

"Was that gibberish your attempt at thanking Selene?"

"No, I'm truly grateful for another chance with a mate. I still can't believe all of this," I whisper as I'm unable to let the hope in.

"Now that we're on the same page, let's go get our man! He's ours, and I'm not sharing. Bitches even glance his way with a hint of interest in their eyes, and I'll claw them out. He is mine!" Wow, she's being earnest.

Most pack members make a point to give our group ample space as we walk through town. Fear mixed with nervous energy lingers in the air, making it easy to detect.

"Hey, are you okay?"

A gentle hand cups my elbow, and instantly, I feel a wave of warmth traveling through my entire body, making me aware of who's touching me. As my mate, he can likely sense I'm currently dealing with internal turmoil. His soft, patient gaze feels like a gentle caress to my soul, easing some of my angst. Goddess, I want to have this man's babies. *Yes! Yes!* My mating hormones chant. *Holy mind detour. Focus, Dana, and say something.*

My mouth opens, then abruptly snaps shut. I land on a lame, "I'm fine." Looking like a fish is the least of my worries right now. *Okay, remain calm and change the subject to the weather, maybe?*

Before I can say anything about the weather, Jax comes through with an assist. "So, I'd say we were good little lads in there and earned that story now."

Oh, thank the Goddess. Never in my life have I felt as unsure about everything as I do at this moment.

Joey's relief is evident. *"Our mate isn't only sexy, but smart. That's a way better topic than the weather, Grandma."*

"Right, well, you weren't being a good little lad when you snarled at Alpha James," I scold him.

"It was a warranted snarl," he defends.

I force my face to remain in a neutral expression. My lips desperately want to curve up, thinking back on how sweet the gesture was. *Am I swooning right now?*

"Definitely warranted," Mickey agrees.

Miguel scoffs, "You should've dragged that Alpha's hide outside for a nice old-fashioned beat down for that level of disrespect."

"Yes, well, maybe next time, but just for your amusement, of course," I tell him sarcastically.

I stop walking and turn toward Jax, trying hard not to get caught in an eye-fucking match with him. It's nearly impossible, but I need him to know this about me.

"I wasn't born into a crimson bloodline; I was blessed by the Moon Goddess, Selene. This tattoo represents my transformation. Little Dana Jo Johnston came from Gamma wolf parents in a conservative Southern wolf pack. At sixteen, a rogue lycan attacked our pack, slaughtering dozens before I killed him. He briefly took me to the other side, where I was given a second chance. The Goddess saw my courage that day and deemed me worthy to be a vessel for one of her crimson wolves. The end." My eyes remain locked on my mate's face, observing how his stunned expression shifts into admiration.

He's the first to speak, "Dana, that's remarkable."

"So how does a sixteen-year-old girl kill a full-grown lycan male?" Mickey refreshingly asks without a hint of skepticism in his voice.

Demi forcefully interjects. "I call bullshit on that tale."

I suppress my urge to burn his eyebrows off because I know the guy's dealing with a lot, but he's still such a dick. Skepticism isn't uncommon among those I share my story with. Often, I choose not to provide details beyond the fact that I was blessed because of this scenario. I don't have the time, energy, or patience to argue the details of my life with cynics.

"You're welcome to believe whatever you want, sir. It's my truth, so I'll not argue it with anyone."

"Show some respect, Demi," Jax's response is laced with barely contained authority.

Demi shoots him an icy look. The conversation quickly shifts internal, given the tight expressions everyone wears as they silently glare at one another. I understand Jax is acting on his mating instincts, but it's causing unnecessary tension, and I don't need anyone fighting my battles.

"How did you kill him? If you don't mind sharing." Dolken's gruff voice cuts through the awkward silence.

I sigh. One life story coming right up. "Well, what I remember most about the day was how miserable the heavy, humid summer air felt. One of those real dog days of summer. It was as if the day already knew it'd be the worst day of our lives, so why not make it a little more unbearable?

My boyfriend, Jeremy, and I were fishing by the stream that ran through the pack when we received a message from our Alpha about a rogue lycan in our territory. Jeremy insisted I take his truck straight home, so I could hide while he went to help." Jax appears relaxed, but stiffens at the mention of another man. *Possessive males.*

"Tucking tail has never been my style, nor is having someone else make my decisions. Being bullheaded, I sought out the threat. When I finally came upon him, the scene of carnage still haunts me.

Jeremy's father, our pack Beta, and his older brother had been ripped apart. The pack Alpha was trying to fight him along with multiple pack guards, but it wasn't sustainable given how badly the Alpha was injured. My Pa, the pack's Gamma, was next in his line of sight, so I just acted on instinct.

Hitting the truck's accelerator, I sped toward him, blasting music and honking to try to distract him. Thankfully, Jeremy had his obnoxious Metallica CD in. There were plenty of weapons in the truck from growin' up in big gator country. I grabbed a silver machete and a silver bullet pistol, tucking the gun into the waistband of my shorts. I put the truck on cruise and jumped out before he took the full-frontal impact.

The hit gave me time to get off the ground and approach him from behind. I shot him twice in the back, which really pissed him off. The huge surge of dominating power he pushed out made everyone in the vicinity fall to their knees. He was on me in an instant, causing me to drop the gun. Somehow, I managed to keep hold of the machete, and I shoved it into his neck.

I attempted to crawl away while he was grasping at his neck, but he caught my thigh with his teeth. He slammed me hard into the ground multiple times, causing me to black out momentarily. I heard my bones being snapped, and his claws sliced my abdomen open. My father launched himself onto his back as I fought to remain conscious. My hand found the cool metal of a gun. At that moment, I knew I was going to die, so I asked Selene to give me enough strength to take the bastard with me. Then I shot him point-blank in the head twice before blacking out. I woke up after being in a coma for a month, fully healed and with no long-term damage."

"Dana, my child. Your journey is not done, my dear. Life's flame will be restored for I choose you to walk among the living once more," I hear *her* ethereal voice in my mind like I always do when reflecting on that day.

A pregnant pause ensues, quickly broken by Miguel. "Destiny's Child's 'Survivor' would have made the story a whole new level of epic."

Mickey smacks his brother upside the head. "Miguel, is that your only takeaway?"

I shake my head. "I disagree. To this day, I still hate that Metallica song, so I'm glad a DC classic wasn't ruined for me."

Miguel nods thoughtfully. "Okay, I can respect that."

"Where in the South did this happen?" Dolken asks me curiously.

"Southern Mississippi."

"Hm, the deep south seems like a strange place for a rogue lycan to be. I'm not aware of any packs in the southern region of the United States since our kind prefer colder, less populated climates." Dolken scratches at his dark beard, lost in thought.

"Agreed. There are none," Jax adds. "Well, maybe a few outcasts around NOLA."

"None of the packs within our region had ever seen a lycan before, nor do they ever wish to again, given the pure devastation he caused. That lycan was completely feral."

"Why are you helping us then?" Demi's question comes out of left field.

"Excuse me?" My tone's politeness is gone, replaced by annoyance.

"Okay, those eyebrows are goners. Please give me the green light," Joey begs.

"Demi, what are you getting at?" Dolken stops walking to frown at the younger lycan.

"Given her history with our kind, I don't think it's smart for us to trust her unquestioningly. How do we know she isn't planning our deaths for revenge?" Turning to look me square in the eye, he continues, "So I want to know why you're so eager to help, even going to the extent of pulling rank over a pack Alpha."

Honestly, I feel pissed, but again, he's been through a lot in one day and it's a valid question. This man knows nothing about my morals or integrity, or that my mate is the lycan right next to him, trying to kill him with his glare.

Anticipating Jax's movement, my arm shoots out, halting his forward progress, but that isn't enough to stop words from leaving his mouth.

"Don't you dare question my mate's character again." Jax thrusts an accusatory finger in his face.

And there it is, the mate's out of the bag, folks. Demi's face morphs into one of horror. His eyes blink rapidly, almost as if hoping to change what he just heard.

Dolken seems unfazed. "I suspected as much," he says.

Mickey's face lights with a large smile. "Well, that explains what's going on with you, brother. Congratulations. I wish you'd said something earlier, because now I have to get a random Miguel-selected tattoo."

Miguel, full-on Cheshire cat smiles. "Oh, my victory prize will be so sweet, dear wombmate."

"Demi, let me be clear, my willingness to help has nothing to do with Jax being my mate." Saying the words 'my mate' out loud feels like a fine wine with a smooth finish that lingers on the palate. It embodies everything you desire in a wine, but it's probably too pricey and out of your beer budget.

"I don't judge or hold a grudge against an entire race of supernaturals based on one's actions. Your sister and other innocent young women have been taken by monsters who think they have the right to do so.

I want nothing more than to find those assholes and inflict pain on them until they beg for the mercy of death. And before I kill them slowly by burning them from the inside out, I'll make sure they know they'll enjoy eternal suffering in the underworld because the Goddess doesn't welcome them home. Right now, those women need someone who cares, who will fight for them; they need hope. You have my word; my intentions are genuine. Now show me what you've found."

"Okay." His bravado finally breaks. Jax meets my eye, nodding before we all continue.

Miguel clears his throat, and I know what's coming. "So mates... Shouldn't you be shouting from the treetops? Or maybe hugging?

Oh, how about crying? Because you're so over the moon, your lost souls have found one another. Wait, I have it, you should awkwardly grope-make out while the rest of us try not to show how uncomfortable we are."

"No," we both reply in unison.

"We'll talk later when we have some privacy," Jax says.

"Last question before I drop the subject. Are you 100% sure you're truly mates? Because I've seen fated couples meet before, and you two have had the most anticlimactic start to a mating, like ever."

"Yes," we both say in unison again, causing us both to chuckle lightly.

I nudge Jax's shoulder with mine. "Is he always like this?"

"Yes," everyone in the group replies at the same time.

"Geesh, tough crowd," Miguel says under his breath.

CHAPTER ELEVEN

Dana

The Vision

To my relief, there are no incidents to report between the lycans and our border patrol when we regroup. I would've been furious if I had to file an incident report. Squad members would have received poor grades on my feedback report cards, which they never requested. The group chooses to split up to continue scanning the neutral zone, while Dolken, Demi, Noah, the twins, and Jax escort me to the portal site. I continually open all my senses, searching for the unknown threat I detected, but the earlier sensation is no longer there.

"Hey, I'm going to shift."

Excusing myself, I leap behind a large pine to start undressing. Joey can perceive more with her heightened abilities, though I'm somewhat concerned about how she'll react to being near our mate. The idea of having another mate is still surreal. As suspected, it takes a lot of convincing before she finally agrees not to go sniffing Jax's fine ass and instead focus on her job. Only one snarky comment from her, and we are off on four paws. Being a gentleman, Jax walks over, gathering my clothing items.

Joey fangirls over his chivalry. *"Our mate's so sweet."*

"Let's be honest with ourselves, he just doesn't want everyone seeing me naked if I have to shift back to communicate."

"Shush, I don't care. It's a sweet gesture!"

Our mate's gaze on my back, the entirety of our walk, is equivalent to a warm physical stroke of my fur. Talk about struggling to concentrate. Joey informs me that Mars is eager to shift, but Jax is holding him back. Carrying our clothes is helping to soothe some of his angst.

Areas of decaying foliage drip to the ground amid healthy spring greenery, revealing the telltale signs of dark magic when we arrive. The lingering scent of rot hangs in the air. The saving grace about being up against dark magic is that it's difficult for the wielder to conceal. Being unnatural, it opposes magic's true nature of giving life, healing, and protecting. Instead, it wields its power like a cancer, consuming the life force and leaving behind decay and death, which are easy to spot.

Joey pauses, taking it all in. *"Hmm, I'll try to connect with Selene on this. I'm not sure what else we can do. It proves the dark witches theory I had."*

Internally, I step back, giving her the green light to do her Joey thing. Being a divine entity, Selene can't pop her fine ass down to the Earthly realm whenever there's our kind's bullshit to deal with. Instead, all blessed wolves contain a direct connection with her, whom she guides. Messages from her can appear in various forms, including dreams, visions, feelings, or direct interactions with our animal.

Jo gently nudges our mate's leg, forcing him to back up. That man's in our bubble again. Chuckling to himself, he reluctantly takes a few steps away from us. Jo sits back on her haunches, giving him a wolfy grin before turning around to lie facing the portal's location.

"You flirt!"

She giggles in response, not even denying it.

Her mirth vanishes as her head lifts and her eyes close. Light of day slips away, and with it go the sounds of the forest's busy afternoon. The connection with the Goddess is instant. Before us, a large lycan male in brown leather holds an unconscious Karissa in his arms, the darkness of night casting a shadow over most of his face.

"Hurry," his deep bass voice is a soft exhale. Light scuffling follows as two more lycans, carrying unconscious women, step through the portal. On the other side, a cloaked figure stands near a dark water's edge. With a simple flick of their wrist, the portal closes, ending the vision. Recognition sparks immediately. Those women are two of the missing she-wolves from Crescent Moon Pack, whose photos I memorized. This is proof that the two cases are connected.

"FUCK!" Demi roars, driving his fist into a nearby tree before dropping to his knees. Waves of panic, anger, and sorrow emanate from him.

"Did he see that vision?" I ask Joey.

"Yes." She smirks, clearly pleased with herself.

Okay. #blessed, I guess. Projecting our abilities to others is new.

Joey's large snout nuzzles Jax's leg again, silently, asking him this time to follow her to a nearby tree. As a good mate, he follows, setting my clothes down before turning to give me privacy. As quickly as I can, I slip into my clothes and then make my way back to the tense group. Demi and Noah are struggling to control their emotions after seeing what happened to Karissa.

"So what can we possibly do now for my sister? They could've taken her anywhere in the fucking world!" Nearby birds scatter in panic, frightened by Demi's sudden outburst.

"You're right," I agree. There's no sugar coating this. "Did you recognize any of those men?" I ask. Different variations of no ripple through the group.

"How'd you see that? What else can you see? How do we get her back?" Noah frantically tosses questions at me.

"I'm not sure. Selene sometimes reveals things to me, but I'm not a seer, so I can't see anything else right now. Do you know any seers?"

Dolken pulls out his phone. "I can submit a request to the Dragon Empire for someone to come out."

"Jax's uncle is mated to a witch, so maybe she can help?" Mickey suggests looking his way for confirmation.

Hopeful eyes turn to my mate. "She specializes in potion-making, but she might know someone. I'll ask her."

Noah responds sincerely, "Thank you, Jax."

"I'll need to update the Moonborn Pack on what I just saw," I tell the group. "Hopefully, they'll provide more support and witches to help, given this evidence."

"We'd greatly appreciate that, and we'd be in your pack's debt."

I wave Dolken's words off. "No debt, sir. All the same cause, remember?"

"Hey, my dad just mindlinked. They found scent-masking potions hidden in my sister's room and a phone charger that isn't for her phone." Demi's handsome face darkens further as he struggles to process the message he just received.

Noah looks like he's on the verge of another meltdown, with elongated fangs as he struggles against his lycan. "Why would she have scent masking?" The words are barely understandable, mixed with his beast's snarls.

"To sneak out," Miguel answers. Bingo. A burner phone, scent masking, and no sign of a struggle.

"I agree. She was likely using it to sneak out to see someone or do something she shouldn't have been." Jax quickly theorizes what I'm thinking.

Joey becomes thoughtful as she works her way. *I believe their pack has a rat, and they need to sniff them out.*

I decide to share this with the group, "My wolf believes someone within your pack might be working with this organization. That's solely based on her intuition, not a vision."

CHAPTER TWELVE

Ajax

Let's Talk About Mating, Baby

Dana mentioning our pack having a member tied to this situation makes my blood boil. My beautiful, smart, angel-faced mate has some of the strongest instincts I've ever encountered. *You had one damn job, Blackclaw: to find this bastard. I* internally chastise myself. *You let innocent women down, along with The Guardians. On top of that, we found our mate and can't do a thing about it right now because we're on a top-secret assignment.* That realization is crippling. The thought of having to walk away from her causes a sharp pain in my heart. I must put my personal life on hold because I promised Andy I'd find this asshole, so that's what I need to do.

Dolken sighs, looking clearly upset. "We should return and speak with her friends to see if they know anything about why she'd have those things."

"I, too, must be getting back. I want to submit our findings here and check on the status of getting witch's aid from my pack. We will keep you abreast. Please do the same and reach out if you need anything," Dana tells us.

"Thank you, Commander Johnston. I know King Anders and Queen Gamila appreciate your willingness to assist us with this case." Dolken steps towards Dana, extending his hand. There is gratitude evident in his eyes.

She clasps it with a small, honest smile. "You're welcome, sir."

The urge to rip off his entire arm for touching my mate is something fierce. Mars starts snarling again. Dolken shakes his head while mumbling something about the ridiculousness of mates, before he walks away.

"Tamp it back, buddy," I warn the beast.

"He's getting his stink on our mate," he protests.

"I'll walk you back," I blurt hastily, before anyone else can talk to or touch my mate.

"Okay." She nods before bidding the rest of the gents a good day.

Mickey and Miguel send me their classic shit-eating grins. *"Take good care of the Commander, Jax,"* Mickey teases via mindlink with an accompanying eyebrow wiggle.

"I will. Now kindly fuck off." Both of my brothers are howling with laughter when I block their connection.

Our walk back toward the wolf pack is met with a blend of comfortable silence and the forest's melody. *How could this extraordinary woman possibly be meant for me? The moon of my eye. The other half of my soul. Am I worthy of such a gift from the Goddess?*

I've never given an ounce of thought to what I would say to my fated mate if I found her. I'm the first to speak up once I feel confident we're out of Miguel's listening range, since his bionic hearing loves to eavesdrop. "So, I can't believe we found each other."

"Yeah. I was shocked once Joey finally told me. I still am," Dana admits, looking sheepish.

"Wait, your wolf didn't tell you immediately?" I chuckle.

"No, she was apparently trying to prove that she's the superior being."

Well, that explains some of her earlier behavior. I find this so amusing.

"Cheeky, wolf," I mock scold.

"She can be a real thorn in my backside sometimes," Dana grumbles.

My stomach knots at the thought of asking her my next question. "Are you someone who wants a mate?"

Her kind eyes grow more contemplative. "Yes, I do. It's just being on assignment means I can't leave right now to figure this out." She gestures between us. "Nor do I know when I can get time off because things are stupidly complicated with my boss. It all leaves me unsure of where to go from here."

Melancholy touches her lips, washing away the warmth. Her tough exterior cracks, revealing vulnerability. My confident, badass mate now shows signs of uncertainty. I hate to see her crumble.

"Mars and I understand. Now is also not ideal timing for us with all that's happening, but we'd like to see where it could go when the time is right."

Mars pitifully whines in protest. He wants his mate now, his patience resembling that of a toddler.

"Joey and I'd like that. There's a lot to talk about, and a ten-minute walk won't give us the time we need to make life-changing decisions. How about after my current assignment, we figure out a plan?"

The devil on my shoulder screams *NO! We want her now; fuck all our commitments.* My favorite angel, Andy, on the other shoulder, scolds me about the importance of upholding commitments. *Do the right thing, Ajax; lives are at stake.* Damn angel.

"That's fair. Considering that our time's currently limited for certain conversations, perhaps we can jump right into extracurricular activities? I reckon that'd be a good use of our ten minutes." I say lightheartedly.

She laughs, rolls her eyes hard, and gives me a shove. "Too far, Blackclaw."

I love hearing my name coming from her lips, even if it's in a sarcastic tone.

"Fine, fine. I'll be a good lad. How about we start with your phone number? So Dana Jo Johnston, may I please have your phone number?" I ask, trying my best to sound like a complete gentleman.

"You may, sir."

Conversation flows effortlessly, creating comfortable companionship as we walk together side by side. Our bond is already quietly weaving its magic, fostering a deep, soulful recognition between us. I want to learn all I can about my beautiful mate during our restricted moment of privacy.

Dana shares details about her life in the Moonborn Pack, including her progression through their military ranks. It doesn't surprise me to learn she's always dreamed of serving with The Guardians. It's a tough organization, but with her gifts, they'd welcome her with open arms. Hesitation to make such a leap stems from fear of leaving her loved ones, so she holds herself back. It's evident by the way she speaks of friends and family that she cares for them with unwavering devotion, especially her brother, Davey. I feel envious of her ability to love so deeply.

I share surface-level details about my age, which makes me several decades older than her, and some information regarding my past lives. When it comes to jobs, I've done more than most. I've worked as a ranch hand, a yacht crew member, a musician, a mercenary, a paranormal tour guide, a dog surfing instructor, and a private island caretaker, to name a few. Hearing Dana's laughter at the absurdity of my past jobs is music to my ears. With a wanderlust personality, I've learned to adapt and find work wherever I can.

Dana is stable with deep roots. *Can my restless spirit find peace in one place? Can we find ways to lay roots together? Or will I always be a tumbleweed, unable to stop from blowing away? Even if that wind blows me away from my mate?* I remind myself that these questions are too deep for our light ten-minute chat.

"Jax, I want to tell you something."

"Anything," I reply honestly.

Dana looks nervous. "Alright, so you're my second fated mate."

Her second fated mate? I didn't see that coming. Halting my steps, I turn to study her face. There's no sign of a lie present. My mind struggles to compute how that is possible because to me, the math doesn't add up. I've never heard of someone having two mates, well, nor have I heard of a fated wolf and lycan pairing. Mars isn't pleased with this admission, and to be honest, neither am I. *What does that mean? Was she mated before us? Do we have to share her with some bastard?*

Mars quickly gets worked up at the thought. *"We aren't sharing. I challenge this other asshole to a fight till the death."*

"Hold on, and don't get your knickers in a twist," I tell him.

"I don't understand," I admit to her slowly. "I've never heard of someone having two fated soul mates."

"Neither had I, aside from the descendants of the Moon God, Alpha," she agrees. "The Alpha's son of my childhood pack was my first fated mate, but our connection broke the day I died in the lycan attack. He felt the bond break and pieced it together. Ultimately, he decided to take a chosen mate over repairing the bond with me."

The word "chosen" feels forced from her pretty lips as if it burns to speak it. I'm certain my eyebrows are touching the fluffy white clouds right now. Did I hear her correctly say someone chose another over her, this goddess incarnate? What a fucking dumbass.

"And we are grateful he is a dumbass," Mars rumbles in approval, glad we don't have to murder anyone for our mate.

"Jo explained that once we were reborn, it altered our life path, thus changing our soul. With that, Selene blessed us with a different mate: you." She smiles softly.

"Wow. Well, I'm one fortunate bastard."

Squeezing her hand in mine, I give her a gentle tug, guiding her into my arms. It doesn't take long for her rigid body posture to relax against me. Some mysterious mate instinct knew she needed the comfort only I could provide. The connection between our bodies creates the most pleasant sensation, making me feel truly alive. I wonder if this is similar to how dormant plants feel after the frost melts and the warm spring sunlight signals it's time to wake up.

"I'm sorry that happened to you. It must've been hard to work through a mate's rejection," I whisper into her hair as I continue to hold her in my embrace.

Her smoky scent embeds itself deeper into my memory as she stays tucked in my arms. Primal instincts direct me to gently press my nose against her neck, offering her extra comfort. I want to nip and suck at that soft, creamy skin, but I fight the urge. She pulls back from our embrace, causing Mars and me both to want to reach for her because we have not had enough. I remind myself it's better this way; the deeper we fall, the more complicated it becomes to walk away, even if temporarily.

"Yes, it was hard on me. Joey helped me get through it, and my brother. After much reflection, I believe it was truly for the best. The pack had conservative views, and women were expected to take on traditional caretaker roles. The two of us would've had a hard time finding happiness because we were caught up in endless fights for dominance. He never would've accepted me being the more dominant, given my crimson blood. Thankfully, I was able to move on from it without experiencing some of the common side effects of a rejected bond, since it broke naturally when I died."

I ponder, "Maybe an unconscious part of him knew you no longer belonged with him." *Because you are mine, Fiery Wolf.*

"Possibly. That's an interesting theory," she says thoughtfully. "Does it bother you that there was another before you?"

"Yes! And I've changed my mind, let's kill the ex-fated douche for good measure."

"No," I tell him, feeling like this is going to be an ongoing discussion between us.

"At least ask if she wants him dead: we aim to please, literally," Mars grins, looking smug.

"No, if she wanted him dead, he'd be dead. Our girl can take care of herself."

"Mars has his panties in a bunch over it. He's currently plotting the guy's murder." She lets out a lovable snort.

"Well, he can wait in line behind Joey. The only reason I've held her back is because then we'd have a pack to run, which isn't high on my priority list."

"I told him you were a capable woman who didn't need our help. However, should you need our services for a little ex-mate roughing up, we're your guys."

CHAPTER THIRTEEN

Dana

Speechless

"*Could he be more PERFECT?*" Jo asks dreamily like a ridiculous cartoon princess finding her true love. She would swoon over a man contemplating murder for us.

Jax does seem incredible, but after having my heart shattered once by a failed mate, I've decided to choose a path of caution.

"*Yes, he seems nice,*" I note.

"Nice? What kind of lying to your best friend about her ugly sweater response is that?"

"I'm trying to be cautious, that's all. I'm not sure we can handle another broken mate bond," I tell her honestly.

"Ajax isn't a dumb pup like Bobby."

"I know. Let's just take it slow, okay?"

"Fine," she mumble-grumbles. *"But have you ever wondered why no were-men could fully satisfy us?"*

Without giving me a moment to think of a witty reply regarding our mediocre dating and sex life, she continues, *"Because we have a SEXY AF lycan mate! No wolf can compare to him, not even all those Omega males in that sex cult searching for their Alpha female queen that one time."*

I cringe remembering too many moonshines, feeling exploratory, making bad choices, and now facing lifelong regrets.

"I don't want to be reminded of that, ever. You know the golden Vegas rule, so let's not bring up those culties again," I tell her.

"Deal, let's keep the focus on our mate. He's so fine. MINE!" Joey is the picture of a happy, tail-wagging pup prancing around in my head.

I can't disagree with her observation. Were-men have always left me wanting more than they could give, but I could never put my finger on it. My assumption has always been that I had horrible taste in men, but maybe it was just the species of men I had wrong.

Jax single-handedly sets my entirety on fire with just one look. As he walks by my side, he puts my soul at ease in a way I've never felt before. His essence is already making a home somewhere deep inside me. This man is mine; together, we are complete.

My animalistic side longs to abandon my responsibilities for him because nothing else matters as much as he does. It encourages me to fuck him from here to home, ensuring everyone we pass along the way knows his name and that he belongs to me from my screams of pleasure.

Fuck, how am I going to walk away right now? Crippling anxiety at the thought strikes faster than a snake capturing me in its fangs. *You can't leave him,* it screams, followed by a small voice that whispers, *but you must.* Right, we have a job to do that takes precedence over our personal lives. *Fuck.*

As we near the Crescent Moon border, I curse the fates once more for sending me my mate with exceptionally shitty timing. *Really, couldn't we have met while we were in Napa or something? Wining, dining, and screwing sounds fan-freaking-tastic to me, fates.*

Shielding my turmoil from Jax is difficult, as I turn to him before I leave. *You can't go with him. It'll be all right.*

Joey whines, *"It'll be alright, but it sucks."*

"Thank you for walking with me. I'll let you know when I'm back home," I tell him.

Grasping my hand, he flips it palm side up before gently placing a kiss on my inner wrist. His tongue darts out for the smallest of tastes, causing my panties to start dampening. The sparkle in his eyes reveals wicked promises of what's to come with that tongue. An approving low rumble is heard in his chest. Possessively, he pulls me to his firm body as his nose explores the crook of my neck.

A moan tries but fails to escape my lips. *No, not happening, but goddess, I want him.* That leathery scent is as heavy as an anchor, and it threatens to pull me down with it. Its potency, combined with the sensual sensation he's causing along my neck, overwhelms me with desire.

"Ahhh," is all I manage to say.

"Christ, I think the '90s dial-up is back in here," Joey complains, causing my lust-filled brain to reboot.

His body begins to vibrate softly as he chuckles at my speechlessness. "Dana, I don't want to let you go."

"I feel the same," I admit quietly.

He pulls back to look me in the eye. "Can I kiss you?"

Joey screams in agreement. *"YES!"*

Self-preservation tells me this is a big no-no. It screams at me, *'It's a trap, run away!' Danger! Sexy Lips Canyon is a steep cliff that you will fall off and never recover from. Game over, babe, because there's no turning back after those luscious lips tango with yours.*

On the flip side, my mating hormones are doing the two-step begging for this man. Chanting *Yes! Yes! Of course, you want to kiss him, fool. There'll be no denying any of his requests. Now do it already, Honey.*

"I'll take your silence as a yes, and kiss you now," he chuckles softly.

Oh, hell's bells, this is actually happening.

"Yes, get it, girl!" Joey cheerleads.

As he lifts my chin, his lips slowly lower to mine. He maintains eye contact to silently signal that I can stop him if this isn't what I want.

Oh, we want it! Shut up, hormones!

When our lips touch, an electric surge ignites, flowing through our bodies, charged by our souls. Something resonates deep inside, telling me this is exactly where I am meant to be: *home*. As the tension leaves my body, it also takes with it some of the barriers I've built around my heart. A desperate desire blazes inside me, but my stubborn self-control keeps me from begging him to ravage me against the nearest tree like the feral beast I know he hides inside. Our kiss is only a brief, fleeting moment before he pulls away, gently nipping my bottom lip.

"Wow. One can never truly understand the power of the mating bond until you experience it for yourself," he breathes as he brushes the tip of his nose against mine.

I feel the same way; no words can adequately describe it. Who knew the equivalent of a G-rated kiss would be soul-shattering? *We're screwed, mate bonds aren't fucking around.*

"My Fiery Wolf is still speechless. I bet that doesn't happen often." I find the nickname he gives me so endearing.

"Never," my reply is a breathy exhale. *Christ, get it together, my ridiculous self.*

We reluctantly pull apart before we can get too lost in each other. Jax leans in quickly to steal a peck goodbye. "I'll plan to stop over tomorrow to see if there are any updates with the case."

"Okay." My stomach flutters at the thought of seeing him again so soon.

"Until we meet again, my Fiery Wolf," he tosses over his shoulder as he walks back in the direction of his pack. That panty-melting grin shows itself to me one last time before he's out of sight.

Damn, how many women before me have gotten lost in that smile? The thought instantly pisses me off and starts leading me somewhere I'm not going. *Nope, not today.* Instead, I focus on the lingering sensation of our kiss.

"Maybe we should follow him, to make sure he gets back safe," Joey howls longingly after he's disappeared in the foliage.

"You know we can't because we have to focus on the missing she-wolves. He'll be back tomorrow."

Tomorrow. The thought brings a smile to my face. I'll eagerly await tomorrow.

CHAPTER FOURTEEN

Dana

Goddess Save the Queen

It takes only a minute after stepping back onto the pack lands for my cloud nine high to be shot down, shattered, and shit on by Squad Leader Kyle. He informs me that Captain Lumen needs to speak to me urgently. *Fantastic.* No doubt an ass chewing is waiting on the other end of the line for me. Finding a private room, I slip in and close the door before dialing his number because no one needs to hear this. Taking several deep breaths, I try to force my already rising temper down. Remembering Jax's Grade A scent does help until the line connects to Brutis, crushing any happy thoughts of my mate.

"What the fuck do you think you're doing collaborating with lycans, Commander?" he barks.

Not skipping a beat, I shoot back, "My job, which is helping find abducted women, sir."

"This is a simple pack secure, in and out, Johnston. You're not there to solve a missing lycan case. Let me spell it out for you so that your small brain can understand. It's simple: your only job is to watch over Luca and intervene if it's necessary for his safety. Is that clear?"

I respond with a low snarl as I'm momentarily blinded by red. Joey doesn't appreciate the way he's speaking to us and wants to rip off his head because of it. My internal fire roars to life, prepared to help her.

"Well, let me spell this out for you this way, sir. If it were your missing mate, sister, or child, would you feel the same way? Just a quick in and out, Captain?"

Teeth grinding comes from the other end. "Those women are never being found, and you damn well know it. Now, stop wasting everyone's time, Johnston."

"And how do you know that, sir?" I challenge him. "Could it be because we aren't thoroughly doing our jobs by searching for them with all available resources?"

More teeth grinding. "Interfere with the lycans again, and you're out of here. I swear to the fucking Goddess. I'll strip you of your goddamn title and rank, Johnston. This bullshit's gone on for too long."

Resorting to threats, classic. "So be it," I reply with a calmness that surprises even myself as I disconnect the call.

Jo's hot temper rages. *"THAT MOTHER FUCKING PIECE OF SHIT!"*

"Whatever happens, we follow our instincts on this. I feel we're meant to help the lycans. The fates aligned and sent us here for a reason."

"Agreed," she says, slowing some of her raging.

Since our mate's soothing energy isn't present to help calm us, the only thing we can do is run; so that's what we do for an hour. Jo needs the release to avoid burning half of northern Canada to the ground. While we run, emotions fistfight one another in my psyche, threatening to overtake us. The urge to find our mate is strong. *What's Jax doing right now? Is he thinking of me?* Luckily, our willpower is stronger. Our job comes first.

What are the next steps we can take to locate these women? Are witches being sent to aid? We are going to find them. How does no one see the evil in Brutis? We should just quit already, tell Brutis where to shove our resignation, and then go fuck our mate into oblivion. That will fix all of our problems. Probably.

"Mate hanky-panky will for sure fix about 99% of our problems, and killing Brutis the other 1%," Jo purrs. The rhythmic, repetitive sound is so foreign it freaks me out.

"No, we can't because that won't help find these women. AND we aren't a damn feline shifter!"

Jo continues her purring. *"I can't help it. Our mate is fine as hell! I just want to rub all over him."*

Exhausted from today's events, we return to the pack for a quick update, meal, and shower. Squad Leader Kyle informs me that Brutis has denied the request for witches' assistance. Taking matters into my own hands, I send a request detailing all our findings directly to Ezekial. *Will Brutis be pissed? Yup. Do I care? Nope.*

When I finally rest, my dreams are a haunting melody of loss. Vivid scenes of losing my job, my pack, my home, Ajax Blackclaw walking away, and finally, losing my heart forever. The grief of it all swirls like a brewing storm that I want to release onto the world. *Why does life have to be so unfair?*

Down I go, free-falling into darkness until I'm completely submerged in a black lake, unable to swim. Freezing water floods my lungs as panic takes over. A sharp pain in my left bicep yanks me upward before I black out. My weakened body is lifted onto the water's surface, which is capable of holding me as it remains solid as glass.

A sharp burn sears my lungs as I cough up water. Looking up through tear-filled eyes, I see a beautiful, pure black wolf with red eyes standing over me.

Throwing my arms around her, I bury my face in her silky fur. *"I love you, Joey, please don't leave me, too."*

Her smooth tongue brushes across my forehead. *"Never. We're a package deal. Now, get on."*

"What?" I ask, confused about what I need to do.

"My back, get on, hurry," she urges.

"Why?"

"Infuriating human, just do it."

Doing as I'm told, I climb on. It's strange trying to comprehend the fact that I'm riding myself. Jo leaps into the air as if she were one of Santa's magical reindeer. It feels as though an invisible rope pulls us high up into the night sky toward a darkened forest off the shoreline.

Our physical forms dissolve away, leaving us incorporeal. I want to scream in panic because I can't feel or control any part of myself. There's nothing inside me capable of making a sound, so I remain tethered to this invisible force, drifting as if dust in the wind. I need to let go of the panic still gripping my subconscious and concentrate on what is being revealed.

We stop, hovering above the ground, and it takes me a moment to see clearly. Below, a warlock and a witch stand chanting in an area of the wilderness that looks familiar. Yes, I passed through here earlier on the way to the portal location. A group of wolves, likely a rogue pack, stands nearby, talking in hushed tones.

"Our contact is certain the female crimson will follow us easily off the pack lands. The witches will bind her fire and trap her in the magical cage they're setting now. Once she's trapped, we head straight for the portal boys because the boss promised a hell of a big payout if we brought him the Fire Bitch." The rogue leader looks down, checking his watch. "We head out in nine minutes; prepare yourself. Everyone needs to ensure their fire-nulling potions are in place before we go."

Contact? They want me? The presence of earlier pricks in my memory. Those slimy scoundrels. Suddenly, we're moving again, but more rapidly, until we reach another pack's land.

"The Silverthrone Pack," Jo's thought is nothing more than a fleeting whisper in my mind.

An uneasy sensation crawls down my spine. Everything feels unnaturally quiet here. A dark, cloaked figure lingers in the shadows, their gaze fixed on a massive mansion. *What are they looking for?* I wonder.

"Dana, you must go now, before it is too late to save the Silverthrone Queen." A familiar ethereal voice's command causes me to jolt upright in my bed. It was *her.*

The smell of sweat is heavy in the air, my sweat. My chest heaves in shallow breaths as my eyes dart around the empty room, searching for the threat. *What the—? Was that real?*

"Yes, the dream was real. We must go now!" Joey urges.

"Is that actually happening?" I ask her.

"Yes!" Urgency from Joey rushes into me.

I sprint from the room, not even bothering to put on proper clothing or shoes, letting instincts drive me. Joey forces a shift the moment our feet touch the cool grass outside the lodge's front door. We take off at top speed toward the direction of the witches.

Notifying our squad members of this trap, I open a mindlink to them all, *"Listen carefully, there are rogue wolves working for the trafficking organization outside the northern border. They plan to take us by surprise in roughly six to seven minutes in hopes of luring me out to a magical containment trap. They're accompanied by two dark magic wielders and a third located outside the Silverthrone Pack. Can someone notify Dolken at the Silverthrone Pack? They want their queen."*

"Yes, I can call him," Angela says.

"Everyone needs to proceed to the border with lethal stealth now so we can take them by surprise. Notify the Alpha, ensure he knows we must remain unheard and unseen until I give the order to move. I'll take care of the witches." I have no time to focus on my competent teammates, knowing they understand what needs to be done.

"We can't let them take the Silverthrone Queen. She's pregnant," Joey tells me.

"How do you know she is pregnant?"

"No time. Be ready!" she snaps.

We slow our pace, ensuring we remain unheard. Jo's midnight black fur easily becomes indistinguishable amidst the shadows of the sleepy forest. Since we can still be scented, let's hope the wind is on our side. We silently comb through the forest's underbrush to the far right of where we saw the rogues lingering. Our best chance at fighting them is to surprise the dark magic wielders while my squad members handle the wolves.

"I'll need to take the witches out quickly so we can get to the Queen in time." Joey confirms my assumptions of what we need to do.

The pungent odor of decay from dark magic hits my nose before I can see its source. Crouching lower, we position ourselves in the darkness behind a large tree, grateful for our night vision but not for our heightened sense of smell right now. The male and female witches are wrapped in one another's arms. I hear their promises of a long night to come filled with ecstasy, driven by the high of their hunt. *Gross!* Overly confident bastards. *Do they really get off on abducting innocent people?*

It's a relief to see there aren't rogues around them. I open my mindlink back up to my squad mates, *"Are you in position at the border? I have two witches in sight."*

"Yes, everyone is in place. We're awaiting your order, Commander," Squad Leader Kyle's voice rings clear.

"Excellent. I need you to lure the rogues your way so I can take out the witches."

"On it, Commander," he says.

Jo stands motionless, her sights zeroed in on our prey. Prey, we desperately want to eliminate. All her muscles are locked into place, bracing for the strike. Internal fire idles beneath the surface, waiting for its moment to be unleashed. A distant howl from the pack's Alpha pierces the quiet night. The witches' heads snap toward our diversion. As the female pulls away from her lover, I surge forward, pushing out a bolt of fire. The flames swallow the male warlock before he realizes I'm here—their prey come to play.

The female's glamoured face contorts into one of agony, followed by rage as she screams his name. Someone is pissed that sexy time is off the table. A curse soars from her trembling fingertips into a tree behind us, annihilating it. Before she can send another our way, Jo is on her, tearing out her throat. To ensure the world is cleansed of her forever, I send a wave of crimson fire coursing through her body, leaving only ashes behind.

"Two witches have been eliminated." I update my pack mates before dashing toward the Silverthrone Pack, our main priority right now. Joey's internal monologue runs rampant as she prepares for a fight. If someone wants the queen, this won't be an easy fight, and I'll not drag my squadmates into this.

"They don't have a scent, but I can sense others here." Joey's thought passes just as a massive lycan hurdles a fallen tree, teeth bared, arms extended, in an attempt to grab us. His advance is narrowly evaded by dropping to our stomach and rolling once. Easily, he pivots his momentum to charge back toward us. Jo forces

the shift from four paws to standing upright in our hybrid-lycan form. The additional shift takes us a few breaths as our legs and arms extend. Our paws transform into long fingers and toes with speared nails. The ability to shift between wolf and lycan forms is likely an upgrade courtesy of the Goddess. *I have no idea how it truly happened, so don't waste your breath asking.*

"Surprise, mother fucker!" Jo snarls at him.

That catches the bastard off guard as my arm swings up with all my force to rip out his heart. It's the quickest way to kill a shifter besides decapitating them. Pivoting, Jo kicks another, sending him into a nearby tree. Then the shit show really begins as we run into a small clearing. There stands around a dozen male lycans, all of whom are very large in stature. Several start to shake as their shift rolls through them. Deep in our stomach's core, tingling begins signaling our flames want to be unleashed. It's the feeling of lava before it erupts. *Bring it fuckers!* Sending out a large blast, we successfully hit three of them.

The screams of the men burning alive drown out the shouts of others calling orders. Some are smart enough to seek cover at the sight of their homeboys' charred bodies.

Flames leaping off bodies into the underbrush have caused several trees to ignite. Our magic easily seeks out the rogue flames. It surrounds them and pulls the fire back into us like a vacuum before the whole forest goes up in flames. We don't need 'Dana Jo caused a forest fire' added to my write-up, which I'll most definitely receive after this. Movement in our peripheral vision snags our attention. A uniformed man is walking in a trance state, carrying an unconscious woman toward an open portal. The Queen.

"FUCK! FUCKITY, FUCK! We need help! I don't hear any help coming from the Silverthrone Pack. JO, JAX SOS NOW! Can we reach him through mindlink?"

"I can do better."

A foreign surge of power pulses through us as our subconscious connects to hundreds of unfamiliar minds. *"ATTACK! ON YOUR QUEEN AT THE SOUTHEASTERN BORDER. COME NOW!"* Joey barks out the command.

"Crimson female! Bind her fire and capture her!" An authoritative, deep bass voice booms from behind the cover of the woods.

Everyone seeks cover again as fireballs alight in our palms. The swift scattering of our assailants clears the way for us to see the third witch. Jo launches a barrage of fireballs that cut through the air like missiles. Her lifeless eyes lock onto ours as she counters, casting spells faster than we can dodge. Diving, Jo manages to avoid the first two curses. They hit the ground in an explosion of rotting earth. Blasting more fire in her direction proves to be a mistake as her magic sinks its talons into ours. She yanks it back like a rope, causing Joey to stumble. A sharp breath escapes us as her invisible claws tear into us.

A dumbass with a death wish tackles us from behind, knocking us entirely to the ground and lighting himself on fire in the process.

The sacrifice of Death Wish gives the witch her opportunity to strike us with one of her fire-binding spells. The magic feels as if shards of glass are being pulled through my veins toward my internal inferno. It's pure agony, but I grit my teeth through the pain as my flames extinguish.

We leap off the ground in time to block an oncoming assault. They will learn we don't need our fire ability to still kill them. Jo's clawed hand plunges into the beast's chest nearest to us, ripping his heart out. Wide, shocked eyes meet ours, followed by a loud thump as his lifeless body hits the ground. Jo bares her fangs at the incoming group of perpetrators.

"We need a plan to stop the witch before she gets the Queen through that portal," I tell Joey.

Dodging another attack, Jo grabs a large fallen tree branch, propelling it directly at the witch, whose attention is now solely on the Queen.

It hits her, and she emits an "umph," knocking her to the ground. Lying where she fell, she releases an ear-splitting scream, not from pain but from anger. Traces of her blood's scent can be detected in the air. *Sorry, not sorry, psycho.*

"I WILL SKIN YOU ALIVE!" she shrieks.

"You can try!" Joey snaps back.

A chorus of distant howls comes from the lycan pack lands. Backup is coming, finally, thank the Goddess. We continue to battle our aggressors in a blur of claws and fangs in attempts to get closer to the Queen. One inflicts a deep laceration on our right biceps muscle before we decapitate him. We come down hard on another's leg, breaking it before leaping the rest of the way to the man carrying the unconscious queen. Joey tucks and rolls, avoiding a flying spell directed at us. The Queen is only a few feet away from the portal at this point.

"Hurry!" the manic witch's voice pitches in hysteria. Wind twists angrily around her, whipping her heavy black cloak.

Finding more downed branches, Jo tosses them at her, causing her to shift her focus back to us. She sends surges of magic into each one, exploding them on contact. We manage to make our way the last several feet to the male carrying the Queen. There's no recognition in the man's features, showing he doesn't realize the threat we pose; he looks to be in a trance. The knuckles of our right hand connect with his temple brutally hard, forcing him to stop. Both his and the Queen's limp bodies fall to the ground, causing us to take up a protective stance over them.

No one is taking this woman on our watch. A sharp bang of a gunshot cracks in the air as powerful as thunder. We don't have time to react before a tranquilizer embeds itself into our stomach.

"No!" Jo howls. *"We aren't going down this way."*

Our clawed hand clasps around the dart, yanking it out along with a fist full of fur. A swarm of enemies descends on us, making us aware that we've been weakened enough to become the prey. The sluggish effect instantly hits us as we fight to keep from being pinned. Slashing blindly, Jo manages to rip one's stomach open before excruciating pain in our left leg causes us to experience a short blackout. Our calf bone has been broken, causing it to puncture my skin.

Adrenaline pumps through our veins, holding the full effect of the wound at bay. Unable to put weight on that leg, we stammer, trying to stay upright. Slowly, we attempt to shift from lycan to wolf form, where three paws are more manageable with this injury. The witch seizes the opportunity to send a powerful blast of magic at us. The force sends our limp body spiraling into a nearby tree. Against our will, my body is forced to shift back into human form.

"Nooo," Joey howls.

The pain becomes unbearable, and my vision begins to fade.

"Goddess, I'm sorry we failed you." Is my last thought before everything fades away, taking me with it.

CHAPTER FIFTEEN

Ajax

Blood and Ash

Pure panic seizes every part of me the moment Dana's mindlink reaches the pack, causing me to frantically leap from my bed. Mars assumes control, shifting and allowing the bond to guide us toward our mate. The thought of losing another loved one transports me back to dark times I never want to revisit. We only have one dominant thought racing through our mind:

protect our mate. Random pack mindlinks start chiming in, asking who sent out the distress call. *Is the threat real? Where's the King? Can pack guards handle it?*

"The threat's real. Anyone who can fight, get to the pack border now!" I shout at them.

Thankfully, Dolken speaks up to confirm Dana's legitimacy before I close the mindlink. I can't focus on the pack idiots right now as my instincts tell me Dana's in trouble. The scent of blood, mixed with burning flesh and rot, is strong on the breeze. Mars snarls, pushing our pace to speeds we've never reached before. We clear the tree line, coming face to face with five lycans and a dark witch.

I open back up my pack mindlink. *"Hurry! Dark witch, unknown lycans, and the Queen's down. I repeat, GAMILA IS DOWN!"*

"I'm almost there!" Dolken answers my call.

Scanning the area, we see the land is scarred with signs of a recent battle – fallen trees, scorched bodies, and decaying Earth. A few feet away, a man grabs Queen Gamila, who's unconscious. Dolken quickly tackles the man trying to carry off his grandson's wife.

We see Dana lying in a crumpled heap of pooled blood near a broken tree with her eyes closed. Instinctively, Mars leaps in front of our mate to protect her. Her safety is all we can focus on. Her naked form shivers, and the bone in her lower leg has torn through the skin.

"Dana, hold on, I'm here," I try to mindlink her, but she's not conscious.

Our eyes meet an unknown male who is currently approaching. Fury erupts inside, causing us to see red.

Mars bares his teeth at the incoming lycan, giving him a clear warning. *"You will not touch our mate,"* he snarls.

The male hesitates when Mickey, Demi, Miguel, and a few others race in to block attacks from the remaining lycans. The thunderous sound of the pack's footsteps forces the witch to retreat through an open portal.

"Coward!" Mars sneers.

He is determined not to let this asshole, who was intent on harming our mate, get away. As the man attempts to flee, Mars charges him. We kick the back of his leg, causing him to stumble, but not fall. He quickly recovers and avoids our back tackle. Crouching, we jump up, blocking his frontal assault. We manage to land a solid hit on his hip, knocking him off balance. Snarls tear from each of our throats as Mars works to pin the other lycan down. We become engaged in a fierce ground battle of snapping jaws and pounding fists.

"Jax, move out of the way," a familiar voice calls into my mind.

I see Cher, Gamila's mother-in-law, raise a long silver blade high, ready to strike. Unwavering determination shines in her steely eyes. Pinning my opponent's arms, I lean back, giving her a clear shot at his neck. His struggles become more frantic against my hold, knowing his end is near. Swinging the blade down with all her might, Cher slices off his head.

"Thank you," I mindlink her. She gives me a single curt nod before running off toward Gamila.

At some point, the portal closed, leaving me unsure of how many managed to escape. Shifting back to human form, I rush to my mate's side.

"Dana! Dana! Look at me!" I cup her angelic face, which is too pale from blood loss. Her unfocused eyes slowly blink open, and her head tilts slightly in confusion. I scoop her into my arms as gingerly as possible, causing her to whimper in pain. The sound shatters my heart.

"What the fuck?" someone shouts among the crowd of pack members gathered.

Dolken races past, cradling Gamila with a dozen additional packmates in tow.

"Pack doctors to the hospital now!" he blasts through the pack mindlink after seeing the sight of both women. *"Everyone spread out to make sure no one else is out there,"* he orders while sprinting toward the hospital.

Mickey and Miguel arrive by my side. "Shit, Commander..." Mickey trails off at the sight of her. Dana's eyes remain unfocused, and her body slumps loosely in my arms.

"Tranq dart," Miguel points to an abandoned metal-encased object on the ground with a long needle.

"I'm taking her to our pack hospital since it's closer, and she'll need surgery. Can you please notify her team members at Crescent Moon?" I ask my brothers in haste.

"Yes," they reply in unison before heading off.

"Hey, look at me, Dana. Breathe through the pain. I've got you," I tell her as I do my best to run while carefully supporting her broken body. More soft whimpers escape as tears roll down her cheeks. She takes rapid breaths as her body trembles. The bone in her calf is fully exposed. This is an injury that even advanced shifter healing requires help to repair. The bone needs to be properly reset before natural healing can begin.

My blood hammers in my ears as Mars rages over the state of our mate. *"You need to move faster."*

"I'm trying. It'll be okay," I tell him, even though I'm not sure I believe it.

"Mate, you came?" Dana mutters through half-lidded eyes, her erratic breathing starting to slow.

"Yes, it's me. I'm getting you help. Hold on," I say calmly, trying to soothe her anyway possible given the circumstances. Her head lolls before shooting up.

"The Queen! Old World Lycs, black itch, oregano," she slurs as she fights to stay conscious.

"Shhh, stay with me. The Queen is safe." Gently, I cup her head, cradling it to my chest as I continue to dodge trees in haste to reach the hospital.

"It's oregano," she insists.

"An organization?" I ask, thinking she is trying to tell me they were that, and not an herb.

"Yeah, organiz..." Her head falls before abruptly popping up again. *Christ! How's this woman still conscious after this much blood loss and a possible tranquilizer?* The fog in her eyes clears as she focuses on my face. She inhales deeply before uttering the most beautiful word in this world, and the old.

"Mine."

With that, she is finally down for the count. Mars releases a contented howl at our mate's declaration. Leaning down, I place a tiny kiss on the top of her head. *"Mine,"* I internally repeat.

Mars forces a shift, allowing us to move faster now that Dana can no longer feel the pain. Nothing matters more than getting her help.

As we travel the rest of the distance, I let the full weight of that one word sink in. In shifter terms, that one possessive word holds more weight than all others. *"Mine,"* she said. She claimed us as hers. The other half of our soul. Was it the blood loss talking, or has she already accepted us as hers? I tuck that away and run.

At the hospital entrance, a group of doctors and nurses wait by rows of stretchers. Setting Dana's broken body down is difficult in my frantic state. As I transition, Dr. Hurts raises one eyebrow in question.

"Who is this she-wolf?" he asks with disdain.

"Dana Jo Johnston, a high-ranking member of the Moon-born Pack military," I tell him. "She was injured fighting unknown lycans on neutral ground while protecting our Queen. Please help her."

Dr. White, Karissa's Aunt, tosses me a pair of shorts before yelling orders at the medical staff about where to take Dana for surgery.

Dr. Hurts huffs. "She needs to be sent to her own kind for healing."

Pleasantries be damned. Snarling, I grab the asshole by the pristine collar of his white coat. "Listen, we don't have time to work through your bullshit wolf prejudices. She's my fated mate, and you will fucking help her, now!" My voice is rough and laced with authority.

The doctor inclines his neck in submission, as he is no match for my level of dominance.

"L-listen," he stutters out through gritted teeth before Doctor White steps in.

"Jax is right, we don't have time for this, get her to O.R. room 2, NOW," she orders two nurses who are standing on either side of Dana's gurney. The two rush off in haste.

"No, all resources must be dedicated to Queen Gamila and injured pack members. They're the priority." Dr. Hurts badly wants to lose his head.

"Gamma Dolken instructed me to help the injured she-wolf. He'll tell King Anders of your insubordination if he catches wind of it," she coolly fires back before jogging after the nurses.

"Oh, he will hear of it," I growl in his face.

Dr. Hurts flounders over his words again. Not waiting to hear some pitiful excuse for his behavior, I run to catch up with Dana. We pass a room overflowing with bustling medical staff, where Gamila is being treated.

"You can wait here." Dr. White gestures toward a vanilla waiting room.

An oversized plant with dusty leaves is stuffed in one of its corners. It has a sad appearance, providing little to alleviate the space's overall dullness as my mind races. The combination of rubber gloves, antiseptic, and my mate's blood lingers heavily in the air. I want to protest waiting here, but I know it'll only delay Dana from getting the help she desperately needs.

Mars' animalistic nature pushes me to stay by her side. *"Our mate needs us. Go with her."*

"We can't. We'll only be in the way."

Mars bares his teeth at that.

"I'm sorry, I don't want to wait out here either," I assure him.

Right now, I'm experiencing a multitude of emotions and can do nothing to soothe the beast's angst. Scenarios of what-ifs quickly escalate to the worst possible outcome. Flashes of my childhood trauma emerge, having escaped their locked cage. My breathing starts to restrict. *Fuck.* I close my eyes, breathing deeply, and searching for a sense of calm. *Our mate is strong; she will survive. The Goddess won't take her away, too.*

"Hey, I thought you might want this," a woman's voice says.

My eyes snap open. Before me, a young female nurse tosses me a T-shirt, accompanied by a saucy smirk. Her squinting eyes, framed by fluttering lashes heavy with makeup, cause my stomach to flip in an unpleasant way.

"Let me know if you need help putting that on," her nasally voice causes another wave of revulsion to wash through me.

"No," my stern reply receives an instant pout of her color-stained lips. Having reached my patience limit with her, I give her my back as I pull the shirt over my head. *Now what? Waiting, fuck.*

My heightened adrenaline desperately seeks an outlet. I force myself to sit in one of the uncomfortable chairs instead of pacing holes in the ugly beige carpet. Stress, anxiety, more waiting, uncertainty, silence; it all quickly becomes overwhelming.

I stand, starting to pace. My sister, Rose, checks to make sure I'm okay before asking about tonight's events. I leave out the part about my mate being involved. I don't have a close relationship with Rose, and I can't handle questions about Dana right now. Unsurprisingly, she and her mate, Draco, didn't get involved. I know why they didn't come, but it still makes me upset, especially since it was my mate who needed help. They stick to their small group, avoiding almost all pack-related events after what they went through at the hands of the former king. I reassure her that everything is fine and go back to waiting.

King Anders rushes in via portal, accompanied by several guards. Soon after, Gamma Dolken emerges into the waiting room. He briefly checks in with me to provide an update on the situation.

"Gamila is in stable condition with no signs of injury, but she needs to stay for monitoring. How's Dana doing?"

"Dr. White took her into surgery about fifteen minutes ago," I tell him.

He clasps me on the shoulder. "Keep me posted. I need to go check on some things."

"I'll do that, sir."

Mickey, Miguel, Dolken, and Squad Leader Kyle arrive together, forty-five minutes into my agonizing wait. Kyle types away on his tablet, taking my statement for his official report. I learn the King had been away from the pack lands, dealing with an issue at an overseas pack. The heavily pregnant queen was left in the care of the pack's Beta, Matt. Unfortunately, all of the royal guards, household staff, Beta Matt, and Queen Gamila were knocked unconscious by what we assume was a sleeping spell. Everyone appears to be fine, but no one remembers how they lost consciousness.

After I recall what I remember from the situation, Dolken escorts Kyle to a secluded meeting room within the Royal Estate. I confided in Kyle that Dana's my fated mate, which is why I'm not leaving this fucking hospital for a debriefing meeting. I also want him to be reassured that she's in good hands while she's here. The young squad leader does nothing to hide his shock at this news.

An hour goes by, and my second parents, Dottie and Frank Fangerson, join Mickey, Miguel, and me. I know they were informed that Dana's my mate, but they don't press for details.

"I thought you might be here for a while, dear," my adoptive mother tells me with a cooler of food in tow.

"Yes. Thank you," I ensure my tone is gentle with the thoughtful woman who helped raise me.

Although they don't express it directly, I can feel their underlying concern for Dana's well-being. I want to send them away, but the extra presence is appreciated right now, even though it does nothing to calm my nerves. Mickey attempts to ease the heavy mood with his light-hearted manner and reassurances.

Miguel, however, jokes, "I'm sure for the Lycan Slayer Commander that was a cake walk, or well, maybe more a cake limp with that leg bone situation." I shoot him a death glare to show I'm not in the mood.

"Boys, only once you have found your destined mates will you understand what Ajax is going through right now. Leave him be, and work on being a strong, silent support system. Key word,

Miguel, silent," Dottie scolds the twins the same as she did when we were young pups.

"Hey, can one of you run to my house to grab my phone in case Moonborn Pack needs to reach me?" I ask the twins.

I need to contact Andy. Normally, I only contact her on a secondary phone with a secure line, but I can't physically bring myself to leave.

"I got you," Mickey says, hurrying off.

Once he returns, I fire off coded texts in the privacy of the bathroom. I detail what I know and assure Andy that I will check the surveillance footage from the capture orbs I placed around the estate. I opt to tell a half-truth about having stuff to care for in the aftermath as an excuse for not doing it now. A quick reply lets me know a small team has been dispatched to scout the area. Guardian Angels have unlimited magical resources, allowing them to go unseen. In this situation, it's necessary to ensure this perp can't flee if they realize the angels are sniffing around.

Soon, it becomes solely a matter of waiting. The minutes tick by painfully slowly. Tick. Tick. TICK. TICK. I resist the urge to smash the damn clock into pieces by shoving my hands into my shorts pockets, and instead, I mentally curse out the obnoxious thing. Mars paces laps in my mind, making sure to share just how displeased he is about literally fucking everything. My head begins to pound. Throb, Throb. THROB. THROB. I can't take it anymore. Shooting to my feet, I make my way to the nurse's station.

"It's been close to two hours; I need an update now before your waiting area gets a much-needed redesign," I say with more force than I intend.

"Well, it wouldn't be the first time," nasal nose replies, not bothering to remove her focus from her computer.

A warm, comforting hand grips my shoulder. "Hey, what Jax meant to say is, can you please get us an update on Ms. Johnston?" Mickey asks politely with his charming smile that instantly makes all the women wet between their legs.

"Oh, hey, Mickey," she perks right up along with her boobs. My scowl is instant. "Sure, give me a couple of minutes." Smiling, she stands up, sashaying off with a little too much sway in her hips.

My nose wrinkles. *Really, man?* It's hard to keep the judgment out of my tone as I mindlink with Mickey. He shrugs, unbothered.

Ten painfully slow minutes later, she returns with Dr. White. The Doctor informs me Dana has been stabilized after losing 900mL of blood, and the compound fracture has been repaired. She has been moved to post-op, where I can see her. They're confident there will be no long-term damage to her leg. Dana will need to be monitored in the hospital for a couple of days before being discharged with a cast for several additional days. With Moonborn Pack's cooperation, they were able to get her medical records updated accordingly. The news feels as if a boulder has been lifted off my chest, allowing me to breathe for the first time in over two hours.

"Thank you, Selene, for looking over our girl," Mars sends his love to our Goddess.

CHAPTER SIXTEEN

Dana

Hospital

Beep. Beep. Beep.

Ugh, go to hell, Satan's beeping. Since when does my room smell like hand sanitizer and roses? Eyelids, why are you so damn heavy? Open now, you little bastards. Ah, I'd kill for a Hawaiian-style pizza. Why's that still beeping? Wait, is that the microwave? Maybe there's a pizza in there. Is that what smells so amaz-

ing? Leather pizza? Is leather pizza a new weird social media trend like putting weird shit in your water? I'll have to ask my baby bro. Eyes, you have two seconds to open. Don't make me pry you open!

"Dana! Focus!"

"Eyelids? Was that you?"

"NO! It's Joey, your wolf. We're in the hospital; the beeping is us. The attack, remember?"

Images of the battle race to the forefront of my mind, shoving past the mental fog. The jolt of adrenaline gives my eyelids the juice they need to open. They rapidly blink to find their focus. I lock onto the source of that irritating beeping. *Yup, it's me.* My stomach weeps a little after hearing it's not, in fact, a delicious pizza.

The marker board on the wall reads "Tuesday, 4/29," and my nurse's name is Gina, accompanied by a smiley face. *Nice touch, Gina.* To the right of my bed, a side table supports the largest flower arrangement I've ever seen. Bright bursts of colors from flowers scatter throughout the room capture my attention. *Is this a hospital or a greenhouse medical center?*

"Dana." Ajax's soft voice from the other side of the room forces my focus away from the floral arrangements.

"My Jax?" *Just wow.* Formulating sentences is very hard right now. Whatever medication I'm on is causing my brain to be the equivalent of scrambled eggs. Grabbing my hand, he flips it over, kissing the inside of my wrist gently. Damn, now my insides are just as scrambled as my brain.

"You're turning me into a giant scrambled egg," I grumble.

"Then I guess I'll have to eat you up." He flashes me a devilish grin, causing my body to heat.

This man knows exactly what he's doing to me. His voice loses its playful note.

"I was so worried about you," he admits. "How are you feeling?"

"Tired. Weak. Confused. Hungry. Wait! Are the Queen and her baby okay?"

"Yes, your heroic actions saved them both. Queen Gamila sent all the flowers to ensure that when you woke up, you felt appreciated. She wishes to be here, but the experience was quite traumatic, so the doc has her on strict bed rest at home."

My soul lightens at this news. The Queen and her pup are safe. That's all that really matters. The greenhouse worth of plants in my room was a thoughtful gesture, but she didn't need to fuss over me.

"A couple of your squad members stopped by to deliver your belongings and a portal spell to return home. Squad Leader Kyle came here right after the incident to write up a report. He was quite worried about leaving you here, but Anders and I assured him you were being cared for and would be safe. There have been a few debrief calls between our packs regarding the incident. I've been told Ezekial wants you to contact him immediately after you wake up."

"Right, he'll want my firsthand account of what happened." *Great.* "Was anyone hurt from either of the packs?"

"No one aside from you."

I rub at my tired face. "Thank the Goddess."

"Let me go get the doctor. She wanted to check on you when you woke up. I say she takes priority over some Demigod." Jax leans down to kiss my forehead before striding his fine ass out the door. *That man is sexy as hell.*

"And ours," Jo purrs.

Moments later, there's a brisk knock on my door. A stunning beauty in a white coat strides in, followed by Jax. *They would make the most gorgeous babies.* The traitorous fleeting thought causes jealousy to surge forward, unlike anything I've ever experienced before. *Shit, feelings, you better get your ass in line right quick.*

Jo expresses her displeasure at me thinking of our man with another. *"Mine. Only we'll be making his gorgeous pups."*

Jax walks straight to my side to intertwine his long fingers with mine, picking up on my change in demeanor. Doctor White, as I learn, launches into a full, detailed play-by-play of my surgery and blood transfusions. My still fatigued brain can't follow all her medical jargon, so I nod along politely.

"Howza? Whatta?" Jo asks, cocking her head in confusion. *"No way our mate would be into Dr. SnoreWhite. Tell this lady we want the abridged version, or better yet, we'll settle for the shitty SparkNotes of the medical textbook wedged up her ass."*

"Joey!" I scold, struggling to hold back my giggles.

"Imagine her dirty talk in bed."

"No, stop." I pinch my mouth together to keep from offending the nice doctor.

"Oh, baby, your male sexual reproductive organ is so extensive. Let's hope your seminiferous tubules are producing strong —"

"JOEY, stop!"

I quickly compose my laugh-cough before gracefully cutting the good Doctor off. "Ma'am, so what I'm hearing is that it was one heck of a doozy. Doctor White, I can't thank you enough for your help. I truly appreciate you and your medical staff for all y'all have done for me."

"You are welcome, Miss Johnston."

"Now, when can this cast come off?" I ask, hopeful the answer is right now.

Unfortunately, I find out the answer isn't soon enough. She wants me to stay overnight, with hopes of removing my cast on Friday. Fortunately, the news is promising about making a full recovery.

I'm thankful for being a werewolf with super healing abilities. *How do humans deal with having casts on for months?* Healing would be even faster in my wolf form, but with a bone injury such as this, it's too risky to shift right now. Surgery and some good old-fashioned rest are my only options.

After she leaves, a sense of foreboding lurks in my gut. I don't want to speak with Ezekial. Jax is kind enough to step out, giving me privacy. He promises to find some food, preferably a Hawaiian-style pizza, which only serves to increase my attraction to him.

I force myself to take several large breaths before dialing the big guy. Ezekial picks up immediately after the first ring. He shows care for my overall health, safety, and comfort with my current location before drilling me for every possible detail regarding the attack, documenting it all for cross-referencing.

"We have not notified your emergency contacts of your injury. Would you like us to do so?"

"No, sir."

"The lycans are incredibly grateful for your service to their queen," he pauses awkwardly.

"But?" I prompt with my least favorite three-letter grenade.

"Your Senior Officer has filed another complaint against you for not following direct orders. It has been decided to place you on a thirty-day medical sabbatical. During which, there will be a thorough investigation into the incident," he pauses again as I process. "Do you have any questions or comments regarding this matter we should take into consideration?"

"Typical Lumen," I bite out.

"Johnston." There is a warning in his tone.

What does he want me to say? "Sorry, Sir."

"Dana, from this report, you had direct orders to oversee a young recruit. Your Senior Officer instructed you not to get involved with the lycans due to the safety implications. These orders were deliberately disobeyed, and team members, including yourself, were put in grave danger. You are lucky your impulsive behavior didn't kill anyone. I am facing immense pressure not to overlook your actions. You are both an asset and a great liability, but there is a pack hierarchy for a reason."

Something inside me snaps. For decades, I've given this pack my everything while struggling with internal politics. I'm not sure if I can do it anymore.

"First of all, sir, you and I both know my current position in that hierarchy is complete bullshit. I'm sick of being deliberately cock-blocked by Captain Brutis, who doesn't operate with the were-communities best interest in mind. It's hard for you to see that when you shut yourself away from the pack."

That earns me a nasty snarl. A clear warning to shut my mouth, but that's not happening today. It's too late. I know this ship is going down regardless of my words or actions.

"Second, danger is part of the job; we all know the risks when we enlist. That's why we swear an oath to protect. Third, being asked to serve as a bodyguard for one of the new recruits, who is very capable, mind you, is an unfair practice toward all other fresh recruits. Lastly, thanks to my impulsive actions, a pregnant woman and her child are safe from whatever horrible fate awaited them.

What if that was your mate and child, Ezekial? What if they could have been saved? I'll never apologize for my decision, so don't ask that of me. I'll await whatever fate you see fit for me."

The glowing ember in my chest fully ignites. All of me is consumed by rage as my heart thunders in my chest, and my hands tremble. I'm so fucking angry, not for myself, but for all the innocents who have suffered due to poor and overlooked leadership calls. A simple in-and-out clean-up job is unacceptable.

More of the Demigod's enraged snarling comes from the other end of the phone, along with the noise of something breaking. "You should explore your options. Seeing as the Goddess gave you a lycan mate, I would say it is a clear sign this is not where you are intended to be." Then the other end of the line goes silent.

Grief. Annoyance. Fear. Anger. Betrayal. Pride. Sorrow. *Did I just commit career suicide? Does it even matter?* Maybe Ezekial's right about the lycan mate thing. I don't belong there anymore.

I sigh, wiping tears from my eyes. *"Damn it. I shouldn't have mentioned his mate and child."*

Joey's rough tide of emotions matches mine. *"Yes, it's hard for him to hear, but he's familiar with that pain and should therefore understand the reason for our actions."*

Direct descendants of the Eden Moon God, Alpha, can have multiple fated mates, but only one at a time. If one mate dies, another is eventually found. Most speculate it's God Alpha's way of ensuring his line continues. Some might envy the prospect of a never-ending line of true mates, but not Ezekial; to him, it's a curse.

After losing three beloved mates and a child, he refuses to take any more. To protect what's left of his heart, he shuts away every inch of himself, only sharing his time with those in his close circle. It's understandable, but the time has come for him to reconnect with the pack or step down from leadership. The absence of an Alpha's presence is felt among our pack and the entire werewolf community. Ezekial needs to see firsthand the problems affecting our society so he can help us fight them. We need him to step up and become that fearless leader who led wolves in The Crossing. It's time.

Jax finally returns with a sausage pizza that has canned pineapple sprinkled on top, a slice of double chocolate cake, and an apple juice. Having my mate near me again helps settle some of my angst. The carefree smile he easily wears fades the moment he scents my emotions in the air. I want to suppress everything and pretend I'm okay, but I don't have the willpower right now. This feeling is completely unfamiliar to me, and I hate being this vulnerable.

"What's wrong? And don't try hiding the truth from me or blaming my shitty attempt at a Hawaiian-style pizza as the culprit for your tears."

"Ezekial and I had a phone pissing match." I wipe at the tsunami of building tears in my eyes. "He isn't happy about me intervening in lycan affairs."

Jax folds his arms over his chest. His eyebrows furrow as he looks at me. "Well, if you didn't, Gamila would likely be dead, and Anders would be making his way to meet her on the other side. He wouldn't survive the death of her." He takes my hand in his. "Dana, you did a really good thing. Don't let anyone tell you otherwise."

"Yes, we did," Jo glows from our mate's support.

I give him a nod in agreement before settling in with my food. I fill him in on my conversation, being careful to side-step the part about potentially losing my job and being packless within a month.

Pride, embarrassment, and stubbornness won't let me share that truth. Not yet, anyway. I don't want Jax to feel increased pressure to mate me because of my current circumstances. Or worse, be disappointed in me for being dishonorably discharged as the pack's number one liability. It's all too much to handle right now.

Dolken visits me in the afternoon. He brings his soothing energy and good conversation. I explain my dream to him through what I remember of the attack.

"You're sure Torr was in a trance?" Dolken asks me.

"Who is that again?" Dolken and Jax are tossing around a lot of new names as they recount the attack, which I'm struggling to keep straight.

"He was the man carrying Queen Gamila," Dolken clarifies.

"Yes, I'm positive," I tell him.

"Hmm. Well, I found his body this morning. It appears to be due to suicide. He was a staff member at the Royal Estate. He was seen by Dr. Hurts last night, and we tried questioning him, but he said he couldn't remember anything. I went to check on him this morning and found him. We did a quick search of his home, which uncovered some incriminating evidence linking him to Karissa and Gamila's abductions." Dolken sounds saddened by this.

"What did you find, if I may ask?" Jax inquires.

"Well, he had lots of documents. From Gamila's typical schedule, a photo of Karissa on his wall, detailed notes about Anders' trip, and the estate layout," Dolken recounts.

"Why would the witches have entranced him if he was willingly working with them?" I toss out.

"Maybe to help him look innocent?" Jax speculates.

I turn that over in my mind. "Yeah, I suppose."

Jax looks deep in thought. "Did you find anything in his house that could help us find where they took Karissa or the missing female wolves?" he asks.

"Nothing. I want to go through it again, though, to see if we missed anything." He still has that lingering sadness.

"Did you know this man well?" I ask Dolken.

"I've known him my entire life."

"And do you think he did this?" I press, curious about what is causing that sadness.

"Well, the evidence speaks for itself," he says simply.

"What do you think was his motive for working with this organization?" Jax cuts in.

"Well," Dolken starts looking thoughtful. "I'm not sure, other than money, or he secretly wanted Anders dead. Killing Anders' mate while she is pregnant would be the easiest way to kill him. Torr was a loner, with not many family members or friends around. He was a hard worker who never complained. I considered him to be one of my friends, so I would've never guessed he'd do something like this, but I've been through enough shit in my life not to be surprised anymore by people's motives. Anders and I believe the witches planned to harvest the soul of the future prince, making it worth the risk of them coming here."

The soul harvesting, I could believe. Dark magic is sustained by taking the life force of a living being. Unborn soul harvesting is a barbaric, unspeakable practice. Consuming a pure soul, such as that of an unborn, allows the witch to absorb the highest amount of power possible through a single sacrifice. Furthermore, consuming the soul of a supernatural being who contains magic yields even more power than a human soul. Depending on the supernatural harvested, it can sustain those consuming it for decades.

Wolf and lycan shifters have been found to produce some of the highest levels of power. Some theorize it's because the sacrificer consumes two souls: the being and the beast. The Guardians have greatly helped eradicate dark magic covens, but unfortunately, they're the cockroaches of the supernatural world.

"And what about Dana?" Jax asks. "They planned to take her, too. Torr didn't even know her. So who was the boss calling the shots?"

"Maybe that presence we felt earlier saw me and couldn't resist the payout they knew they'd receive, or it was, you know, my charm," I joke, trying to clear the murder from Jax's eyes.

"You were a greedy bonus prize," Jax snarls, unable to hide Mars in his eyes. I love my man's protectiveness.

"Yeah, I'm not sure." Dolken seems to ponder this, but only looks more exhausted. I'd guess he hasn't slept much recently.

"You look tired," I tell him.

He laughs with no humor in it. "Yeah, I could use a lot of sleep. I fear that since eradicating King Andras and his cronies, I've let my guard down; we all have, and it's welcomed in other enemies."

Leaning forward, I squeeze his hand. "Don't waste good energy beating yourself up over it. Take what you've learned and use that knowledge. Create more alliances outside the lycan race for starters, and get better wards in place to alert you of threats outside pack lands."

"You're right. Thank you for what you did to protect my family. I don't know what I would've done without them," his lower lip quivers slightly. "The Silverthrone Pack owes you an enormous debt."

"Again, it doesn't, and you're welcome, Dolken."

Time in the hospital passes quickly with cat naps, easy conversation, and the constant companionship of one very sexy lycan. For the most part, I feel welcome by the staff tending to me, no doubt under strict orders from the royal family. The twins stop a handful of times, bringing cheap entertainment and various baked goods their mother prepared. According to them, she's been stress baking, which I don't mind. That woman can make a mean snickerdoodle cookie.

Miguel creates a spectacle, recounting numerous times how my bone looked outside of my body. Starting with only graphic details, but soon morphing into an elaborately spun tale. He paints a story fit for a Hollywood action film, of me killing an enemy lycan by piercing his heart with my protruding leg bone through a roundhouse kick to the chest. To my horror, Mickey tells me the outrageous story has already been circulating through the pack.

On Wednesday, Dolken came to extend a dinner invitation to me on behalf of the King and Queen for tomorrow evening. The invitation also includes a place to stay with amenities for as long as I wish. They're aware of my medical leave, but I'm unsure if they've been fully informed of its extent. Part of me wants to decline their offers because it's all too much, but I want to stay here longer. Dolken insists they'll not take no for an answer, so I accept.

Jo is ecstatic! *"Not only will we be pampered by royalty, but we can also spend more time in our mate's pack. I want to meet Mars so badly."*

Ideally, we want to stay with Jax, but he hasn't invited us to do so. Not being invited to stay with him hurts. It leaves me wondering and spinning Miguel-style fictions in my head. We both originally agreed that we had other things going on, and the timing wasn't right for us, but now things on my end have changed with my sabbatical. I'd rather he tell me to leave if this is inconvenient for him than leave me wondering.

"Dana, stop with the insecurities. We don't know everything Jax has going on in his life, or what's in his head, so maybe this is a good alternative. Being at the Royal Estate will give us time to take things slow, yet still be close to our mate."

"You're right," I agree with the great, wise wolf who lives in my head.

We still have heavy mate business to sort through, and space will be helpful for that. Together, we've been dancing around the topic. Our conversations have been safely centered around getting to know each other. With this hospital crawling with busybodies and gossip spreading faster than wildfire among the pack, it's not the place for life-altering conversations. But deep down to the root of my soul, I know my choice.

CHAPTER SEVENTEEN

Ajax

Ground Rules

After much disagreement, Dana finally had me throwing up white flags in surrender. If the stubborn mule wants to crutch out of the hospital, then that's what Dana Jo Johnston will do. I quickly learned that once my mate's mind was set, you were hard-pressed to change it. She refused a wheelchair or to let me carry her out like a *"damn fragile princess."* Furthermore, she refused to let me drive her *"only 300 feet"* to the Royal Estate. Mars even tried pleading with her to no avail. Goddess help me, because I love her fiery spirit. She left me with no choice but to follow her like an obedient mate, all while listening to Mars' nonstop stream of complaints.

"Look, pal, I don't like it either, but this is what she wants. You want her to be happy, right?" I ask the large, whiny beast.

"Yes...I still don't like it," he files the same complaint.

"How about, if she lets us, we can care for her later in the privacy of our home?" I suggest.

"Yes!" He perks right up at the thought of that.

The only reason I'm allowing my mate to take this field trip is because I've been looking for a way to get into the estate to release capture orbs to record those higher up within the pack. After notifying Andy of what transpired with Torr, she sent me a message back saying "not our man", leaving me still tied to this mission. She scheduled a call later this afternoon to further discuss how they know Torr isn't who we have been looking for. I feel angry knowing this asshole is still out there.

Chester, one of the lead estate guards, greets us when we arrive. He is someone I have spent a significant amount of time investigating. After months of vetting him, I was finally able to remove him from my suspect list. My instincts point to someone higher up in the pack hierarchy. After recent events, they showed they were in a position that allowed them to know Anders' private schedule. Potentially one of his personal guards.

Chester engages in easy small talk as he guides us to Dana's designated room. Staying present in the conversation is quite challenging for me, as my stress levels rise with each step. I fucking hate this place. It houses too many terrible memories for my family. Mars is teetering on the edge of losing his shit already. After seeing our mate badly injured, being cooped up in the hospital, this place, and leaving her here, he's at his breaking point.

"I don't care if we need an in. Get her out of here and take her to our house, now you idiot!" he rages at me.

"I know, but we must do our job before we can have our mate." I remind him.

At that, he bares his teeth. *"I don't care about the job right now! Our mate's upset we haven't asked her to stay with us. I can sense it. You're causing her to feel rejected. And if the perp is in this estate, we don't want our mate anywhere near here!"* Hysteria is coming through loud and clear in his tone.

Mars isn't wrong about Dana's feelings. She seemed uncomfortable about accepting the offer to stay here.

"She'll understand one day when we can tell her the truth. Now, deep breaths, Buddy. This isn't you. Where's my calm and loyal companion?"

He follows my suggestion, taking some deep breaths to bring himself back down to a highly stressed but less hysterical level.

"Okay, we can check it out, but if anything seems off, we'll grab her and run. Even if she is kicking and screaming at us to let her crutch herself out."

"I agree," chuckling, imagining that.

Prioritizing my duty over my mate goes against all my instincts. No part of me wants her here, in the place my sisters both considered a prison under Andras' rule. My thoughts pivot quickly to that dark place in my mind I so rarely go. The horrible memories of the former King Andras coil around me like a thorny bush, hell-bent on making me feel the pain.

The man murdered my parents on this estate's lawn in front of the entire pack and forced my sisters into unwanted marriages. The last time I was here, I stood in the front yard watching the powder white snow turn red from my parents' blood. A man held my arms too tightly, forcing me to have a front row view at the King's request. Another held my sister Rose next to me.

"Jax, don't look, don't look," Rose yelled at me through her tears.

My heart rate quickens as the panic creeps in, causing Dana to glance my way. Damn, that woman sees too much.

"Breathe! Breathe, keep it together," Mars tells me. *"You're stronger than those memories."*

"I know. It's just this place."

It's been over sixty years, and I can still clearly see the look on my parents' faces just moments before their deaths, if only I allow it to surface. I've made strides, seeking assistance when needed, but I'll always carry it with me.

"Here you are," Chester chirps merrily, helping break through the panic. "The Queen's arranged for new clothing and toiletries to be placed in your room. She insists you help yourself to anything; just ask for assistance if you wish to go anywhere on the grounds. If you're hungry, there's a stocked fridge available, or you can call the kitchen staff. Here's a list of numbers. They're also saved in this phone." Chester hands Dana a typed-up white sheet of paper and a new cell phone to borrow while on the pack lands.

"Dinner will begin at 6:00 P.M., so someone will arrive to escort you fifteen minutes before that." Chester turns to face me. "Ajax, will you be joining for dinner?"

Fuck. I'm expecting Andy's call at that time. "Unfortunately, I can't make it." The words are forced from my lips.

"Okay, I'll leave you to it. Ajax, call when you need an escort out." With that, he strolls out of the suite.

Dana crutches into the room, letting out a low whistle. "Davey and Charles would shit a glitter ball if they saw this place." I can't restrain the small chuckle that escapes me.

The room has a contemporary style. A soft, caramel-colored leather seating arrangement is positioned in front of a linear gas fireplace. Above it, an abstract forest landscape is displayed. To the right of the seating area is a spacious, renovated kitchen with all the amenities. Double doors at the back of the room lead to a spacious bedroom, bathroom, and walk-in closet, all designed for a queen. A mixture of new furniture scents reveals this space hasn't been lived in. It was probably one of the former King's wives' living quarters that was renovated after his death. New paint and flooring can't erase the unhappy memories this place holds.

My gut twists. *Did one of my sisters live here? Not now.*

"Seriously, this place is bigger than my apartment. Oh wow!" she drawls, opening the generously stocked wine fridge. "And this place has way more expensive wine than my apartment."

I really want to feel happy about how adorable my mate looks right now, gushing over wine, but I can't quite get there. The past darkness inside these walls weighs too heavily on me.

Dana reaches out a hand to grasp mine. We've grown familiar with light, innocent touches from our time in the hospital. The desire to touch and be near each other has already proven to be overwhelming at times. Her simple gesture helps ground me.

"Hey, enough about wine. Talk to me. Where'd you go back in the hallway, and just now?"

Before I talk myself out of it, I quietly admit to her, "It's this place. It brings back trauma from my childhood. I know you're a strong, capable, independent, Alpha female who makes her own decisions, but please don't stay here. Will you come stay with me instead?" I plead, as grief threatens to overpower me. Grief is the one thing I'm an expert at running away from, but not at this moment.

Abandoned crutches thud to the floor as Dana's warm arms wrap around my waist. Smoky lavender mingles with my scent, helping to calm my panic. Squeezing her tight to my chest, I inhale a deep breath of her before placing a tender kiss on the side of her neck. The contact causes her to shiver. Electrical currents surge through my body, fueling me. Reaching up, I cup her angel face and kiss those soft lips. She opens her mouth slightly, inviting me in for more. Not accepting her invitation is difficult, but my mind can't focus here.

"You can have more of that if you stay at my place," I say, wiggling my eyebrows to try to defuse some of the heaviness. I need to hear her say she will stay with me.

She smiles. "Okay, you convinced me."

Pure joy rushes through me. Scooping her up into my arms, I place one more kiss on her perfect lips before finishing the rest of her accommodation tour. She protests but eventually stops, knowing she will not win this battle.

We settle in at the kitchen island, enjoying sandwiches we found in the refrigerator. Summoning all my courage, I decide it's time. Dana and I need to have a serious conversation about mating. *Where do we start?* More than anything, I wish to tell her every-thing, but I can't. It's complicated. Christ, now I'm beginning to sound like a social media relationship status. Dana deserves to know where I currently stand, and Mars' angst is wearing on me.

Mars is the equivalent of a toddler; he wants his mate, and he wants her now, everything else be damned.

The beast pouts. *"Stupid commitment, that angel had to have known we would find our mate while on assignment. She knows everything. Are you sure she isn't a demon?"*

Hmm, he has a point. That angel is sneaky as hell. Did Andy know?

I shift uncomfortably and hesitate, unsure how to start this conversation, when Dana beats me to it.

"So, should we talk about the mating elephant in the room?"

Damn, does she also have some blessed gift for reading minds?

"I can't read minds if that is what you're wondering," she smiles.

"Well, I think you can." I poke her in the side playfully.

She shakes her head with a gleam in her eye. "I wish. Your energy shifted. I assume that it has something to do with our mate bond, which we haven't spoken about." Cradling both her hands in mine, I decide to plunge right in.

"You're right. For starters, every instinct in me is screaming to get you the hell out of here. The only place I want you is in my den. Where I know you're safe and that your every need, whether it's feeding you or fucking you, is met by me alone. The thought of your smoky scent mixing into my space makes me rock hard. You're mine, Fiery Wolf." Possessiveness is thick in my voice. Her sweet arousal blossoms in the air, signaling she likes my forwardness. *Fuck, here comes the equivalent of a cold shower.*

"But there are things I need to work through before I can fully be yours. I'm unsure how long it will take, but I promise that I'll be all in on the day I commit to you because you deserve nothing less."

She nods, sadness evident in her eyes. "I understand. Thank you for being honest with me."

The word "honest" stings. I hate not giving her the whole truth behind my reluctance; more than anything, I wish I could tell her about my commitment to this mission.

Deciding it's best to press on, I bring up our living situations. "There's also the matter of our home packs. Hell, we live in different countries. Now's not a time I can easily leave here, and you seem very committed to your pack duties. Are you ready to walk away from that?" More sadness dulls her eyes, and I hate that I caused it.

"You're right, I'm not sure. Since I have time off, maybe we can continue getting to know one another and figure it out along the way?" she suggests.

"That sounds perfect." Hope blossoms inside me. Maybe we can figure this out. Please, goddess, let me find this person before our time together is up.

"Just a forewarning..." She nervously giggles, and I find it adorable. "You'll learn quickly, I can be a real stubborn pain in the fanny."

"Oh, I'm fully aware of that after leaving the hospital. Let me assure you, I'll never grow tired of your fire. That's who you are, so don't change."

She beams at me before wrapping her arms around my neck.

"We'll see, Mr. Blackclaw." Leaning in, she brings her lips to mine in a slow, lazy kiss.

Quickly, our innocent kiss escalates to a raging inferno. Damn, I want her, all of her. She pulls away before we get lost in the moment.

"Maybe some ground rules would be smart," she proposes.

"Right," I reluctantly agree. I don't want rules, I just want her. But they might be good for me.

"How about I swear on my Pup Scout honor not to get carried away in hot, steamy, sexy time and mark you." Her devilish wink is the cherry on top, making me chuckle. I love the way she makes me laugh so freely.

"And I won't tolerate you being with another." My command is sharp. Instantly, I smell more of her arousal, telling me she likes it. "So we will remain exclusive until we make a decision about official mating."

"I agree," she says, still brainstorming. "Oh, and I think we should allow each other time and space if we need it for a decision." I hate the thought of being apart from her, but I agree.

"Do you think we should avoid using the word mate, especially in public, since it can be confusing to people if we haven't officially, um, done the deed?" she says with an adorable blush on her face.

I chuckle, "Sure. Add it to the list."

Mars makes it very clear he won't be following that one. *"Why did you agree to that? We aren't calling our mate anything besides mate!"*

"That's a good list, anymore you can think of?" she asks me.

"Yeah, maybe no maiming, castrating, or killing the other for choosing to reject the bond," I joke, but it doesn't land. Hurt flashes in her eyes before she pushes it away. I quickly pull her into my arms.

"Sorry, bad joke," I whisper.

She looks up at me. "Was that clause specifically for Joey?"

I push some stray hair away from her face. "Probably," I admit.

"Well, I think we need to keep it," she forces a light tone.

We spend the day into the late afternoon cuddling and napping in each other's embrace. In the end, neither beast is happy with our set of ground rules, but they have to live with them so we can move forward with our relationship.

I see myself out instead of requesting a chaperone as advised. I've walked these halls hundreds of times as a child when my father was the Beta, which will be my excuse if I am stopped. Mars heightens our senses, and thankfully, no one is too close by.

My hand finds the warm metal case nestled in my front pocket that has been spelled to look like a pack of gum. I slide it out and quickly flip the lid. The twenty-five capture orbs take flight, fading from a faint shimmery blue to invisible. They are a blend of magic mixed with technology. They are programmed to seek out living beings and follow them. The tiny magical balls can record years' worth of footage that is sent back and stored within a special laptop where I can view it all. May they finally find something useful.

CHAPTER EIGHTEEN

Dana

Royal Dinner Date

It's exactly 5:45 P.M. when a knock sounds at my door. Thanks to my talented style team, I wasn't forced to sport my Moonborn Pack uniform or pajamas to dinner with the lycan royal family. Instead, they dressed me in a fitted Prussian blue satin cocktail dress with bronzed florals. The knee-length spaghetti strap dress gathers at the left hip, flattering my curves. The dress is stunning.

"You look hot, ugly, cast, and all!" Joey hype-girls me.

"Aw, thank you."

I can't wait for Jax's reaction when he sees me in something other than my uniform or drab hospital attire. Most of all, I want him to see the sexy little number underneath the dress. The thought of him ripping it off me later has heat shooting down south. An annoyed huff escapes me as there's another knock at the door, pulling me out of my sex-filled daydreams of my mate. *Fuck, not mate, just Jax.*

"See! Those rules are stupid." Joey sounds more like an irritated teenager talking back to her mom than an animal.

"No, they're not. It'll take time to adjust to the mate one in particular."

"MATE, MATE, MATE, MATE, MATE, MATE, EVERYBODY!!" she shouts into our mind.

"Shush it, furball!"

"Just use the damn term, because I sure as hell will be."

"Fine, you win, but internally only, are you happy?" I ask her.

"Mildly," she replies, and I have to suppress an eyeroll.

I lean on my crutches and open the door. On the other side, a tall, imposing red-haired man stands. He's about the same height as Jax, with a rectangular face covered in a couple of days' worth of neatly trimmed stubble. Overall, he appears relaxed, wearing a plain white button-down shirt, blue jeans, and brown shoes that match his eyes perfectly. The sugary sweet smile aimed at me has my instincts telling me it's a façade.

"Hello, you must be the infamous Dana." The words smoothly roll from his lips.

"Yes, sir."

"I'm Matt Minos Storm, Pack Beta. It's truly a pleasure to be meeting such a remarkable creature as yourself," he gushes as he extends a hand to shake.

Taking his warm, calloused hand in mine, I give it one firm shake before dropping it. Joey hesitantly sniffs the air as if trying to avoid smelling something rotten.

Pulling back, she bares her teeth. *"I don't like this guy."*

My internal radar spikes; I agree something is off, a potential threat, it warns.

"It's nice to meet you, Beta Matt." The pleasantries are forced from my mouth along with a practiced smile. *Thanks for the involuntary beauty pageant smile lessons, Ma.*

"If you will, please follow me," he says while closing the door behind me.

"Thank you, sir." We start toward the west side of the estate.

"Please, call me Matt." His face lifts in a delighted expression, but I'm unsure of the genuine emotion in his eyes. "So, how long will you be gracing us with your presence, Miss Johnston?"

"I'm not sure. Doctor White's checking the healing progress of my leg tomorrow, so I should know more then."

"I see, well, I have to think your pack is anxious to get an asset such as yourself back quickly."

I internally snort, *yeah, if only.*

"They've placed me on a medical sabbatical to ensure I feel my best when I return to active duty. Your king and queen so graciously invited me to stay, which was very kind of them." Hopefully, most of my time will be spent with the special someone who sets my soul on fire.

"Queen Gamila has a kind heart. How long is this leave of absence for?" he asks.

"It's 30 days."

"I bet someone back home will be glad to have more time with you while you recover," he pushes.

Abruptly halting on my crutches, I turn to face him. "Why, Beta, are you trying to get rid of me already?" My face is an innocent mask with one eyebrow raised. Joey huffs. She doesn't like this man, nor does she care who knows it.

He, too, wears a mask of perfect innocence, shielding any of his true feelings. "No, not at all. Forgive me. I'm trying to understand why a lone wolf would be interested in staying with a lycan pack, especially after she was attacked outside our borders by our kind. Unless the rumors are true," he leaves the assumption hanging.

"Look, if you have something to ask, Beta, just do it."

"Okay, seeing as I've never heard of a lycan and werewolf fated pairing. I want to know if the rumor of Ajax Blackclaw being your fated mate is true." The way he says Jax's name tells me there's history there, and not a good one.

The hot temper in me wants to tell him it's personal and to go kick rocks. I can't pinpoint why this guy has my defensive walls sky-high, but I don't want to tell him anything, and I never second-guess my instincts.

Sensing my hesitancy, he plasters on another glucose-infused facial expression. "I apologize, I think we've gotten off on the wrong foot, or should I say crutch," he forces a laugh. "My job's to ensure everyone's safety, so I want to know your intentions for staying on our lands longer than necessary."

"Yes, we have a fated bond," I hesitantly confess before continuing.

His face lights up in surprise at that statement. "Interesting," is all he says on the matter.

"Any updates on Karissa?" I ask, changing the topic.

"Unfortunately, no." He hangs his head and sighs, expressing great sadness. "We found nothing in Torr's house regarding where to find her. I've been praying to the Goddess that she'll help bring sweet Karissa back to us." His perfect response falls flat.

"Wow, get that man an Oscar," Joey mumbles. *"For worst performance because I ain't buyin' it."*

"Rest assured, Beta, I believe Selene is watching. One day, those who dare to hurt her innocent children will face her judgment," I say sweetly.

Matt's eyes widen ever-so slightly before he nods. The remainder of our walk is completed in silence. Neither of us wants to be in the other's company. His upper body is stiff, and his strides purposeful. Joey stays alert, taking up a fighting stance in my mind's eye. She knows there is no way we can shift right now, but she refuses to show weakness in his company. Finally, after what feels like an eternity in unspoken tension, we arrive at our destination.

Exiting an inside corridor, we step into an exclusive, serene outdoor patio. The space is designed to foster an intimate atmosphere. A dark-stained wooden pavilion stands tall in the center, decorated with white sheer drapes tied to its legs. Twinkle lights fall in waves across the interior roof, while a modern glass chandelier hangs in the center, casting a warm glow. Underneath the massive structure sits a rectangular table that comfortably seats ten. Surprisingly, no commentary comes from the furball in my head as she stays focused on Matt.

Tall shrubbery lines the back stone wall, offering more privacy. To the right of the patio, a decorative fountain is carved into a smooth slate wall. Water flows from the open mouth of a lycan's head into a small, illuminated pool below with a soothing pitter-patter. To the left, a stone wall extends from the floor to the pavilion ceiling, featuring a fireplace as its focal point. Oversized, comfortable chairs with colorful pillows brighten the space.

Queen Gamila and King Anders are comfortably seated near the cozy fireplace. Detecting our presence, their heads snap around toward us. Queen Gamila is stunning. Her dark hair, olive skin, and almond-shaped light brown eyes suggest Middle Eastern descent. She waddles over faster than any pregnant woman should to hug me tightly. Her firm baby bump pokes my flat front. *Hello, little prince.*

A small sob escapes her. "Oh, Dana!" Going with it, I hug her back, trying my best not to be awkward or to drop my crutches. Behind me, I hear Matt's retreating footsteps, exiting the way we came.

"Good, we scared him off," my guard wolf says confidently.

Thank the Goddess he doesn't seem to be staying for dinner, the knot that had formed in my stomach disappears. I've no desire to fake pleasantries with him over dinner, no ma'am.

"How are you feeling?" Queen Gamila asks with an English accent, giving me one last squeeze before pulling back to examine me from head to toe.

"My leg is healing quickly, and, with any luck, this will be coming off tomorrow, Your Majesty," I tell her, gesturing to my bulky leg accessory.

She waves a dismissive hand. "Please, call me Gamila. No formalities are needed here, and that's fantastic news. Thank the gods, you're alright!" She wipes at her tears. "Truly." Her words ring sincere.

"Are you and the baby doing all right?" I ask her.

"Yes, we're both doing well, thanks to you."

King Anders steps beside his mate, stroking a loving hand up and down her back. He glances briefly at her before turning his attention to me. In that tiny glance, I can see the depths of his love for her. Jax is right; he never would've survived her death.

"Commander Johnston, we can never repay you for what you did. I also want to apologize for not personally checking on you in the hospital, but I couldn't physically bring myself to leave my mate's side. I hope you can understand," he explains.

"I understand. No repayment is necessary, and please call me Dana."

"From what I've heard, you were well looked after by your mate in the hospital." Gamila sends me a teasing smirk. I'm unable to prevent myself from smiling at her words.

"Yes, Jax made sure I was well cared for."

"So, the rumors are true? Jax is your fated mate?" Gamila asks sounding more like a gossiping teenager than a sophisticated royal, as her title suggests. It makes me like her even more.

"They're true. He's my fated mate."

She squeals. "What! How's this possible? I want to know everything."

"Gamila," Anders warns, causing her to pout. "Come sit." He ushers us both toward the table.

"Fine, we can talk about this another time when someone isn't around," she whispers conspiratorially to me.

The two cozy up next to one another, while I sit across from them. Candles, bread baskets, and small floral arrangements sit atop a crisp white tablecloth. As we settle in, we continue with pleasant small talk.

"Grandpa Dolken said you knew I needed help from a dream. Is that true?" Gamila's still puffy red eyes eagerly burn into mine.

"Yes, I saw you in a dream, then Jo, my wolf, knew where we needed to go. It's hard to put into words, but Jo is gifted. I often refer to her abilities as my 'Joey senses'; they're likely a goddess-blessed inherited trait." A waiter enters at this moment carrying a bottle of red wine. *Oh, I don't mind if I do.*

"As a blessed wolf, do you have these types of dreams often?" asks Gamila curiously.

"No. That was the first time I had dreamed about something. The Goddess is mysterious and calls out in different ways to me."

"That's quite remarkable. Are you willing to share with us how you became goddess-blessed?" Anders asks.

"Yes." Plucking a roll from its warm basket, I start my back story while buttering the hot carbs I can't wait to eat. Anders and Gamila sit intensely listening, as if they might miss some critical information if they move.

Gamila is the first to speak once I finish. "I don't know what to say besides...you're incredible."

Anders looks at me appraisingly. A new curiosity sparks in his intelligent green eyes. "What is it?" I prompt before taking another mouthful of bread.

"Agnar, my lycan, notices something in you. Almost attuned to a kinship."

"That's probably because I carry traces of lycan DNA. Medical professionals define me as a conundrum. They can't say for certain why or how my DNA was changed. Either from the Goddess or the lycan who bit me." Wolves and lycans can only be created the good ol' fashioned way, not from a bite, so it will always remain a mystery.

"Do you remember any physical attributes about the lycan who attacked you?" Anders' tone is eager when he asks.

"Well, this might sound unbelievable, but Joey confirmed it happened. When I died, I traveled to the realm of our creator, Selene. There were three figures present. I believe one was the man I killed. He had long auburn hair, green eyes, a powerful aura, and a tattoo symbol on his bare right pec."

I can still see him clearly, the large man with auburn hair and sharp green eyes standing next to *her*, *"Thank you for setting me free,"* his voice deep and alluring.

"Was this the symbol?" Anders asks eagerly, pulling the neck of his shirt aside to display the same tattoo splayed on his chest.

"Dun, dun, dunnnn...the plot thickens," Joey muses.

"Umm, yes, that was it. What's its meaning?" A million questions take flight in my mind.

"It's the crest of the Silverthrone King. Only the rightful heir bears this mark. Would you mind looking at a photo of my grandfather, King Nelus Silverthrone, to see if he was the one? He went missing in the 1950s and has left a gaping mystery."

"Yes, I'll take a look," I agree.

"Rumors say his disappearance was caused by his power-hungry son, Andras, who was my father. Nelus didn't believe his son was ready for such responsibility, and Andras was never shy about how desperately he wanted the throne." Disdain is evident in Anders' words when speaking of the man who fathered him.

Chester bustles in several minutes later, extending a hand with three photographs. "Here, sir, these are the best quality ones I could find on short notice."

Just one look at the first photo causes my breath to hitch. Smiling back at me is the man I killed, happily attending a formal dinner party. *I killed a Lycan King?*

"Well, butter my butt and call me a biscuit. That's him alright," Joey confirms.

"It was him," Gamila states, reading the shock on my face.

"Yes, it was him."

Now Chester's the one with shock on his face. A muscle ticks in Anders' jaw. Anger flickers behind his eyes, and I'm unsure if it's aimed at me. *Do I need to run? Or more like, crutch away quickly?*

"I don't know what to say. I'm truly sorry for your loss. Please understand…"

His face softens as he raises a hand to stop the apology spilling from my lips. "My anger isn't directed at you or your actions. Ask anyone and they'll tell you my grandfather was a kind and generous king. My rage is directed at my piece of shit father, who I know down to my bones played a hand in my grandfather's demise. My hope as a leader is to leave a legacy as respected as King Nelus."

Gamila rubs his back comfortingly. "Your father is dead, my love, and he is in hell, where he belongs for his crimes. Knowing some of this truth about Nelus helps bring closure, which we're grateful for."

"Our pack buried your grandfather's body in an unmarked grave just off pack lands. I can accompany you to the spot one day." I offer it as an olive branch.

Gamila's eyes soften. "Thank you, Dana, that's kind of you." She turns to her mate. "We'll have his remains moved and commission a headstone here so he can be with his pack."

"Yes, and we can share the news at the next pack meeting," Anders agrees somberly.

Servers bustle in, breaking some of the heaviness surrounding us. They serve fresh mixed greens salads and a hearty lamb stew before our main course of filet mignon. Our conversation shifts to strategies for finding Karissa before turning to a lighter place. Gamila peppers me with questions, making me feel as if I'm doing way too much talking, especially about myself. Anders, being a dutiful King, sticks to professional-level questions.

"How is it living under the Wolf Demigod's rule?" he asks.

"It's alright. Ezekial and I often butt heads, but his old stubborn behind needs someone to challenge him, respectfully, of course," I share truthfully.

Gamila breaks out in a full belly laugh. With how pregnant she is, I'm concerned she might laugh the future prince right out.

"I like you. I respect someone who tells it as it is and who isn't afraid to question those in power. We're going to be lifelong friends, I know it," she says while dabbing away her tears of laughter. "Also, first name basis with the Wolf Demigod, hmm?" A saucy smile is splayed on her pink lips as she raises a questioning eyebrow at me. This queen loves her tea.

Anders nudges her arm. "From what I've heard, he's taken a vow of celibacy, never to mate with another again."

She adorably wrinkles her nose. "Well, to each their own, I guess."

"Anders is right, and we don't have that type of relationship. We've built a friendship over the years, but he'd probably call it more of a tolerance. He admitted once to sensing some importance in me. I feel like if not for that, he'd have tossed me out on my behind by now. But there's no way I'd let him do that without putting up a fight," I say teasingly.

"Is he the type of leader who'd let you fight, or shut you down quickly by asserting his Alpha dominance?" Anders asks, trying to gauge Ezekial's character better.

"Pssh, he could try," my cocky wolf comments.

"His dominance doesn't work on me or my wolf, so he'd have no choice but to let me fight," I flash them a confident grin. "In fact, no one has been able to control us with their Alpha dominance, another strange quirk that baffles doctors. Their best guess is it's a genetic mutation."

"WHAT!?" Gamila shouts, clapping her hands in excitement. "Try it on her, Anders! Please! Please! Would that be okay, Dana?"

He cocks his head, studying me for any signs of a lie.

"You can try, but I don't think you will have any luck," I goad.

Leveling me with a hard stare, he commands, "Stand up."

The command is sharp, causing a little niggling sensation in the back of my mind, which I easily push aside. Holding his gaze, I tell him, "No."

The King's eyebrows shoot up. "No?" he repeats. "No" is probably a foreign term to him, same as for Ezekial.

Gamila giggles. "Oh, my gods? This is crazy. I've never heard of such a thing."

"You're a fascinating one, I'll give you that," Anders says, seemingly impressed.

"That's a way of explaining it," I chuckle, light-heartedly.

The rest of the dinner goes smoothly. I feel strangely comfortable and forthcoming with them. Gamila might be right about the lifelong friends vibe. Deep in my soul, there's a knowing I was meant to meet them. The couple invites me to their unborn child's Blood Oath Ceremony, being held this Saturday evening.

The event's a big deal in the lycan community and dates back to the Old World. They explain how the ceremony is customary for the future heir. The parents choose guardians to swear a blood oath to the child, offering their lifelong protection and allegiance. The event's timing is meticulously planned to align with the moon cycle, before the child's expected birth. Being invited is an honor, as, according to them, I'll be the first-ever wolf in attendance. I humbly accept. Excitement bubbles up in anticipation of the event. I want to learn all I can while I'm here about their kind, especially knowing I'm strangely connected in more than one way.

CHAPTER NINETEEN

Dana

I Would Crutch 500 Miles

The royal couple walks me to my room, where we part for the evening. I check my loaner phone, which I'd left on the table within my suite. There's an unread text from Jax. Giddy butterflies flutter in my stomach. Opening the message, it reads:

Jax: "Hey babe! I hope dinner was amazing. Can't wait to see you around 10:00 P.M. I'll call you when I'm done at The Horde to pick you up."

Me: "Call? Okay, boomer! Your old age is showing."

No response comes back. *Now what? Do I wait around in my room or track down my lycan at this Horde place?* The thought of seeing him perform excites me, making the decision easy. Turning, I exit the room, but there's nobody in the vicinity to ask for an escort.

"Hmm, should I call someone to walk me out, or is it okay to walk myself to the front door?" I consult with Joey.

"I vote we just leave. I want to see our man now, even if we have to crutch 500 miles to do so," she casts her vote.

"Well, maybe someone can give us a ride. Let's look at the contacts list."

"Suit yourself," she replies before jumping into a modified version of "I'm Gonna Be (500 Miles)."
"And I would crutch 500 miles and I would crutch 500 more just to be the mate who crutched 1,000 miles to fall down at your—"

"Hey, is everything alright?" A familiar masculine voice comes from my right, startling me. Joey's remix comes to a record-scratching halt.

I whirl around awkwardly on my crutches. "Shit, Chester, you scared me. I was just, um..." I let the thought trail off. *What do I tell him? My wolf was serenading me? Poorly, I might add, and she says I can't sing.*

"You sure as hell can't, and we have the childhood beauty pageant participation awards to prove it."

"Not the time to unpack that childhood trauma," I snap back at her.

"Sorry to startle you, Miss Johnston. I didn't think it was possible to sneak up on the Lycan Slaying Commander." There's a mock tease in his voice. I narrow my eyes at him in return. Typically, it isn't easy to sneak up on me, but I was a little preoccupied with my all-consuming thoughts of Jax and the performer in my head.

"I was trying to find my contacts list for a ride. Can you tell me where The Horde is located?"

Chester's nose wrinkles. "Why would you want to go to that shit stain?"

"Who doesn't love a good dive bar?" I retort.

"You don't strike me as someone who'd enjoy sitting in a smelly old bar on a Thursday night, full of old men with nothing better to do while waiting for their boring eternal lives to end. Oh, and who hold heavy prejudices against your kind," he says, smirking.

"Wow, what a charming description of this place. It sounds rather fun to me. I grew up working at a "shit stain" bar, as you so eloquently put it, waiting tables. Old, crotchety lycans won't easily intimidate me. The old, crude ones are the most fun to break."

"Really?" He points to my leg. "Even with that cast and set of crutches, you want to brave it?"

Oh, right. I frown, looking down at that damn cast I'm still sporting. "Nope, not seeing an issue," I lie. "Maybe we'll all become friends and have a drunken cast signing party."

He humors me with a soft chuckle, not buying my bullshit. "It's on the far northern side of the pack lands if you wish to go."

"How long would it take me to crutch there?"

Now that earns me a genuine laugh. "It's probably a good ten miles."

Joey quickly points out, *"That's better than 500 miles."*

"Come on, I'll give you a lift there. I assume Ajax will be there to give you a ride back?"

"Yes, and thank you for the ride."

Together, we make our way outside to Chester's truck, where he helps me in like a gentleman. He pauses, scanning my attire. "You know you'll stand out even more wearing that fancy dress, right? Do you want to change before we leave?"

"Changing is too much of an effort," I grumble. "No matter what I wear, I'll stick out in the place."

Closing my truck door, he walks around and climbs into the driver's seat. The engine roars to life. "Okay, but don't say I didn't warn you. Also, I'm not sure if Ajax will approve of you wearing that little number in there."

"Yes, noted. Are you always such an obnoxious walking warning label?" I ask, pulling another laugh. My fiery side is getting the best of me. Being away from Jax's comforting presence and not being able to shift has started to make me feel twitchy. It's a strange sensation, feeling so trapped within my body.

"Just looking out for you since you're new around here. The King and Queen will not be pleased if anything happens to their cherished guest."

"I'll be fine. I have my fire magic and Jax if anything goes down."

"Well, you two being out in public will definitely stir more gossip. It wasn't something I believed until I saw it for myself today," he admits.

My curiosity gets the better of me. "Tell me more about all this gossip?"

He looks at me seriously. "Do I seem like one who gossips?"

"Chessy, stop lollygagging and spill the tea already."

He gives me a dramatic sigh. "Fine. The rumor mill says you two are fated mates. Some witnessed Ajax nearly kill Dr. Hurts for refusing to help you when you were injured. Most don't believe this mate story is true because why would the Goddess mate a lycan with a wolf? No offense."

"None taken. Tell me more," I press.

"Some believe Ajax's made up the mate's story to get you the help you needed from the medical staff. At least, that's what they're hoping because those who care about bloodlines are appalled that someone with such a high pedigree, like Ajax, would even be seen with you. Those individuals are mainly the ones who have tried to pawn off their daughters on him for good breeding. And finally, you roundhouse kicked one of the invaders with your leg bone, killing him, or some crazy shit like that."

Fucking, Miguel.

"Wow. Y'all need hobbies around these parts. And what do you think about our fated mate bond?"

"I don't care. It's not my business."

"Well, I knew I liked you, Chessy, from the moment we met."

He frowns. "I'm not loving the nickname."

"You'll get used to it," I assure him.

Chester pulls into the parking lot of an all-brick building with flaking white and green paint. An illuminated sign in front announces we've arrived at The Horde. Only a few vehicles are scattered around in the gravel parking lot. On either side of the building are volleyball courts and designated fight rings with seating. Neon signs in the front windows broadcast that they serve Molson Canadian, Labatt Blue, Corona, and PBR. I open the truck door, hopping out onto my good foot, while thanking him one last time for the ride.

"Have fun tonight, stay alert, and remember not to pick fights. You can't win on crutches," he warns.

Jo huffs. *"Sure we can't..."*

"Yes, sir. Thank you for the ride."

"I hope your second ride this evening is better." I didn't miss the devilish grin or the sexual innuendo behind his words.

"Make sure to take it all back to the gossip mill, Chessy." With that, I shut the door and start crutching toward the entrance. Even as he drives off, I can hear his cackles. Such a funny bastard.

A couple of beefed-up dudes stand out front smoking cigarettes, Old World by the look of them. Their eyes rake over me as they take a drag. Being the overly confident bitch I am, I push a little of my Alpha aura out, letting them know not to fuck with me, crutches, and all. Awkwardly, I maneuver my crutches through the heavy wooden front door. Thanks for the help, assholes.

Once inside, I inhale a large lungful of musty, stale liquor smell mixed with the scent of old wooden floors and an overwhelming amount of testosterone. There's a large hand-carved wooden statue of a lycan next to the door, holding a raised sword with an open, snarling mouth. The craftsmanship is impressive. The overall vibe inside is wood cabin meets organized hoarder.

A variety of shit cakes the walls: old license plates, weaponry, photographs, currency, animal hides, and the list goes on. What catches the eye is a decorative sword with elaborate embellishments, hung on one wall. It features a huge moonstone embedded in its silver hilt. Something about it resonates within me. I'm not sure why, since only The Incredible Hulk's size could overshadow it.

My focus moves from the walls to the patrons. A raised section, bordered by a waist-high wooden railing, sits above the main floor. Two pool tables are surrounded by small crowds, with money stacked nearby as spectators laugh and taunt the players. Some pause what they're doing to stare as I pass by.

Upon a quick scan of the place, I detect no immediate signs of a threat. Pushing my aura out again helps me maneuver some of the heavy glares. A few even curl their lips in a snarl. I lift my chin in a gesture of dominance and keep moving. Feeling again through my senses, I pick up curiosity, respect, lust, and even disgust. The latter likely from the old wankers who still hold large prejudices against my kind. *Mental note, don't sit by those assholes unless I want to be escorted off the pack grounds by Chessy.*

As I crutch farther into the bar, my attention locks on Jax, who's on a small corner stage strumming a '70s classic with a few bandmates. Physically seeing him releases the anxious energy I've been carrying. Our eyes meet, revealing the heat and dark promises he holds within those deep blues. My body warms at the thought of staying with him tonight.

"Mmm, mine," Jo starts up a soothing, rhythmic purr in our mind. Seriously? Cue her heart-shaped love eyes.

"Stop acting like a frickin' cat! We need to stay alert for possible threats." I must admit, it's hard to focus on anything other than him.

Damn, this man is already taking up some major real estate within my soul. Jax is the reason behind me staying in a lycan pack, instead of heading home to my support system to figure out my next move. It's the logical and responsible thing to do, but I don't want to be rational. He's the only one I want to recount tonight's dinner events with. The person I want to open up to and share all my secrets and fears with. I want him, fuck everything else, he's mine as I am his.

As my mind and soul align on our mate claim to Ajax Mars Blackclaw, the urge to strangle all unmated females in this joint becomes overwhelming. Goddess help me. There's a table near the stage with three young women, one of whom seems a bit overzealous about watching my mate play. Of course, she is supermodel beautiful with a full display of tits. Whoever unclasps that bra later will be disappointed to find it's half empty. Pushing hard, I tamp down the territorial rage. Instead, I focus on my breathing. *Calm, remain calm. This is not me.*

"If perky tits keeps looking at our mate that way, we might go back on our word to Chester," Jo snarls in disgust at the female's attention-seeking antics.

Several patrons I pass give me curious glances. Probably wondering why the smell of burning wood is wafting off me in waves. *Don't call the fire department, y'all, it's just me wanting to shank a bitch for looking at my man. Mating jealousy is great, not.* I need to think about anything else. Joey starts sending images of us naked in the woods under the moonlight. Me on my knees sucking our mate's —*OKAY! Things just went from hot-headed to hot and bothered real quick.*

"Thanks, wolf."

"You're welcome!" Joey chirps, overly pleased with herself.

Calm down, Dana. I chant this to myself over and over. I watch several nostrils flare. Damn it! It's sometimes so embarrassing to be around people with supernatural senses. Pretty sure they can smell how turned on I am right now, just crutching into a bar full of cranky-looking old men.

Brutis. Brutis. Brutis, I chant.

"Stop thinking about that bastard!" Jo barks.

"Well, stop sending me nudies!" Thankfully, the need between my legs starts to alleviate. *"Jo, we need to keep our damn hormones in line while in this snake den! Got it?"*

CHAPTER TWENTY

Dana

The Horde

I avoid the clusters of customers engaged in conversation and find an unoccupied area around the bar. The metal-legged stool scrapes unpleasantly along the floor since I can't lift it properly. The bar itself is shaped in a large oval situated in the center of the tavern.

A stunning female lycan with Dolly Parton-sized breasts bustles over to take my order. Her midnight black braided hair falls over the shoulder of her neon pink tank top, in sharp contrast. Neon polished nails with floral designs match her outfit perfectly. She wears confidence like a second skin. There's no question about who's in charge here.

"Yes, they're real. No, you can't touch them," she says with a sly grin. *Damn, she caught me staring, but I don't know how anyone can ignore those neon melons.*

"That's a bummer, since I was feeling experimental."

Her perfect symmetrical smile widens, "Oh, honey, I'm not for beginners."

I crack up, I think I'm in love with this woman. "Fine, you caught me. Do they make an excellent secret hiding place?" I muse.

"Now don't go giving away my best-kept secret," she winks.

"Yes, ma'am."

"None of that, call me Cher. I'm not old enough to be a ma'am."

"My apologies, Cher, southern roots grow deep."

"Now what'll it be? Anything you want is on the house, for saving my future grandbaby and his mama." *Grandbaby?* Homing in on her scent, I pick up similar undertones to Anders.

Unable to contain my curiosity, I ask, "Are you Anders' mother?"

"Yes, that's my baby boy."

It's adorably sweet that she still calls her son, the King, "baby." I'm also a bit dumbfounded by how it's acceptable for the King's mother to run a dive bar. I'm liking the lycans more and more.

"Okay then, an old-fashioned would be divine," I tell her. "Thank you!"

Cher bustles off to assemble my drink. I sense a familiar presence nearby that causes a tingling awareness. When I turn around, I see the Fangerson twins approaching, both looking as if they stepped straight out of GQ magazine. Physically, they are identical, but style-wise, they couldn't be more different.

Miguel's medium-length chestnut colored hair is styled back to perfection. He struts confidently like he owns the goddamn place in a loose black and white floral button-up, with one side tucked in. His toned legs are on display in tight black skinny jeans that hit right above the ankle. Matching colored Vans and a large, jet-black watch tie the look together. Mickey sports a buzzcut and radiates lumberjack sex appeal. The red flannel he wears with the top three buttons undone screams, I have a large ax and I know how to use it.

"Hey Smokey, who started a fire in your woods?" Miguel asks in a way of greeting, as he takes the seat on my right. Snarky bastard.

I force myself to hold back a smirk. It's hard not to love the guy. Mickey pulls out the seat to my left.

"Miguel's right, the whole place smells like a damn campfire," Mickey points out to my horror.

I decide it's best not to talk about it. Letting my mind go there will only piss me off again, causing it to get even more smoky up in here.

"My favorite M&M pairing. Come to watch your brother play?" There, a nice change of topic.

"Yeah, totally smooth," Joey says dryly.

"DJ, that sounds like a deflect." The devil to my right taps a contemplative finger to his lips. "Let me guess. You're considering crisping a certain beauty in the front with her boobs on full display for your mate?" Miguel hits me with a prove me wrong gleam in his eyes.

Damn, he's very perceptive. I let fire show in my eyes. A silent warning for him to shut the fuck up!

"Nailed it," he continues, unfazed by my silent wrath.

"Nothing to worry about there," Mickey reassures. Then he drops his voice to barely a whisper. "Tiffany needs to get over her obsession with him. If she sees you two together, she'll know the rumors are true and back off."

My blood boils at my confirmed suspicions. I hate this jealousy driven by an invisible bond we share. *Relax, inner crazy, you need to calm down.*

"You let me know if either of these boys is bothering you. Especially this one." Cher thrusts an accusatory finger in Miguel's direction while setting down my drink.

Miguel grabs his chest in mock hurt. "I'm the little angel, Mick's the devil."

The twins then start bickering like children. I snatch the cold beverage off the bar and give it a small stir with my cocktail straw while I enjoy the sibling banter. The first sip provides a pleasant burn in the back of my throat. That's delicious. Cher makes eye contact with me as she taps her temple twice, silently asking me to mindlink with her. Joey opens our mind to Cher's.

"Hey," I squeak, trying to sound perfectly fine and not like my jealousy is driving this ship.

"Ah, so strange how you can connect with us when you're not a pack member, but I'm glad you can. Don't listen to Tweedledee and Tweedledum here. Miguel can't resist stirring a pot even if it's full of hornets. You have nothing to worry about with Tiffany. She's very young, and dare I say, desperate to mate. Everyone can see how Jax only has eyes for you, dear. AND if he fucks it up, we can castrate him together."

Her kind words help to lower my crazy. *"Is that a promise?"* I chuckle.

"Yes, now let's drink on it." Cher makes quick work of pouring out two large whiskey shooters before handing me one.

Miguel straightens, looking around. "Hey, where's mine?" he pouts.

Ignoring him, Cher raises her glass to mine in a toast. "The world may see us as bitches, but the truth is, we have low tolerance for bullshit and don't play well with others. Cheers to continuing to raise hell wherever we go."

"Cheers to that! Oh, and your amazing tatas!" I add. We both laugh before clinking our shots together. Miguel instantly starts in on Cher about not getting an invite to our bitches' club.

"Cher, what kind of establishment are you running? Serving her kind free drinks?" A burly mountain-looking man cuts in from his place on the other side of the bar, killing all playful banter.

Jo assesses the man at a low threat level. *"Our kind! Tell him we would be happy to file his complaint up his ass,"* she spits.

"Okay, Jo, we need to have a serious conversation about your level of ridiculousness."

Murder flashes in Cher's eyes. "She's a damn hero who saved our Queen and pup. Now shut the fuck up, and get out of my bar!" Snatching the soda gun, she sprays it directly at him, forcing him to dodge before hightailing it out the front door.

"Next time it'll be my shotgun with silver bullets," she hollers after him.

Snickers ring out throughout the bar.

"Anyone else who has a problem, leave now. I won't tolerate your bullshit." Whoa, talk about an instant woman crush. I hope we become friends because Cher's a frickin' incredible force.

"Dana, feel free to put anyone in their place if they get disrespectful and use your fire to do it." With that, she turns to help a new customer waiting on the other side of the bar.

I focus my attention back on Jax performing on the stage. The entire interaction with Cher didn't go unnoticed. I could feel Jax's eyes on me, along with his concern. It's unfathomable to think about how attuned I am to him, even without a solidified bond.

"Damn, our man is talented. I bet those fingers could play us better than that guitar," Jo singsongs.

"Okay, keep it in your pants, wolf. Public. Place. Large crowd. Remember?"

Mickey clears his throat, looking from me to Jax. "He's a good one, you know." *Aw, well, isn't he a decent wingman?*

"Some minor commitment issues, but yes, absolutely," Miguel adds. *Note to self, Miguel isn't a good wingman.* Mickey slaps his twin in the back of the head.

Miguel throws a hand up, acting confused. "What? No one is perfect, brother. Why pretend otherwise?"

I wonder if these commitment issues are what Jax needs time to work through?

Lowering his voice, Mickey is back to whispering, "It stems from his childhood trauma. Please just be patient with him. Support, challenge, and ground him. Be the home he doesn't realize he's searching for."

I nod in response, fully processing his words. *Be the home he is searching for.* I know Jax has admitted to past traumas, and I hope one day he will feel comfortable enough to share the details with me. Are they what drives him to change lives so often? Is he running from the pain of the past? Too many questions. For now, I need to focus on being a safe place for him.

"So, will you hold the mating ceremony this summer? Or in the fall? Don't hold out on me, girl, because I'll need ample time to plan my outfit."

What? Is Miguel being serious right now? Jo reaches out telepathically, deciding it's best to take this extremely personal conversation internally.

"Y'all, we have no set plans for mating."

Mickey, having just received a beer from Cher, chokes due to my sudden mental invasion.

"Oh, sorry about that, Mickey."

"No worries, it's still strange you can connect with us telepathically," he says, wiping beer droplets off his chin with a napkin.

"I know," I agree. *"I wanted to bring this conversation internal. No mating talk out loud. We don't need to feed the pack gossips anymore."* Case in point, a full bar of shifters with supernatural hearing. *"We're taking things slow to get to know one another, before we decide if we're going to accept the bond."*

Just admitting that is painful. I push the hurt away quickly, not wanting to linger too long on the thought of another broken bond.

Miguel looks as if I just told him he has ketchup on his Gucci shirt.

"What!" Mickey semi-shouts. *"You two are fated mates and perfect for one another. I've never heard of anyone R-ing the bond. I can't even say that vile word."*

"Seriously, what's the point of pissing around the bush? This is fate. You want someone else coming over and pissing on your bush? I don't think so. Jax probably needs a little push," Miguel says, having finally overcome his shock.

"Pretty sure that isn't how the saying goes," I point out, but I understand what he's getting at. Honestly, my mind and soul have already decided on buying the bush. Deep down, I know we would make it work logistically. Jax seems more hesitant, and I feel he's not ready to commit. It causes me to feel unwanted frustration. I understand needing more time, but what's wrong with my bush?

Jo face-paws in embarrassment. *"No more shrubbery references for the love of the Goddess."*

"Eh, yeah, you're probably right," I chuckle.

My traitorous mind starts working in overdrive, weaving toxic webs. *It's you*, it shouts. Is he trying to come to terms with not receiving a beautiful lycan mate from a strong bloodline? No, it's definitely my level of dominance. That was always the problem with males in the past.

Mickey helps shut up my negative inner monologue. *"I think it seems reasonable to take your time. I'm sure you two will work things out."*

Sassy Miguel tosses out his unwanted two cents. *"Seems stupid to me."*

Mickey smacks his brother upside the head for a second time tonight. *"No one asked you, devil spawn."*

"People go their whole lives without finding their fated mate. How long do you think you'll remain blessed when you piss off Selene by swiping left on our boy?" Ouch. *"Wait! Unless I have this all wrong. Are you and Selene besties? Has she been sending you options, like a were-bachelorette? Can you put in a good word for me? I'm not looking for much. Just one tall, ultra-handsome, muscular, Tom Ford Oud Wood scented, dimpled, tight assed, margarita lover, naughty talker, giant—like big-penised sex god. Oh, and who loves '90s jams,"* Miguel finishes gazing off dreamily, no doubt thinking of his future unicorn of a mate.

I give him my best sarcastic slow blink, *"Right, I'll make sure to place your tiny mate order next month, during Selene and my monthly sleepover, where we watch romcoms, drink wine, and talk about boys."*

"You're the best!" Miguel flutters his eyelashes at me.

I can't help but laugh at the ridiculousness of this male. *"But in all seriousness, this is a life-altering commitment. I'm unapologetically who I am. Jo and I can be difficult, which has ruined plenty of our past relationships. She'll not fully submit to anyone, not even our mate. He needs to feel comfortable accepting all of that,"* I explain.

"You two are doing what's best for you, which is all that matters. Ignore Miguel, he's always been a do first, ask questions later with no regard for consequences guy."

"So what, I have no regrets," Miguel quickly defends.

"Oh, do share some of these epic tales, Mickey," I encourage, bringing our conversation out of our heads.

"Let's see, he lost his virginity in our parents' car. He did nothing to clean or air it out. Dad chewed his ass, and mom all but gave it away the next day to some unknowing human family." Mickey shakes his head.

Miguel shoots back, "They got over it, eventually."

"How about the 'Bootylicious' tattoo splayed across your ass?" Mickey asks his twin.

Miguel pretends to toss long hair over his shoulder. "Well, I have a nice ass, so why not highlight it?"

"There was the poodle looking perm he got in the '80s that smelled rancid for a week." Mickey wrinkles his nose as if he can still smell it.

"The higher the hair, the closer to the Goddess." Miguel points upwards.

"I need to see pictures!" I demand.

"Even better, in the '90s, he wanted frosted tips. Being a cheap ass, he made our mom do it. She ended up dying a blond landing strip on top of his head. That I do have a framed copy of," Mickey grins.

"You have to admit, Mick, I still made it look cool."

"Keep telling yourself that, bro."

The M&M duo continues to entertain me between the band's sets. From the sounds of it, Frank and Dottie deserve the damn moon for having dealt with their son's shenanigans this long. They're mischievous little creatures who worm their way into your heart without you realizing it.

Mickey seems to be a solid presence who will always have your back, no matter what. Miguel might be my bestie soulmate, given his love for '90s pop culture. He made me swear I'd bring him along the next time I visited Mississippi. He dreams of visiting a honkytonk where he can line dance in his matching rhinestone-studded cowboy hat and boots. Dancing isn't my forte, but seeing the looks he'll get would make it worth it. The guy went so far as to text me a link to his favorite online dancing tutorials to help me prepare. *Yeah, that's a polite pass for me.*

I encourage the two of them to visit Moonborn Pack. They would never turn down lycans willing to lead training exercises. At night, they could explore the bustling nightlife. Men and women would throw themselves at them, which seals the deal in their minds.

The band takes a little pause between their next set. Jax picks up his beer and takes an easy swig. He leans in, talking with the three other members in hushed tones. When he turns around, his eyes lock with mine, and he gives me a beautiful smile. His beer bottle makes its way back to the floor, and he swings his guitar into place.

"Alright, folks," Jax says into the mic, and the crowd silences. "This will be the last song from us this evening. I want to dedicate it to a special Fiery Wolf Commander."

"Aww," Jo squeals. She and I both go mushy inside.

No one says anything, likely taking Cher's threats seriously. Jax closes out his set with "Song of the South" by Alabama. Even without a fiddle, everything about it is perfect. It takes me straight back to fond childhood memories of dances after mating cere-monies. My mother would force me into a poofy, uncomfortable dress I despised, but they were meant for twirling in the cool grass as the music played way too late into the night. If I didn't have this bum leg, I would prove to Miguel how bad my dancing skills still are.

"In this moment, I'm grateful for the cast," Joey says.

I can't keep the giant smile off my face as he plays on. Tears start to build behind my eyes. *Shit, no crying. It's just dry in here; haven't they heard of a humidifier?* Jax's thoughtful gesture sends my heart soaring. It's been a long while since I've felt this level of happiness.

Finishing for the evening, Jax quickly thanks the crowd and packs up his guitar. On the outside, his easy-going persona shines, but I don't miss the intense focus on me behind his gaze.

The jukebox kicks up with "Milkshake" by Kelis, causing most of the bar to groan in protest.

"Fucking Miguel, every goddamn time," a nearby patron sneers to his friend.

"Well, my geriatric kin, seeing as I seem to be the only one in the bar capable of using technology, that's just how it will continue to be," he announces loudly.

Sliding his phone over with the Jukebox app open, I see the "Thong Song" queued up next. I snag his phone, adding Britney Spears and Spice Girls songs to his playlist, to good, and thoroughly piss the crowd off.

"Yes, Queen!" He high-fives me as a possessive hand encircles my waist, and turns my chair.

Leather and cedarwood envelop me like a hug. *So fucking yummy.*

"Fiery Wolf, please tell me you didn't crutch all the way here."

Jax's nickname for me may seem like an insignificant thing, but he created it just for me, and I love hearing it come from that kissable mouth of his. The thought leads my dirty mind straight to the gutter.

My brain screams for me to toss myself on him, and to lay claim to what's mine. Fuck him right here on the bar top, not giving a damn who sees. *Sex on top of the bar, what would that be like?*

Jax's nostrils flare, scenting my lust. A grin tugs at his plump lips. Leaning in, he whispers, "What are you thinking about right now?"

I try to remind my hormones for the millionth time that they need to chill! Public. Place.

Clearing my throat, I casually say, "Chester was kind enough to drive me here."

"As for my second question?" The sultry purr in his whispered words gives me goosebumps.

In a very deliberate, unhurried gesture, he plays with loose hair pieces along my neck. Tingles spark along where our skin touches. Being naturally stubborn, I won't give him the satisfaction of admitting out loud how badly I crave him.

"Oh, just thinking about the dentist," I tell him, before taking a swig of my drink.

His laughter rings out around us, causing patrons to glance our way. "Right. So, you weren't daydreaming of me ripping this pretty dress off you later?" he asks in a low, seductive voice.

"Definitely, not. I was thinking of my dental hygienist who nearly flosses my gums off, I mean, who doesn't enjoy a good time at the dentist?" I look at him with my best mask of innocence, continuing our cat and mouse game.

"Well, I'll have to show you actual fun later. You look beautiful, by the way," he tells me while still twirling a piece of my hair.

"Thank you," I beam at him.

Mickey kindly scoots down a stool, allowing Jax to settle in next to me. The slight tension in his features eases as he no doubt feels the calming presence of our bond. Cher brings him a beer while gushing over how phenomenal he was, as always. She's a mixture of total badass and pack mom. Cher floats in and out, checking on drinks or just shooting the breeze with the guys and me.

Jax keeps his hand lazily draped along the back of my high-backed stool. His massive body faces toward me, with one booted foot propped on the metal footrest of my chair. The gesture looks relaxed, yet possessive. It's his way of signaling to everyone in this bar that we're together. It doesn't go unnoticed, earning him a few death glares from patrons upset with him for downbreeding, no doubt. Jax seems unfazed, without a care in the world.

Joey, on the other hand, wants to sink her teeth into them, downbreeding her furry ass. She's a damn limited edition upgrade – *Hello! Fire magic!* Picking up on Joey's rising irritability, Jax helps to soothe us by pressing his warm hands into pressure points along my shoulders.

"I'm here now, rest," he whisper-coos to Joey. She lovingly brushes against my mind, pleased by his words. Being reassured our mate will protect us from any threats, she finally recedes, curling up in the back of my mind.

"That's better," he continues to coo.

"Wow. You're a Joey whisperer. No one has ever gotten the fire beast to relinquish any control."

He grins cockily. "Good, I'm honored she trusts me enough to be the first."

"I meant to tell you earlier, you were incredible out there. Thank you for the song. It reminds me of fond memories from growing up."

"I'm glad you enjoyed it. It was between that and a Shania Twain song, which I knew you'd love, but I couldn't get the boys on board with it."

"Lost opportunity, Blackclaw," I joke.

After finishing a second dark draft, Jax stands to bid the group good night, insisting I need rest. According to him, my leg needs to be elevated. In a non-mate bond scenario, I'd tell someone to get bent for giving me orders related to my body. I know he's coming from a genuine place of concern over my well-being, so I easily agree to leave without a fuss.

On our way out, we are met with whispers and several hate-filled comments. Something about "wolf whore" and "what a waste." Joey perks up at this; she's ready to throw down, bum leg and all. Jax stays by my side, looking as cool as a cucumber. How is he so composed? Dominant Alphas aren't known for their Zen state of mind. I might need some pointers from him.

"Ignore them. They're not worth it, Jo," Jax says openly, not attempting to hide his remark from others.

He's right; getting into a crutch fight with some drunks would be a foolish way to get kicked off the pack lands and separated from him. I take a deep breath, trying to calm my heightened state.

Two males block our path, stopping us right before we reach the exit. Calm state, gone. Instinctively, I bare my teeth at them, feeling very fatigued and fed up with the nonsense.

Then the words fly out of my mouth. "If this is about my crappy bloodline messing up good breeding material in your pack, you can fuck off now."

Both men look back at me with wide eyes. Unease rolls off the older of the two. Jax's sexy, lopsided grin makes some of my anger fade. What's so amusing about this?

"Well, I guess the rumors are true," the younger of the two mumbles under his breath.

"Dana, this is Remus and his son, Allen." Jax points toward the door. "Let's take this outside, shall we?"

Remus nods. "Okay."

On the way out, I can feel the entire bar boring holes into the back of my skull. Well, no one missed that interaction.

"Remus and I grew up together," Jax adds color for my benefit.

Once outside, Remus turns to us, clearing his throat awkwardly. "I apologize for disrupting your evening. I was hoping you could tell us if there have been any updates on Karissa, since you've been helping with her case?" His genuine concern is readily apparent.

My posture and heart soften because she evidently means something to this family. A pang of guilt for baring my teeth racks through me. I need to stop letting my mating emotions dictate my actions.

Jax's face turns regretful. "No, we don't have any leads right now on where to find her."

Remus' face falls. "My daughter Isla has been best friends with her since they were in diapers. She's struggling with all of this. Barely eating, not sleeping, and battling extreme anxiety to the point she refuses to leave the safety of our house, even though Torr is dead and can't take her. I promised her I'd get an update, and I feel bothersome constantly asking the Whites."

"I've put the Lycan Guard in contact with some resources from the Moonborn Pack, hopefully, combining efforts will help," I add, trying to shed some hope on the ever-growing, more desperate situation.

Remus looks at me with kind eyes. "Thank you for your kindness with Karissa's search, and your efforts in saving Queen Gamila. I don't want to think about what would have happened if King Anders fell."

A shared solemnness settles over the lycans. From what I've observed, pack members all seem to prefer their new king and queen over the former.

A thought suddenly strikes me. "Would you be okay if we stopped over and I met Isla? I've taught women's defense classes before, and I could teach her some moves. Maybe that could help her feel a little safer."

Remus scratches at his overgrown beard, looking unsure. Likely, pondering if he wants his daughter to spend time with the were-woman hanging around the pack, telling strangers to fuck off.

Allen speaks up, "Dad, I think Isla would want that."

"I think it's an excellent idea," Jax agrees.

"Okay. I'll text you tomorrow after I speak with her to confirm it is something she wants," Remus finally consents.

Jax guides me to a well-maintained early 2000s-looking Toyota SUV as we part ways. The bumper's home to a speckling of fishing stickers. A few of my favorites are "Fish Magnet", "No Drama Piranha", and "I jerk it every chance I get." I can't help but burst into laughter as I take a moment to enjoy the sticker collage.

"Mr. Blackclaw, am I going to be competing with fish for your attention?"

"No, beautiful. Most of these gems were an added perk from the previous owner. I snagged her for a great price at an estate auction. Mickey and Miguel think it's hilarious to continually add more."

He points to "I'm a Hooker", and another one I missed of a boat being hoisted from the water that reads, "I Hate To Pull Out". Unable to contain myself, I roll into another fit of laughter. Jax shakes his head, murmuring "assholes" under his breath, before assisting me into the car.

He's unlike any dominant male supernatural I've ever encountered. Most love to express their masculinity and BDE through what they drive. Giant trucks, loud motorcycles, expensive cars, lots of flash, and extreme speed, not old Toyotas with tacky bumper stickers. This is another quirk I adore so much about this man.

"Now, buckle up, beautiful, because you're staying at my five-star den tonight. It has the best service in town to meet any need you may have."

The suggestiveness gleams in his darkened eyes. Leaning down, he places a lingering kiss on my lips. That leathery scent mixed with alcohol on his breath sends my hormones into a frenzy. Again, I curse my busted-up leg. I would 10,000% be car fucking his brains out right now, if it wasn't for this cast.

"I've wanted to kiss you all night but wasn't sure if you'd be okay with that, given our audience," he admits.

"I've never cared about what others think of me." *Aside from you.* "So in the future, kiss away."

Flashing me a devilish grin, he starts the car and drives off toward his home. My stomach flips with eager anticipation of what the night might bring. I hope more of those intoxicating kisses are on the menu.

CHAPTER TWENTY-ONE

Ajax

There's a Snake in My Pack

Dana's scent of arousal fills my car. It's downright mouth-watering, causing my cock to painfully strain against my pants. It doesn't want to take things slow; no, it wants to be buried deep inside our Fiery Wolf's tight, wet pussy as she clenches around us. Uncomfortably, I shift in my seat, which does nothing to alleviate the straining appendage. I still can't believe she braved The

Horde to see me. No one willingly spends time with those old bastards unless they are one.

"Our mate missed us," Mars gushes.

"No using the 'M' word," I scold him.

"I'll use the word all I want, because I wasn't the one who agreed to those ridiculous terms."

The last thing I want to do is fight with Mars after the night we've had so far. My body is still humming from the rush of having our female see us play for the first time. How her face lit up at the song I dedicated to her will forever be ingrained in my memory. My hope is that more firsts can soon be internally filed away alongside that keepsake.

Mars rumbles his approval, *"Yes, like taking our mate to our den for the first time."*

The bastard's been itching to care for our female within our space. All damn day, I've had to listen to him, go on and on about the ways he wants to please her.

"You feel the same way!" he argues.

"Fine, you're right." I hate admitting when the beast is right, but I'm feeling over the moon right now to bring Dana to the privacy of my home.

Giddy excitement rolls through me, causing more blood flow to my dick. *Easy boy.* I have to use all my willpower not to pull the car over right now to claim my mate. *Damnit. No 'M' word.*

Mars is instantly on me. *"I cannot wait to consum-mate with our MATE!"*

"Shut up!" I yell at him.

"What are you thinking about right now?" Dana's playful voice pulls me from my dirty thoughts. Her soft hand strokes my forearm, with a smirk playing at the corner of her rosy mouth.

I decide to be semi-truthful with her, leaving out my car sex fantasies. "Mars won't shut up about getting you home so that we can take care of you."

She gives me a knowing look. "Well, isn't he a little sweetie?"

Mars preens at her words, being the oversized golden retriever he is. He already lives for her praises.

"How was your dinner?" I ask, remembering she hadn't said anything about her evening with Anders and Gamila.

"Insightful, actually." Her eyes alight. "You'll never guess what I learned, even I can hardly believe it."

"Oh yeah?" I prompt.

"Anders asked me to look at a photo of his missing grandfather, King Nelus, and he was the feral lycan who attacked my pack when I was sixteen."

My eyebrows take up residence in my hairline at this revelation. I wasn't expecting that.

"Wow, you're positive?" I ask, dumbfounded. "What are the odds of that?"

"Yup, I'm positive." She gives the P a cute little pop. "When I was in the realm of our creators, Nelus was there in human form alongside the Goddess and Jo. Nelus thanked me for setting him free. Jo confirmed it happened, and I didn't dream it up when I was in a coma."

"Damn, Dana, that's incredible, all of it." *Just like you. I wonder how I'll ever be worthy of such a powerhouse mate as her.*

"We'll spend every day proving we are worthy if that's what it takes." Mars expresses our inner feelings of strong determination.

"I've never heard of anyone speaking directly with the creators. I can't wrap my mind around it," I admit.

"It took me a very long time to process. I still hear *her* voice so clearly, Selene. She said to me, Dana, my child. Your journey is not done, my dear. Life's flame will be restored for I choose you to walk among the living once more. It only made sense after Jo awakened, and she confirmed it wasn't my imagination. The details aren't something I openly share, as it seems almost sacrilegious to speak of, and I don't like to draw attention to myself or my unique situation. People already blow smoke up my ass, thinking I have some special goddess hookups. Like tonight, while you were playing, Miguel placed a teeny tiny mate order for me to deliver to Selene. Apparently, he believes we're best friends who have monthly sleepovers."

I shake my head. That's Miguel for you. "Noted, so no blowing smoke up your perfect ass, but maybe other things?" I glance her way, raising an eyebrow in question.

"Only if you play your cards right, Mr. Blackclaw," she jokes.

"Oh, I know I will, Sweet Cheeks."

We continue our drive toward my place with the carefree lyrics of The Eagles' "Take It Easy" playing softly through the car speakers.

"Can I ask you something?" Dana says, not turning her gaze from the sights of the pack lands passing by her window.

"Anything," I answer without hesitation.

"What's your impression of Beta Matt?" Her question genuinely takes me by surprise.

"Did he join you for dinner?" It's a struggle to keep the detest out of my words. There's a slight snarl woven into them. The thought of that self-absorbed asshole sitting next to my mate at dinner pisses me off.

"Look who's dropping mate bombs left and right now." That earns my beast an internal bird, which he finds hilarious.

"No, he only escorted me to dinner."

Good, that news helps tame some of my internal rage, but I still don't like any scenario involving him near Dana.

"I'm picking up an undertone from both of you regarding the other, and it's not sunshine and rainbows," she grins.

"There's always been tension between us, but it worsened when I moved back to the pack last fall. Matt feels threatened by my presence, which has caused some minor conflicts between us. Naturally, he assumes I only returned to challenge him for my rightful place as pack Beta. That may have been my birthright, but destiny had other plans for me. He sees me as a snake waiting for the right moment to strike him."

"He seems more like the snake," she mumbles, piquing my interest.

"What makes you say that?"

"Something felt off. His mannerisms didn't seem genuine to me. Jo also didn't believe the façade he was selling. She was sniffing him as if he were day-old garbage left in the hot sun."

I throw my head back in laughter. "Best thing I've heard all day. That's my good girl, Jo."

Mars feels pride over his mate's assessment of our nemesis. *"He's the rat! We need to investigate him further."*

I wonder if I should report this to Andy. She would require evidence; the angel doesn't operate on a feeling. During my call with her tonight, I learned a seer within our organization confirmed that Torr was framed. The seer wasn't shown who was behind the setup. She described the person as shrouded in darkness, and she believes they are being masked by the dark witches involved.

Matt's being moved to the top of my investigation list, since I haven't been able to clear him as a suspect. Maybe the capture orbs will return something on him, or perhaps I can send his name to Andy to look into his background further. So far, I haven't found anything about where he originated from. He showed up with Anders and helped him overthrow King Andras, then took up the role of pack Beta. All I have been able to collect is the two met while working as mercenaries for The Dragon Empire and became as close as brothers.

"Do you know his whereabouts when Karissa was taken?" Dana asks.

"Away for pack business." Both events give him a perfect alibi. That doesn't mean he didn't have a hand in the game.

"Well, I still don't trust him for some reason, and for what it's worth, I think you'd make a much better Beta than him."

I shrug her words off. "You're too kind." I entwine her hand with mine and squeeze it. Our mate bond appreciates the contact, emanating rippling pulses from where our skin connects.

"Why don't you want the pack Beta position?" she asks, clearly not willing to let the topic go.

I falter slightly. For starters, I have a secret job you don't know about.

"I don't know. That path was stolen away a long time ago, but now that it's a possibility again, I'm not sure if it's something I want."

"Well, you should at least think about it, but only if it's something you want. I'll pretend it's not because I really want to see you knock the fake smirk off Matt's face."

"So, you're using me for cheap entertainment?" I joke.

"Pretty much."

"Tell her we'll do it. I've been thinking we should consider it after we leave the Guardians."

"Mars, said he would do it for you and Jo."

"No." She shakes her head with amusement in her eyes. "You have to do it for you, not us."

That beaming light on her face fades to a sober expression. "You haven't told me, did you hope to find your fated mate?"

"YES!!" Mars shouts to the universe with zero hesitation.

I want to wholeheartedly agree with him after meeting her. Having her presence in my life has already helped repair some of my fractures. For the first time, since I was a seven-year-old boy struggling with depression and PTSD from losing my family, I feel a sense of home. *But before meeting Dana, did I want to find her?* I'm not entirely sure.

Having a fated mate means having to feel things, big things, as I'm finding out. Things that scare me. I barely knew her when she was almost killed, but I know to my very core that if I'd lost her, I too would have been lost forever. There would've been no running from that level of pain, only following her in death.

"One day, I wanted to meet someone. Fated mates are scarce among lycan kind, so I never allowed myself to hope. Mars had been riding me to at least look, but I wasn't in a rush. Then this fire goddess appeared out of nowhere, blocking my path, snarling in all her glory, and I thank Selene for sending me you."

"As do I," her honest confession feels both euphoric and surreal. As if I'm in a dream where I'll wake up and realize I'm not fortunate enough to be among the few who find their destined mate.

CHAPTER TWENTY-TWO

Dana

5-Star Den Review

After our scenic drive through the pack's residential area, we pull into the driveway of a quaint white split-level home sporting black shutters. Darkness blankets everything, but it's still clear that the outside is well-cared for. Butterflies in my stomach start to flutter in anticipation. I'll be entering his space, which could someday become our space. *Can our two very different lives merge?*

"Of course they can, he's our other half," Jo confidently replies to my inner monologue.

"And so was Bobby-douche," I toss back.

"Ugh, no thinking of that dumbass. Jax is our true path. Now get your head in the game and clear those cobwebs," she cheers. That thought causes my libido to spike. Damn, horny wolf.

Jax parks the vintage Toyota in an otherwise barren garage before guiding me into the lower level of his home. His leathery scent welcomes me and tempts me to stay forever. On the far wall is a sliding patio door leading to the backyard, which has a top deck sheltering the area. And is that a hot tub out there? Yes, please.

Drums, guitars, a piano, and at least ten other instruments are neatly arranged around the lower level. Jax confirms he can play them all. And why not learn every instrument known to man when you are blessed with immortality? The walls are littered with music memorabilia, including gold records and awards.

"What are all these?" I ask, pointing to several golden albums.

"They are songs I wrote that have won awards for topping music charts."

Say what? Could the man be any more casual when talking about how incredibly talented he is?

"You wrote this song, this extremely popular song, the entire world knows?" I say dumbfounded, pointing to one of the gleaming records.

"Yes." He casually shrugs. Wow. Add that to the long list of Ajax Blackclaw. Hella good songwriter, check.

"Were you also a member of the band?"

"No. Mars and I mutually agree on many things, but that was never one of them. Playing deafening sold-out stadiums while living on the road in a tightly packed bus, and not knowing when our next shift would be, wasn't something we could ever find common ground on. Instead, I settled for writing music and selling it to artists."

"Oh my gosh, is that you with Freddie Mercury?" I fangirl.

"Yes. I met him in the '80s," he says as if it's just another day for him.

"Wait, I'm not seeing any Spice Girls or my girl, Britney, up here." I send an accusatory look in his direction.

Fighting a grin, he wraps two strong arms around me. "No pop for me, beautiful. Rock and roll owns my heart."

"And apparently fishing," I quip. Together we share a laugh.

"Come on, let me get you upstairs. You need to change into something more comfortable and prop your leg." With that, he scoops me into his large arms, crutches and all.

A yip of surprise sneaks out of me. Happy tingles warm along where our skin touches. Jo instantly kicks up her happy purrs.

"I can manage some stairs, you know," I halfheartedly grumble. The independent woman in me is struggling to accept our new reality of mates in shining armor, doting on me.

"Yes, yes, you're no damsel in distress. I know, but I want to carry you. Now, stop fussing." His hot breath warms my face. Unable to help myself, I lean in, kissing him lightly while running my hands through his tousled dark hair.

"Thank you, and Mars, for caring for us. No boyfriend has ever cared for me."

Jax snarls at the mention of past lovers. I boop him on the nose. "What I mean is Jo and I have a hard time being vulnerable around others, but we feel comfortable with you caring for us. Please be patient with me."

His soft chuckle sends delicious vibrations through me. "I've got patience."

When we reach the hardwood base of the first-floor landing, he bolts straight toward his bedroom. Along the way, he plays half-assed tour guide, nodding toward the kitchen and telling me what's behind some closed doors—bathroom, spare room.

Jax's elbow connects with the light switch on the wall of his bedroom, revealing a tidy space with a deep forest-green accent wall. A king-sized bed features a soft matte gray comforter and oversized pillows neatly arranged across its simple dark oak headboard. Matching dark oak nightstands with side lamps flank either side of the massive bed. Across the room are two doors, one to an ensuite and another to a walk-in closet. I'm shocked one door doesn't lead to an extra music room overflowing with instruments.

"Miguel decorated it, and most of my place. He wouldn't let me buy furniture at the estate sale where I got my car. He said I couldn't have some elderly dead man's musty furniture stinking up my house with his 'old people smell'."

This makes me laugh. "He has a fair point." *Note to self: thank Miguel.*

"I'm a bit nose blind after traveling around to so many places. But I won the debate about the car," he says proudly.

That leathery, masculine scent of Jax is most potent here, and thankfully, it's not tainted with old man smell. Its powerful aroma invades my nose, causing wetness to instantly start pooling south. My entire body begins to buzz with pent-up primal desire. My womanly bits chant for us to seal our bond, causing my traitorous wolf to quickly join their team.

"Seal the bond, seal the bond," Joey chants. *Ugh.*

"Sex, yes, but no sealing eternal bonds. All wolves and body parts need to calm down."

Jax's tongue travels a path up my neck. He whispers before laying me down on his soft comforter, "I hope you are thinking of the same things as I am."

"Oh, and what would that be, Mr. Blackclaw?" I ask with feigned curiosity.

"First, we need to get you comfortable." Standing, he sets my crutches aside before entering his closet. When he comes back, he hands me an oversized T-shirt to change into before leaving his room. I quickly take off my dress and slip on the soft cotton shirt. This sexy lycan of mine will have to work for it, no sneak peeks. Listening carefully, I search for Jax's location within the house. It sounds like he's in the kitchen getting water.

Joey encourages me with a vigorous *"Do it!"* as I wrestle with a naughty idea in my mind.

Hastily, I slide my damp, silk thong down my legs and over the cast. Only a tiny G-string or commando works favorably with this leg accessory. Grabbing the pillow on his side of the bed, I slide my panties under the pillowcase before tossing it back into place.

Joey giggles mischievously, *"We're so gettin' some tonight."*

Jax strides in carrying a couple of glasses of ice water and an extra pillow. Mars' dark eyes roam over every inch of me. That penetrating gaze leaves goosebumps in its wake. There's no denying the hunger in his gaze, which makes me feel powerful in a whole new way. Those animalistic eyes lingering over my breasts don't go unnoticed by my nipples; they perk right up - *Hey, Sugar!*

"Yup, Jo, so gettin' some," I slowly drawl.

"Does Mars want to play?" I tease, because I surely do.

His voice comes out deeper, intermingling with his beast, "We like seeing you in our clothes and safe in our bed. Your aroused, smoky scent mixing with ours is, gods..." Nostrils flaring, he pauses to inhale deeply.

My vagina continues to act on her own accord, firing up, thrumming with need, and making a wet mess on his comforter. Typical needy bitch things.

"Fuck, Dana, I'll be right back." He turns and uses lycan speed to dash from the room.

There better be a good reason for leaving me here right now, real hot and bothered, like he forgot the whip and handcuffs. My horniness reaches its peak thinking about him handcuffing me to his bed. *Ugh, but I've got ninety-nine problems and my cast is number one!* Without it, I would've pinned him against the wall the moment we arrived and fucked his brains out. Hobbling around awkwardly on one foot really kills that vibe.

A few seconds later, he is back holding a kitchen chair?

"Umm, what's that for?" Clearly, not what I had in mind.

Walking over to my side of the bed, he sets it down. I raise a questioning eyebrow at him.

"It's to elevate your leg."

Before I can reply, his strong hands grasp my hips, pulling me to the edge of the bed. The movement causes my shirt to ride up, revealing my lack of underwear. My honeypot is on full display for him for the first time. I make no effort to cover myself as I stay propped on my elbows. I've never been self-conscious about sex or my body. We're shifters; it comes with the territory. Watching him take in these new parts of me brings me to my sexual breaking point.

"Come on, get to the good stuff, our leg is fine." Jo puffs in annoyance, and I couldn't agree more.

"Jax, my leg's fine. I have more pressing needs."

He blinks, finally pulling his gaze away from my bare core. A few additional seconds are spent fussing like a mother hen over my leg placement until he appears satisfied with its position. *Mates...*I don't have the heart to tell him my leg prop reminds me of getting an annual pap.

Leaning down, he gently pushes my legs open. Kneeling between my parted legs, he places tender kisses on my inner thigh up to my tattoo.

"Have you not been wearing any panties all night?"

"Nope." He'll discover that white lie later, hiding in his pillow.

He pushes me flat on my back as he crawls up my body. His strong arms support his weight as he hovers above me. As he ascends to my lips, our mouths meet with a fierce intensity unlike our former kisses, which have been sweet, exploratory ones. His tongue dives deeper into my mouth as I wrap my arms around his shoulders, urging him closer. The bastard holds strong, not giving me a single inch. A low growl escapes me; one might say I'm used to getting my way. The kiss breaks for a moment as he tosses his shirt aside.

"Pants too," I get out, trying not to break our kiss.

He pulls his lips away from mine to look me in the eyes. "No, I'll be the one giving orders tonight."

Mars flashes again in his eyes. Joey rises inside, challenging her male, her equal. In the blink of an eye, his sharp canines are biting gently into my shoulder through the T-shirt I'm still wearing. His heavy weight slowly pushes down on me, allowing me to feel his straining cock. A strong hand makes its way to my throat, lightly squeezing. I'm pinned in this predator's hold, and I fucking love it. The pressure of his bite intensifies, making me cry out. The feeling is incredible. I don't mind a little pain with my pleasure. That dominating aura of his continues to crash into me as his teeth stay locked in place.

Jax's true power is masked well behind a carefree shell he presents to the world. Right now, though, he wants my submission. Leaning my neck forward, I run my tongue along the base of his neck, tasting his skin. My hands roam freely along his hard chest down the length of his body. Coarse chest hair leads to a happy trail I gladly follow below his pants. Goddess, he's massive. Larger than any wolf male I've been with.

"This is mine," I declare, giving his stiff erection a firm squeeze. A low rumble of desire vibrates in his chest. "And I want it, now," I demand, stroking him slowly.

"Not until you relinquish control. Let me be in charge tonight."

"Hmm, submission, can I get the definition?" I ask while continuing to pump him with my hand.

"Yes, stop fighting me, because I can tell you like when I'm in control."

Trying a new tactic, I grasp the ends of the shirt to pull it over my head. He can't say no to boobs, right? A large hand stops my progression, proving me wrong. Baring my teeth at him, I snarl, letting him know just how sexually frustrated I am.

"None of that, my Fiery Wolf. You're the most exciting gift I've ever received, and unlike a greedy kid who rips open their presents quickly, I want to unwrap you slowly. Savoring every fucking moment."

I understand, as he, too, is the best gift I've ever received. His right hand slowly slides up my inner leg before grazing over my dripping wet core. I moan in response to the sensation of his touch.

"You're so wet for me." Lazily, he starts stroking his finger up and down my core. "Tell me I made you this wet," he commands.

"You made me this wet," I whisper.

That warm hand leaves me to travel up to his lips. His eyes close slowly as he groans in satisfaction, tasting me for the first time. We shifters are dirty freaks.

"Taste more of me," I plead.

Sliding down my body, he kneels before me. Warm breath fans my sensitive skin as his nose runs up my inner thigh. Jax takes a deep inhale of my scent before his tongue finally makes contact with my throbbing bundle of nerves. The sensation is unreal, causing me to jerk. Strong hands grip me firmly in place while his tongue continues to explore the most intimate part of me. I don't hold back, allowing my moans of pleasure to echo off his bedroom walls.

"Yes! More!" Commands start to spill from my lips.

Slipping two fingers inside me, he strokes my magic spot, sending me right over the edge into an incredible orgasm. My vision darkens for a moment at the intense pleasure. Damn, most men can't find a G-spot even with a compass and a map with *"X marks the G-spot"* in bold red lettering. Instinctively, he knows the layout of my sensitive, hidden places.

"Come here." I gently tug his hair, leading him back up to my mouth after I come down from my high. My taste lingers on his lips. "My turn to make you feel good." I grasp the waistband of his pants, ready for them to disappear.

"Ours!" Jo's in complete agreement.

"Fuck, Dana," his voice is low and rumbly. "Not tonight, there will be plenty of time for that after you are better. Right now, you need rest."

Stubborn male only thinking about my needs. "It counts as resting if I lay here while you bring that glorious appendage between your legs to my mouth." I give him a full, toothy grin.

He laughs, shaking his head while climbing off me. Jo starts howling in protest, and I agree with her.

His warm hand squeezes my thigh lightly as he stands. "Come on, cuddle with me."

My protest is unable to leave my lips because he leans down to place a finger on them, silencing me. "None of that."

The thought of him giving me pleasure while I leave him with blue balls for the night doesn't sit right. As his mate, I have the same instinctual drive as he does to ensure he is cared for in every way.

Joey's not ready to give up. *"Tell him we don't do as we are told!"*

I debate it. Now that I let my body settle in, the fatigue weighs on me. The fight leaves me. *"I'm pretty tired."*

Jo huffs. *"Grandma."*

I let Jax scoot me into the center of the bed. Large pillows are placed under my leg to prop it in a comfortable position. Once he's done fussing, he comes to snuggle on my left side, but not before he finally loses his pants. His large erection is on full display through his boxer briefs. Holy Mother Moon above.

The fatigue I was feeling a moment ago quickly dissipates and is replaced with white hot lust. The need is almost unbearable as my entire body burns for him. Smelling my desire, Jax's chest rumbles; no doubt, Mars is also pleased with our body's reaction to him. I look at him with pleading eyes.

"You better put those lusty eyes away, Smoke Show." Scrubbing a hand over his face, he turns to instruct the smart home device to turn off the lights. Deliberately, he settles in lying with his body facing away from me. I hear sniffing, then some rustling.

And 3-2-1.

"You snuck your panties into my pillow."

"Just a little inspiration for your wet dreams tonight."

"Stubborn female, you need rest."

"What I need is you inside me. This mating instinct is unrelenting. You must feel it too. Besides, I promise to lie here, RESTING, while you do all the work."

Snaking one arm around his neck, I tug his well-built frame closer to me. My free hand roams his body. Even in the dark, I can see his resolve slip away. He lets out a sigh of defeat before settling over me. *And got him!* Cue Jo's happy dance.

The sound of boxers being removed from his body and thrown aside brings me more joy than successfully purchasing Taylor Swift concert tickets – yeah, I cried. His heavy weight settles on top of me again, as he nestles himself between my parted thighs.

"This isn't how I imagined our first time," he admits.

"Oh, and what did you imagine, Mr. Blackclaw?" I ask while brushing his hair back away from his face.

"More along the lines of a dominance battle leading to tearing of clothes and breaking of furniture. You'd finally submit, allowing me to bend you over this bed. I'd spank that plump ass of yours, before plowing into you so hard you saw stars."

Secretly, I wanted that too. I believe the balance to our power struggle will be found in the bedroom. We'll clash in primal lust, fangs, and passion until one submits. For me, I want him to earn my submission.

"You've thought a lot about this," I say.

"There's no way I couldn't have dreamed about every part of you. The thought of any other man ever thinking of you the way I have makes me see red."

The possessiveness causes more liquid to pool between my legs.

"You may say you don't like my dominance, but your body calls your bluff."

I nod, unable to speak. A smile carves through his full lips before he passionately claims my mouth. Those artistic fingers begin working my sensitive core again. *Vibrator era is officially over.*

That wicked mouth moves lower, nibbling along my neck. The talented hand that is effortlessly playing me like one of his instruments slides under my shirt, moving higher to find my breast. Finding one of my nipples, he massages around it before circling it with his finger like a hungry shark. Through the shirt, he starts a gentle nip and tug motion. He mimics the gesture on the right with his hand.

The tips of my nails slide along the landscape of his body, creating a map of our new favorite territory. Before I take his shaft, I run my hand through the wet heat, eagerly running out of me. I glide the coated hand over his pulsating cock along the curves of veins up to its smooth head.

My body is more than ready for him. Using the hard tip of his cock, he slides it back and forth over my clit, eliciting more moans of pleasure from me. Unable to take it any longer, I grab his hips and position myself just right for him to slip inside.

Taking the hint, he finally enters me; the stretch is most welcome. Moans escape both of us at the feeling of our connection. Everything about this feels right with our two souls uniting in the most intimate way. Our lovemaking quickly shifts from passionate to frantic, in our lusty, mating-induced state. Our mouths taste and nip one another in between our cries. His thick length slams into me, hitting just where I need him.

"Jax, more!"

The pad of his thumb finds my clit to rub in pressured circles that push me into my second orgasm tonight. Jax follows quickly after me with his own release. I scream out his name as the most explosive orgasm of my life shatters my soul. His teeth elongate, sinking a fraction into the top of my shoulder where it meets my arm. Love biting, luckily, not fully marking. The sensation again pushes me into another orgasm as he continues to pulse inside me. We both lie there panting as our waves of pleasure start to subside.

Once his body relaxes, he retracts his fangs and lifts my shirt sleeve to examine the puncture wounds. Carefully, his tongue traces over the bites to aid their healing. I run my hands through his silky hair as he tends to me. He softly kisses my shoulder before meeting my lips for a tender kiss.

"Did I hurt you?" he asks.

"No."

Sporting a goofy smile, he hangs his head, letting his forehead meet mine. "Good. That was. Wow, incredible."

"And that was just the missionary position, while I'm still half clothed, and barely able to move. No wonder mates fuck like rabbits."

Our soft chuckles fill the now quiet room, as we poke fun at the ridiculousness of our kind. Freshly mated couples are often given a couple of months off, no matter their position in the pack, to get their hormones in check. This allows them to settle the mating urges and go through their first heat together, which is triggered by the fully formed bond.

"I can already feel the addiction to you," he tells me.

We stay in this position for a while, with him still inside me, and kissing before my exhaustion forces us apart. Jax fusses with my leg position, which I'm too tired to care about, before snuggling in next to me. My last fleeting thought before sleep overtakes me is that he is *mine*.

CHAPTER TWENTY-THREE

Dana

Smut and Eggs

"*Dana, wake up!*" Joey sing-songs as she prances around my mind. If only I could swat her away like an annoying fly.

"*I'm tired... Wait, is that bacon I smell?*"

"*Yes! But what's even better than the bacon is our sexy lycan, currently preparing it for us. Now get up!*"

"Okay, fine, you win," I whine.

Forcing my fatigued bones off the overly plush down mattress is a challenge. I snatch my crutches from the floor and head into the bathroom to quickly freshen up. On my way to the kitchen, the bright morning sun shines through the windows, giving me a better look at Jax's home. Eclectic art, I suspect from all his world travels, decorates most of the space. I hope we can visit some of his favorite spots together someday.

Traveling for fun is rare for me, and I don't consider going to Florida as well-traveled. The more time I spend with him, the more I realize how compatible we are. My strong dedication to duty is rooted in my blessed essence. My workaholic tendencies could benefit from his free-spirited nature. He's a partner who reminds me to take time for myself to recharge because burning out won't solve all the problems in the supernatural world.

Rounding a corner, I reach the kitchen where soft music plays from hidden speakers. An Ajax hundred-watt smile greets me. The sight is contagious. I hope my returning smile gives him the same mushy feelings I have, like a warm, gooey lava cake. He sets his phone aside and pulls me into his sturdy arms for a morning kiss.

Pulling back, but keeping me at arm's length, he asks, "Did you sleep well?"

"Amazing. You earned your five-star den review."

That earns me another brilliant smile. "Excellent, I knew I would."

His warm hand lands on my lower back to usher me towards the breakfast buffet he set up. There are fruits, eggs, meats, and pancakes at the ready on his table overlooking the back patio. Drool might have just slipped from my mouth onto the table. It smells that good. My stomach lets out a thunderous rumble at the prospect of eating all of this.

I pat my front. "Well, my stomach approves of this breakfast feast you've prepared for us."

"I'm not sure what your favorite breakfast foods are, so I made everything I had in the house. Come sit." He pulls out a chair and sits before gliding me sideways onto his lap.

"Jax!" I protest as I awkwardly adjust over the growing bulge I'm sitting on. "Is this necessary?" My crutches are tossed ungracefully to the ground.

"Yes, I'm taking care of my—" he cuts himself off abruptly. I give him the look that says, 'You almost dropped the mate bomb'.

"Of you. Let me take care of you." He lifts a bacon strip and brings it to my lips, waiting for me to open. His left hand tickles my side, causing me to squirm. "Open up, stubborn female."

The greasy piece of meat reaching my taste buds takes away all other thoughts bouncing around my brain. *So dang yummy.* I'm left with a deep-rooted feeling of contentment at this moment. *Wow, maybe all the world needs is more bacon; it's truly a miracle drug.*

"Tell him we prefer his sausage for breakfast," Joey pants suggestively.

"No! That sounds like a line from a bad porno."

"Fine, how about the best part of waking up isn't Folgers, but his sausage in our cun-"

"Wolf, don't finish that thought, for the love of the Goddess."

"You're no fun." Jo switches up her antics by pushing X-rated images to the forefront of my mind. She gives me teasers of what we should be doing with his sausage.

My body starts to heat of its own volition. Dormant flames perk up, prickling under my skin. They, too, have a mind of their own. I picture them asking, *"Did someone say sex? Because we are here for it!"* The moisture between my thighs confirms it for them.

Jax's face looks just as strained as his pants. "Smoke Show, if you keep that up, I'll bend you over this table and eat you for breakfast."

"Is that a promise?"

"Anything for you, beautiful." The arousal wafting off him has dark promises of smut with my eggs. *Fuck the food.* Our mouths collide in a dominant embrace. My right arm wraps around his neck to tug at his hair.

A large warm hand slides under my shirt to tease my breast. His mouth breaks away to slide down my neck, sucking and nipping along the path he travels.

"Fuck Dana, I can feel your wetness through my pants."

Lifting me by one arm as if I weigh nothing, he gives his pants a quick jerk, and they slide down to the floor. As he lowers me back onto his lap, he turns me to face the table. Strong hands force my legs wide apart. With my back now to his front, his hands rub up and down my parted thighs. Down they go and then back up with one finger, taking a detour through Vagina Falls and Clittopia. That finger slides up the seam of my vagina to my clit, bringing with it my warm liquid. Christ, I've never released so much fluid down south before.

One of his powerful hands grips my waist while the other cups my core, playing with me. Beneath me, he slowly rocks his hips, slickening up his hardened member. I recline into him, arching my back to push my chest forward. My tongue traces the curve of his ear as my right hand holds steady in his hair.

I nibble his earlobe. "Can I take this damn shirt off yet?"

He nips back. "Not yet."

This makes me growl my disapproval, and he sends a warning growl right back at me.

"Hands on the table," he orders.

My hand reluctantly leaves his hair to play along.

"Good girl." He continues to coat himself in my wetness, sliding back and forth along my entrance. "Are you ready for me?"

"Yes," I pant.

"Are you sure?" There's a tease playing along his words.

"Yes," I snarl, frustrated.

In a quick, fluid movement, he lifts me before thrusting himself fully inside me. The sudden invasion, mixed with his dominating aura, causes me to cry out in pleasure. Running his hands under my shirt, he finds my bare breasts. His thumbs and index fingers pinch down on my nipples, tugging them forward.

Every part of me hums with need for his touch. The delicious sensations he's eliciting envelop me and beg for escape. I try to take over by rocking my hips, needing the throbbing in my center to ease. One of his strong hands stops my pursuit of a quick release, while the other grabs a fistful of my hair. Gently, he eases my head back so I'm gazing into his two perfect blue orbs.

"While you're injured and in my den, must I remind you who's in charge?"

I scowl back at him.

A wave of his dominance washes over us. "If you need to assert your dominance outside of here, so be it, but while you're in my den, I'll be taking over the reins. Unlike some males, my pride and masculinity aren't easily weakened by my female wielding more power than I do. Now, no more of that. Stand up and bend your perfect ass over my table. Understood?"

For a moment, Joey and I are rendered speechless. *Holy goddess, that was sexy.*

"Are you going to be okay with this?" I ask Jo.

"Only for our mate will I do this. Heck, I'd even be willing to Omega roleplay in the bedroom occasionally if it makes him happy."

What in the Kentucky Fried Chicken is happening? Joey's willing to take on the role of a submissive wolf?

With that declaration, I stand up, putting pressure only on my good leg and doing as I'm told. I place my hands on the table, take a wide stance, and push my ass back, hopefully giving this man the best view of his life. Jax quickly pushes aside our forgotten breakfast before his muscular frame towers over me. His hot breath fans over my ear, sending goosebumps across my skin. The feel of his nose running from my ear to the crook of my neck leaves tingles in its wake.

"Down on your forearms, Fiery Wolf," he commands.

I let my elbows lower to the cool surface of the table.

"And you're going to stay like this, unless I tell you otherwise."

I slightly push my hips back farther. A sharp crack fills the silence. Pain stings my right ass cheek where his hand made contact. Even with the pain, a small moan falls from my lips. *Damn it, I do love being put in my place.*

"Dana," there's a warning in his tone.

What can I say? I'm a rule breaker, not a follower. Deciding it's best to obey, for now, I give a small, "Yes, Beta." Luring my mate into a false sense of submissive-security sounds fun, and once my leg is fully healed, we can really play.

"Good girl," he coos.

Bending down between my spread legs, his hot tongue licks me from front to back. *Fuck.* When he rises, his strong arms lift me by the hips, ensuring no pressure is being put on my healing leg. That thick cock relentlessly slams into me, giving my overstimulated body precisely what it's craving. I hope naughty breakfast becomes a regular on the menu.

CHAPTER TWENTY-FOUR

Dana

Jealousy

After our round of smut, we get back to our eggs. The overbearing mother-hen forces me to eat more than necessary, claiming my body needs the extra calories to heal. After which, he helps me get presentable for public eyes. Neither of us had the foresight to bring extra clothing from the Royal Estate for me to change into. Talk about an obvious walk of shame. Oh well, the busybodies around these parts will love the fresh tea. Remus reached out this morning to let us know Isla agreed to speak with me about self-defense lessons. We plan to stop there later this morning after I hopefully get this cast removed. Not willing to take any chances, I have my fingers, toes, and eyes crossed.

Our first stop is the Royal Estate, where I change into a new flowing maxi dress. From there, we make our way toward the hospital. On our way out, Chester informs me that the Queen would like to invite me to lunch this afternoon. Since we're striving for bestie goals, I accept, though my mating hormones are riding me hard to turn down her offer. They prefer we blow off everyone for our mate and his talented D. *Sorry, hormones, not today.* Arriving at the doctor's office, we check in, then take a seat in the waiting area.

"I'll be right back," Jax excuses himself to the restroom.

The nurse's death glare directed at me isn't missed once he is out of view. In fact, she looks like one of the groupies from The Horde last night. Being the charming bitch I am, I glare right back. Joey takes this as a blatant challenge, baring her teeth.

"She wants our mate! Let's take this outside," she snarls.

Is that this woman's problem? Maybe they're former lovers. The thought triggers a sharp stabbing sensation in my chest. Angry flames threaten to erupt across my skin. *Relax, deep breaths. This isn't you; it's the uncompleted mating bond,* I try to remind myself. Yet, it does nothing to stop the vivid images my mind conjures of them together. She finally loses our dominance stare down, lowering her eyes in a submissive gesture, as she should.

Still, a menacing warning growl begins to build deep in my chest when a warm pair of hands wraps around my shoulders. They draw my attention to my new favorite pair of eyes that have concern etched in their gaze. A cool wave of energy flows through me, calming my raised hackles. Jax's touch is the ice to my fire. He lifts me straight into his arms, not bothering with the crutches. In several long strides, we step into a one-stall bathroom, giving us a little more privacy for this awkward talk we're about to have. I'm struggling with this new jealous side of myself.

Setting me down, Jax cups my chin, tilting my face so I am looking at him directly.

"Hey, deep breaths. Tell me what happened," he says soothingly, further calming my smoldering jealousy.

"Oh, just that nurse. Likely an ex-lover of yours, given the death glares she's sending my way."

Oh. My. Goddess. Why? Why did I say that? I wish I could reel all that word vomit back in. *God's damn mating hormones, can you give a girl a break? I want this man to see the real me, not the crazy Shifter Love Island version you're making me out to be.* Whoever thought of leaving single shifters on an island to make trashy TV was brilliant.

"Dana, I can assure you nothing has ever happened between us. She's not my type. Also, she's screwed around with Mickey, so that's a hard no for me. He's a borderline manwhore, don't let his sweet demeanor fool you."

A small smile springs to my lips at the mention of Mickey being a manwhore. What girl wouldn't want to be knockin' boots with a lumberjack god?

"I won't lie to you, she's very close with Tiffany. The woman who can't take a hint, and who was at the show last night. I saw Tiffany briefly, eh, maybe like five or six months ago. She's a lot younger and eager to settle down. I was clear I didn't want anything long-term with her, but she still makes advances."

Smile gone. Crazy, activated. Jo flashes her fangs. *"I'll kill her! Problem solved."* She wants blood. Specifically, Tiffany, perky boob's blood.

"Hold on, Crazy Train, that was in the past. Be rational, we all have a past," I tell the beast, attempting to calm some of the extra rage she's stirring up.

"Hey, trust me when I say, I only have eyes for you," he whispers as his hand tucks a strand of hair behind my ear, causing my heart to melt.

"Jealousy over a man is new territory for me. This damn mating call is making me act out, so I'll have to work through it," I tell him honestly.

He gives me a devilish smile. "I don't know, I kind of like it."

Lightheartedly, I push his stupid smiling face away. "Get over yourself. Also, next time I see Mickey, I'm going to tell him you think he's a manwhore."

"Go ahead. He's self-aware, so it won't be a surprise to him." Leaning forward, he kisses me. "You good?"

"Yes," I say, a little breathy and craving more of his kisses. *Hmm, maybe a quick bathroom romp? Eesh, this is a hospital, gross. Rein it in. We have standards.*

"Good, let's get that thing off so we can have some real fun tonight. Mars is dying to meet Joey."

With that, the arrogant wolf inside me preens. She, too, can't wait to meet her mate.

Doctor White is pleasantly surprised to find my leg has already fully healed faster than she initially anticipated. Seeing as I'm a wolf, it should have taken a day or two longer, according to her textbook brain. I've always been an abnormally fast healer. Random lycan DNA floating around in my blood, I'm sure, helps. Whatever the actual reason, I don't care. *RIP, cast, you will not be missed.*

The doctor suggests I still take it easy for the next few days, just as an extra precaution. Jax seems happy about this news, probably because he gets to helicopter mom me a little longer. Doctor White enforces a strict no-fighting rule. Not a problem, seeing as my wolf is now embracing Omega roles as of this morning. Finally, we're told not to shift unless it feels right for our body. To stay safe, she recommends I wait an extra day or two.

Joey disagrees with this news. *"Yeah, not happening, seeing as my male and I have a date tonight."*

I laugh, *"You do you, girl."*

After my doctor visit, my spirits are lifted as we head to Isla's home. Finally, I feel like my whole self again. Hopefully, it'll help Jax and me take more positive steps in our relationship.

After a short drive, we arrive at a charming green two-story house with flowering plants carefully maintained out front. Remus greets us at the door and informs us that his wife has stepped out to pick up some groceries. His son Allen lounges on the couch and gives us a small wave when we enter their home.

"Isla is in her room. Let me see if I can get her to come out," Remus says, looking unsure.

He looks at Allen as if he might help, but he keeps his focus on the sports game he's watching. I sense that neither man is sure how best to support her through this. They move cautiously, like someone dealing with a wounded wild animal.

I clear my throat, "If it's alright, Remus, can I have a moment alone with her to introduce myself and to tell her the plan I have in mind for what we can work on?"

Hesitation shows through the slight frown on his face.

I do my best to comfort him, "I know I'm a stranger to you and this pack. But I've been a teenage girl before, so I'd like to check in and see how she's feeling, and that might be best without a crowd of men hanging around."

"That seems like an excellent idea," Jax chimes in.

Remus looks a little more at ease after Jax's agreement. "Sure, let's go see if she is okay with that."

I follow him up polished wooden stairs that creak beneath our feet. He pauses outside a door, and I can hear a television show softly playing from inside the room.

Remus gently knocks. "Isla, Dana is here. Can we come in?"

"Yes," she calls back.

Remus opens the door to reveal a girl with sandy colored hair, fair skin, and green eyes, matching the photo of her mother I saw downstairs. She could be her clone. I find myself imagining what Jax and I's children might look like. Hopefully, a replica of him, because that man is beautiful. *Whoa, holy brain tour.* Quickly shoving those thoughts aside, I return my attention to the task at hand, Isla.

Her hair is twisted into the perfect messy bun atop her head. Clear signs of exhaustion mark her youthful face. She's lounging in a Canadian Hockey League sweatshirt with black leggings while watching an episode of the highly popular supernatural dating show Mated at First Sight.

"This is Dana, Jax's mate," he introduces me.

Joey forces out an obnoxious fake laugh. *"Clearly, the pack didn't get a list of your stupid rules."*

"Shut it."

I don't have the heart to correct him.

"Dana wanted to talk to you about her self-defense class plans. Is it okay if she talks with you in here, or do you want to come downstairs with us? Your brother and Jax are down there. Mom is at the store."

She glances over at me, and I offer her a small smile. "Whatever you are most comfy with," I reassure her.

"We can talk in here," she says softly. I'm not picking up any signs of fear with me in her presence, which is a good sign.

"Okay, I'll be downstairs if you need me," Remus tells her before leaving the room. He does a poor job of hiding his uneasiness.

"Mind if I sit?" I ask, gesturing toward the end of her bed.

"Go ahead."

"My brother, Davey, has an extravagant watch party at the start of every new season because it's his favorite." A smile spreads across my face at the fond memories.

"Karissa was that way about this show, too. We always binge-watch the new seasons together." Her face falls at the mention of her missing friend. Tears build in her eyes, and her voice breaks. "Sorry, it's been hard. I want to hope she's gonna come back, but I've heard all the whisperings, and the chances of her returning seem impossible." At this point, tears are streaming down her porcelain cheeks.

I come sit by her and wrap her up in a tight side hug.

"I'm so scared for Karissa, and selfishly for myself. I don't want to get taken too. I'm, I'm sorry," she sniffles.

"Hey, never apologize for how you're feeling. Don't fight those little rascals. Even if they're the unpleasant, yucky ones we prefer to avoid, we need to acknowledge them and let them pass. It's understandable that you also feel scared after all that has happened."

She nods silently in my embrace. I stay silent next to her, rubbing a hand up and down her back soothingly. We remain like that for a little while, as she gently sobs, releasing all her fears.

"Sorry, I didn't mean to cry on you when you came to talk about self-defense." I can sense her embarrassment.

"It's okay, I wanted to check in with you first to see how you were feeling. It seems like you two were very close."

"Yes. She's the only female my age. She's six months older than me." She wipes the remainder of her tears with her sleeve.

"Can you tell me about her? What's she like?" I ask.

"She's outgoing, intelligent, and supermodel beautiful. All the boys at school fight over her attention. Her life mission has been to push me out of my comfort zone. I don't care for large crowds or a lot of attention. I tend to be kind of awkward and prefer to stay in, but Karissa isn't like that. She always seems to know exactly what to say, what to wear, and what to do." She drops her voice to a whisper, "We want to attend college together at the Supernatural Institute in England next year. She's been riding me hard to talk to my parents about it." Isla pauses. "Well, until recently," she states as if just noticing that change in her friend's behavior.

"How has it changed recently?" I prod gently.

"I don't know, she just hasn't brought it up lately. Maybe I'm overthinking it."

I shake my head no. "Always follow your intuition," I encourage her.

"Well, most females around here mate young in their early to mid-twenties because they feel they have some duty to our species. That's not what either of us wants. We want the freedom to see the world before taking a mate. Karissa knows I'm too chicken to tell my parents I want to leave the pack. They're stricter and more traditional than her parents. She's been on me nonstop for months, hyping me up to talk with them. The girl can be relentless, but lately she hasn't mentioned it. I don't know why." She chews her thumbnail, suddenly looking nervous.

"Hey, what's on your mind?" I lightly press.

"It's probably nothing, but I just thought of it. On a recent shopping trip to Grande Prairie, we, um, met a vampire," she admits sheepishly.

"He was our age. I thought he was too much, but Karissa thought he was cute, so she got his number. She mentioned texting with him a little, but nothing else. That was around the time she stopped begging me to ask my parents to move. I don't know. What do you think?"

This gives me pause. I don't know Karissa well enough to make a judgment call.

"She should talk to Dolken about this," Joey offers her two cents.

"I think our closest friends sometimes know us better than our own family. If you say her behavior seemed off, then I think you should tell Gamma Dolken about it."

She continues to chew on an already worn-down nail. Her rising anxiety is palpable.

"Our parents are going to be upset." She takes a deep breath, trying to push her tears down. "But, if it helps find her, I can deal with my parents being upset."

"You're a good friend, Isla. How about you tell your parents after this, okay?"

"Okay," she mumbles, still looking on edge.

I work to change the subject, hoping it might ease some of her stress. "You and I are similar in ways. I come from a conservative wolf pack in the southern U.S. No one ever left. Everyone mated young, and women took on traditional roles. Worst of all, women weren't properly trained on how to fight if we were attacked.

The environment was stifling for anyone who thought differently or wanted something different with their life than what the elders told us we wanted. At eighteen, I decided to leave for Moonborn Pack, where I've been ever since. I knew it was the right choice for me. My old pack didn't support my goals or help me become the best version of myself. You're young with a long life ahead of you. I think you should follow your dream. Do what makes you happy, even if it's difficult and upsets others, mainly your mama," I say with a mild grimace. "If going to college, even for a little while, will make you happy, you should do it. If you don't like it, you know you have somewhere to come back to."

There is a new light shining in her eyes. "Thank you." She offers me a small smile.

"You're welcome. Now, I'm not sure how long I'll be here, but how about I stop over every day for a couple of hours so we can work on some self-defense training. Does that sound good?"

"Yes, thank you for agreeing to work with me," she tells me sincerely.

"You're welcome. Okay, let's go talk to your parents about this vampire. Oh, and maybe don't tell your mama, I encouraged you to leave her." I give her a little hand pleading gesture with puppy-dog eyes.

"I won't tell her."

When Isla and I finally emerge from her room, we find all the Reeds, including Isla's mother, Nancy, in their living room being entertained by Jax. Animatedly, he waves his arms around, telling a tale from one of his many adventures. The man's so damn adorable, I can't help but grin watching him. Once his story is over, he slides up to me and wraps one arm around my waist. His warm lips find mine for a fleeting kiss. Nancy looks put out by Jax's open affection.

I clear my throat, "I'll be back tomorrow to start some self-defense lessons with Isla. She'll need a can of pepper spray, as well as a couple of small silver knives with sheaths that she can keep on her person."

"Okay, we can do that," Nancy says, looking unconfident, glancing from me to Remus.

Remus agrees, letting his head hang. "I think we can get those things. Training is ah, something we should've already been doing with her." Guilt wafts off him as he rubs at the back of his neck.

"Yes, well, all the women in the pack should have better training," Jax chimes in, and I want to kiss him for it. Because yes, they should!

"I agree," is all I say, holding back the urge to get on my soapbox about the importance of women's training.

Silence stretches for a couple of beats. I stand as a silent support next to Isla as she nervously nibbles on her lower lip.

"So, should we get going?" Jax asks me.

"In a minute." I look from him to Isla. I make eye contact with her and give her a reassuring nod. All of us can hear the anxious rhythm of her heart.

"Um, dad, can you ask Gamma Dolken to come over?" Isla's voice is shaky. "I remembered something he might want to know about Karissa. Um, when we went on that shopping trip, Mom, a couple of months ago, well, we met a vampire."

Nancy looks horrified. "A vampire!" Her voice rises several octaves.

Allen makes a face. "A vamp," he says in disgust.

Remus looks a mixture of shocked-horrified. He puts a hand around his wife, giving her a look.

"Yes, and well, we just talked to him, and Karissa got his number. I know she texted with him a little. Um, and well, Dana thought I should tell Gamma."

"Yes, someone should search her phone for any history between them," I cut in, trying to take some of the heated looks off of Isla.

Nancy looks confused. "But they already confirmed Torr was involved in her abduction."

"Even if it feels insubstantial, we should rule it out, seeing as we have no leads on where to find her." Jax jumps in, and I nod my agreement.

Remus looks at Karissa with gentleness in his eyes while Nancy appears to be on the verge of a meltdown. "Okay, I'll mindlink Dolken and ask him to stop over," he tells her.

Jax and I leave before Dolken arrives, feeling the Reeds need some privacy with their daughter. Once in the car, I fill Jax in on what Isla and I spoke about. For some reason this vampire feels important, and I think while it's hard on Isla, she's doing the right thing by bringing him up.

Jax leaves me at the front of the Royal Estate for my gal pals' lunch date. He has a few items to attend to this afternoon but will pick me up after. Jo perks up with a cat-like stretch at the mention of returning to his home for the evening. Today, she has spent most of her time resting in preparation for tonight. She's beyond ready to run free with her mate. The thought sends a flutter throughout my stomach. With the anticipation building for this evening, I'm not sure how I'll be able to focus at the Queen's lunch.

CHAPTER TWENTY-FIVE

Dana

The Queen's Garden

I spend thirty glorious minutes indulging myself in my estate room's luxurious shower spa. There's a new yellow sundress in the walk-in closet I slip into after pulling myself away from my new favorite spot in the world. A girl could get used to having a shower spa and a stylist on staff.

Shopping for clothing isn't one of my favorite pastimes. Davey and Charles do the majority of it for me, since my uniform and sweats don't classify as a wardrobe. I feel a pang of guilt thinking about them. I should really fill them in on everything that's happened over the last several days. Davey will be pissed that I didn't tell him the second I laid eyes on my mate. I've never kept anything from him, but this is all fresh, and I'm not ready to bring more opinions into our complex relationship.

I dry my hair and apply a light dusting of makeup I found, before heading to lunch. A palace guard leads me through the corridors to the Queen's Garden. My damn southern DNA makes my empty hands twitch.

"One always brings something to contribute, but don't use your favorite Tupperware; you might not get it back, like when Sally Jones kept mine," I hear Memaw scolding me in my head. All of us in the Johnston family have had years of our lives wasted that we'll never get back, listening to Memaw drone on about frickin' Sally Jones. *Okay, hide nice Tupperware and don't trust anyone named Sally Jones, life lesson learned.*

When we arrive at the northern side of the estate, we walk down a long hall before stopping outside a stunning dark mahogany door. Intricately carved flowering vines flow elegantly across its polished surface. The Egyptian-themed room it opens to is even more astonishing.

It's rich in colors of deep blues and browns. Sculpted Egyptian gods stand as sentinels throughout, with small accent pieces intermingled. The focal point of the room is the striking canvas painting of Anubis, positioned over a fireplace nestled between bookshelves. I wonder if Gamila's family is from Egypt? I'm not familiar with lycan packs in that area of the world. I will add that to the list of things to learn about my future bestie.

Two guards stand posted next to massive wrought-iron doors. Each door features decorative blue lotus-stained glass panels. They push their heavy frames wide, revealing several more guards stationed just inside the doors.

Jo lets out a low whistle as we take it all in. *"The Queen's Garden lives up to its name."*

"Wow," is all I can manage to say, seeing it for the first time.

"This upstages the shower you're ready to move into."

I give Jo a nod in agreement. *"Yeah, I'll give you that."*

A dome constructed of glass and metal encloses a vibrant display of colorful plants, shrubs, and small trees. Butterflies lazily meander about their day in this paradise. Polished riverstone pathways weave their way through the enchanting garden. Three trellises draped in vines create charming archways to pass under while guiding you further into the unseen garden. The final opening leads to a pond featuring a cascading waterfall, providing a calming background noise.

Graceful koi fish can be glimpsed beneath floating lily pads. A wooden bridge offers a dry crossing with a scenic view of the pond's surface, which is dotted with blue and white lotus flowers. The dark blue shades of their petals and the striking contrasts of their yellow centers match those of the stained glass doors.

A large white hexagonal gazebo with vibrant blue plush chairs and twinkling lights sits in the back right corner. Inside, tables offer a selection of food and refreshments that range from green juice to glazed donuts. The earthy, floral scents of the garden intermixed with the delicious wafts of the food bring happiness to my soul.

Gamila stands to give me a welcoming side hug. "I'm so glad you could join me today."

"Me too," I reply, genuinely happy to see her again.

She turns toward the massive buffet. "Make yourself comfortable and help yourself to any of the food. Seriously, please eat. Since I became pregnant, the staff has started serving portions that could feed an army. It's a little insulting."

I have to laugh because she isn't exaggerating about the quantity of food for the two of us.

"This place is incredible, beyond incredible. Is there a gift shop where I can get a souvenir magnet or something to remember it by?" I joke.

That makes her happy. "Unfortunately, no gift shop, but feel free to take photos. Anders gifted it to me, and no one else is allowed in without my permission. The room's spelled to always be a perfect eighty degrees."

"Wow, eighty degrees does sound amazing for some moonlit romps in the dead of winter. Sign me up." *Well, there goes my good southern manners.*

"You're refreshing," she grins. "I sometimes feel suffocated by how fake people act around me, just because I have a sparkly tiara in my closet. If they only knew Anders found me working as a burlesque dancer at the Velvet Underground, they might feel differently."

Choking on the sip of wine I had just taken, I manage to cough out, "What! Really?"

The Velvet Underground is a paranormal nightclub in New York City, where all the dark and lethal supernatural creatures come to play. Sex, drugs, alcohol, fight rings, basically any shady shit you could think of all under one roof.

"Yes. My upbringing was complicated, causing me to flee my home pack at a young age. I hustled, begged, borrowed, stole, and sold my soul. Fortunately, I love to dance, so it was an easy way to make money at the Velvet Underground. Anders came in one night on a job, while I was performing onstage in a very tiny rhinestone thong with matching decorative pasties. The male lost his shit." She flashes a wicked smile.

The snort laugh that escapes me is not cute in the slightest. "There's no way that wasn't an iconic shitshow."

"Oh, it was. It's not how I envisioned meeting my soulmate." She pauses, looking lost in the memory. Her face brightens as she looks at me. "Your turn. You and Ajax have been causing quite the stir in these parts. Now that my mate isn't around, give me all the details." She waits patiently.

"Well, he's actually my second fated mate."

Her mouth drops open in shock. "What!?" She squeals like a schoolgirl. "I've never heard of anyone having multiple goddess-given fated mates." *Join the club, girl.* "Explain, please."

I share details of Bobby, what led me to meet Jax, Jo's little prank, and briefly about how we're taking things slow.

"The timing of destiny is never wrong. The soul call isn't something one can easily walk away from. I have no doubt you two will figure it out. It's clear you are both already mad about one another." Her hopefulness is reassuring.

The next hour passes by in easy conversation. I learn she is part Egyptian, hence all the cultural artwork. I tell her about my conversation with Isla earlier today. Gamila feels extremely conflicted about their upcoming Blood Oath Ceremony due to Karissa's disappearance. She doesn't feel right celebrating her child when another's child is missing. I do my best to reassure her because the show must go on. The event has always been meticulously timed to occur on the full moon prior to the child's birth and can't be postponed. I offer my assistance in keeping watch during the event, since many of the pack will be busy attending. She appreciates my offer, but is adamant that she wants me present to witness it.

Eventually, Gamila's friends, along with Cher, her mother-in-law, join us. It's terrific seeing Cher again; she's such a hoot. Cher's like the hip aunt with tattoos, a motorcycle, and a secret bottle of Jack stashed in her bra. I learned she was the second of the deceased King Andras' seven wives. She managed to escape while pregnant with Anders in the back of a food supply truck, with the help of her father, Dolken. The pair sought refuge at The Dragon Empire in Las Vegas, Nevada, in exchange for life sentences of servitude tied to Andras's lifespan. Only when he died was their contract considered fulfilled. Greedy dragons.

Due to its massive scale, workers are always in high demand. The Dragon Empire is untouchable by other supernatural factions, giving them an upper hand when making bargains. They play in the gray and are seen as a step above the Velvet Underground, with some spec of morals. The mighty operation consists of four hotels, gambling rings, live entertainment, clubs, bars, prostitution, you name it, they have it. It's unique, as it houses direct portal access to other realms.

I lose track of how many bottles of wine our group polishes off, and the food, well, we haven't even made a dent. Conversations with the women flow naturally from pack politics to men, and everything in between. I never expected to form such easy bonds with non-wolves.

Joey starts to get restless, having been away from Jax all afternoon. The melty drama queen whines to me, desperate for some playtime with her man. Which, I wholeheartedly understand.

"Okay, let's mindlink him," I tell her, but before I can, my body hums to life, sensing our mate's nearness. Anders steps into view with Jax in tow.

Joey squeals.

"So, this is where my mate has been all afternoon. Caught up in a gaggle of women," Anders jokes before leaning down to kiss Gamila passionately. Her eyes instantly turn dreamy.

"You're just jealous, son. She prefers our company better," Cher teases before giving him a quick squeeze. When she pulls back, she pinches his cheeks.

He grumbles, "Mother, really?"

"Yes, really," Cher tuts at him.

Jax walks straight to my side with a broad smile on his handsome face. One of which I can easily return. He pulls me up and guides me into the side of his hard body.

"Hey, beautiful, are you ready to head out?" he asks.

"I believe I am, Mr. Blackclaw."

Jo starts in on me, *"Tell him if it was up to me, we'd have left three hours ago. Imagine all we could have done with him in that timeframe."*

"Not the time or place, horn dog. Besides, I had a nice time."

After our goodbyes, we stop at my room in the estate to toss a few items into an overnight bag before heading to Jax's place. My anticipation peaks as I eagerly await to see what the night holds for Joey and Mars' first meeting.

CHAPTER TWENTY-SIX

Dana

Unwrapping the Present

Being the most amazing man in the world, Jax had already done the prep work for our dinner. Once we arrive, he tosses seasoned steaks and baked potatoes on the warm grill. While we wait for dinner to cook, we catch up on our time spent apart this afternoon. Everything about this simple moment feels like home.

There's nowhere else in the world either of us is supposed to be right now. We are safe, cherished, and cared for by one another.

The scent of incoming rain weighs heavily in the air. Grabbing our plates of food, we head to the lower covered patio below the deck. The lower level features a gorgeous hardwood outdoor dining table and a hot tub, which I'm eager to use. After our dinner, we grab a couple of beers to enjoy while watching the light rainfall. Listening to rain droplets pattering to Earth with my mate by my side brings me tranquility; it's a foreign state for me. I decided it's a safe space to ask some deeper-level questions that have been weighing on my mind.

"Nooooo, I want to play. You're gonna kill the mood," Joey whines.

"Hush, you'll have your fun later tonight." Hopefully.

"Jax?"

"Hmm?"

"Will you tell me what happened to your family?" I gently prod. Jax releases a heavy sigh before nodding. Providing what comfort I can through physical touch, I clasp our hands together. My thumb rubs soft circles over the back of his smooth, sun-kissed skin while he collects his thoughts.

"It's a traumatic story. One that I do want you to know. Are you sure you want me to share it now?"

"No," Joey protests.

"Yes," I say without hesitation.

"Okay. Well, the Blackclaw bloodline served as the royal family's personal guard for generations spanning back to the creation of our kind. Most often holding the title of the King's Beta. King Nelus guided our ancestors, and some of the old wankers who are still here, through The Crossing, creating a new start for our pack on this land. During that process, he lost his mate and heir.

Eventually, he was able to have another son, Andras. Speculation, as you've heard, is that Andras had a hand in his father's disappearance. He was power hungry, and with dear old dad as a roadblock, he sought to remove him. Unfortunately, for our people, Andras was rotten to his core.

After he was crowned, he started collecting wives. My eldest sister, Edith, became one of his brides. My parents and most of the pack were conflicted about these arrangements, seeing as he had other wives, and the number of females was low. It caused tension between my parents. They knew Andras wasn't a good man, but bearing an heir to the royal line is considered an honor, so they didn't resist. Edith frequently reassured them that she was fine and understood her duty, but she ended up committing suicide when she was twenty-two."

The rage I feel toward Andras quickly morphs to grief at the news of Jax's sister. His face takes on a haunted expression, and I'm unsure of what to say to make him feel better.

"I'm sorry," I whisper lamely.

Jax places a tender kiss on my hand. "I didn't know her well because I was so young. Edith's death devastated my parents. My dad started drinking, and my mom completely shut down. The King didn't handle the loss well either. It wasn't out of love for my sister, but rather from the loss of pedigree within the bloodline.

In retribution, he demanded that my second sister, Rose, take her place. At the time of Edith's death, Rose was only sixteen. My parents opposed this because she was so young. He agreed to wait to marry her until she was of age, but forced her into the palace immediately. He was afraid my parents would try to flee with her. My father turned against the king in anger, which ultimately cost him and my mother their lives. I was seven at the time, and I watched them die right there on the snow-covered front lawn of the Royal Estate."

Tears trail freely down my face. My heart clenches in pain at the thought of Jax, an innocent little boy, being forced to witness his parents' murder.

His warm hand pushes away my tears. "Andras wanted to kill me, too, ending my disgraced father's legacy. Rose, along with others, begged him to spare me, because I was just a young child. In the end, I was stripped of everything. My parents, home, birth rank, and family's legacy. Mickey and Miguel's parents took me in while they tried to reach my only living relative, my father's younger brother, Kazrith. Uncle Kaz was a lost soul who traveled the world. It took four years for someone to get in contact with him."

Pausing, he pulls me onto his lap. He holds me tight as he continues to wipe loose hair and tears away from my face.

"Do you wish to hear more?" his low voice asks.

Meeting his eyes, I tell him, "Yes. I want to know it all."

Reaching up, I bring his lips to mine, hoping to convey the words I can't seem to find. Searching inside, I locate our forming bond to send him a pulse of my love. He doesn't have to be alone in his trauma. I'm here now, if only to listen.

"Wow, I can feel your energy." He points to the center of his chest. "Here. It's incredible. I didn't know that with an uncompleted mate bond, I'd be able to feel you so clearly."

I give him a small smile. "I didn't either, but we're both newbies at this, so we can learn together."

"I'd like that." Leaning in, he pecks my lips before continuing his story. "So, back to my uncle. The man who had a lot of his own baggage, which he didn't know how to process, got me. A young kid with my own major baggage. Needless to say, he wasn't prepared for me. His coping mechanism was to wander the world to take in new experiences that helped him forget the ones that had hurt him. If you're not happy where you are, you could move on to another place. Easy as that.

He secured a home base within the Scottish Highland Pack so I could attend school. They were kind enough to look after me when my uncle was gone for long stretches. I hated the loneliness during his absences. Occasionally, my uncle would take me with him, but it caused me to miss too much school and him to get in trouble with the school leaders. I didn't mind missing school, of course. At one point, he mentioned sending me to a boarding school, but I threatened to run away and never speak to him again.

There were some big emotions I didn't know how to handle as a child, and neither did Uncle Kaz. Fortunately for us, the Highland Pack had wonderful people who supported us both. We were the Alpha's mate's special project. I do believe that woman is more stubborn than you," he chuckles, seeming lost in a memory. "Then, once I reached adulthood, traveling became my way of life too."

"Does your uncle still travel often?" I ask.

"Not so much. My uncle found happiness when he married my aunt. She's a witch. He told me that if I wander enough, I too will find my home."

I search his face. "And do you feel like you have found it being here in your original pack?"

"This place is something I didn't realize I was missing. Coming back here opened my eyes to the loneliness that burrowed in a long time ago. I became desensitized to it. Now that it's gone, I'm unsure if I can return to my former lone-lycan ways. Being here has also led me to you."

The look he gives me causes my entire body to alight. The sensation is different from my crimson fire. The burn is one created solely of self-need.

I narrow my eyes at him. "And how many panties have dropped for that pick-up line?"

He chuckles, "It's most certainly worked in my favor before."

Jealousy flares its ugly head, causing crimson flames to blaze in my eyes. A completely uncontrolled and illogical response, I, too, have a past. Nevertheless, Jo wants the names and addresses of these bitches for her hit list.

"Is that jealousy I smell, my Fiery Wolf?" Amusement is evident in his tone.

Unable to deny it, I choose to say nothing. Through our bond, I feel his calming, cool energy, which spreads from the center of my chest through my limbs, soothing away any hurt I felt over his past encounters.

Cupping the back of my head, he turns me to face him while massaging around the base of my skull. *Ah, that feels lovely.*

"You can't tell me men aren't falling at your feet." A statement, not a question.

Oh, if only he knew how untrue that statement is. No, men are running away crying, but he doesn't need to know that little tidbit right now.

"Make him work for it. We need to ensure he never thinks of anyone but us ever again," Jo hisses.

I make a noncommittal sound as I stand from his lap.

"Where do you think you're going?" He reaches for me, but I easily dodge him.

I deliberately lean forward, giving him the perfect view of my chest as I whisper, "Making you fall at my feet."

It's officially time to unwrap Jax's present, but also make him work for it a little longer. I back up slowly, making sure to give him a full body view. My hand slides down the back zipper of my dress.

When it reaches the top of my ass, my hands glide the straps over my shoulders, allowing the dress to fall freely to the ground. Standing before my mate in nothing but a lacy thong, I mentally thank the palace stylist for the assist. No way would any of my uniform undergarments classify as remotely sexy.

A deep, satisfied rumble crawls up his throat. Those animalistic eyes are fixated on my bare chest while they shift from his bright blue to gold. Mars is near the surface, also enjoying the show.

"Your turn. Clothes off," I demand.

"I'm good." There's a challenge in his words. Walking forward, I grab the collar of his shirt, ripping it wide open. He raises an eyebrow, giving me a "was that necessary?" expression.

"Now, I have a better view," I tell him.

And damn, his ripped upper body is quite the spectacular view. I hold his gaze as I let my hands roam over my body. Starting with my breasts, I pluck at my nipples before disappearing lower to that favorite spot between my legs. Things are already heated down there. I moan at the contact as I rub slow circles over myself.

Jax unzips his pants, releasing his straining cock from his tight jeans. The tip is slick with some pre-cum. He starts to stroke himself, his eyes never leaving my body.

Pushing two fingers inside, I coat them in my liquid heat before raising them toward my mouth.

"Come here so that I can taste you." His command sounds more animal than man.

There's so much authority lacing his words, my body naturally takes a step forward before my sex crazed brain catches up. *Nope, I don't think so.* Popping my fingers into my mouth, I slowly pull them out. Then, in a blur, I shift, letting Joey take over. She sprints towards the woods, releasing a howl into the night. Our body celebrates returning to its animal form and being liberated from the confinement of just our human shape.

Joey speeds up, and I can feel her excitement for this moment. *"Let the chase begin, my lycan,"* she mindlinks him.

CHAPTER TWENTY-SEVEN

Dana

The Chase

Behind me comes a loud snarl before I hear the sound of shredding clothes. *I tried to warn the stubborn male.* Knowing the chase has begun, Jo picks up the pace, weaving through trees. The rain has become a soft mist, releasing a deep, damp Earthy scent. All animals in the vicinity flee, sensing there are predators nearby. Our bond hums, notifying us that Jax is closing

in. The approach is silent, yet I feel his hunger. Slowing Joey hopes
to lure him into a false sense of victory before picking up the pace
in a new direction.

Our body shifts further into our hybrid form when we near a
large tree we can hide in. Leaping up onto a branch, we crouch,
waiting. Running past in a blur of speed, Mars abruptly stops
scenting the air for our trail that went cold. Our lycan stands over
seven feet tall with a dense black coat. As he turns, Joey leaps
down, landing on his back, causing us both to tumble. Recovering
quickly, we roll up into a natural semi-crouched position. For the
first time, he sees what we can become. Mars stands as still as a
statue, stunned, before tilting his head adorably in confusion.

"Surprise." Jo swoons over his attention before picking up a
downed branch and tossing it directly at him.

We take off at full speed again, not ready to end the game of
chase. Mars' hunt for us lasts another mile before strong arms
encase our middle, taking us to the ground. Landing with a loud
thud, our bodies skid through the underbrush of the forest floor.
Mars' golden eyes meet our crimson ones. He bares his teeth, demanding our submission, but Joey bares her teeth right back, not
giving it to him.

The two engage in a playful battle of love bites, sniffing, and
rubbing, which quickly turns possessive and claiming. Joey's typically sarcastic monologue is replaced with only animalistic noises.
In a swift motion, Mars flips us onto all fours before plunging

himself deep inside. Jo howls in delight before completely pushing out my consciousness.

My eyes flutter open to reveal a wet forest canopy above. I'm lying on my back, naked, with no recollection of how much time has passed since the pushy hussy took over. A warm, hard chest is pressing into me. The swirling aroma of leather and cedarwood helps kickstart my brain. Jax's wet, winded body on top of mine comes into focus.

"Hey," I whisper, stroking his messy, damp hair that has remnants from the forest around us.

"Hey..." His eyes roam over my naked body, lying here on the damp ground.

His attention snags on my lips, lifting the fog from his eyes. He lunges, crashing his mouth with mine. Excitement pulses through me, knowing it's now our playtime. The thick forest surrounding us absorbs the sounds of our pleasure. Warm arousal starts to seep between my legs while my entire body heats. It feels like I'm burning from the inside out.

"I need you inside me now!" I order.

"Goddess... your scent is strong. We need to get you home before another smells what's mine." He is all possessive male when he says this.

Pulling me up into his arms, he turns, heading in the direction of his house at full speed. I take the opportunity to lick along the soft skin of his collarbone. My sharp canines scrape along his marking spot that I so desperately want to sink my teeth into.

"Fuck," he groans.

When we reach the bottom patio, he sets me on my feet, causing my whole body to protest at the loss of contact. Our mate bond at work desperately wants his naked bits touching mine. We're wet and covered in dirt, but I don't mind. He's perfect either way.

"Mine." Jo's animalistic urge pushes through, making our voice sound gravely.

In a blur of speed, he pushes me over the wooden outside table. His hand spanks my bare ass, and damn, I do like being dominated a little too much. Those strong arms on either side of me pin me in place.

"You naughty wolf, you didn't listen to your doctor's orders about not shifting," he tsks into my ear.

I shrug. "Well, it turned out fine, didn't it?"

Around us, the rain has picked up, coming down in angry sheets. Soft lips graze along my earlobe, causing my body's blaze to amp up several more notches. I burn for him, my mate.

I turn over my right shoulder to face him and then shove him back. I prowl towards my prey, never breaking eye contact. My hands connect with his shoulders, pushing him again, harder this time. His backside connects with the hot tub.

"On the cover, Beta," I command.

He gives me a sultry smirk. "As you say, Alpha."

Muscles in his biceps bulge as he lifts himself to sit on the edge of the cover. His legs are spread wide in anticipation of what I plan to do to him. He is fully erect, with the tip slick with pre-cum.

"You're so fucking huge, Jax. This cock is mine." Bending forward, I take the tip of him in my mouth. Using my other hand, I stroke his thick length while sucking. I create a rhythm of sucking him down and then back up, swirling my tongue around his tip. His strong hand tangles in my hair.

"Fuck, baby," he curses low with his head thrown back. "I need to be tasting you, come here," he says, tugging at my hair.

My mouth reluctantly releases him. Strong arms pull me to straddle him as he lies back. I kiss him deeply before shifting positions to give him an unobstructed view down south.

Firm hands grasp my ass, massaging it. A teasing, warm tongue licks me painfully slowly, causing me to shudder. His sharp teeth graze my inner thighs before his tongue returns its attention to my sex that's dripping for him. My moans of pleasure increase around his cock, causing vibrations that add fuel to his desire. I use my fingers to add pressure to that sweet spot behind his balls.

Pushing my ass back farther, I start to ride his face, causing him to react by bucking his hips. I relax my throat to take him deeper with each thrust. Pressure builds, eventually sending me into an orgasm. Jax, too, is pushed over the edge, releasing his hot seed into my mouth. Unlike past encounters, I enjoy his sweet taste and suck him down without hesitation.

"You're incredible, Dana," he says breathlessly.

"Back at ya, big guy." I collapse onto my side with my left arm and leg sprawled lazily across his body. His twig and berries give me a scenic view from here. I let my left hand roam his lower half, feeling the stiff V of his abs, toned thighs, and heavy balls. The cover gives no warning before collapsing under our weight. We topple onto one another as the center of the hot tub cover meets the water. Warm water washes over the top.

"Oh shit," Jax laughs.

We maneuver off the broken top, chuckling to ourselves. It takes only a moment for our eyes to connect and for the heat between us to reignite. Power oozes off him as he fully unleashes his dominance.

"Come here, I'm not done with you." His voice is deep and thick with this animal's presence.

He pulls me up into his arms, and my legs straddle him. We collide with the lower-level sliding door, unaware of our surroundings because we're too wrapped up in one another. Jax shoves the door open harder than necessary and stumbles in. My back connects with the wall before his mouth is back on mine. His large erection slides in with ease, his desire mirroring mine.

"Yes!" I cry out. Fucking fuck yes! In a quick motion, I'm tossed over the saddle-colored sofa arm.

"Gods, you feel so amazing," Jax groans as he thrusts into me from behind.

I cry out at the incredible sensation. I'm so close to the edge already, but an urge pulls me back. I need to see him when he comes undone from our all-consuming passion.

Giving my hips a hard thrust back, I turn, catching his waist to toss him onto the couch. I jump onto his lap, sliding him back inside me before I begin riding him. Throwing my head back, I push my chest forward. Lowering his mouth, he bites one of my nipples. My climax hits so hard my vision blurs, tremors rack my body, and my teeth elongate. Jax follows with an additional thrust. I look upon his face of pure orgasmic bliss, knowing I did that. Our eyes connect in a universe-aligning moment. This is where we belong, forever.

Jo shoves forward, pushing me down into that sweet spot between his neck and collarbone.

"Mark what's ours," the devil in my head shouts.

At this moment, a hurricane of emotions threatens to drown me. Our sole focus becomes to claim our mate, bonding us together forever. The storm winds sweep away everything else, raging through my emotional state. My teeth graze the spot where our mark will be displayed for the rest of our lives. *This is MINE.*

Jax stiffens. "Dana." Wrapping his hot hands firmly on my forearms, he tries to push me into an upright position. This helps clear some of the mate-bond induced haze.

"Joey, no!" I command. *"He's not ready! Marking another against their will is punishable by death, and you know that."*

She snarls, lashing out at me as I try to shove her back. It reminds me of our early days together when I had no control over the beast. She thrashes and claws, forcing me to squeeze my eyes shut as I endure the pain.

"Do it now, or you'll lose us another mate!" Her words slice open old wounds.

"No! You're wrong." I want to help her see reason, but she's too feral right now. *"Marking him without consent will lose him forever. Now, back the fuck down! We need to give him a little more time."* Digging deeper, I lace my words with authority.

Inside my mind, I push her with all my might to lock her deep inside, so she has space to calm down. Uncontrollable tremors shake my body as we face off.

"Joey, back down," Mars' voice emanates in our mind.

Finally, we're getting through to her. She retreats, allowing my shaking body to relax. Jax's strong arms hold me as I fall limp onto his chest. A long, melancholy howl sounds in the depths of my mind. Failure isn't part of Joey's DNA. Disappointment, anger, unworthiness, and fear of losing another mate radiate from her. Her emotions hurt my heart because I, too, worry about those things.

I squeeze my eyes shut, begging tears not to fall. *What crazy person cries after the best sex of their life? Not this girl.*

"Deep breaths." Those warm hands rub up and down my exposed back. My body is now cool, the fire inside having receded to a normal level.

Though he hasn't asked for an explanation or apology, I feel one is due. "I'm sorry, I lost control of Joey. She isn't always easy to coexist with, given her strength. With the natural urge to mark you, and fear of losing another mate, it overrode all her logic. If Mars hadn't gotten through to her, we'd be in a world of trouble right now. You and I agreed to wait, which I respect, and I'll continue to honor that vow until you're ready."

"You don't have to apologize. Mars is frustrated, too. Our animals will never understand nor accept our decision to wait."

I lean forward, hiding my face in his neck while I try to wrangle stupid tears back.

"Dana."

I look up at him, still feeling ashamed.

"You want our bond and have no reservations?" he asks.

I look him in the eyes and confidently reply, "Yes, I want you forever."

Smiling, his hand brushes away one stray tear. "I hope to be there soon. Please have patience with me."

All I can do is nod as a pang of rejection cracks across my heart. Self-preservation instincts start reviewing blueprints to construct a protective wall around it. *No! Stop! None of that. He wants us; he just needs more time. Everyone moves at their own pace.*

He carries me bridal style to his room, where he prepares a warm bath for us. The master bath features a nice, deep jacuzzi soaking tub. We both need a cleanse after our time spent rolling around on the muddy forest floor.

Snuggling in each other's embrace as the warm water jets relax our bodies, we talk until everything feels right between us again. Jo swears to the Goddess that she'll keep her fangs to herself while we continue to postpone our official mating. With that out of the way, we get back to the good stuff of exploring one another's bodies. All I want is to memorize every inch of him and become the ringleader of his pleasure.

CHAPTER TWENTY-EIGHT

Dana

Morning Meditations

Gentle kisses wrapped in his leathery scent touch my face, pulling me out of a deep sleep.

"Hey, time to get up." Jax nuzzles my neck.

"No," I protest, swatting at him.

"Get up, human! My radar is picking up on a high likelihood of sexy time in our near future!"

"Come on, beautiful. I've got a surprise for you." Turning to face the clock on the nightstand, it reads 5:00 A.M. *What the—?*

"Five A.M.? No surprise is worth getting up this early. I'm going to have to pass." Rolling over, I snuggle back into the cotton sheets that are fresh with our intermixed scent. *Ah, so yummy smelling.*

"You can't tell me Joey isn't already up and ready to go. Jo, can I get an assist here?"

"GET UP!" Joey shouts obnoxiously.

"Nope, she's sleeping like a log."

"Liar," he says in exasperated humor.

"UGH, fine," I roll back over to look at him. "She wants to know if this surprise involves the rock-hard member between your legs and multiple orgasms?"

Amusement twinkles in his eyes as he shakes his head. "Later, but only if you get your butt up now."

A soft peck lands on my lips before he hands me a green smoothie in a mason jar. I eye it with suspicion before giving it a hesitant sniff. I want to ensure he's not one of those people who drink grass all in the name of health. Hints of spinach, banana, strawberries, and coconut are a relief.

"Fine, I'll get up, but only because you're sexy and it's hard to say no to you."

"That's my girl."

Crawling out of bed, I sip the green drink and toss on proper attire for a *"light hike,"* making sure to complain the entire time.

My efforts are rewarded when I'm presented with a mouthwatering breakfast burrito.

Outside, we follow a winding, narrow path through the woods, hand in hand. There's a chill in the air since it's the ass crack of dawn. We walk for a solid twenty minutes before we reach a clearing where we sit on the new spring grass. Jax pulls me into his lap where we hold one another while watching the sun rise over the forest's tree line.

"How are you feeling this morning?" His question breaks the comfortable silence surrounding us.

"Perfect, and you?" I ask.

"I'm feeling great."

It makes me happy to hear this. I snuggle into him, enjoying the warmth of his body. "Do you come here often to watch the sunrise?"

"Almost every morning. After which, I stretch and meditate. Maintaining the level of self-control Mars and I've mastered has taken decades of practice and a solid routine."

"Is that your secret to always being Mr. Laid-Back, calm as a cucumber?" I joke.

"It's some of it. My hope is we can have a morning routine together. You might find it helpful."

Frowning. "What makes you think I don't have my own tranquil morning routine?"

"Do you?" he asks curiously.

"Sleeping in seems like a solid routine to me."

"Sleep is always good for the body, but does it help ground you and calm the hotheaded beast inside?" he challenges.

"Hey!" Jo surges forward to shoot dagger eyes.

"Not helping your case, Big Energy."

"Look, I won't judge what works for you or ask you to change. As you know, in my childhood, I held deep emotions around my family members' deaths. Even as a young lycan, those unchecked emotions pushed Mars to give in to our animalistic nature too often. Uncontrolled power, emotions, or anything can lead to destruction. I've seen it take too many lives. True power lies in maintaining control of our actions. All I want is the best for you. I can't imagine the complexity of having an animal inside, along with the fire magic coursing through your veins."

He isn't wrong. However, it hurts my pride to admit it. Joey can be a huge, dominant, unreasonable pain in the ass at times, causing us to fly off the handle. Hell, our job is hanging in the balance right now, but in all honesty, we both dug that hole together.

Joey gives a nod. *"Ride or die, human."*

"Yoga and meditation aren't something I've ever been interested in. I usually find my grounding by beating the shit out of someone on the training grounds or releasing the flames. And as of lately, fucking you surely Zens me out. But I'm open, so teach me your ways, Master Lycan Jedi."

Happiness spreads across his face. "Let's try it every morning for the next week. If you decide it's not for you, that's totally okay."

"Deal," I say. My hands run up his thighs and make sure to stop at my favorite destination between his legs. "Shall we seal it with a quickie?"

After our sunrise romp, we head back for a round of stretching and meditation. I really suck at meditation. How can anyone calm their mind? I'd like to see Gandhi give it the ol' college try with another presence in his mind. Especially when said presence likes to have a non-stop running commentary on how bad you are at meditating. Meditation might lead me to finally lose my mind.

Eventually, I give up, interrupting Jax to confide in him about my lack of mental calmness. In turn, he scolds Jo like a naughty pup. I'd say there's a fifty/fifty chance she listens to him about the importance of helping me clear our mind, instead of causing more chaos with her comedy hour.

Jax calls it early on today's lesson. We each pick up a hot mug of coffee and return to the upper deck to savor it on a cozy outdoor sectional. The wood of the frame matches a small coffee table seated in front of it. My theory that Jax built these furniture pieces, along with the table below, gets confirmed. A soft white blanket hangs over one of the couch arms, just waiting to be snuggled in. Thankfully, Jax had his retractable awning open last night, which helped keep everything dry from the storm. Sipping our coffee, we listen to the birds serenade us with their morning melodies. *Gosh, I want to stay here forever.*

Ajax

In this simple moment, I feel my mind, spirit, and body have reached harmony. A soft morning breeze rustles the trees, adding to the melody of the forest animals. Warmth from Dana seeps into my side, where she is currently snuggled close. Her smoky floral scent carries to me, along with another one of my favorite scents: the Earth after rain. My mind is clear; it wants this woman forever.

Dana sits completely still, her breathing rhythmic and slow. She has a soft, tranquil expression on her face as she looks toward the forest. Through our strengthened bond, I feel nothing weighs on her as she reflects on the new day. Something tells me my Fiery Wolf has little time to slow down and absorb a simple moment such as this. I know this firsthand, as that has been my life for the past ten years while serving The Guardians. The work is necessary but soul-depleting. Sensing she's being watched, she turns her softly crinkled eyes my way.

She pokes my cheek. "What's that goofy look for?"

"I'm just happy. This moment feels perfect."

"Perfect." She hums thoughtfully. Unexpectedly, she reaches for the blanket on the arm of the couch and tosses it over our laps.

I raise a questioning eyebrow at her. "Are you cold?"

"No," her reply is quick and sure. Next, her hand grabs my coffee before setting it on the side table. I continue to stare at her in confusion.

"I want to make it even more perfect, but I don't want coffee spilled on my head in the process."

Her hand slides into my joggers, giving me a good squeeze. The little vixen holds my gaze as she ascends to her knees. My cock stiffens at the thought of her swallowing me whole again. Pulling the blanket completely off, I toss it aside, unwilling to miss the show.

"Hey!" she complains. "If the M&M duo shows up, it's on you, Bud."

"I'm willing to take the risk." All shifters have heard the ridiculous stories of mate connections. Most people are aware of the risks associated with unannounced visits to new mates.

Intense eyes hold mine as her tongue runs the length of my shaft. Slouching into the sofa, I push my hips forward, allowing my lower body to stretch out around her. Claiming some control, I lace my hand through her hair to help guide her mouth.

"Yes," I groan.

It doesn't take long before I'm battling the growing pressure begging to be released. I'm not ready for it to end yet, but her talented mouth wins, gifting me with my second orgasm for the morning.

Mars rumbles his approval at our mate caring for us this way. *"Goddess, we're so lucky to have been blessed with her."*

"Yeah, I'm not sure what we did to deserve her," I agree with the beast.

Rising from her knees, she helps slide my pants back up in case anyone would be stupid enough to pop over. Remnants of what she just drew from me linger on her lips that gently meet mine. Settling in beside me, she returns to sipping her coffee while admiring the forest below. This woman has no idea how perfect she is, or that she already owns my entire soul.

Agony rolls in, reminding me, I can't have her, not yet, because I have a job to do. I made a commitment that I'm struggling to focus on because of the beautiful distraction that is my mate. *Get focused, Blackclaw...*but internal pep talks do nothing.

Mars starts trying to come up with a solution. *"We need to find more time to work, like after our mate goes to bed and in the early morning. We know she isn't a morning person. Maybe we should do morning meditations every other day? Then on the off day, we get up extra early to review capture footage."*

"Yeah, maybe that could work. I do have a lot of footage to review." I feel exhausted thinking about it. *"Maybe I should connect with our squad brothers. Evan would know what I should do."* I debate,

feeling as if I need to confide in someone about the struggle I'm dealing with.

"Evan would tell you to stop thinking with your dick and not understand how much mating instincts hijack your life. The bond's there to bring two people together, like fate said it's meant to be, no matter what. It's incapable of factoring in outside circumstances," Mars reasons.

"You're right. Let's give it a little while longer to see if we can get caught up on work; if not, I'll call them for advice."

"Okay. We also need to check with Dolken to see if he spoke to the vampire," Mars reminds me.

"Shit, you're right. See, I can't focus around our, Fiery Wolf."

Mars' determination to hang on to her and succeed in our job lights a fire inside me. I grasp onto that hope because selfishly, I'm not ready to let her go.

CHAPTER TWENTY-NINE

Dana

Blood Oath Ceremony

Who's this woman staring back at me in my reflection? She's radiant, and so stinkin' happy. Way happier than I've ever been.

Guilt worms its way in, reminding me that women are missing and I've failed at finding them. Guilt loves to put pressure on my shoulders, and I allow it to do so freely because I was given a second chance. The Goddess chose me; what are the odds of coming back from death? Selene is counting on me to make the Earthly realm a better place for our people.

But tonight I shove the guilt away, remembering Charles' words, *"I know that blessed crimson DNA of yours drives you to protect others above yourself, but know you're allowed to choose yourself and your happiness."*

"Not every case can be solved. Let's enjoy our time tonight," Joey agrees.

I look at my reflection with resolve in my eyes. Tonight, I am going to allow myself to be happy.

An elegant black, floor-length velvet gown hugs my curves perfectly. The long-sleeve dress is simple, featuring a flattering sweetheart neckline that accentuates a hint of cleavage. A revealing slit along the side exposes my toned leg without any sign of protruding calf bones. Black ankle-strapped heels with a crystal-encrusted band lay over my toes, adding four inches to my height. *Why can't tactical boots or Crocs be formally acceptable?* Heels are so impractical, not to mention painful. I hard-passed on the silver pointy-toed pumps that, according to my personal stylist, "would look the best". She can keep those bunion bakers far away from my feet.

Finishing off the look are the most glamorous pair of Art Deco diamond and drop pearl earrings that Jax surprised me with earlier. His sister was kind enough to lend them to me at his request, as they belonged to their mother. The thoughtfulness of the item sent my heart soaring, and tears to my eyes. *What's with the waterworks lately?* The mate bond has really had me feeling all the feels and caused me to become an emotional sap. *Frickin' mate bonds.*

Gamila insisted I use one of her hair and makeup stylists for the event. The talented stylist beautifully enhanced my natural look, making me feel confident without pushing me out of my comfort zone. My makeup bag consists of some clumpy mascara and tinted chapstick. I was impressed that she was able to fill a fully loaded cosmetic suitcase on wheels. She styled my hair in loose curls that cascade effortlessly in golden waves over my shoulders. All the fuss felt like too much, but I truly appreciated it.

My brother and Charles would be soaking up every second of this pampering without concern. The thought of my brother causes guilt again to pierce my chest. *Soon, I'll tell them. There's no need to fuss over it now.*

A knock at the door of my estate suite has my pulse quickening. Nervous energy associated with blossoming love rolls through me at the thought of being back in the arms of my man. The notion is crazy, seeing as we spent the entire day together, aside from getting ready for the event. Jax even joined me at my training session with Isla, working through the same maneuvers with her parents. My wingman, my ride or die, my mate.

"Come in," I call out.

Having become so familiar with him, my body starts to ignite the moment he reenters our space. My handsome lycan strides in wearing a form-fitting classic black suit and tie. Damn, the man can rock a suit. The usual dark strands of his messy hair have been tamed with a little product for tonight's formal event. Those ravenous eyes on me reveal signs of the beast that lurks inside. Jax in a suit oozes confidence, with a spice of sex that demands your attention. This might be my favorite version of him because this suit doesn't hide his true power; it exudes it.

"Yummy! A perfectly fitted suit on him is my version of male lingerie," Joey drools.

"I agree!"

"Um..." He clears his throat. "Wow! Dana, you look stunning. Beyond stunning, I don't have proper words to tell you how beautiful you are."

"What? No poetry or hymns from a former life of yours you can recite regarding the depth of my beauty?" I mock with a hand to my chest in feigned hurt.

"I'll add that to my next life goals." The distance between us vanishes as I'm caught by the waist and pushed back against the wall. Sliding a flowing strand of hair behind my ear, he admires his mother's earrings.

His eyes turn tender. "I knew they would look perfect on you."

"I love them. Thank you for getting them for me to wear tonight."

"You're welcome."

He leans in to brush his nose on mine. It detours down to the crook of my neck, where he takes a deep pull of my scent. Pure sexual desire pulses through our incomplete bond, fanning the embers of my desire.

"My stylist might castrate you if you mess up her makeup job," I warn, knowing where this is heading.

"It's a gamble I'm willing to take." One hand moves lower under my dress slit to squeeze my ass. Growling, he pauses, "And where are your undergarments, lass?"

I can't help but tease, "Undergarments? I think you just aged yourself, Mr. Blackclaw."

"Are you calling me old?" The challenge is clear in his tone and by the way he squeezes my ass harder.

"Well, you are older than my parents." That earns me a hard spank on the backside. Our age difference doesn't bother me because, when you're immortal, it matters very little. My man, while in his seventies, looks to be only in his thirties. If he were human and only a decade away from a nursing home, it'd be another story. Most shifters continue to look around thirty to forty years old throughout their adult lives.

Giving in to our desires, we make quick work fucking against the pretty, powdered, blue wall. Afterward, we hastily freshen up in the en suite bathroom before arriving fashionably late to the cocktail hour ahead of the main event.

The silver and dark blue-themed event hall gleams with pride as it welcomes all its guests. The estate's ballroom is bustling with pack members in elegant tuxedos and gowns for this evening's black tie event. Instantly, I decide I'd rather retreat to the comfort of Jax's place than face the cool stares of our critics.

There's an additional layer of stress tonight since I'll be meeting Jax's sister and brother-in-law for the first time. Not to mention, I'm the only werewolf in attendance. *Super.* Bring on all the stress. Vigilant Joey is already scanning our surroundings for signs of a threat. Jax offers his elbow, reassuring me without words. I give him a grateful squeeze on his bicep in return.

No surface was forgotten in the meticulous planning for tonight. Carefully arranged, lavish floral displays featuring moon-flowers symbolize luck and prosperity for the unborn prince. Banners of the Silverthrone Crest are sprinkled around the hall, reminding its visitors whose home they're in. A second-story balcony is used solely by palace guards who diligently scan the crowds below, some of whom I recognize from my brief time inside these walls. Large round dining tables draped in dark blue are filled with seated guests, scattered across the glossy, checkered wood floors. Massive overhead chandeliers cast a warm glow over the room, creating a more intimate atmosphere.

The ceiling is as breathtaking as the Sistine Chapel. A painted masterpiece of the Moon God, Lycaon depicts lycans in animal form paying homage to their original creator in various ways under a starry sky. Taking a picture might draw too much unwanted attention to me. *Perhaps there's a gift shop in this part of the estate where I can purchase a souvenir magnet.*

Joey huffs at me. *"Will you give it up on the gift shop already?"*

I remind her, *"Our pack has a gift shop, so it isn't that far-fetched."*

Servers hustle past us to replenish the buffet table that has a long line of hungry lycans, all of whom have bottomless stomachs. Mine grumbles at the selection of roasted meats I can smell, begging us to join the lengthy line. The far wall consists of floor-to-ceiling windows, some of which are retractable. Several are open to the outside, allowing the cool night breeze to filter in. Children play freely in the green space, screeching with delight.

Soft music is playing through hidden speakers, but it's hard to make out with the cacophony of life occurring at the event. Howls of laughter roar from various points throughout the room. The atmosphere's energy is higher than I expected, considering the recent events around the pack. Curious pack members send a variety of looks our way. Most people get that blank, far-off look on their faces that is common when mindlinking with another. Others don't even bother to hide their snide remarks.

"What's the wolf doing here?"

"I see he hasn't marked her yet. He must have some doubts."

"Because he knows he can do better than a dog."

"I don't even believe the fated mates story."

"She isn't even that pretty."

Ouch. Joey's temper flares, throwing gasoline on our internal flames. The urge to wave a flaming middle finger in their direction is strong, but I practice restraint. The King and Queen invited me as a guest. It would be dishonorable to turn their ceremony into a flaming fight ring.

"It would make it more memorable," Jo argues, just itching for a fight.

"No, rein it in. Try some meditation since you're so good at it," I tell her sarcastically.

I take a deep inhale and lift my head a little higher while sending out a fraction of my aura as a warning. Jax pulls me closer to his side as a silent reminder of his favorite saying, "ignore them, Smoke Show". Jo lets out an overly dramatic sigh, fighting with her instincts. Instead of dishing out several beatdowns, she decides to sing. Launching into a remix of Taylor Swift's, "Shake It Off" as we continue through the crowd of judgmental onlookers. *FML.*

"Shake it off, Shake it off
And the haters gonna hate, hate, hate, hate, hate,
And bitches are going to get stitch, stitch, stitch, stitches,
And I'm just going to flip, flip, flip, flip, flip.
Flip them off. Flip them off."

"Wow, T-Shifter, quite the tune there. You really need your own side show," I tell her.

"I know!" she says confidently.

Finally, we spot a table with familiar faces who are happy to see us. Mickey and Miguel sit beside a couple who I presume are their parents. The woman stands abruptly after spotting us.

"Jax!" she squeals in delight. The voluptuous, dark-haired, dark-eyed beauty pulls him into her clutches.

Then her attention turns to me. "Dana? Wow, you're positively stunning, my dear, and tall for a she-wolf. Oh, and your mother's earrings, Jax! They're perfect," she gushes as she pulls me into a bone crushing hug. A quick inhale tells me she's related to M&M.

"How are you feeling, dear?" Her worry reads genuine. My intuition tells me she feels and processes emotions at a deep level. Her sons inherited this trait from her, though they mask it well.

"Ma, remember you should tell someone who you are before throwing yourself at them," Miguel says dryly, as if he's seen his mother do this a hundred times before.

"Right, right." Her hand waves dismissively. "I'm Dottie, these three rascals' mother. The handsome man sitting there is Frank, my mate."

Frank continues to sip on his beer but gives a little wave.

I give her a warm smile. "It's nice to meet you both. By the way, thank you for the amazing cookies. They definitely helped my recovery."

"I'm so glad you enjoyed them. Come sit, you two, we saved you each a seat." She waves us forward. Dottie retakes her seat next to Frank. Flanking Frank's left is Mickey, followed by Miguel.

"We were all so worried about you after the attack. I sent prayers to Lycaon and Selene for your recovery," she tells me.

"Turns out Dana didn't need your prayers, Ma, because she's besties with the Goddess," Miguel whispers conspiratorially to his mother.

My eye roll is automatic as I take the silver-covered seat on his left. The last thing I need is goddess slumber party stories spreading around these parts. "Don't listen to him, he's spewing nonsense," I say.

The right corner of Frank's mouth tips up. "He's done that since he was a pup."

I reach for the water pitcher on our table and notice the twins with matching sly grins.

"Jax's been spewing things as well, seeing as you both reek of each other's dirty bits. Thanks for making us all smell it," Miguel complains.

I pinch Jax's leg beneath the table, reminding him that he's the one responsible for this ridicule.

"Not sorry." He gives my leg a little pinch back.

"Pretty sure everyone has already smelled them with all the rutting they've been doing around the woods," Mickey adds.

"Boys! You leave them alone. The mate bond is just weaving its magic." Dottie gets a far-off, dreamy look in her eye. "You know, I remember when your father and I first—"

"Mom, stop that thought right there. We don't want to hear it," Mickey barks.

Miguel shudders. "Gross. I don't need to add Mom and Dad bumping uglies stories to the list of traumas I need to unpack with my therapist."

Frank huffs, fatigue crossing his face. "Miguel, do we need to remind you of the car situation? Your mother is still traumatized from that."

The Fangersons are quite an entertaining group. Their bickering provides the much-needed comic relief that helps me relax in these surroundings. They accept me so easily as one of their own, which brings out the warm fuzzies inside.

"Hey, have either of you two heard any updates on Karissa's case?" Jax mindlinks with Mickey, Miguel, and me.

"The vamp's number was easy to find in her phone. We think she deleted their text exchange since there was none, and Isla mentioned them texting. Her parents are getting phone records. Dolken tried to call the number, but his phone was off." Mickey updates us.

"Of course, the dude's name is Sly. Like, tell me what supernatural being you are without telling me," Miguel side tangents.

"Right, and Tech man is trying to trace his number to a home address," Mickey adds.

Chester's hurried arrival cuts our conversation short. The guard stands tall, a picture of professionalism in his official royal silver and dark blue uniform.

"Excuse me, sorry to interrupt." Chester turns to face me directly. "Miss Dana, the King and Queen would like an audience with you."

Jax's mouth tightens into a line. "At this hour?" he asks, sounding as confused as I feel.

Chester places a reassuring hand on his shoulder. "Yes. It's all good, I can assure you there's nothing to worry about regarding your mate."

"What could they possibly want that they couldn't wait until after their ceremony?" I wonder.

"Maybe they're considering taking you up on our offer to help stand guard during the ceremony," Jo considers.

"Yes, that's probably it."

"We really must get going," Chester urges me.

"Um, okay," I say. Before Jax can fully stand to join me, Chester stops him. "Sorry, Ajax, only Dana."

Hesitance mixed with a healthy dose of frustration can be felt from Jax's side of the bond.

"It's fine," I whisper before quickly kissing his lips. "I'll be back."

"Chester, please escort her back here right after this meeting." Damn, with that commanding tone and suit, my man's sex appeal is off the charts. Chester gives him a nod before turning to escort me from the crowded ballroom. It feels like everyone is watching us, leading to more whispers all around.

"The dog isn't allowed to stay," someone snickers under her breath.

"Please just let me kick that one person's ass?" Joey begs with puppy-dog eyes and all.

"No! Sing your song again, or do something not related to harming pack members."

CHAPTER THIRTY

Dana

The Vow

I'm in disbelief to learn that the King and Queen have chosen me to be one of their unborn son's Blood Oath Protectors. They assured me the vow wouldn't require me to follow the male around for the rest of my life, acting as his personal bodyguard. Instead, I'd be considered an ally to their family. Someone they trust and who holds my loyalty in the highest regard. They know if called upon in time of need, I would come.

From what I understand, to be chosen is one of the highest honors among the lycans. Often bestowed only upon other family members, lycan nobility, or their kind's most elite warriors. I remind them several times that I'm a werewolf. This being such a big deal and all, I don't want them to hastily make a decision they later regret, like a face tattoo.

Gamila quickly dismisses my hesitations, reassuring me with her confidence. "It's time to set aside old prejudices. Without your heroic actions, who knows where this little one, or I, would be right now. You're a protector, *our* protector. I can feel in my soul you'll always be connected to us."

Gamila's a forward thinker, which is precisely what the lycans need. "Oh, and not only will you be the first werewolf but also the first woman ever to receive such an honor. Go big, I guess." The gleam in her eye speaks volumes. This little rebel loves to push the boundaries.

Joey puffs and preens at the Queen's words. Pride practically radiates from her midnight fur. Goddess, this will inflate that large head of hers even more.

Joey struts around in my mind's eye. *"Damn right it will! You can't stop this level of awesome."*

"Okay, tone it back, tacky bumper sticker. And what if the prince turns out to be a psychopath like his grandfather, Andras? We don't want to be tied in some magical bond with that."

Joey's confident in this decision without any reservations. *"I have a good feeling about this. Let's do it."*

I sigh, not needing much of a push on this. *"Okay, I'm in too."*

Searching out Jax in our mind, we quickly mindlink him, letting him know our shocking news. Pride and admiration flow through our connection, swirling within me and confirming the emotions I feel. I wish more than anything that Jax could be here with me as I wrestle with this imposter syndrome, trying to convince me I don't belong here. His calming presence would definitely squelch it.

Cher approaches, beaming, in a show-stopping silver gown that highlights her figure perfectly. She pulls me into her chest.

"Dana, you look lovely this evening." Dropping her voice, she whispers into my ear, "I told them they would be the biggest dumbasses on this planet and Eden, if they didn't choose you for this honor. Most of the pack elders were upset with it and fought against their decision. I told them, fuck those old bastards, it's your baby and your choice."

Her sassy attitude makes me smile. "Well, thanks for the referral."

Being as I'm utterly ignorant of the process, she gives me a full rundown of tonight's events. The King and Queen have selected five protectors: two are from high noble bloodlines, great-grandfather, Dolken, Beta Matt, and me.

Jo fluffs up in disgust at the mention of Matt's name. *"The only thing the King and Queen will regret is choosing that hoodwinker."*

My thoughts are the same. There's something off about the Beta. The idea of that man being anywhere near the little prince causes my hackles to rise. Matt catches my hard stare directed his way and gives me one of his perfected candy smiles.

"Congratulations, Crimson, on such a high honor," his voice carries over the room for all to hear.

"You as well, Beta." I nod in acknowledgment before turning away. The other two males don't even spare me a glance. *Assholes.*

We're all required to change into nothing but a heavy, dark blue velvet robe that will be easy to shift from. The robes are beautifully crafted, containing silver stitching that incorporates the symbols of the Moon God, Lycaon, and the Goddess Selene. Tiny shimmering moonstones are scattered throughout, capturing the gentle glow of our moon tonight. The King and Queen wear similar silver robes, but with blue stitching. Gamila's outfit is distinctive due to a large opening in the front, putting her baby bump on full display. Her firm belly features a silver-painted design of five crescent moons encircling the Silverthrone mark.

The time passes quickly, bringing us to the big event. Guests have been directed outside to the large lawn next to the ballroom, where they can sit in the arranged chairs or stand freely. Large, soft-glowing candles in glass votives illuminate the walking path. The aisle opens into a sizable circle outlined with the same votive candles. The design's simplicity doesn't diminish its beauty. An elder from the pack, dressed in a red velvet robe, waits patiently in the center, ready to guide us through the ceremony. In a single-file line, we follow the parents-to-be, with little old me bringing up the rear.

My body senses my mate's nearness, but it's soon overshadowed by the cold pricks of awareness from hundreds of eyes. Most of the crowd wears appalled expressions directed solely at me.

By the time I reach the inner circle, sweat has formed around my body thanks to this heavy robe. The graceful night breeze offers no relief in this situation. My skin feels itchy, though I contemplate if that's a side effect of the hard glares directed my way. I adopt my best poker face, revealing nothing to my critics. Jo bares her teeth at the audience's lack of respect.

"Jo, haters gonna hate, sticks and stones, whatever. We expected this type of reaction. Now let's just concentrate so we don't make a fool of ourselves by missing something."

The pack elder begins the ceremony by bestowing a blessing on Gamila and the little prince for a safe birth. Then, one by one, the chosen protectors are called forward to present ourselves in front of the royal couple. Dolken stands first, with his hands extended and elbows bent. Already scarred palms from past battles, face upwards as he recites the oath back to his loved ones. King Anders carefully runs a silver dagger vertically down his palm, leaving a permanent reminder of his vow on this day. Dolken reaches forward and places his bleeding palm on one of the painted crescent moons on Gamila's stomach. Magic takes hold, causing the blood to travel along the silver moon's line, turning it red. Cher told me each protector is rewarded with a short glimpse into the prince's future as the blood magic takes root.

What will I see? The thought causes knots to form in my gut and dread to wash over me. From what Cher has heard, the glimpses consist of only a few brief seconds of the protector with the future King. *It's nothing crazy. Relax, Dana.*

No more than four seconds pass before Dolken's face lifts. "I saw my great-grandson be crowned," he announces softly. Gamila heaves a sigh of relief. I never thought about what would happen if a child never made it to wear the crown. The next three chosen pass quickly. We learn that the future king will be a strong fighter and well-educated. Matt's words feel vague, as he tells Gamila and Anders that his people will love him. My instincts sense a lie, but Anders and Gamila appear blinded by the reassuring "vision" regarding their son's future.

Finally, my turn arrives. My hands shake with pent-up adrenaline, so I ball them into fists. *There'll be none of that.* Walking forward on silent steps, I hold my head high. *I'm meant to be here.* Gamila's face shows reassurance, while Anders' does nothing to make me feel at ease.

The air seems to be still. *Is everyone collectively holding their breath, or is it just me?* I take a deep breath before reciting my oath to ensure my words carry power.

"Before God Lycaon, Goddess Selene, and these witnesses, I Dana Jo Johnston, blessed crimson wolf of Moonborn Pack, vow that for as long as my heart beats, I will protect and never cause harm to the future King of Silverthrone. I shall answer his call without hesitation, never abandoning in fear, nor wavering in loyalty, but standing firm by his side. With this vow, I seal it in not only my word, but with my blood."

King Anders rapidly slices my left palm. The area of my skin where the knife's tip touched burns as the silver leaves its permanent mark. *At least it isn't a face tattoo.* I place my hand gently on the last remaining shimmering silver moon. Immediately, my vision turns white, and all my senses shut down.

I want to panic, but I refrain. The bright white of my vision slowly recedes, allowing my eyes to refocus. Before me stands a handsome man in his early twenties, dressed in a perfectly fitted tux, smiling down at his stunning mate. His dark eyes and thick dark hair are the same as his mother's. *Whoa, this is the future king's mating ceremony?* My heart beats faster as I watch the couple. They're fated mates. I'm not sure how, but I know this to be true. Their love is powerful, and being fortunate enough to witness it moves me to tears.

They're a timeless picture as they stand outside behind a large wooden table decorated with flowers and levitating candles in this very area. The setting sun casts a gorgeous pink glow across the skyline. The scene steals my breath away. My attention is pulled back to the woman at his side. A lycan by her build, delicate but strong, blonde hair, and familiar features. Her dress is a simple A-line lace gown that falls off the shoulders. Nothing about it screams royal wedding, but no dress could be more perfect for her. *How do I know that?* I struggle to place the familiarity, but when I try to enter into the archives of my mind, I feel only static. The answer bobs beneath a glass surface that I can't penetrate.

"Jo, can you catch her scent?"

"No, my smeller isn't working here, but the Prince is trying to gain your attention."

My attention snaps to him. "Hello, is this thing on? I have an important announcement here," he says, hands waving wildly in my direction.

When did he get a microphone? His beautiful bride, along with the surrounding wedding guests, slowly fades away until the two of us remain.

The Prince flashes me his perfect white teeth. "Finally. Dana, we don't have much time. I already have a request for you. One that will cost you a sacrifice but benefit many."

Say what? Cryptic message much?

"Okay," I hesitate, unsure about this situation. It feels like I'm walking into a trap.

"Only you can eliminate one of the five who doesn't belong," he tells me.

Ahh. My stomach drops at his words. "Matt," I whisper.

His reply is a simple, "Yes."

The future Silverthrone King wants me to kill Beta Matt? Fuck.

"What has he done? How do I find proof of it? Do you want me to kill him now?" Questions start pouring out of me.

"He's a danger to my family, and no, do not kill him now. You must wait until he has revealed his true self, along with what remains unseen. That's the only way."

"Are you sure about this?" I ask skeptically. "What about your father? Won't he in return, murder me?" *Do I sound a little hysterical?*

"Yup, you do," Joey confirms.

"Not if you wait until the right moment. And speak of this request to no one. Fate has chosen you, now trust it." He has so much wisdom behind those dark eyes that are fixed on me. "Okay, Dana? Can you do this?"

I sigh dramatically in defeat. "Okay, unborn prince, since I don't think I can outrun fate." *I didn't read the fine print before signing up for what I just agreed to.*

"Until we meet again," he says, his tone eager.

The scene comes back into focus as he twirls his mate into a low dip. Long blonde curls free fall as she throws her head back in laughter. The groom seizes the opportunity to trail kisses up his bride's exposed neck. Again, tears spring to my eyes as I soak in the love they radiate.

As the scene fades, my heart starts to ache. It feels too soon, I'm not ready for this moment to end. My mind spins like a truck stuck in the mud, trying to comprehend all of it. *Why me?*

Joey knows. *"The cost of our rebirth."*

"Your wolf will help guide you... Trust her, she will hear my guidance for purposes unfulfilled." I hear Selene's words all those years ago.

The Goddess's price for my rebirth. Joey is right, from what I have heard, there is always a reason for the Goddess granting someone a second chance at life. Maybe this is our purpose. To kill this guy and protect the safety of the future Lycan Prince. The thought is too heavy to hold right now.

My senses slowly return, and I open my eyes to a horrified-looking Gamila. "Dana, what happened?" she demands, roughly grasping my shoulders.

Concern is blaring all over her pretty face. Anders puts a protective arm around her waist before shooting me a warning glare to choose my following words carefully. *What's happening?* Absent-mindedly, I begin wiping at my damp cheeks.

"Oh," I mumble, staring down at my wet fingertips. *Right, no one else came out of their vision crying, only smiling with joyful news.*

"Pull it together, human half, you're stressing the Queen."

"I, ahh. Um," I stutter before closing my mouth. Pausing, I take a breath while collecting my jumbled thoughts.

Joey groans, *"Wow, a goldfish could explain better than that."*

Goddess, why did I get blessed with this pain in the ass?

"Focus! The Queen!" Joey snaps.

"Sorry. Gamila, I can assure you it was nothing concerning. I mean, he was kind of a smartass. Which, my money's on him inheriting from his father," I try to joke to lighten the tension, but sound more like I'm rambling around the question.

Anders narrows his eyes at me. "Why are you crying?" his tone is sharp and commanding.

Flustered, I press on, "Seeing him and his beautiful mate at their mating ceremony brought happy tears to my eyes. That's all. I swear." Hushed conversations erupt throughout the crowd.

Anders looks even more horrified by this. "His mate? You saw her?" he presses.

"Y-yes?" More gasps from the peanut gallery. *Oh. Oh shit.*

"Jo, did I just reveal too much?"

"Yup, smooth move, goldfish."

"Miss Johnston, that can't be what you saw," the pack elder says condescendingly. "No one has ever seen the future king's mate, the future queen. That's privileged knowledge only the creators hold. Information such as that would be dangerous in the wrong hands," he warns me sternly.

"Inform this fossil that we are blessed by such goddess, thus she entrusted us also to hold this knowledge."

"Jo, I'm not pulling that card. Clearly, I fucked up in my flustered state of mind." I can taste the angst wafting off the soon-to-be parents. I try humor once again.

"Well, no need to fear. I'm horrendous at drawing, so you don't have to worry about me plastering her wanted posters around town."

Do they honestly believe I would do anything malicious with this information? The thought hurts, but I have to remind myself we are only newly acquainted. Taking Gamila's hand, I give it a gentle squeeze to try to ease her worry.

"And you insinuate I'm a smart ass?" Anders grumbles under his breath. He gives the pack elder a slight nod. I hope that gesture signals we shouldn't continue this conversation any further in front of the entire pack.

The elder clears his throat, gesturing for me to return to my original place among the five. I make sure not to make eye contact with Matt, though I feel his eyes as I pass.

For the final part of the ceremony, we must shift into our animal forms for their oaths. No one present aside from Ajax knows I can take on a wolf-lycan hybrid form. That side of myself is often hidden, as my wolf side is naturally more dominant. It requires extra energy, concentration, and control to use, which can mean the difference between life and death in a fight. This is my dirty little secret that I keep close to the chest. It has never failed to earn me the element of surprise.

"I'm having second thoughts about all these lycans knowing our truth," I confide in Joey.

She doesn't share my hesitation. *"Don't be chicken shit. Show them we belong."*

"But we'll lose the element of surprise among them if we ever need it."

"Yes, but maybe we'll start getting the damn respect we deserve. Dana, there's this whole other side of ourselves we rarely embrace. It's time. I'm sick of hiding who we truly are, and I can't wait to see their shocked faces!"

"Fine," I sigh, resigned to it. *"But you better be right about this, almighty blessed one."*

The others begin their shifts. Being pureblooded lycans, their transformation flows directly from standing. I haven't mastered that party trick yet. For me, we can only push the additional shift from our wolf form. Turning on my heels toward the long aisle, I throw myself into the change. Several in the audience sneer. One party pooper in the second row mutters, "fucking dog."

With that, Joey takes the reins.

"Teach them a lesson if you must, but PLEASE make it a minimal scene," I beg her.

We prowl forward as our bones start to rearrange for a second time. The sensation of hundreds of people focused on me causes my hackles to rise and flames to test the strength of their cage. Stepping onto my right and then left hind leg, we raise fully vertical before turning to glare at the man. The crowd emits a loud wave of shock.

"Surprise, mother fuckers!" Jo smirks.

Our crimson eyes blaze red as Jo searches out the man in the second row within the sea of spectators. The fire that always dances under my skin escapes momentarily, skipping along our fur before I firmly shove it back down. Our eyes lock with the asshat's, and Jo releases a menacing, dominant growl. Easily, he bares his neck in submission, as do most of the surrounding crowd members. The smell of fear flooding the air is a high that Jo never wants to come down from.

"Joey," Jax sends us a warning through mindlink.

"Oopsy, maybe a little too much?" she giggles.

"Yes, but very impressive and sexy as hell, I must say. We'll discuss your punishment later," Mars tells her, causing me to internally chuckle. He likes his mate's dominance.

Pulling our attention back to the royal parents, we walk to retake our place within the inner circle. All the male protectors have their eyes firmly locked on Joey as she saunters up. All the beasts exhibit signs of unease, knowing they aren't at the top of this food chain.

Gamila's mouth is slightly ajar, and Anders' sharp scowl could cut glass.

"Sorry about that, boss," I mindlink him and Gamila.

"How the hell are you doing that?" Anders rumbles.

"We can discuss it later," I inform them.

"Oh girl, we're so discussing the fact you failed to mention being a flaming hybrid badass bitch!" Gamila adds.

Rounding out the ceremony, Anders cuts each lycan's palm, collecting their blood along with ours into a ceramic bowl. The king dips his finger into the blood mixture, using it to trace the Silverthrone emblem's design. The remaining blood is burned with a final blessing, sealing our vow amongst the gods until our final breath. *Fuck.*

CHAPTER THIRTY-ONE

Dana

Rose

The ceremony concludes, and I desperately need a moment to process away from everyone. Hell, I'm probably going to need some wine, a therapist, and a year alone on a deserted island to process all of that. I make my way to the changing room, where I find a private restroom to claim shelter. I try to calm my reeling mind with calming breaths. *Come on, meditation lessons.* Did I unknowingly put a target on my back by exposing the truth about seeing the future king's mate?

My mother's unhelpful criticism pops into my head: "*You need to think before you speak, Dana Jo.*" I snarl, *fuck off, mother.*

Okay, focus, Dana, there are more pressing issues. What in the seven hells am I going to do about eliminating Beta Matt? Why couldn't he have asked one of the others to do his dirty work? Like, gee, I don't know, his great-grandfather!

"*Not a good choice, as he, too, is fooled by Matt's charms.*" Damn it, Joey is right.

Jax's soft voice and gentle knock tear me from my thoughts. "Hey, can I come in?" I fling the door open, revealing myself looking a little crazed.

"Are you alright? I can sense your distress," he says, locking the door behind him.

It takes one head-to-toe look at me before he quickly closes the distance between us. I am crushed against his warm chest. That leathery cedarwood scent of his washes away my manic thoughts like the tide. Nuzzling into his neck, I inhale the intoxicating pheromones of my mate, which helps my body relax. They're wonderful, better than any drug I've tried.

"I'm overwhelmed," I confess, not leaving the safe space of his neck. "Something I'm not good at admitting, but it's best not to discuss it here."

Soft lips meet the top of my head. "I understand. That was an incredible honor you received tonight. One of the highest among our kind, and with it comes great responsibility. It's a lot for anyone. I'm unbelievably proud of you, my Fiery Wolf." His strong hands stroke my back.

Tears brim in my eyes at his sincere words, but I hold them back. No one outside my family has ever told me they were proud of me for all I've accomplished. My soul swells a little more. *No crying. No crying,* I internally chant. *Add "mate's pride" to the growing list of items to reflect on later.*

"Please just take me home to your bed," I whine-beg.

There's a low rumble in his chest. "Nothing in the world would make me a happier man, but it's customary for the honored to stay. Many will want to bestow blessings of their own upon you."

"Bless me? Or ask me a million questions I don't want to answer?" I continue to whine like a child.

Chuckling, he cups my face, "I'm sure a bit of both. My sister and Draco are also waiting to meet you."

"Okay, but I'm not a natural charmer like you, Mr. Black-claw. My fake happy pageant expressions and BS tank are currently running on empty. I'll be giving off major fuck-off vibes."

"Don't sell yourself short. Just be yourself and all will be fine." He nuzzles my neck, holding me tight.

"Will you stay by my side?" I beg with my best pleading eyes.

He brings his lips to mine in a tender kiss. "Yes. Now, let's get out there."

Returning to the party, I must admit that with my mate at my side, I feel semi-recharged. His calming scent shovels away any of my growing anxieties, looking to tag along. Jax weaves us through the crowd toward an outside garden where his sister and brother-in-law wait.

They're kept waiting even longer as numerous pack members greet us. Everyone seems more curious than disappointed about the hybrid who has been hanging around. Several ask if I'll be officially joining the Silverthrone Pack, which leaves an uncomfortable sensation in my chest. With Jax by my side, he easily guides conversations away from topics we aren't ready to discuss openly.

We finally make our way to the fragrant, blossoming gardens behind the Royal Estate. Scattered pack members meander along paths, enjoying the showcase of floral sights. A beautiful woman with the same shade of sable-brown hair as Jax peers longingly into a tiered marble water fountain. She stands tall in a simple black midi dress, yet her posture is rigid. The man beside her has a bulky, muscular frame that looks barely contained by his white button-up shirt. Continually, his eyes scan the area as if the ghost of Andras will appear at any moment. Jax had shed more light on their story to help me understand Rose's sometimes standoffish personality.

One of the king's other wives, a close friend of Rose's, stabbed her multiple times in her lower abdomen with a silver blade. That woman then took her own life. Rose was ultimately dismissed due to her ruined womb. Draco was her former Royal Estate's guard, with whom she fell in love. They became chosen mates, but together they have never been able to have a child.

The pair tends to be reclusive due to their past traumas. They venture to significant pack events infrequently. The only reason they've stayed in the pack is because of Draco's large family presence. With all of Rose's family gone or living far away, she's left with little support. My heart broke hearing her story.

"Rosie. Draco," Jax calls as a way of greeting before bringing his sister in for a bear hug.

"Thank you for waiting. I'd like you to meet Dana." *My mate* is what I wish he had said. A slight pang of hurt pierces my heart. *You agreed to this, Dana. No, using the M word.*

"Hello, it's so nice to meet you," I say with the best smile I can muster. I extend a hand out to Rose to shake. *Gosh, is that too formal for my potential future sister-in-law?* Her facial expression is impassive as she looks me over, not giving off any feel-good vibes.

"Screw it, actually, I think hugs are in order," I embarrassingly announce as I go in for the squeeze. She's stiff under my touch. Pulling back, I turn to Draco, extending my hand for a firm shake. I decided it's best to avoid any more awkward hugs this evening.

"It's nice to meet you, too. Congratulations on your honor." Rose's tone is cool, but I don't detect any insincerity.

"Thank you." I give her a small smile.

Draco's protective internal wall doesn't seem as sturdy as his mate's, giving off a more friendly vibe. "Must say it was a bit of a surprise. I've never heard of a wolf getting such an honor before."

Jax wraps an arm around me, pulling me closer to his warmth. "None have," he brags with a cocky smirk on his lips.

Rose continues to study me. "Are you part lycan? I've never heard or seen a hybrid before, but anything is possible, I suppose."

"No, both my parents are wolves from Gamma bloodlines. My guess is it's an upgrade from Selene."

Draco's current scan of the area abruptly halts to focus on me fully. He looks confused.

"So, the rumors are true? My brother has a fated wolf mate? I figured after your display tonight, they were wrong about your heritage." Rose sounds almost disappointed.

Not that what she thinks about me matters, but it still stings all the same. Jax wraps an arm around my waist, pulling me close to his side. The touch is soothing to my fractured pride.

Lowering his voice, he explains, "Yes, we're fated mates, and I don't give a shit about her werewolf bloodline."

"Right, sorry, I didn't mean it that way," Rose backtracks. "I'm happy for you both." She looks at Jax with happiness shining in her eyes.

"My back story is a long-winded one; maybe we can talk more another time about it," I suggest.

Jax takes that suggestion and invites us over to their place for dinner tomorrow to continue this conversation in private. Graciously, they agree. I promise them a delicious Memaw homemade pie recipe for their hospitality.

We wish them goodnight before heading back toward the festivities. The sound of the bustling reception, still in full swing, darkens my mood. "Can't people just go home already? Gamila must be exhausted." I glower towards the sound of all the noise.

"Come on, my cranky one. My senses tell me you need food, Miguel's sarcasm, and a stiff drink pick-me-up. Then once you're done charming over my pack members, I'll take you home and reward you for your good behavior." Mars briefly flashes in his eyes as he leans in to nip my ear. The promise in his tone sends an excited chill down my spine.

Pack member introductions continue well into the night. Overall, it's tolerable, even pleasant at times. True to his word, Jax never leaves my side the entire time. He sent his brothers on multiple food runs for us. I seemed to have formed a line that would put the ones at theme parks to shame.

Miguel finds my suffering humorous. "Why didn't we get this woman a booth ahead of time, where she could've at least sat and signed autographs too?"

The Fangersons are a wonderful support system and awesome beings all around. They stay close, offering silent support and some crowd control. In Dottie's mind, I'm already a member of their family. She has all sorts of ideas for our future girls' outings together. Motherly warmth radiates off her in waves, filling some of the voids left by my own mother. I'm thankful Jax had both her and Frank as parental figures growing up after the loss of his parents.

Seeing familiar smiling faces pass through my line causes warmth to bloom in my chest, knowing I haven't been here long, but I've already formed connections to the pack. Cher stops to give me a talkin' to about not confiding in her, Anders, or Gamila, but mainly her, about being a hybrid. She also makes a fuss about what I saw in my vision. I repeatedly reassure her that there was nothing else I saw in the vision, and the woman's description will stay private. It's only after agreeing to another garden lunch that she seems satisfied enough to leave. She informs me I'll be spilling all the skeletons in my closet. Then she marches off into the crowd.

"You gonna tell her about the Vegas Omega sex cult?" Jo snickers.

"Ugh, probably."

Draco's extended family offers blessings, followed by a barrage of questions. I'd bet all my money some will crash our dinner tomorrow night just to ask more questions.

It's unfortunate I didn't have more time to better prepare for this event. I would've printed a pamphlet to hand out, featuring "frequently asked questions" with noncommittal Magic 8-Ball-style responses.

1. Are you two fated mates? *It is decidedly so*

2. When will you complete the mating bond? *Unknown*

3. When are you officially joining the pack? *Reply hazy, try again later*

4. Is one of your parents a lycan? *No*

5. Are you truly best friends with the Goddess? *Fucking Miguel*

When the time finally comes to go home, I send a silent thank you to the universe. I'm beyond exhausted. Sitting alone in a room, staring at a wall, and watching paint dry sounds wonderful right now. My mate in shining armor scoops me into his arms.

"Jax, we look ridiculous. I can walk," I weakly protest.

"You're spent, let me carry you."

"Fine," I halfheartedly grumble, not having the strength in me to fight him. Instead, I rest my head against his hard chest, letting my body fully relax, knowing he's got me as we walk to the fish-mobile.

CHAPTER THIRTY-TWO

Dana

Days Ahead

Dinner Sunday evening at Rose and Draco's is lovely. Six uninvited members of Draco's family join us. Rose is much more relaxed in the security of her own home. Her self-protective walls are still standing tall, but I think with time I'll get them down. Much of the evening revolves around me being peppered with questions. Scarlett, Draco's six-year-old niece, has all the best ones.

"Miss Dana, what's the Moon Goddess like? Is she really your friend? Does this pie really have potatoes in it? Do wolves pee on fire hydrants? Because Oliver told me they did."

Oliver is her eight-year-old brother who clearly has a strong imagination. *Ain't no wolves I know peeing on fire hydrants.*

"Oh, and will you show us your fire magic?" She gives me the most adorable pleading look.

"Scarlett, stop bothering Dana," scolds her mother.

"It's okay," I reassure her. Then I turn my attention back to Scarlett, "I don't know the Goddess personally, so we aren't friends. I did meet her once for a couple of seconds."

"Wow!" Her large, doe eyes go wide.

"Yes, the pie is made with actual sweet potatoes. It's much yummier than it sounds. Lastly, I'm not aware of any wolf shifters who pee on fire hydrants. We try to avoid resembling puppy dogs as much as possible."

"Well, Colin at school told me he saw one peeing on a fire hydrant the last time he went into the city," Oliver protests with his arms crossed and chin jutted out.

"Oliver!" his father scolds.

"I'm sure it was a dog, Little Man. Werewolves are large creatures that wouldn't be walking around city streets in their animal form. It's forbidden by supernatural law," Jax says, ruffling the boy's hair.

"Hey!" Oliver exclaims before launching an attack on Jax. He easily catches the pup in a headlock before tossing him over his shoulder and hauling him outside for a little wrestling match. I don't miss the way Rose smiles longingly at them as they go.

Draco's family's curiosity leads me to share my entire backstory, along with the workings of how a large pack like the Moonborn Pack operates.

"So you're telling me your pack has created supply chains with other supernaturals across the world using portals to import and export goods?" Draco's father asks, scratching at the facial hair along his cheek, appearing to have a hard time with the idea of doing business with a different supernatural faction.

They're all very sheltered here in the northern woods and disconnected from the reality of the entire supernatural community. The pack has no ties to other non-lycan supernaturals, and most of their resources come from humans. My impression is King Andras kept the pack purposely ignorant, as that makes it easier to control people. Now, King Anders and Queen Gamila are struggling with the fact that change is hard for people. It sounds like they are taking baby steps to build trust and get people comfy with change. I'm happy to provide Draco's family with enlightenment and encouragement for branching out beyond just the lycans.

The days following the dinner are spent in a haze. Most of the time we are held up in Jax's house, fucking, fucking in animal form, or eating whenever we can find the strength to, well, stop fucking. One night, my mate surprises me with an after-dinner show. He strides out of his closet with nothing on but assless chaps, cowboy boots, and a matching cowboy hat. His guitar is conveniently positioned over his bare front. He does a little spin, allowing me to get a peek at his perfect ass.

"I still had these lying around from my ranching days."

"I'm glad you do." I can't hold back my smile. "And what are you going to play me, Mr. Blackclaw?"

"Well, little lady." He tips the brim of his hat to me as if he wandered out of some old western film. "I was thinking Toby Keith's "I Should've Been a Cowboy," he gives me a lopsided grin, and my insides instantly melt.

I lounge at the end of his bed as he starts strumming. Music is Jax's soul. He pours everything he has into it. His light shines so bright when he performs, even when it's a show only for my eyes.

When his song ends, I crawl off the end of the bed onto my knees. My hand slides up under his guitar, where I find him already semi-erect. My hand slowly begins to stroke him, causing him to release a little groan that fuels me on.

I look up at him through my lashes. "Please, play another one."

I lean in, nipping the skin of his thigh. Being a good mate, he does as he is told, and I make sure to express my gratitude with my mouth around his thick length the entire time. Unable to say no to that, he obliges with more songs.

The more time we spend together, the more impatient our bond grows, pushing us to complete it. Honestly, I'm unsure how long we can keep it at bay. The urgency it causes is now an ever-present nagging feeling. *Do it. Come on, you know you want to. Just complete me.*

Mating hormones make it easy to get lost in one another and difficult to remember responsibilities. Every day, we manage to find the willpower to tend to our assigned tasks, like my training sessions with Isla. It brings me pride to see her growth and to know I helped her find that confidence.

Karissa's case, along with the missing female wolves, weighs heavily on my mind. I see people giving up. The effort to track down the vampire is still ongoing. Many on the case believe it isn't related to Karissa's disappearance, considering what was found in Torr's house. Squad Leader Kyle informed Dolken that there had been no movement regarding the missing female wolves in the area and that their squad was being deployed to another case back in the States. I grieve the loss of my Moon-born Pack resources that are typically at my disposal. It all tears at my conscience. I should be out there doing more, but how?

"We insert ourselves into the lycans' investigation," Joey suggests.

"True, Jax did mention there are witches coming today."

"We're going," Joey says without hesitation.

I'm unable to reach Jax for the details of the witch's arrival time, so I get it from Mickey. Dolken leads a group of three women down towards the forest line. I stand there waiting in the chilly rain.

I give them a little wave. "Hey, mind if I tag along? I was just out for a walk."

"Sure you were," Dolken says teasingly as the breezy wind pelts rain into my face.

Some damn rain won't stop me. "Hi, I'm Commander Dana Johnston from the Moonborn Pack. We also had female wolves taken through this portal by the same organization," I introduce myself to the new faces.

On the way, I explain my vision to them. The three witches create a shield from the rain, which is greatly appreciated. Crystals are meticulously placed around the area, along with symbols they carve into the earth. Dolken and I stand back and observe as they try a mixture of chanting and potion spells.

"I'm sorry, we can't see anything," one of the witches tells us with a solemn look on her face. "This is heavy dark magic. I suspect this coven is very old."

When I return to Jax's home, he is still gone at band practice. I want him here to console me through feelings of defeat. He's gone often, conducting pack training sessions, playing at The Horde, or partnering with the Lycan Guard on Karissa's case.

Our early morning meditation abruptly stopped. When I asked about it, he said he wanted to try my sleep-in approach. It's strange because I don't see him sleeping in the mornings, and he appears more tired. I found him up early one morning before dawn, working on a laptop, which he abruptly closed. That easy smile crept on his face, and he told me he was working on a new song that I couldn't peek at. For some reason, I didn't believe him, which made unwanted questions creep in.

Meanwhile, the unborn prince's words spin in my head. Jo and I still haven't come up with a plan to kill King Anders' bestie, without him in turn murdering us. *Thanks for the shit task, Little Fetus Prince.* I'm so regretting that vow, and he hasn't even been born yet.

My looming thirty-day review hangs over me like a dark rain cloud. I still haven't found the strength to confide in my mate about it. I'll do it soon, just like calling Davey.

When did my life become such a crap shoot?

Oh, and did I mention the whole mate decision thing?

Jax has not committed. But I know what I want: to be with him, be near my brother, and still do work for the Moonborn Pack, but not on such a demanding schedule. I want to create a cadence that divides our time between the packs. That is, if I'm not banned from the Moonborn Pack. Knowing that as long as Jax is by my side, whatever my next step may be, it will all be okay.

There's truly no one else for me. I am certain. He's thoughtful, funny, sexy, and damn good at making my complicated vagina come like no other before him. The perfect laid-back, fun-loving balance to my controlling, dominant side. No one has ever cared for my needs the way he has. This feeling is still foreign to me. I'm the blessed wolf who kicks asses while taking names, with or without the help of others. The pain in the ass who doesn't take orders even from the Wolf Demigod himself. The one fighting to prove to everyone that Selene's decision to give me another chance at life isn't in vain.

If you strip all that away, what's left underneath? Like many, I have that psychological desire to be loved. With some self-reflection, I see it's the essential self-nutrient I've been missing. Since my first mate's rejection, I've ignored it. I have led myself to believe it's something I don't need. It lies in a state of dormancy, overlooked by all my accolades. Jax changes all that. He's my equal who's there to lighten the load, bridge my gaps, understand my flaws, but not run from them. I love him down to the marrow of my bones. Though he says he isn't ready, his love shows through his actions.

Self-preservation won't stop knocking. *Get the fuck out of here. He isn't committing at the same level as you. That isn't normal; something is off. He either doesn't want you or he's hiding something.* Stubborn as I am, I flip that self-doubt the bird.

I'll take my chances...

CHAPTER THIRTY-THREE

Ajax

Secret Meeting

The clock on my nightstand reads 5:02 A.M. Even with my mate secure in my arms, I feel on edge. There's a knot in the pit of my stomach because it knows something bad is coming. Just an annoying, nagging gut feeling. The Uncle Kaz conditioned part of my brain is tossing red warning flags, urging me to flee. *Get out of here and head to some paradise where you can happily ignore the turmoil of your feelings. It's safe there,* it whispers.

For once, I push back on the urge. *No! We can't run from this. Instead, we need to stay and fight for what we want, our mate.* If the Goddess chose me as Dana's other half, I'll spend every day proving I'm worthy of such a gift. Together, I know we can have true happiness, but right now, my commitment to the Guardians is standing in our way.

The bond grows relentless, strengthening with each day we spend together. The urgency to mark our mate is becoming almost too difficult for Mars and me to handle. Everyone, and I mean everyone, in the pack can't understand how Dana and I have spent over a week together without completing it. I even question it at times. *Why can't we? She's our mate! It's fate, for fuck's sake! Dana wants this too.*

Then I force myself to remember that completing a mate bond adds another layer to our already complex situation. We don't need to add things like mating heats into the mix. *Heats. Oh, that sounds amazingly wonderful, but right now we're short on time.* I curse the fates again for giving me such a precious gift I can't fully accept right now. I've spent the last several nights awake, holding Dana in my arms, knowing what I must do. I just physically can't bring myself to do it. The thought alone sends ripples of agony through my body.

"NO, you will not send our mate away from us!" Mars protests for the fifteenth time this morning. He stalks around in my mind's eye, torn between his duty and instincts.

"What choice do we have? She's a distraction, and we haven't been able to catch up on our duties. Dana's also smart and knows we've been keeping things from her."

At times, her hesitation shows itself. It seems to me she has been ignoring it. Something that must be incredibly difficult, given her intuition.

Mars gets hopeful. *"Talk to Andy, explain. She'll understand. Maybe she can get a better spy in here to finish the mission?"*

"We can't just abandon the mission. Andy's counting on us, along with the innocents who've been taken. We must see this through. There's no one else like Andy said with natural ties to this pack."

"Fine, but we need to explain our situation. If we could tell Dana, she would understand our time away, or even help us," he rationalizes.

At this point, I'm out of options because my mate and I can't exist in limbo for much longer. I must tell her the truth about my mission, or she must leave. Bile rises in my throat at the thought. Swallowing it back adds to the already uncomfortable sensation in my stomach.

"Fine, we can talk to Andy," I agree. The possibility of obtaining permission from her lights a small spark of hope that soothes the crushing sense of loss at the thought of sending our mate away.

Quietly, I untangle myself from a sleeping Dana and slip into my closet. Crouching down, my hand searches out the secure phone line I keep hidden behind my dresser. My shaking fingers fly over the keys as I type out a message to Andy requesting a time to speak ASAP. Thankfully, her quick reply confirms a meeting tonight at 3:00 A.M. on the east side of the pack within the neutral ground. Usually, one would want more specific instructions about the meeting place. I know from experience that wherever I end up is where she will meet me. Firing off a quick confirmation, I slide the phone back into the cutout nook behind the dresser. Standing abruptly, I come face-to-face with a sleepy-eyed Dana.

"Good morning," she drawls in a slow, carefully neutral tone.

"Hey, good morning." I strive to sound steady.

She looks confused. "What are you doing?"

Tossing on an easy smile, I pull her into my arms for a morning hug. I take a deep inhale of her smoky scent, hoping it will calm my nerves. "Just looking for something that fell behind my dresser yesterday, I just remembered it." My easy lie feels slimy. "Do you want to grab some food and head out for a morning walk?" I chirp in my best upbeat tone.

"Okay," she agrees as she yawns, snuggling her face into the crook of my neck. The gesture helps settle my unease. Thank the Goddess she left it at that.

I listen to Dana's soft rhythmic breaths as I anxiously lie awake in bed. My heart rate is currently elevated, causing blood to thunder in my ears. *Relax. Deep breaths. There's nothing to be nervous about.*

"Other than a powerful, all-knowing archangel who could easily ruin our lives," Mars points out.

"Love the optimism, buddy."

Over the next twenty minutes, I continue to work on steadying my breathing before slipping from bed. I head to the lower level to exit through the patio slider door. Earlier today, I hid a pair of shorts, a T-shirt, and my second phone behind the couch. Pulling out the phone, I check to see if I have any new messages from Andy before stepping into the brisk night air. I secure the phone in the zipper pocket of my shorts before letting the shift ripple through me. Mars grasps our clothing in his clawed hand as he takes off toward our meeting spot.

Our senses don't pick up on other pack members in this vicinity out for a late-night run or patrolling. The last thing I need is someone spotting me. Arriving at a small clearing a little before 3:00 A.M., I quickly shift back and put on my clothing. While I wait, I close my eyes, seeking out Dana through the bond. We've strengthened it enough that I can visualize it in my mind's eye and probe along it. From her end, I make out a calm, steady strum, which is a good sign she's still asleep.

Before me, a golden portal spirals open to reveal Andy's familiar office. Her dark chocolate brown eyes assess me, missing nothing before she steps aside, allowing me entrance. Without hesitation, I rush through the portal, which abruptly closes behind me.

"Ajax," she greets in her customary manner before proceeding to take a seat behind her desk.

Large wings with golden tips extend outward before draping over her low-back chair. Andy sits with her hands clasped, resting on the desk. Behind her, a large picture window frames a fluffy, clouded, sunny sky. The sunlight shines in, highlighting her olive skin, which emanates a shimmering ethereal glow.

"Thank you for meeting with me, Andy," I reply, taking a seat in a leather chair across from her.

"Did anyone see you?" she asks.

"I didn't sense anyone while I traveled here."

"Good, now what's the urgent matter you wished to speak about?"

"I wanted to speak to you about my fated mate. I found her," I let that declaration hang between us.

She gives a tiny nod of acknowledgment, as her face remains blank, giving away nothing. I press on, explaining everything to her, "I wish to obtain your permission to tell my mate the truth about my mission. We can trust her. She's a Commander in the Moonborn Pack and a goddess-blessed crimson wolf. She has extraordinary instincts and might be able to assist in the case."

I hold my breath as Andy begins to speak with a sympathetic expression on her face. "Ajax, she hasn't been vetted through our organization. You know of our strict protocol. I cannot grant this request."

Grinding my teeth in frustration, I run a hand through my hair, holding back my anger. It takes every inch of my willpower not to rage at the divine being before me.

"What do you want me to do? I can't tell her the truth or send her away," I snap.

"You can send her away, and you will. Challenging situations arise all the time that we must face full-heartedly. We are Guardians, that is what sets us apart. We make the hardest sacrifices for the greater good. Duty above all, Ajax. This will be a true test of your Guardian oath. Based on what you told me about her, she sounds sensible. Once she can fully understand the truth, she will forgive you."

Mars whimpers at what we have to do. The mating bond rises to the challenge, urging me to keep fighting for my mate. White hot anger blazes through me. I feel the urge to punch a hole in the wall to release it, but I hold it all back. Always the mask of control. Resigned to my fate, my head hangs, my fists ball, and tears threaten. All I can do is give her a quick nod, since no civil words will come out right now.

"I have resources looking into where the pack Beta originated based on the small bit of information you shared with me," she says.

Again, I only nod. A portal is summoned back to the clearing. Andy's hand stops me before I pass through. I turn to look at her.

Her eyes are filled with determination. "We are close, I can feel it."

I don't bother saying anything as I storm off into the darkness. Mars and I both feel too agitated to talk any further. We need to get out of here.

"I'm sorry, we tried," I mutter. Mars doesn't bother replying as there's nothing to say.

I make my way back, rehearsing different scenarios in my mind about how I'm going to ask my mate to take a break for an unknown period and without a valid reason. I turn through verbiage that's less likely to spark feelings of rejection. *Fuck. Who am I kidding? No matter what I say, my mate will feel rejected.* Andy's words play over in my mind about her forgiving me. *How will she be after having already been rejected by another mate?*

"FUCK!" I snarl, punching an innocent nearby tree, shattering a part of it with the force of my rage.

Emerging from the forest and into my backyard, I spot Dana in my oversized T-shirt sitting on the top deck. The white outside blanket she has clutched around herself. The woman is a beacon in the moonlight with her eyes trained on me. That sour sensation is back in full force. Bile rises in my throat again, souring my stomach. Continuing through the lawn, I walk up the deck stairs to her, unsure of what I'm going to say.

"Hey, are you alright?" she asks, rubbing at her chest. "I felt your anger."

"Yes, I'm alright," I manage to say calmly.

"Talk to me. What's going on?"

I decide to tell a half-truth to buy myself a little more time. "I couldn't sleep. Karissa's case has me extremely frustrated. I've seen situations like this before, and we were able to shut them down within days. Karissa's a child, afraid and alone. We have failed her, and I fear she will endure a doomed fate at this point." I pause, looking away from her assessing eyes out into the darkness.

Turning back to meet her warm gaze, I watch her process for a long moment. She grabs my hand and leads us inside. Closing the patio door, we continue down the hall to my bedroom.

She finally speaks as we sit at the end of my bed. "I don't know how to find her. We know Karissa's location is being blocked by powerful magic, so we need more powerful resources to counter it. I feel speaking more openly with Dolken about getting Guardian involvement might be the best course forward. They're the best option for finding dark witches."

If only she knew Guardian involvement was already at play in the background.

"That is a good suggestion." Another lie to my mate.

Turning toward my nightstand, the clock reads 3:27 A.M
. "Come on, let's get some sleep. These are big problems better
suited for the day."

"Okay," she agrees before climbing under the sheets.

I stand, stripping off my shirt and pushing my shorts to the floor.
My body slides under the cool sheets to Dana's side of the bed.
I pull her close to my chest, breathing in her intoxicating scent.
Everything inside me wants to tell her I love her, but the meaning
would only be spoiled by cruelty. Only an asshole would confess
their love and then ask the person to leave the next day. I want the
first time we say we love each other out loud to be a joyful moment
in our history, not a painful reminder of what comes next.

Instead, I squeeze her tighter to my chest, stroking one hand
through the silky blonde strands of her hair. My fracturing soul
wants us to memorize the way every part of her feels. Anxiety hits
even harder, making my heart race. Internally, I'm screaming, *I'M
SORRY! I'M SORRY!* Dana nuzzles deeper into the crook of my
neck, sensing the dam of secrets building between us. There is no
way she doesn't see them.

"Jax."

"Hmm?" I croak out, trying hard to keep my shit together.

"Why does it feel like this is our end?" Her voice is nothing more
than a melancholy whisper.

Because it is, for now, I so desperately want to reply. Grasping
her chin, I guide her soft lips to mine, pouring every ounce of

my love into this kiss. She parts her mouth, allowing my tongue access to hers. Our tongues meet in a slow-burning dance, savoring every second in the other's embrace. We both cherish this moment, sensing it might be our last. The deeply emotional adolescent part of me, which I locked away years ago, wants to turn on a raw and emotional last song. Allowing my future self to evoke the memory by either playing or listening to it.

Grasping the neck of my oversized shirt, I tear it away from her body. Tonight, I fully submit, giving her complete control over what may be our last time together in this intimate way. Rolling to my back, I pull her on top of me, memorizing every inch of her. From her angel face down to her toned forearms, the soft curves of her perfect breasts, and those defined abs she's dedicated years to perfecting.

Her lips find mine again as she begins to slowly rock her hips, coating my cock in the heaven between her legs. Noises of pleasure leave her as she slides me in deeper. That tight pussy works me thoroughly, alternating between rocking, bouncing, and swiveling her hips. She wears the power of complete control like a second skin. Our eyes lock on one another, conveying the many emotions we aren't ready to speak out loud. Love, sadness, fear, and hope are reflected at me. Not breaking eye contact, we find our release together. Exhausted, we fall into each other's arms, holding onto the other tightly as our breathing gradually steadies.

"Jax?"

"Yes."

"Tomorrow we need to have an honest conversation, okay?" she says quietly with sleep lacing her words.

"Okay," my reply's barely audible. Mars releases a long, sorrowful howl before retreating away. *I must do this.*

Chapter Thirty-Four

Dana

Drinking Fixes Problems, Right?

When I woke this morning, Jax was already gone. On his cold pillow lies a little note reminding me that today is the last training session, which will end at 3:00 P.M. My stomach sinks, and I feel absolutely beside myself. Jax has been off for a few days, and his demeanor last night screamed that he was hiding something. I also noticed a faint feminine scent on him. I didn't push it, but today, I need answers. Lack of trust is starting to worm its way in, deep. *Did he go for a run? Was he sneaking around?* My stomach wrenches. *Shit.*

I briskly make my way into the bathroom, where I splash some cold water on my face. *Breathe, Dana. You're making up stories.* It's hard to relax when I can feel Joey's anxious energy building inside me too. She's been relatively quiet on the matter. Jax has her trust and loyalty, but she, too, can't help but see that something is off. I can't sit here all day dwelling on the stories in my head, or it might drive me to my wits' end. My nervous pacing leads me back to the bedroom. *What can I do today? A run, maybe?*

"That won't take all day," Jo chimes in while weighing our options.

"You're right." I bite my thumbnail. *"Maybe I should call Davey? I think he can offer advice, but he'll also lecture me for an hour straight for not telling him about our mate already."*

"True, he'll also call out that Jax's behavior isn't normal. Are you ready for that?" Joey paces around, just as unsure about our next move.

"No. Maybe. I don't know." My stomach starts to knot.

"Just admit it," Joey pushes.

"Fine, that's exactly what I'm afraid of. Can we survive another mate rejection?" I need to know what she thinks. Sometimes Jo feels like a built-in fortune teller, so I need her to tell me we will be okay.

"I'm not sure, but we need to know what he has been keeping from us to know."

I continue my anxious pacing. A pile of crumpled clothing next to the bed catches my attention. *Don't do it*, I tell myself. Then I do it. Picking up Jax's shirt he was wearing last night, I bring it to my nose. Taking a deep inhale, I find that faint feminine scent I detected last night. I can't place the type of flower or herb. Jo expresses her displeasure with a snarl.

My subconscious decides it's a good time to start reciting helpful past words from my mother. While I was growing up, she believed I would always remain mateless due to my dominant and difficult nature, unless I changed. *"Male wolves want a nice submissive partner. Dana, you're a bit unlovable at times. You don't have a single friend at school! I know this because Amber told her Ma, who told me, of course. After all, we're worried about you, dear. Now, take Amber, she's such a sweet, kind-hearted girl. Popular, beautiful, and understands her place in the pack. She'll make the perfect mate and mother one day."* SHUT UP MIND!

"Don't listen to your mother's vile words. You know that was her depression talking. The Goddess created us exactly how we're meant to be. If that's bothering our mate, then good luck to him finding someone better." At that, I smile. If Jo had fingers, I picture her sassy snapping, bye-Felicia-ing his ass right now.

"True that, sister," I tell her.

Bending down, I reach for his shorts to toss them along with the shirt into the dirty laundry hamper. To my surprise, they have weight to them. Unzipping the right pocket, I find a cell phone, and not his regular one. *What the hell? Why would he have a second phone?*

Then a memory from yesterday morning comes to me of Jax looking behind his dresser. It was rather strange. Being an older home, it doesn't have a newly crafted walk-in closet design with built-in cabinetry or dresser drawers. Instead, it houses what I'd guess is a thrifted antique-looking dresser pushed up against a side wall. After closer inspection, I find it inconspicuously a few inches from the wall. Crouching down, I run my hand around the back, stopping when I reach a cutout.

Peeking out is the tip of a charger that fits this phone. Nothing good I can think of would warrant him having a hidden phone. Then a nauseating thought hits me like a sack of bricks: is he somehow connected to the disappearances? Karissa had a secret second phone too. My heart plummets to the floor. *Please, goddess, no, it can't be my mate. That might kill me.*

Sliding to the ground, I slump over, letting the tears come. *No, I don't believe it, I won't believe it.* The unborn prince only warned me of, Beta Matt. He never warned me about my mate. *Would he have told me if Jax was the bad guy, too?*

I wipe at my face, hoping my wolf can console me. "*What have we gotten ourselves into now?*"

"Tonight, we confront Jax about all of it. I don't believe he's involved, but he's clearly hiding something. You also need to tell him about our 30-day investigation that might cost us our job, you've been putting off," she says.

"Okay," I hate the resignation in my voice. Joey's instincts settle me a little, but not my churning stomach.

"We need to get out of his house to clear our head," she wisely advises.

"You're right. Ahh, umm, oh, I got it! Miguel distraction, he has off today. Maybe we can get a drink with him, and then we can grow a pair and call Davey after," I suggest.

"Yes, that's perfect," she agrees.

Taking a final glance at the locked phone, I leave it among the clutter on the dresser top. I make my way into a scalding shower that I hope will help me compose myself. The water burns my skin, but I'm too numb to feel it.

I let my mind reach out to Miguel. *"Hey, what're you doing on your day off?"* I ask in my best normal, non-mental breakdown sounding voice, I can muster.

His reply is instantaneous, *"Friends reruns and a nap."*

"Wow, sounds like you need a hobby," I tease. *"Want to meet for a drink?"* Or ten... *"at The Horde in say twenty minutes?"*

"First, naps count as hobbies. Second, it's 9:00 A.M., so what's the occasion for this day drinking excursion?"

"Does one need a reason for a good day drinking excursion?" I avoid the question by hitting him with one.

"True, and?" he prompts. The man's intuition is so annoying.

"Maybe I just want to hang out with my lycan bestie while singing poor renditions of pop diva classics."

"Fine, you convinced me only because you just agreed to karaoke. Meet you there in twenty." He cuts the connection.

Twenty minutes later, I walk into The Horde, inhaling a lungful of that glorious musty dive bar scent. Some might think I'm crazy admitting this, but I would totally buy an air freshener of that scent.

"That would be marketed as an air un-freshener." Jo chuckles at her joke.

"Touché," I agree. *"I'm still buying it."*

Miguel already sits cozied up to the bar in a crisp white short-sleeve button-up and snug aquamarine-colored shorts. He casually chats with Cher, who looks to be restocking liquor bottles behind the bar. I'm pleasantly surprised to see her here this early in the day. A few other patrons meander about, but overall, it's relatively quiet. *Well, well, I'm not the only morning lush in town.*

"Hey!" I greet them as I pull out a stool.

"Hey, girl, hey," Miguel replies before taking a sip of his fruity cocktail. The sugary sweet scent of his coconut rum assaults my nose.

"Hey!" Cher calls back, looking genuinely happy I'm here. "I'm surprised to see you here this early. I'd expected to see you later tonight when Jax has his set." *Oh, right, it's Friday, already? Who knows if we'll even still be together by this evening?* The thought makes my heart squeeze so hard that my tear ducts start to prickle. *No! Those traitorous bastards.*

"Oh yeah, well, I didn't have any plans today while Jax helps with the last training session, so I thought Miguel and I could warm up the Jukebox for tonight."

She studies me briefly. "Great idea. Hey, can you two help me carry some boxes that are in the back?"

"Sure," I easily agree.

Miguel squawks at her, "What kind of boxes? They better not get a speck of dirt on my Versace shirt." *What? Who in their right mind wears Versace to a dirty old bar?*

"They won't," she assures him with an eye roll.

Exiting from behind the bar, she leads us down the back hall where the bathrooms are located. She unlocks a door next to the men's room which leads to a small hallway with more doors. Our party of three enters the first door on the left, a storage closet. The room smells strongly of chemical cleaning supplies and has an undertone of sex. *Gross.*

"Cher, did you bring us to your sex closet for a threesome? Maybe you don't know this, but I don't swing the V-way." Miguel wrinkles his nose in disgust. "Gross! I'm picking up on hints of my brother's scent." With that statement, he overly dramatically gags. "Did you two fuck in here?" Now that he mentions it, there is a faint scent of Mickey juices in the air that I could have gone without smelling.

Cher gives him an unapologetic shrug. "Sometimes I fuck people in here, like your brother. Anyway, that's not why we're here."

"There has to be a better place in this bar for a secret conversation than your closet of sin," Miguel deadpans.

"Shut it, this isn't about you, surprisingly." She turns, looking solely at me. "Now, Dana, spill what's going on?"

"Nothing, really," I say too quickly.

"Really?" Miguel snorts. "Because everyone could smell your tears and sorrow the moment you walked in."

Cher shoots Miguel a stern look for that one. "What Miguel means is that you seem off. I know we haven't known each other long, but we're your friends, you can trust us to help you with whatever is bothering you," she presses.

Plastering on a strong front, I try hard to seem perfectly normal. "It's nothing I can't handle."

Cher narrows her eyes at me. "I call bullshit. If there's one thing I'm good at, it's reading people, and you need some support right now."

All of me is too tired to keep up this act. I contemplate what to tell them. It's between Jax and me, period. After last night, and now the secret phone, I have too many questions with no answers.

I also don't want to pin all the blame on him when I, too, haven't been entirely truthful.

I sigh. "Jax and I are just complicated."

"Explain," Cher and Miguel blurt at the same time.

"Well, we haven't agreed on completing our bond, and it's wearing on us both."

"No part of me understands the hang-up between you two. You're both clearly into each other, so what's the big fucking deal?" Miguel throws his hands up.

"Exactly," Cher nods.

"We're going to talk after the training session this afternoon about where we stand. I don't know. He seems hesitant. Maybe we need time apart to truly understand what we want," I admit while wiping away tears. "Anyway, I'm feeling a little stressed. So right now, I want to have some drinks and a little fun, since I might not be here much longer."

Cher pulls me into her motherly embrace. "We're here if you need anything."

Miguel's long arms stretch over the top, pulling us into a group hug.

He leans back from our hug to make eye contact with me. "If my dumbass brother doesn't figure his shit out soon, I'll kick his ass."

"Thanks for the support, you two." I'd be lost without them right now.

"Come on, let's go cheer you up. I don't think Cher's sex closet is helping," Miguel complains. Breaking apart, we make our way to the door. All my tears have been wiped away, but I'm sure my burning eyes still hold traces of them. *Excellent. I hope this news doesn't spread around.*

"So, how long have you and Mickey been hooking up?" I ask, unable to hold back my curiosity.

"I don't want to hear about that," Miguel dramatically whines.

"Better cover your ears then," Cher gives it right back. "He's been in my usual rotation for a couple of years now."

"Rotation? Damn, get it, Queen Mother!" I can't help but envy how seriously badass this woman is.

"Sexy Crimson Wolf. You have a list of men," she winks at me.

"Ah, no, actually. I'm not sure why everyone assumes that. My dominance has the opposite effect of a turn-on. I do have a nice vibrator rotation," I joke with them.

"Well, complete your mate bond and you won't have that problem anymore," Miguel tells me.

Cher slaps him upside the head for me. "Light his fancy shirt on fire."

"Don't you dare!" He growls. I believe this is the first time I've seen him completely serious.

The next several hours give me the much-needed reprieve from my worries. I don't get the time to call Davey. Cher stays the whole time, making easy small talk while feeding us way too much free alcohol. Calming liquid courage is the best way to open up about everything bothering me, or it's possibly making things even worse. I guess we'll find out soon.

CHAPTER THIRTY-FIVE

Dana

Our End

After too many drinks, a tiny kerfuffle with a burly mountain man who believes all female wolves are whores for lycan dick, and Miguel's performance of Tina Turner's classic hits, we're finally heading to the training grounds. Currently, I feel good. Cher sent us on our way once she heard things were starting to wrap up at today's session. A sea of men can be seen sparring throughout a large open field when we arrive. While they're nice to look at, seriously, where are the women? *Wait a minute, ah nope, just a dude with a long ponytail. Come on, lycans, do better.*

"Let's go show them a thing or two a woman can do," Joey urges me.

"Ahh, probably not the best timing," I advise. She grumbles something under her breath, clearly not agreeing with me.

My eyes easily seek out Jax leaning in to hear something Mickey is saying. *Mickey Manwhore,* I laugh to myself. Jax's head snaps up in our direction, sensing my nearness. The bond gives a little hum due to our proximity. I sway slightly before smiling and waving, looking like a poor rendition of Miss America. *Shit, time to sober up, Dana.* I can do it in a matter of seconds if I call my flames forth to burn off any remnant of alcohol. Feeling inside, I greet my lovelies and push them forward. The flames perform an intricate weave, diving over and under my skin, drawing the attention of those around us.

Their sudden presence startles Miguel, who's leading this circus. "Shit! Put those away! My blood alcohol level is so high right now, I'll go up within seconds. And this is my favorite shirt."

Winking, I reassure him, "No, you won't, I got ya, Versace." Several sparring pairs stop to eye me wearily. Continuing through the crowd, we finally make our way to Jax and Mickey's side.

"Put us in, coach." Miguel mock salutes the two.

Jax gives us an incredulous look. "Have you two been drinking?"

"Yup-p-p!" Miguel pops the P annoyingly, earning a disapproving look from Jax. Mickey just looks amused. *Well, fuck.* I want to admit I needed to relieve some stress because of him, so get over it, bucko.

"We had a liquid brunch," I blurt out, not so helpfully.

"And Cher took us to your sex closet, Mick." Miguel wrinkles his nose in disgust. "I can never un-smell that."

Mickey roars with laughter. He's not bothered by his brother's lack of a filter.

Jax reaches into his pocket to pull out his actual phone, checking the time. His usual carefree demeanor isn't present. Instead, it's replaced with a no-nonsense air. Searching the bond, I don't feel anything, as if he has closed it off to me. My stomach twists. *Why's he being cold?* He didn't even bother to greet me in his typical fashion. That coldness feels like an icicle to the heart. *Maybe he's in professional training mode. Yeah, I will keep lying to myself with that.*

"We're almost done. Maybe you two should go sit down and sober up a bit," he advises us.

"Yes, sir." Miguel gives another mock salute before sauntering off toward a long metal bench. I'm not sure how to act right now, so I stay quiet because if I speak, it probably won't be the right thing to say.

"Wow, Jax seemed upset. That isn't like him," Miguel mumbles so only I can hear.

"Yeah, he has been off," I agree.

We take a seat on the extremely uncomfortable bench. The hard metal bites into my ass, causing my frustration to only rise. *What's going on with him? What's he keeping from me?* My stomach uncomfortably flips some more.

After a couple of silent minutes, Miguel stands. "I need to take a piss."

"Okay," I absently mutter as he walks off.

My thoughts drift back to my mate. Last night, he didn't deny it when I asked if it was our end. Instead, he proceeded to kiss me so passionately that my head spun. There was so much desperation behind his actions. Through our bond, I felt his love spilling out of him and into me, even though he's never said it aloud.

"Well, well, the all-star's been benched," a male voice says behind me.

Uneasiness prickles along my senses. Joey surges forward, ready for the threat. When I turn around, Beta Matt stands there, looking smug with that plastic fucking smile.

"Gosh, is there trouble in paradise, crimson wolf?" His words are laced with sarcasm.

At this moment, I'd like nothing more than to punch the perfectly molded expression off his face. Joey's top lip curls up, sending a silent warning. I shoot Matt a withering look I hope conveys the "fuck you" I'm feeling, before turning my attention away.

Undeterred, he invites himself to take a seat next to me. Anger rolls through me caused by his nearness. *What does he want? Wait, is this the moment, Little Fetus Prince? Send me an obvious sign now if you want me to kill this creep. Okay, I'll hold here awaiting your wisdom and signal. Thanks.*

"I don't think this is the time or place," Jo offers.

I feel so much relief. *"It was worth a shot,"* I tell her.

Matt has a purpose behind this encounter, but what is it? Playing his little game, I bite out, "Can I help you with something unrelated to my personal life, Beta Matt?" Okay, luckily that didn't sound too bitchy.

Ignoring my question completely, he trudges on, his voice low for only my ears. "I'm not surprised by the status of your mating, seeing as your mate is a womanizer. Female pack members fall for his fake charm regularly."

Matt has finally taken off the mask, revealing a bit of his authentic self. A warning growl rumbles in my chest.

"I will kick his ass right here, right now." Joey's eyes blaze with rage.

"No, *keep it together. He is goading us, and he wants a reaction."*

But why? Is it his hatred for Jax? Nevertheless, neither Ezekial nor Anders will approve of us giving Beta Matt a beatdown because of some smack talk.

"I don't care! No one talks shit about our mate!" Joey continues her low warning growls directed at Matt.

"Beta, please kindly leave me alone," I tell him.

Ignoring me again, he trudges on with his conquest, "I'm sure Jax hasn't told you about how many women he has fucked around here."

My anger blazes, causing my flames to enter this fight. They want to rumble. *Little Fetus Prince, can I please kill him now?*

"Beta, let me clarify: I don't care who's come before me. We all have a past, and that's where it will forever stay." I give him a glimpse of my own perfected fake smile.

He chuckles darkly. "Don't be so sure about that. Has he told you what, or who, I should say, he's been keeping from you?"

His words are cut off by a ferocious snarl coming from a very pissed off looking Jax. "Get the fuck away from my mate, now."

The threat is low, deep, and all-predator. Claws start to pierce through his shaking fingertips, as black hair slowly sprouts along his forearms. Worry lines crease Mickey's handsome face, who is following close behind him. Others don't seem fully aware of the confrontation yet.

Matt has a mischievous twinkle shining in his cold eyes, telling me he has a trick up his sleeve. "Ajax, so glad you could join us. I was just about to fill your mate in on the secret you have been keeping from her." Then he gives a disapproving tsk.

I look to Jax, who has an unreadable expression as he holds eye contact with the Beta.

"But by all means, if you wish to start something, I'll be happy to exile you from the pack finally," Matt tells him.

Ah, and there it is.

"I said get the fuck away from my mate," Jax repeats, finally earning the attention of several sparring companions who are closest to us.

Mickey comes to grasp his upper biceps. "Jax," he hisses. "Calm down."

I move to walk toward my mate when Matt grabs my forearm painfully, jerking me back.

Oh, hell no! Whirling, I slap him across the face.

Jax lunges but Mickey and Miguel, who is finally done pissing, manage to pull him back.

Turning, I bare my teeth at Matt as crimson blazes in my eyes. "Let me go, or so help me, I'll make you."

Matt smirks, silently accepting my challenge.

Jax fights against M&M's restraints on him. "Don't fucking touch her!" he bellows, causing some bystanders to run over to assist the twins.

Leaning in, I decide to poke the bear back. Keeping my words hushed, I say, "Matt, I see the real you. It's nice you're finally showing the true you that's been hiding in there. How long before everyone else sees him?"

The slightest ripple of shock cracks his plastic face before he smothers it. He finally releases my arm. "Oh really, the real me?

Let's talk about your real mate, who has been hiding a pregnancy with his girlfriend from you."

Wh-what? My brain shuts down as I try to process Matt's words.

Jax is expecting a pup with a girlfriend? Is that whose feminine scent he carried last night? And why he has a second phone because he needs more time to figure out stuff? A secret pregnancy? My heart fractures, and I feel absolutely sick. Joey lets out distressed yips.

"You god damn liar!" Jax shouts, pushing the full force of his power out. Wiggling free of the others' grasp, he lands a direct punch to the left side of Matt's face. The two start exchanging blows, as I stand in shock.

Shouts rise from the chaos of the crowd that has formed around us, but I can't comprehend what they're saying. My blood is thundering frantically in my ears, drowning out the noise. *How could he keep this from me, the other half of his soul? How could he lead me on?* Maybe I'm broken, seeing as my soul seems pretty janky with two soul mates. *Or is Matt lying like Jax claims?* I need to talk to him alone and get out of this damn crowd.

Jo starts to rage inside, urging us to help Jax. She feels the same emotions as I do, but still doesn't like others hurting our mate. My flames beg and plead to be released.

Jax grabs Matt by the shirt, throwing him hard to the ground. Seeing an opening, I grant their wish. They leap from my body, creating a ring of fire around Matt. His face turns ashen at the sight of them. *Smart man, because goddess knows Dana Jo can be a wild card.* Jax abruptly halts his forward progress, breathing heavily. He has a busted lip and a torn T-shirt, but Matt looks worse off. The crowd's angst increases.

"ENOUGH!" I shout over them, letting the full force of my dominant aura out. The rowdy crowd instantly silences. In an authoritative, calm voice, I announce, "We don't want any trouble. Let's all calm down. I'm not going to hurt Beta Matt, I just wanted to stop the fight."

Matt sneers, "Bullshit! You all saw them attack me."

"What the hell is going on here?" Dolken's voice carries over the masses. I extinguish the ring of fire confining Matt. He breaks eye contact to focus on an incoming Dolken.

"Ajax and his mate were threatening my life," Beta Matt explains to Dolken.

Murmurs ripple across the onlookers. What will they say happened? Does Jax have peers who will stand up and tell the truth? Or will they cower to the Beta?

Fights are not uncommon among pack members, given our nature. But his statement is ridiculous on so many levels. First, it wasn't an actual fight to the death situation. Second, the asshole started it all. Lastly, the number one rule of being a shifter is not to come between mates.

Dolken turns his concerned features to Jax. "What happened? Explain."

"The Beta is spewing lies about me having a secret girlfriend and he grabbed my mate without her consent," he bites out.

"Gamma Dolken. Can we please speak to you about this in private? I can assure you, we weren't looking to harm Beta Matt. Things quickly got a little heated," I try to explain.

Dolken opens his mouth to speak, but Matt talks over him. "Given this unwarranted, life-threatening attack on a pack official, Dana Johnston is hereby exiled from the Silverthrone pack, and Ajax Blackclaw will stand trial for his actions."

What the fuck? There are more gasps and murmurs from the witnesses standing around us. Dolken looks in shock.

Joey is enraged. *"That lying piece of shit!"*

"Beta Matt provoked this fight!" Mickey defends. Members in the crowd can be overheard taking both sides.

Matt forges on before he can be interrupted again. There's so much malice behind his brown eyes as he looks directly at me. "Dog, you have twenty minutes to leave the pack lands before guards are notified to kill you for trespassing."

Joey bares her fangs, so over this asshole. *"I wish this were the right time to kill the bastard!"*

Dolken sputters before throwing himself in the path of a lunging Jax, who has murder in his eyes. Dolken, Miguel, and Mickey quickly prevent him from reaching his target.

"Calm down before you do something stupid like your father!" Dolken's gruff words sober Jax a little.

I stand there, shocked by the whole situation unfolding.

"Don't you dare threaten her, you lying piece of shit!" Jax bellows, looking on the verge of shifting.

"Beta Matt is not lying," a feminine voice rings out over the crowd. The group parts to reveal the very pretty, too much cleavage, groupie from The Horde I saw on the first night while watching Jax play, Tiffany. She beams brightly at my mate as she cradles her flat stomach. "It's true. I'm pregnant with Jax's pup."

My fractured heart finally breaks with that declaration. He's having a child with her. Someone who is not me. That child will always take precedence in his life, and it should. My mate kept this from me, just stringing me along this entire time. *Why would he be so cruel? Goddess, I'm a fool.* It physically pains me to look at either of them. Joey whimpers in defeat, something she's never willingly done. She knows as well as I that there's no going back from this. This is our end.

Jax's face is one of horror mixed with rage. "Tiffany, stop lying! You aren't having my child, and I'm positive a quick doctor visit can prove it! Did the Beta put you up to this?"

"No, you need to stop lying!" she shrieks through her tears. "This has gone on too long. I gave you the space you asked for to reject her. Is a wolf worth ruining our chance to be a family?" She gingerly dabs at her eyes.

Joey's anguished cries reverberate throughout my soul. The pain causes vomit to rise. *Do not throw up here.* Turning toward Miguel,

I look for backup, but for once, he remains silent. *Did he know about the baby, too? I don't think so.*

Jax mindlinks me, pulling my thoughts away from Miguel. *"Dana, please, I don't know entirely what's going on right now. Likely a ploy by Beta Matt, but I swear to you she isn't my girlfriend or carrying my pup! Please believe me. I love you! I only want you! I wouldn't lie about this,"* He frantically begs for me to listen.

"I don't know what to believe," I reply weakly. *"You've been hiding things. And don't deny it, I found your hidden phone today. Tell me the truth about what you've been hiding."*

"I, I..." he sighs, looking so broken.

It's hard for me to look at him when I ask, *"Tell me you weren't going to ask me to leave?"*

"I can't." Defeat rings through his words.

My tears are back, but I refuse to cry, not here in front of that fucker, Matt. Anger at the Beta and the unfairness of this situation replaces my sorrow. I have fucking lived through one mate's rejection, and I can damn well do it again. My resolve hardens.

"Lock him up!" Matt barks at some men standing nearby. He looks completely unhinged, but I can't focus on that right now. All my focus is on not dying of a broken heart in front of this crowd.

"Tick tock," Matt's taunting voice rings in my mind.

Joey's snarls directed at Matt are ferocious. I feel her fighting through the heartbreak and urge to kill the Beta.

This is goodbye. *Am I really walking away from my mate? I must.* My internal flames soar at the rising panic the thought provokes. Wrestling my emotions back, I stand tall and lift my chin.

Matt conveniently shoves a portal spell into my hand. "Have a good life, Commander," he says condescendingly. "I'll send your belongings and a detailed report of this incident to the Wolf Demigod personally," he flashes me a genuine smile, and it takes all my willpower not to punch him.

"No!" Jax continues to fight off those trying to contain him. "We wish to speak to King Anders now!"

"Babe, you need to calm down, it's stressing me and our baby. Let her leave. I know we can work this out." Tiffany's words scrape like nails across my soul.

Mating instinct urges me to fight and kill anyone standing in my way of what belongs to me. It makes me see red, reviving my fight and flames beneath my skin. I bare my teeth at her, causing her to tremble in terror. Others move to form a protective barrier around her, now turning on me.

"No, no, no. Jo, we need to leave now, before we do something we regret."

"I can't leave my mate," she whimpers.

Joey, too, is no longer willing to roll over and accept defeat so easily. Her energy feels feral. She hysterically claws, wanting to be released. The sensation makes me feel as if I'm being split in two from the inside out. My head throbs, just adding to my list of afflictions right now.

Dolken quickly steps between Tiffany and me with his hands raised, trying to ease the tension. He looks pained as he says, "Gamila has started laboring, and we have orders not to disturb either of them. Beta Matt is in charge in the interim."

"How convenient," Miguel mumbles under his breath.

Jax is visibly distraught as he continues to battle with Mars internally. Mickey's trying his best to calm him, but there's a lot of fear in his normally kind eyes.

"Time to go." Matt smirks at me.

Jax lunges again, but is pushed back now by the eight men surrounding him. What do you say to the person who not only broke your heart but also your soul? The person you will never recover from? I hope you have a great life with your girlfriend and baby, or thanks for breaking my fucking entire being, asshole? Neither.

I open a private mindlink with him, *"Jax. Please stop before you get in serious trouble. It's okay, this is where we say goodbye. I, I need to go. I think that's what's best."*

"No, it's not okay. This isn't how we say goodbye. I'm not letting you go. Dana, don't go! I love you. I'll tell you everything! I swear, please, trust me."

"You're going to tell me everything now at the eleventh hour?"

"I, ah," he snarls in frustration. *"I can't. But soon, I promise to tell you everything. You just have to trust me, please!"*

It's too late, bud. Tossing the spelled rock on the ground, I tell it where it needs to take me. "Open a portal to Moonborn Pack Portal Travel Center, located in Oregon, United States." The magic in the stone shimmers as it expands, growing until there's a magical gateway before me. The center of the portal swirls with vibrant lights of white and blue.

Unable to stop myself, I glance from Matt to Jax for one last look at the man I love. I feel unable to breathe due to my emotions suffocating me. His face is wet with tears as he continues to battle those restraining him. *Good-bye, my love,* I send out into the universe. Then I turn and walk toward the portal.

"Get the fuck off me! Dana STOP! Don't go!" His frantic screams are hard to ignore as I force myself to keep walking.

"Bye-bye, Fire Bitch, you won't be missed," Matt taunts in my mind.

Fire bitch. There's a deep sense of knowing and clarity as the words echo inside. The rogue werewolf leader's words come to mind, *"...the boss promised a hell of a big payout if we brought him the Fire Bitch."*

"Do it!" The devil inside my head encourages.

All of me feels numb. *"It'll get back to Ezekial, and we'll for sure be kicked out."*

"Do it! They need to know!" The angry devil pushes me harder.

I open a mindlink to the entire Silverthrone pack. This will be the final nail in my Moonborn Pack coffin, but I can't seem to bring myself to care at this moment. *"Beta Matt is connected to Karissa's disappearance. Get the rat to talk, and maybe you'll be able to save her from whatever fate he dealt her."* With that, I step through the portal and into the Portal Travel Center (PTC) outside the Moonborn Pack's lands, officially broken in every way possible.

This has been Wolf of Crimson, Book 1 in The Crimson Flame Series. The adventure continues in Book 2, Wolf of Vengeance.

www.ingramcontent.com/pod-product-compliance
Lightning Source LLC
Chambersburg PA
CBHW071736110726
47908CB00006B/1611